About the Authors

Susan Meier spent most of her twenties thinking she was a job-hopper—until she began to write and realised everything that had come before was only research! One of eleven children, with twenty-four nieces and nephews and three kids of her own, Susan has had plenty of real-life experience of watching romance blossom in unexpected ways. She lives in western Pennsylvania with her wonderful husband, Mike, three children and two overfed, well-cuddled cats, Sophie and Fluffy. You can visit Susan's website at www.susanmeier.com.

Ellie Darkins spent her formative years as a committed bookworm devouring romance novels. After completing her English degree (which had Mills & Boon on the syllabus!) she decided to make a living from her love of books. As a writer and freelance editor her work now entails dreaming up romantic proposals, hot dates with alpha males and trips to the past with dashing heroes.

A busy wife and mother of three (two daughters and the family dog), **Donna Alward** believes hers is the best job in the world: a combination of stay-at-home mum and romance novelist. An avid reader since childhood, Donna always made up her own stories. She completed her arts degree in English literature in 1994, but it wasn't until 2001 that she penned her first full-length novel and found herself hooked on writing romance. Donna loves to hear from readers. You can contact her through her website, ~~~~~~~~~~~~~~~~~~~~~~ page at www.myspace.co~~~~~~~~~~~~~~ publisher.

One Winter's
COLLECTION

September 2018   October 2018

November 2018   December 2018

One Winter's Night

SUSAN MEIER

ELLIE DARKINS

DONNA ALWARD

MILLS & BOON

Published in Great Britain 2018
by Mills & Boon, an imprint of HarperCollins*Publishers*
1 London Bridge Street, London, SE1 9GF

One Winter's Night © 2018 Harlequin Books S.A.

The Twelve Dates of Christmas © 2014 Linda Susan Meier
Frozen Heart, Melting Kiss © 2014 Ellie Darkins
A Cadence Creek Christmas © 2013 Donna Alward

ISBN: 978-0-263-26842-3

MIX
Paper from
responsible sources
FSC® C007454

This book is produced from independently certified FSC™ paper to ensure responsible forest management.

For more information visit: www.harpercollins.co.uk/green

Printed and bound in Spain
by CPI, Barcelona

THE TWELVE DATES OF CHRISTMAS

SUSAN MEIER

For my sisters...may we always take care of each other the way Olivia, Eloise and Laura Beth do.

CHAPTER ONE

THERE WAS ALWAYS too much month left at the end of Eloise Vaughn's money.

"Here, put these crackers in your purse." Laura Beth Matthews gathered a handful of crackers from the party buffet of their newly married friend, Olivia Engle, and shoved them at Eloise.

She gasped. "So now we're reduced to stealing crackers?"

"Five crackers are lunch."

Eloise sighed but opened her Chanel purse and let her roommate dump the crackers inside.

"I'm sorry, Coco."

Laura Beth said, "Coco?"

"Chanel…" She shook her head. "Never mind."

Hoping no one saw the crackers falling into her purse, Eloise glanced around the Christmas party at the women wearing shiny cocktail dresses in shades of red and green and the tuxedo-clad men. Subdued gold and silver decorations gave the Engles' penthouse a sophisticated glow. The clink of ice in glasses, laughter of guests and the air of importance—wealth and power—wafted around her.

For fifty cents she could work this room and probably leave with a date. But she didn't want a date. She'd had the love of her life and had lost him. Now, she wanted a job, a good-paying job, a permanent position that would support her. Unfortunately, her degree didn't seem to translate well into actual work. In lieu of a job, she'd take another roommate, someone to help with the rent on the apartment she shared with Laura Beth. Then the pressure would be off, and the salary from the temp job she currently had at a law firm would be enough that she and Laura Beth could buy food again.

But she wouldn't find a roommate here. All of these people could afford their own condos. Maybe two con-dos…and a beach house.

Laura Beth studied the remaining food. "It's too bad we can't pour some of this dip in our purses."

Eloise shoved her purse behind her back. "I draw the line at dip. No dip. Not on the inside of my Chanel."

"You do realize you could sell some of those overpriced clothes, handbags and shoes you own and probably eat for an entire year."

"Most of my stuff is five years old. No one would want it."

Laura Beth sniffed a laugh. "You make it work."

"Only because I know how to change a collar or add a belt."

"So update your stuff and then sell it."

She couldn't. Not that she loved clothes and dressing up so much that she'd die without accessories. It was more that these clothes were the last piece of herself she had. The last piece of the starry-eyed college junior, one year away from graduating, who'd run away and married her Prince Charming.

Her heart pinched. Prince Charming seemed like an odd description. Especially given that she and Wayne had had their troubles. After they married, her wealthy parents had disowned her, and Wayne couldn't find a job. So she'd had to work as a waitress, and they'd fought. A lot. Then he'd been diagnosed with pancreatic cancer, and in what seemed like the blink of an eye, he'd died. Overwhelmed with grief and confused that death could be so swift and so cruel, she'd gone home, hoping her parents would help her cope. But they wouldn't even come to the door. Through the maid, they'd reminded her that they had disowned her and didn't want her and her troubles visiting their doorstep.

At first she'd been crushed, then she was sad, then she got angry. But that only fueled her determination. Come hell or high water she intended to make it. Big. She didn't know where or how, but she intended to make it. Not just to show her parents, but so she could be happy again.

"I'd like you to meet my cousin."

Ricky Langley glanced up in horror as his lawyer walked up to him with a thirty-something woman. With her hair in a tight black ball on the back of her head and her bright red dress clinging to her curves, she eyed him appreciatively.

"Janine Barron, this is Ricky Langley."

"It's a pleasure." Her voice shivered just the tiniest bit, as if she were so thrilled to meet him she couldn't quite catch her breath.

Another man might have been pleased—maybe even proud—that his lawyer liked him enough to introduce him to a relative. But since his son had died, he'd been besieged by a loss so intense that thoughts of love, romance or even meeting somebody weren't anywhere on his radar.

He said, "It's nice to meet you," and managed ten minutes of polite conversation, but when he found an opportunity, he slipped away.

He wove through conversation groups as he walked across Tucker Engle's sleek living room. Although Tucker had married six months ago, his New York City penthouse still claimed the sophisticated furnishings of a bachelor pad. Chrome and black leather furniture sat on white shag carpet atop dark hardwood floors. The Christmas tree Tucker had decorated with his new wife, Olivia, glittered with all silver and gold ornaments. The cherrywood mantel over the fireplace boasted one stocking…for Baby Engle. Not yet born, the child hadn't been named. They wouldn't tell the sex either. It was all to be a grand surprise.

He pursed his lips as his breathing stuttered. He thought of the one and only Christmas he'd shared with his son. Blake had been born December twenty-seventh, so he was two days shy of a year on his first Christmas day. He'd clapped when he'd seen the tree lit with brightly colored lights that reflected off the tinsel. He'd eaten Christmas cookies. And he'd gone just a bit bananas when he'd awakened Christmas morning to find tons of gifts all for him. He couldn't talk, so he squeaked and squealed for joy. He had torn off wrapping paper, liked the boxes better than the actual gifts and in general made a mess of Ricky's pristine penthouse.

It had been the best Christmas of Ricky's life. And now he had nothing.

He sucked in a breath. He shouldn't have come to this party. He might be eighteen months into his grief, but some things, like Christmas celebrations, would always level him. Worse, he had twelve more of these events on his calendar. Ten parties, one wedding and one fraternity reunion. Last year, six months into his grief, he could reasonably bow out. This year, people were beginning to worry.

He turned to race away from the mantel and bumped into somebody's purse. He swore he heard a crunch as his hands swung around to catch his victim.

"Damn it! I think you crushed my crackers."

The scowl on the blonde's beautiful face surprised him so much he forgot he was too unhappy to talk with anyone. "You have crackers in your purse?"

She sighed heavily and tucked a strand of her long yellow hair behind her ear. "Not usually." She glanced at his tuxedo, gave him a quick once-over, then shook her head. "Never mind. You're a little too rich to understand."

"Oh, you took crackers from the buffet table for lunch next week." At her horrified look, he inclined his head. "I used to be poor. Did the same thing at parties."

"Yeah, well, this was my roommate's idea. Typically, I'm not the kind of girl who steals."

"You're not stealing. Those crackers were set out for the guests. You're a guest. Besides, it's the end of the night. Once we all leave, the leftovers will probably be thrown away. Or given to a homeless shelter."

She squeezed her eyes shut in misery. "Great. Now I'm taking crackers out of the mouths of homeless people. I hate this city."

He gaped at her. "How can you hate New York?"

"I don't hate New York, per se. I just hate that it costs so much to live here."

She suddenly straightened. Right before his eyes she changed from a frantic working girl into a princess.

Her shoulders back, her smile polite and subdued, she said, "If you'll excuse me, I want to say goodbye to Olivia and Tucker."

He stepped out of her way. "Of course."

Three things hit him at once. First, she was gorgeous. Her gold dress hugged her high breasts, slim waist and round bottom as if it were made for her. Second, she was refined and polite for someone reduced to taking the extra crackers from a party. Third, she'd barely given him a second look.

"Ricky!"

Ricky pivoted and saw his attorney scrambling toward him.

"I understand your reluctance to get back into the swing of things, but I'm not going to apologize for trying to find you someone. If you don't soon start dating, people are going to wonder about you."

Hadn't he just thought the same thing himself? "I hope they come up with some good stories."

"This isn't funny. You're a businessman. People don't want to sign contracts with unstable men."

"Being single doesn't make me unstable. I can name lots of men who did very well as bachelors."

"Yeah, but most of them don't have a children's video game line they're about to release."

He turned away. "I'll take my chances."

His attorney caught his arm and stopped him. "You'll be wrong. Look, do you want support when you take this new company public next year? Then you'd better look alive. Like a guy worth supporting."

His attorney stormed off at the same time Cracker Girl walked by, her head twisting from side to side as if she were looking for someone.

A starburst of pleasure shot through him, surprising him. She *was* beautiful. Physically perfect. And with a conscience. Although taking crackers from a party didn't rank up there with grand theft auto, he could see it upset her.

He laughed and shook his head, but he stopped midmotion. Good grief. She'd made him laugh.

With the party officially winding down, Eloise retrieved her black wool cape, a classic that never went out of style. By the time she reached the elevator, Tucker and Olivia were already there, saying goodbye to guests.

The plush little car took the couple in front of her away. She smiled at Olivia and caught her hands. "It was a wonderful party."

Pregnant and glowing with it, blond-haired, blue-eyed Olivia said, "Thanks."

"It was great seeing your parents too. Where did they run off to? I tried to find them to say goodbye but they were gone."

"Dad wanted to be in bed early so he and Mom could get up early. We're all going to Kentucky tomorrow."

"Celebrating Christmas from the last Friday in November to January second," Tucker said with a laugh.

"You're taking more than a month off?"

"Yes!" Olivia joyfully said. "Five weeks! We're coming back for one party mid-December, but other than that we'll be in Kentucky."

Eloise smiled. She'd wondered why Tucker and Olivia had had their Christmas party so early.

"It's going to be such fun. We'll sleigh ride and skate." She smiled at her handsome husband, a dark-haired, thirty-something former confirmed bachelor she'd fallen in love with in Italy. "And drink hot chocolate by the fire."

"Sounds perfect." *For Olivia*. The woman lived and breathed the fairy tale. But Eloise wanted a real life. With her husband dead and most of the magic sucked out of life, all she wanted to be was normal, to get a job and *never* depend on anyone but herself again.

She glanced around. "Have you seen Laura Beth?"

Olivia caught Eloise's hand and pulled her to the side. "She left ten minutes ago with one of Tucker's vice presidents."

Eloise's chest tightened. "Really?"

"They were talking stock options and market fluctuations when they said goodbye to us. I overheard them saying something about going to a coffee shop."

"Oh."

"Do you need a taxi?"

She licked her suddenly dry lips. A taxi? Obviously Olivia had forgotten how much a taxi cost. The plan had been for her and Laura Beth to take the subway. Together. She didn't want to ride alone this late at night and couldn't believe Laura Beth had ditched her.

Still, that wasn't Olivia's problem. If anything, Eloise and Laura Beth had vowed to keep their financial distress from their now-wealthy friend so she wouldn't do something kind, but awkward, like pay their rent.

"Um. No. I don't need a taxi." She smiled. "I'm taking the subway."

"Alone?"

"I love the subway." That wasn't really a lie. She did love the subway. It was cheap and efficient. But at night, alone, it was also scary.

"Oh, Eloise! I don't want you to risk it. Let Tucker call his driver."

"We're fine."

"*You're* alone."

Drat. She'd hoped Olivia wouldn't notice that tricky maneuvering use of "we" to make her think she had company for the subway.

Tucker caught Olivia's hand to get her attention. "Ricky's leaving."

Eloise turned to see the guy who had tried to tell her stealing crackers was okay. He had dark hair and dark eyes, and he looked amazing in a tux. Sexy.

She sucked in a breath. Noticing he was sexy had been an accident. She refused to notice any guy until she was financially stable.

Olivia stood on tiptoes and kissed his cheek.

All right. He was tall. It was hard not to notice someone was tall.

He straightened away from Olivia, and Eloise frowned. It was also hard not to notice smooth, sexy brown eyes that had a sleepy, smoldering way of looking at a woman. And that hair? Dark. Shaggy. So out of style she should want to walk him to a hair salon. Instead, she was tempted to brush it off his forehead.

Wow. Seriously? What was wrong with her? She had not intended to take note of any of that. But the guy was simply too gorgeous not to notice.

"Good night, Ricky. Thanks for coming to the party. I hope you enjoyed it."

"It was great."

He kissed Olivia's cheek, and Eloise stood there like an idiot, realizing her mistake. When he'd walked over, she should have taken advantage of Olivia's preoccupation and slipped into the elevator. Nothing was worse than the guilt of a former roommate who hadn't just found the love of her life but also her calling. While Eloise and Laura Beth floundered, Olivia had hit the life lottery and was married, pregnant and a manager for young artists. And now she couldn't stop worrying about her former roommates.

Eloise didn't want to be anybody's burden. She was smart, educated. With the right job, she could be happy as a clam. It was finding that job that seemed impossible. Until she did, she'd be poor. And Olivia would worry.

Olivia glanced at Eloise and, as if just seeing the obvious, she gasped. "You've met Eloise, right?"

The guy named Ricky looked over at her. "I bumped into her by the fireplace."

"She's on her way home, but her friend left early." Olivia winced. "Talking business with one of Tucker's employees."

Eloise supposed she shouldn't be angry because that might lead to a better job for Laura Beth, but she knew the next words coming out of Olivia's mouth before she even heard them.

"You have your limo, right?" She put her hand on her tummy, looking beautiful and Madonna like, the kind of woman no man could refuse. "You wouldn't mind taking Eloise to her apartment, would you?"

Eloise immediately said, "No. I'm fine."

At the same time, Ricky said, "Actually, I think I owe her a favor."

Olivia beamed. "Great."

The elevator doors swished open.

Ricky smiled at her and motioned to the door. "After you."

She stepped inside. As the doors closed, she waved to Olivia. "Thanks again for inviting me."

Tucker and Olivia waved back, looking like the perfect couple. "Thanks for coming."

The doors met and the little car began its descent.

"So…your friend dumped you."

"We're both trying to find jobs that pay better than what we have so we can afford our rent. She was talking business with one of Tucker's executives. I can't fault her for that."

"How long have you been in New York?"

"Three years."

"That's a long time to still be scraping by."

"We were fine until Olivia left us."

Even though she had a good excuse for her poverty, embarrassment rumbled through her. She might have been born into money, but she'd gone to the school of hard knocks. Paid her dues. Gotten her education in spite of her grief and confusion. Now all she wanted was a job.

Was that really so much to ask?

Ricky waited in silence as the elevator descended. From the tension crackling off Eloise Whatever-Her-Last-Name-Was, he could tell she wasn't happy that he was taking her home. Actually, he could tell she wasn't happy period. Her financial situation was abysmal. Her friend Olivia was living a great life. Her other friend had deserted her.

She had a lot of pride. Which he couldn't argue. He had a bit of pride himself. But he wasn't going to let a pretty single girl ride the subway alone after midnight. Especially not one who had made him laugh.

The elevator door opened and she sped out into the frosty cold night. He ambled behind her. When she reached the sidewalk, she stopped dramatically.

He wasn't the only one who had called for his limo. Four

long black cars sat in a cluster in front of the building. No way for her to pass. No way for her to hail a cab.

He paused behind her, slid his arm around her shoulders and pointed at the third one down. His fingers accidentally brushed the back of her neck, and the tips tingled at the feeling of her soft, soft skin.

He cleared his throat. "I'm number three. Just accept a ride."

She straightened regally. "All right."

When they reached his car, Norman, his driver, opened the door. She slid inside. He slid in beside her. A minute later, Norman's door closed and the engine hummed to life.

"Wanna give me your address so I can tell the driver where to take you?"

She told him, then sat staring at her coat while he used the internal intercom system to inform Norman.

The next five minutes passed in silence. Finally, unable to bear her misery anymore, he said, "I really was as poor as you when I moved to the city. I don't mind taking you home. This isn't an imposition. It isn't charity. It's a happy coincidence that we were leaving at the same time. Please, stop feeling bad."

To his surprise, she turned on him. "Feeling bad? I don't feel bad! I'm mad. I'm sick of people pitying me when all I want is a decent job. I'm educated enough to get one, but no one seems to want me."

"What's your degree in?"

"Human resources."

"Ouch. You know human resources functions can be folded into administration or accounting. And that's exactly what happens in a recession."

"I know. Lucky me."

She had enough pride to fill an ocean. But she also had a weird sense of humor about it. Enough that he'd almost laughed again. Twice. In one night. Both times because of her.

"Now, don't get snooty. Surely, there are other things you can do."

"I've waitressed, and apparently a degree can also get you a lot of temporary secretarial work because right now I'm in a six-week gig at a law firm."

"That's something."

She sighed tiredly. "Actually, it is. I don't mean to sound ungrateful. I know others have it a lot worse."

He was one of those people who had it worse than she did. But he didn't share that—not even with people who almost made him laugh. She'd go from treating him normally to feeling sorry for him. And for once, just once, he wanted to be with somebody who didn't feel sorry for him.

He glanced at the floor and was nearly struck blind by the glitter of her shoes. His gazed traveled up her trim legs to the black cape she wore. Her shiny gold dress peeked above the coat's collar.

For a struggling woman, she dressed very well. Of course, her clothes could be old. Or she could have gotten them from a secondhand store.

But even if she'd gotten them from a thrift store, she'd known what to choose and how to wear it. Actually, if he thought about it, she had the look of every socialite he'd been introduced to in the past year.

Except she wasn't one. She didn't have any money.

"What Laura Beth and I really need is another roommate."

He spared her a glance. "That shouldn't be too hard to find."

"Huh! We've tried. We never seem to pick someone who fits with us."

He turned on the seat. "Really? Why?"

"The first girl we let in had a record we didn't know about until her parole officer called."

He chuckled, amazed that she'd done it again. So easily, so effortlessly, she could make him laugh. "I dated somebody like that once. Turned out abysmally."

"Yeah, well, Judy took my coffeemaker when she left."

"Ouch."

"The references for the second one were faked."

"You need Jason Jones."

"Excuse me?"

"That's the search engine I created. Well, I came up with the idea. Elias Greene actually wrote the programs. It investigates people."

"Really?"

"Yeah. It's great. It'll tell you things you never even realized you wanted to know." He smiled politely. "I'd let you use it for free."

She squeezed her eyes shut in distress. "I don't want your handouts. I don't want anybody's handouts!"

Yeah. He could see that. He didn't know where she'd come from, but she had guts and grit. She wanted to make it on her own.

"We could bargain for it."

She gasped and scrambled away from him. "Not on your life."

He laughed. Again. Fourth time. "I'm not talking about sex."

She relaxed but gave him a strange look. "I don't have anything to bargain." She petted her coat. "Unless you're into vintage women's clothes."

"Nope. But you do have something I want."

Her gazed strolled over to his cautiously, wary. "What?"

"Time."

"Time?"

"Yeah. I have ten Christmas parties, a wedding and a fraternity reunion coming up. I need a date."

CHAPTER TWO

ELOISE STARED AT Ricky Whatever. "I don't even know your last name."

"It's Langley." He smiled at her. Those silky brown eyes held her prisoner. "And yours?"

"Vaughn."

He reached out and shook her hand. "It's nice to meet you, Eloise Vaughn."

"So you have twelve places to go for Christmas and you want me to go out with you?"

"No. I want you to be my date. Big difference."

She eyed him askance. "I'm not sure how."

"There'd be nothing romantic between us." He winced. "Except to pretend that there is. I need space. A reason to bow out of conversations. Bringing a date to parties has a way of giving a guy options."

She studied him, realized he was serious and said the thing he was dancing around but wouldn't quite say. "And you want people to stop fixing you up all the time. With someone at your side, they'd leave you alone."

"It's more complicated than that. Really what it comes down to is easing myself back into the world and into my social circle. A date at my side would be like a living symbol to my friends that I'm fine, and they can all stop worrying about me."

Eloise got comfortable against the supple leather seat. He talked like a guy coming off a bad relationship. Nobody wanted to have to go to parties when they were smarting from a breakup. He probably didn't want to have to explain where his ex was. Or, worse, have to flirt or be flirted with.

"So you're looking for ways to be able to go to parties without being social."

"I don't mind being social. I just don't want to have to be too social. Look, I'm not in the market for something romantic, so you'd be perfectly safe. You might even enjoy yourself. Meet some new people. Make some work contacts."

Yep. Anybody who wasn't in the market for something romantic was still hurting over a bad breakup. But he'd also said the magic words. Work contacts. The employment market was so tight she couldn't even get interviews. But if she could meet the higher-ups of some companies, she might impress them and maybe open a door for herself.

"And I don't have to do anything but smile and be polite?"

"And pretend to like me."

She already sort of liked him. He was handsome and just a little bit scruffy, the way a man was when there was no woman in his life. And he was honest. So pretending to like him wouldn't be hard.

"We'd need a story."

"A story?"

"How we met. Why we're dating."

"Why don't we just say we met at Olivia and Tucker's party and hit it off?"

"It's only half a lie. We did meet at the party. But we didn't exactly hit it off. We barely spoke."

"We're talking like two friends now."

She thought about that. "Yeah. I guess we are." She sucked in a breath. "And you'd help me find a job?"

"You don't want to use Jason Jones to find a roommate?"

"A roommate is temporary. I want a permanent solution. I want a career."

His brow wrinkled. "Are you asking me to hire you?"

She gaped at him. "God, no! I don't want to be the girl in the office who got her job by dating the boss. Sheesh! Talk about instant pariah. I want you to get me job with one of your friends."

"I can't get you *hired*, but I could help you make contacts."

She shook her head. "If I'm going out with you—" She did the math in her head...ten parties, one wedding, one fraternity reunion "—twelve times, then I'm getting twelve dates' worth of help."

"What do you want me to do? Run an ad saying that someone should hire you?"

"I don't care what you do. Pick your friends' brains to see who's looking for an HR person and get me interviews, and I'll go out with you *twelve*," she deliberately exaggerated the word so he'd see the significance of the big number, "times."

His eyes told her he was doing a bit of mental calculating—proving he took her seriously—before he stuck out his hand to shake hers. "Deal."

She took it. "Deal."

They reached her apartment building. She slid out of the limo, and he did too. "You don't have to walk me upstairs."

"Someone could be hiding—"

She put her hand on his chest and was surprised that she met a solid wall. He was a lot stronger than he looked. Probably all muscle under that trim tux.

Now that they were going to spend a lot of time together, that meant something. She took in his handsome face. The fine lines that created his chiseled features. Those beautiful brown eyes.

A strange feeling worked its way through her. It took a second to recognize it, but it was attraction. Real attraction. Not just the I-think-he's-handsome feeling. But more like the I-could-sleep-with-him-someday feeling.

Which would only wreck their deal and was the last thing in the world she wanted. She'd gone the route of love. Now she realized having a job was a more secure happily-ever-after. Plus, he'd said he wasn't interested in anything romantic. She couldn't be either.

She removed her hand. "This is where I draw the line. I'm fine walking myself upstairs. And you need to believe me."

"But—"

"No." With that she turned and strode into her building. He was handsome, but neither of them was in the market for a romance. And she needed their deal. She hadn't been able to make job inroads for herself. He might be able to help her. She wouldn't risk being alone with him outside her apartment door when there was so much goodnight-kiss potential. She might be strong, but she wasn't perfect. She'd learned a long time ago that a smart woman didn't tempt fate.

The next morning she woke confused. Or maybe disoriented. She hadn't gotten drunk, so she didn't have a hangover. But that meant she also didn't have an excuse for agreeing to go on twelve dates with a stranger.

Although he wasn't really a stranger. He was a friend of Olivia and Tucker's. Someone Olivia liked enough that she'd gone up on tiptoes to kiss his cheek. Olivia would have the scoop on him.

She grabbed her phone from the bedside table and headed for the kitchen. After throwing together a pot of coffee in an old drip coffeemaker instead of her sleek one-cup one stolen by Judy, she speed dialed Olivia.

"Hi, this is Olivia Engle. You've reached my voice mail. Please leave a message after the beep."

Drat. She'd forgotten Olivia and her family were leaving early for Kentucky. She wouldn't have her phone on. Heck, she might not turn on her phone for the entire month of December. What had she said? She and Tucker would be having family time?

She tossed her phone to the table before she sat. So much for asking Olivia about Ricky Langley.

Laura Beth trudged into the kitchen. Her long brown hair lay in disarray on her shoulders. Her green eyes were barely open. "Who were you calling?"

"Olivia. I needed some insider information, but then I remembered she's flying to Kentucky today."

Reaching into the cupboard for a cup and a tea bag, Laura Beth asked, "What kind of insider information?"

"A little background on a guy. I think I may have found a way to get a job."

Laura Beth's eyes widened. "Really?"

"Yes. And, by the way, thanks for deserting me last night."

"Sorry. Bruce heads Tucker's newly created IT department. I went for coffee and got an interview."

"Yeah, well, the guy I met last night wants a date for some parties."

"Oh my God, you're not—" Her eyes grew as big as two dinner plates and she couldn't finish.

"Not *that* kind of date. Ricky Langley seems to be coming off a big breakup, and he doesn't want to go to his Christmas social engagements alone. So he asked me to go to all his parties. In exchange, he'll introduce me to influential people and pick their brains about job openings."

"That sounds almost as promising as my job interview. Maybe more promising because you could get a couple of prospects."

The comment eased away the little bit of confusion Eloise had had about this deal. Ricky was Olivia and Tucker's friend. He hadn't made a pass. He'd made a deal. She liked deals. She liked giving something to get something. She absolutely hated charity.

So she'd try this, giving him one date to prove himself. And if he didn't, she'd end it.

This did not have to be something to stress over.

He called around ten o'clock, apologetic because the first party he needed her to attend with him was that night.

"Already? It won't even be December for two days."

"My friends start early." He paused, then said, "Is that a problem?"

"No. It's fine. It might be Saturday, but I don't date and I don't have enough money to go out myself." She winced, realizing how pathetic she sounded. "I meant that to be reassuring, not whiny."

"Yeah. I got it."

"So what time will you pick me up?"

"Around eight." He hesitated, not sounding any more sure of this weird arrangement than she was, then added, "This party is being thrown by my banker."

"Any idea how I should dress?"

"I think the same way you did for Tucker and Olivia's party." He paused. "You looked nice."

The simple compliment gave her far too much pleasure. She shook it off. "Thanks. But that was a cocktail dress. If this event is formal, I may need to wear a gown."

"It's black tie at the Waldorf."

"I'm wearing a gown."

"Fine. But don't be waiting in the lobby of your building. Let me come up. I don't want my driver telling his other driver buddies that I make my dates meet me on the street."

She hadn't wanted them to get too personal, but the whole point was for this to look real. He was right; it would be odd if she was waiting for him in her building lobby. "Okay."

She headed back to her bedroom to find something to wear. With twelve cocktail dresses, several ball gowns and just about anything he needed her to wear for any occasion, she had plenty of possibilities. Except everything she owned was out of style.

She pulled a red gown from the rack. She would think bankers would like red... No. No. Green. Like money. With a laugh, she reached for a green velvet gown. It would need tons of updating, but she didn't care. In the past few years, she'd developed a way with scissors and a needle and thread. She'd gotten so good at refurbishing old clothes that she'd actually bought a secondhand sewing machine so she could make real alterations.

Smiling as she went in search of her scissors, she realized she was really looking forward to going out. She would meet people in a position to hire her. But also she had a reason to dress up. To socialize. Maybe even dance. It would be fun.

She couldn't remember the last time she'd had fun.

As long as Ricky Langley really was a gentleman, this arrangement could be good for a bundle of reasons.

He arrived a little before eight. Still excited, she opened the door, and her eyes widened. She'd forgotten how good-looking he was. Dressed in a tux with a black top coat, he was so gorgeous, so sophisticated, he could have been the king of a small country.

She quickly pulled herself together. His amazingness did not matter. She did not want to be attracted to anybody. She wanted a job.

"Let me get my coat."

Nodding, he strolled into her apartment, but she didn't give him a lot of time to look around. It wasn't that she was ashamed of her living space. Actually, she was proud of the fact that she had come as far as she had with absolutely no help. But she was eager to get out the door and go to a party. In a pretty gown. Something she'd made even prettier.

She flipped her cape over her back and walked toward him.

"You look incredible."

Pride sizzled through her. He wouldn't have said that if he'd seen this dress five hours ago. "Thanks. I loved this dress when I bought it." They walked to the door, and she closed it behind them. "So it was fantastic to have a reason to bring it up to date."

She led the way down the stairs.

"You updated your dress?"

"Yes. I took off the collar and the belt and did a little something to the back."

"Oh."

She glanced over her shoulder at him. "You don't have to worry that I'm going to embarrass you. I don't have money to buy new things, but I have plenty of old things I can fix or update. And I've gotten very good with a sewing machine. No one will even notice that this dress used to look totally different."

The conversation died, and they stayed silent on the drive to the Waldorf. The building façade had been covered in white lights, which were also woven through the branches of the fir trees standing like sentinels on both side of the entryway.

Memories of the time she'd come here with her parents flooded her. It had been her first formal party, and she was so nervous at meeting her dad's friends and business associates that she'd sworn real butterflies were in her tummy.

Mind your manners.

Don't speak unless spoken to.

You are a guest. The daughter of a wealthy man. Your comportment should say that.

The doorman came over and opened the door of Ricky's limo.

She drew in a breath and let him help her out. That's when she saw the other attendees. Furs. Diamonds. Hair coiffed to perfection.

She slid her hand down her cape, which looked foolish compared to the furs being worn by the other women exiting limos, and turned to Ricky. "I'm guessing the guy knows a few wealthy people."

He smiled, motioning for her to walk under the portico and to the steps leading to the hotel. "Expect a camera or two on the way in. A photographer for the society pages will take a shot of everyone in the hope of getting something for tomorrow's paper."

She faltered. "Oh." Her mother might live in Kentucky, but she got all the New York papers so she could "keep up" with her own kind. She lived and breathed the society pages.

Fear shimmied along her nerve endings. She couldn't seem to make her feet move. She hadn't seen her parents in five years. Not since they'd disowned her. But if they saw her at a society event with a wealthy man, God only knew what they'd do. Happy she'd finally come to her senses, would they call her? Pretend nothing had happened? And if they did, what would she do? Was she lonely enough, desperate enough, to pretend it was okay that they hadn't cared that her husband had died and that she was struggling to get her bearings?

She squeezed her eyes shut. Why hadn't she thought of this?

Ricky's voice came to her slowly, softly. "You don't mind getting your picture taken, do you?"

She popped her eyes open. "It depends on where it will end up."

He took her elbow and guided her up the steps to the entryway. "Probably nowhere. We'd have to be important enough for a society columnist to want to comment on us."

"And you're not important?"

Another uniformed hotel employee opened the door and they walked inside. "Last year I was everybody's charity case. This year, I'm nothing. You're safe."

Relief poured through her, but it was short-lived. Not only was she in a dress from five years ago, updated by collar-and-belt removal, but also no one could predict who a society columnist might deem important to write about. If Ricky Langley hadn't dated anybody in a year, his suddenly appearing with a woman might spark curiosity.

As they walked through the ornate lobby, she saw a camera raised toward her, and as smoothly as possible, she ducked behind Ricky.

He turned. "What are you doing?"

"Oh, I just thought because you have the invitation, you should go first."

He frowned. "The lobby is wide enough that we can walk side by side."

Seeing the photographer's attention had been caught by another guest, she laughed. "Of course. I'm sorry."

They entered the elevator and rode up to the ballroom in silence. Ricky noticed that she'd kept hugging her cape, almost as if she was trying to hide it, and winced a bit internally. She clearly believed she didn't belong here and was embarrassed.

But wariness overcame his worry. This was their first date. He wanted her to have a good time and meet perspective employers, but he was more concerned with how his friends reacted to *her*. If they didn't believe their dating was real, then all bets were off, and she wouldn't have to worry about how she looked.

The doors opened, and they walked out of the elevator together.

He caught her gaze. "Let me take your cape for coat check."

She slid it off and handed it to him. He shrugged out of his top coat and gave the two to the young woman manning the station.

They turned to go into the dimly lit foyer that would take them to the ballroom, and a photographer snapped their picture. Eloise's face drained of color. He would've sworn she swayed.

At Tucker and Olivia's party, she'd given him the impression she was as close to a princess as a woman could be without actually being royalty. Yet she was suddenly shaking in her shoes.

"Are you okay?"

She faced him with an overbright smile. "Yeah. Sure. I'm fine."

He knew she wasn't. Her eyes shone with fear. Her face was pasty white.

"You're not afraid to meet these people, are you?"

She sucked in a breath. "I need to meet these people."

"So what's wrong?"

"I hate to have my picture taken."

Which explained all the questions she'd had about the photographers…but raised new ones about why she wouldn't want her picture taken.

Before he could say anything, regal Eloise reappeared. She straightened to her full height. Her expression shifted. The green dress that she'd altered slid along her curves like decadence incarnate. She turned and headed for the entrance to the ballroom, and Ricky's eyes bulged.

The neckline might be normal in the front, but the back dipped to the bottom of her spine. Smooth yellow hair flirted with her naked skin, swishing back and forth.

His mouth watered.

How the hell had he missed that her dress had virtually no back?

Realizing he wasn't following her, she stopped and faced him. "Do you like getting your picture taken by people you don't know?"

He raced to catch up with her. "I've been getting my picture taken by strangers for so long I guess it doesn't faze me anymore. Especially because they rarely turn up anywhere."

She shook her mane of yellow hair down her back and strode ahead again. "Fine."

Watching her walk away, he stood frozen. The smooth material of her dress caressed her perfect butt so well the fact that she didn't like getting her picture taken faded into insignificance. At Tucker and Olivia's he'd noticed she was gorgeous, but in that dress she was a showstopper.

Which was perfect. One look at her and everybody would totally understand why he had come out of his self-imposed social hiatus and was going out with her.

Imagining his friends' reactions to her, he bit back a cheesy grin and caught up to her right before the desk where he'd present his invitation. There could be a million reasons why she didn't like getting her picture taken, and most of them were innocent. He wasn't going to ruin what could be the perfect return to the party scene with unfounded suspicions.

"If it's any consolation, cameras are off-limits in the party."

"Yes. It is a consolation."

He presented his invitation at the discreet desk by the entry, and they were routed to the greeting line for the host and hostess.

Paul Montgomery's eyes lit when he saw Eloise. "My darling, however did you get this guy to finally break down and bring a date somewhere?"

She laughed and slid her arm through Ricky's. "We met at the party of a mutual friend."

"Tucker and Olivia Engle," Ricky said, shaking the old

man's hand. "She's a friend of Olivia's. I'm a friend of Tucker's."

"Oh, we love Olivia," Mrs. Paul Montgomery said, leaning in to air kiss Eloise's cheek. "She simply glows with her pregnancy."

Eloise smiled. "She certainly does. She will make an amazing mother."

Their twenty seconds of greeting time expended, Ricky and Eloise were guided to the next section, where they were given their table number and a hand-carved Christmas ornament as a gift from the Montgomerys.

The huge ballroom shimmered with laughing, talking people. Rich red velvet drapes billowed from ceiling-high windows and glittered festively as if they'd been sprinkled with stardust. Round tables boasted gold tablecloths and huge centerpieces of calla lilies and evergreens accented by a ribbon of gold that wove through them.

Ricky took Eloise's hand and guided her through the sea of round tables. "That went smoothly."

"Our story's very believable."

"Then we'll stick with it." He paused, turned and caught her gaze. Now that he'd realized the impact gorgeous Eloise would make on his friends, a bit of fear tugged at his gut.

"We're seated with some of my best friends. I don't want them to know you're a fake date. These are the people I most want to reassure that I'm fine. Dating someone is the living, breathing symbol of that. If we're convincing enough, they won't ask questions. They'll see I'm fine."

"Okay."

"But if anybody even suspects you're a fake date, I'm going to look pathetic. This has to be as real as possible for my friends to buy in. That means I'm going to put my arm around you."

She nodded.

He sucked in a breath. "And we're going to dance because I love to dance, and it will look odd if I bring a date and don't dance."

She straightened the collar of his tux, then tightened his bow tie, the gesture both casual and intimate. His nerves shivered. Not from fear of her touch, but from easy acceptance of her fingers on him. Which scared him to death. She was gorgeous and, probably like every other man in this room, he wanted to touch her and be touched by her. Their situation might be fake, but that didn't mean he wouldn't get the feelings.

"Relax. Not only do we seem to be compatible, but I have dated a guy or two. I know how to act."

He sniffed a laugh. "Sorry."

"It's okay. We're actually doing better than people on a real date because we're not afraid to be honest."

He fought a wince. She would not be pleased if he'd honestly tell her that her little ministrations with his bow tie had shot white-hot need through his veins. "I guess that's true."

"So if either one of us does anything wrong, we know we can be honest and tell the other one."

Okay. As long as they weren't admitting things like awakening hormones, he could get on board with that. "That's good."

She took his hand. "We are going to ace this."

He led the way to the table and introduced Eloise to his first business partner, Elias Greene, and his fiancée Bridget O'Malley, the couple getting married on Christmas Eve. As they sat down, another friend, George Russell and his wife, Andi, joined them.

When introduced, Eloise smiled and nodded, and the knots in Ricky's stomach began to unravel. He expected the husbands to fawn all over her, but he would have never guessed the wives would instantly like her.

Andi leaned over and caught Eloisa's hand. "I love your dress."

She laughed. "What? This old thing?"

Andi sniffed. "Okay. Don't tell me where you got it."

"Actually, I do a lot of my own designing."

Andi's mouth fell open. "You made that?"

"I bought it, then sort of reorganized it to suit my tastes."

Ricky liked the way she stuck with the truth. She didn't announce that she was broke, but she didn't pretend to be someone she wasn't. He took a sip from his water glass, his nerves settling and his faith in their deal reviving. She was doing very well.

They ate salad, filet mignon and simple baked potatoes, and an elaborate chocolate mousse creation for dessert, then Paul gave a toast that was more of a thank-you for coming and blessing to all in the new year, Then the dancing started.

Eloise turned to him with a smile. "I know you're dying to dance."

For the first time in his life, he wasn't. Her dress had no back. He was going to have to put his hands on *her.*

But his friends expected him to dance, so he gave her points for being a step ahead of the game.

He rose and took her hand. They threaded through the tables to the dance floor and kept going until they were in the center of the throng of people. This far into the dancers, they couldn't be seen by his friends at their table or even by anyone curious enough to seek them out.

As he pulled her to him, he let his hand fall to the small of her back and found soft, supple skin. But a quick mental review of her dress told him that if he were to lower his hands until he found fabric, he'd be fondling her butt.

Leaving his hand where it was, he cleared his throat. "Interesting back on this dress."

She laughed and winced. "Sorry."

"Oh, no. It's not a problem." *Most guys would kill for the opportunity to touch you like this.* But, of course, he didn't add that out loud. He looked down into her smiling face. "You seem like you're having fun."

"Honestly, the steak alone with worth the evening for me."

He twirled them around. "Not much steak in the diet of someone scrambling to make a living."

"Or champagne. Or even salad most days." She caught his gaze and smiled. "Thanks."

His heart flip-flopped. It had been a long time since he'd made someone happy. It humbled him that this woman was so broke she thanked him for food.

He winced. "You're welcome. But we still have to introduce you to a few people tonight, so you get your side of the arrangement too."

"Maybe tonight should just be my getting-my-feet-wet night." She glanced around. "Is this your usual crowd?"

"Usual crowd?"

"You know. Are these the people who typically get invited to the events you attend?"

Puzzled, he let his gaze ripple from face to face of the people on the dance floor. She was right. He did have a "usual" crowd. He'd see most of these people again and again until January second, when the party circuit would end.

"Yes. But other parties will have additional guests, depending on the event. You won't see any of these people at my office party. You'll see one or two at the fraternity reunion. You'll see them all at Elias and Bridget's wedding. And you probably saw most of them at Tucker and Olivia's."

He twirled them around again, and she laughed.

His gut tightened. Every instinct he had came to life. He couldn't remember the last time *he'd* made someone laugh. Or the last time he'd had fun. But he was having fun now.

When the music ended, he removed his hand from the softness that was the small of her back and immediately directed her to the couple beside them, Mimi and Oliver French.

She politely shook their hands. "I think I read about you in the *Journal* last week."

Oliver feigned humility. "I don't know why they wrote that piece."

Eloise laughed. "Because your firm made billions of dollars for your clients last year."

Mimi playfully swatted her husband's arm. "He's such a goose. Never likes to take credit. But we did have a banner year." She smiled at Eloise. "So tell me, dear, where did you get that dress?"

"A little boutique a few streets over from here," Eloise said with a smile. She didn't mention that it had been five years ago on a shopping trip with her mom. Or that the dress had been a conservative gown with a full back, high collar and slim belt to accent her waist. Andi might have loved hearing that, but Mimi behaved a little too much like Eloise's mom. She wouldn't see talent. She'd sniff out desperation.

"I must take a look at their stock."

"You really should."

"Eloise has only been in the city a short time," Ricky said, obviously having decided three years was a short time.

Oliver said, "Really."

"Yes." She smiled pleasantly. "I got my degree, and now I'm job hunting."

The band began to play. The couple smiled and turned away to dance again.

Ricky put his hand on the small of her back and they moved in time to the music.

"That went well."

"It did, but it feels odd." With the gooseflesh raised on her skin from his hand warming the small of her back, her voice came out a little huskier than she intended.

His eyebrows rose. "Feels odd?"

She carefully met his gaze. "Like I'm asking for a job."

He swung them around. "Okay. There's problem number one for you. You should be proud of the fact that you're looking for a job."

"I feel desperate."

"And that's problem number two. Do you think these people got to the top by not being able to smell desperation?"

"I know they can."

"You've gotta get rid of that."

"Okay."

The dance ended, and their conversation was cut short by someone else who came up to talk to Ricky. Unlike the Mr. and Mrs. French, this guy was not interested in Ricky's date. Not at all. Proposing a new business venture, he'd barely reacted when Ricky introduced her.

Eloise looked around. The winking diamonds shimmering through the crowd on throats, wrists and fingers told the story of just how rich, just how important, these people were. Yet Ricky looked totally comfortable. Listening as he explained that he couldn't invest because of the upcoming release of his new line of children's video games after which he would take that company public, she realized he was so casual because he was so smart. He belonged here. He was as sharp as any billionaire, any magnate, any tycoon.

Ridiculous pride surged in her. The whole group wanted to know his thoughts on something, but he was with *her*.

She shook her head to clear it of the unexpected thought. He wasn't with her because he liked her. He was with her because they'd made a deal, and he'd only made a deal because he needed protection. She was nothing more than a symbol to his friends that he had moved beyond the breakup that must have really hurt him.

She had best remember that.

After the set of waltzes, the band began to play a slow,

mellow tune. Expecting Ricky to bow out and direct her back to the table, she was surprised when he pulled her close.

She met the solid wall of his chest as his hand slid up her back, raising gooseflesh that she prayed he couldn't feel. Snuggled against him like a lover, she had to fight the urge to close her eyes and melt into him.

He's not a real date.

He's not a real date.

He's not a real date.

She rolled the litany through her brain until it sunk in. She'd had her Prince Charming and he was gone. If she didn't find a way to stop her reactions to Ricky, she might just lose the chance to continue going out with him.

Then there'd be no job. No future. Just endless days of temp jobs, struggling for rent money and eating packaged noodles.

CHAPTER THREE

REMINDING HERSELF OF her dire straits did not stem Eloise's attraction.

Dancing with Ricky and watching him between dances, it was obvious that he was strong and smart. And he treated her like royalty. He brought her drinks, eased her into most conversations and basically behaved as if she were someone he cared about...like a real date.

Was it any wonder she was having trouble separating fact from fiction?

The second time they slow danced, she'd felt a stirring inside her that went beyond attraction. She liked him. A lot. So she spent a little extra time in the ladies' room, reminding herself again this was only a deal, not a relationship.

But every time they slow danced, her reactions increased. Warmth flooded her when he held her. Pinpricks of delight raced through her when he did something sweet. He smiled at her when he held her cape for her at the end of the night, and her heart about shot out of her chest.

She groaned internally, finally figuring out what was wrong. Her brain might know this was only an act, but her body and her hormones reacted as if it were real.

Sliding into the limo, she sat as far away from him as she could.

As Norman started the engine, Ricky tapped his hands on his knees, studied her for a few seconds and finally said,

"Tomorrow night's event is a private dinner at the home of an investment banker who is also a college buddy."

From the far end of the seat, she smiled politely. "Sounds nice."

"I don't think you'll need to wear anything fancy."

"Probably not. A cocktail dress should be good."

"Great."

The conversation died, and Eloise leaned back. It was clear from his nervous gestures that he wasn't feeling any of the attraction she felt. So, if he'd noticed her over-long glances or the way she snuggled into him when they danced, that might be why he was so uncomfortable with her now.

She winced. Gazing into his eyes, nestling into him when they danced, she was breaking rule number one of their bargain: no romance. And if she didn't watch herself, he could end this deal.

To head off the curiosities of his driver, she politely let him walk her to her door—up all four flights of stairs, just in case the chauffer was the type to sneak into the building and check on things.

Outside her apartment, she smiled. "I had a great time." Too great. She'd been so angry with her parents and just plain life in general for so long that she'd never anticipated she'd actually enjoy going out again. Or that she'd be so attracted to someone again. And now here she was nervous, with their deal in jeopardy, trying not to look smitten.

He shoved his hands into his trouser pockets. "Thanks. I had a good time too."

She cleared her throat. "So. Um. Okay." Stammering. Great. Now she looked like an even bigger fool. Knowing how to end this torment, she caught the gaze of his dark, sleepy eyes and simply said, "Good night."

He stepped back. "Good night."

She turned, opened her door and jumped inside.

Braced against the solid steel, she groaned. What the

hell was she doing? She needed a job! Since when did she let a man tempt her like this?

They were in an arrangement. They were not dating. She could not lose this opportunity to make contacts that might net her a job just because her hormones had unexpectedly awakened. Particularly because *he* was not feeling anything for her.

And wouldn't that be humiliating? Her growing to like a guy who'd essentially hired her to be a date?

She'd had her fair share of mortification in her life, thank you very much. She wouldn't be so stupid again.

Ricky jogged down the stairs. Eloise had been the absolute perfect date. Gorgeous. A cuddler when they danced. She even had *him* believing she liked him. She was so perfect, he found himself humming as he jumped back into the limo.

But the second he realized he was humming, he thought of Blake and cursed. What right did he have to be happy when his son, his baby, was gone? He'd been as responsible for the death of his beautiful baby boy as Blake's mother had been. He did not deserve to be happy.

As Norman pulled the car out into the street, his phone rang. He automatically pulled it from his pocket and glanced at caller ID. His head research and development guy. He had to take it.

"What's up, Tom?"

"I'm sorry, Ricky. We hit a snag."

"A snag? We're in production. There shouldn't be any R&D snags."

"Which is why you might want to call your lawyer. A manufacturer in Berlin has just released a game exactly like game number two in your three-game package."

His stomach fell. "Are you kidding me?"

"No. I have a team comparing the games. Unfortunately,

it will take days. But that gives you time to call your lawyers and bring everybody into the loop."

"I want to know the very second you have a verdict."

He disconnected the call and dialed his lawyers.

At six the following evening, he hung up from yet another
call with his R&D team. He hadn't slept, hadn't eaten. He
felt like his phone was growing out of his ear. Exhausted,
he considered not going to Tim and Jennifer's dinner party.
But, in the end, he knew missing the quiet gathering of
friends might spur more questions than he cared to deal
with. Until he figured out whether he and a German manufacturer had come up with the same game at the same
time, or one of his employees had sold his idea, he had to
pretend nothing was wrong. And, luckily, he already had
Eloise Vaughn in place.

He knocked on her door. She opened it with a smile and
immediately handed him her black wool cape.

Sliding it on her shoulders, he said, "You look great."

She did. Even in a simple black dress and pearls, she was
a knockout. His eyes might be heavy from lack of sleep,
and his brain dead from conversations about patents and
corporate spies, but he still could see she was gorgeous.

She turned and smiled at him. "You look great, too."

He glanced down at his black suit with a white shirt
and thin black tie. "Think I'm okay for a dinner party?"

"You have squarely hit semiformal. You'll be fine."

She headed for the door and all but ran down the four
flights of stairs to the building lobby. Tired, he could barely
keep up with her. He wondered again about the wisdom
of not canceling this party. He hadn't had any sleep, and
her running was odd, as if she were trying to get this night
over with. That wouldn't be good at all for their charade.
She raced outside to the limo and, after Norman opened
the door for her, slid in.

Two steps behind her, Ricky got in beside her. "You're in a hurry tonight."

"I'm just nervous."

"Don't be. Tim and Jennifer are very casual." He stifled a yawn.

Relief swooshed through her. Not just because he'd eased her fears about the dinner party, but because he'd almost yawned. He wasn't nervous around her anymore. If anything, he seemed bored, which had to mean she was successfully hiding her attraction to him. As long as she played it cool, the deal would not be in jeopardy.

She straightened on the seat and smiled at him. "I'll be fine."

Ricky's cell phone rang and he sighed. "I have to take this."

She waved her hand in dismissal, grateful for any chance to look like a woman who wasn't interested in him. "No problem." She smiled. "Take the call."

He clicked the button to answer his phone, and she glanced out the window at the city, which was beginning to dress up for the holiday. Tall Christmas trees had been erected in the lobbies of office buildings, their lights twinkling in the darkness. Shop windows featured elaborate Christmas displays. Salvation Army bell ringers stood beside street vendors with carts covered in tinsel. Steam rose from manhole covers.

Ricky was still on the phone when the driver pulled up to a luxury apartment building and opened the door. He talked as he got out of the limo, talked as they walked to the door and finally disconnected the call when the doorman offered them entry.

"Sorry about that."

Fake date smile in place, Eloise happily said, "It's fine. Really. You don't need to apologize." She gave him a significant look. "Remember?"

He frowned. "Right."

Drat! Now she'd gone too far in the other direction. Instead of reassuring him, she was behaving like a hired hand. Exactly what he didn't want.

They rode up in the elevator in silence. The doors opened onto a plush penthouse. A huge Christmas tree stood in front of a wall of windows. Bright lights and tinsel had been strung around the tree, and that theme continued on coffee tables and archways. Two red stockings decorated the marble fireplace mantel. Awash in lights and color, the main room had a warm, cozy, old-fashioned Christmas feel.

Tim and Jennifer welcomed them with hugs, got them drinks and slid them into the group of couples in front of the elegantly simple marble fireplace.

Conversation flowed easily until the butler announced dinner was served. The hostess pointed out seats at the long mahogany table set with fine china and crystal. Once everyone was comfortable and salads had been served, the lively discussion resumed.

Something light and airy floated through Eloise. Amid the colorful Christmas lights, tinsel and easygoing people, she totally relaxed. This was her second meal, good wine and simple conversation in two days, but, best of all, the odd tension between herself and her fake date had evaporated. With no dancing or touching of any kind required, she didn't have to worry about her attraction or his lack of attraction. All she had to do was talk. And that came easily.

After dinner, the men retreated to the den for a cigar.

Proud of herself for controlling her attraction to Ricky, Eloise breathed a sigh of relief. But when she turned to the women seated with her in front of the fireplace, she found herself facing four round-eyed wives.

"I thought he'd never date again."

Glad for the chance to really play her role and fulfill her commitment, she smiled as she picked up her wineglass. "Oh, he wasn't such a tough nut to crack."

Jennifer's face fell. "Sweetie, it was four months after the tragedy before he even *spoke* to anyone."

Eloise kept her facial features neutral, but internally she winced. Wasn't *tragedy* a bit of an odd way to refer to a breakup?

Muriel, who owned a string of restaurants and was married to Fred, who Eloise had learned was the prankster of their fraternity, said, "Fred was positive he was going to lose everything. All his businesses and all his prospects for more business. But then…" She turned to Jennifer. "What was it? Six months in, he finally picked himself up and got back to work."

And wasn't missing six months of work a bit extreme for a breakup?

Surely she'd misinterpreted.

"He missed work for six months?"

"Oh, sweetie, I don't think he ate for six months."

Her heart stuttered. This had been no ordinary breakup. Everything inside her wanted to ask what had happened. But she caught herself before she opened her mouth. She was supposed to be dating Ricky. These women assumed she knew—assumed *he'd told her*—about whatever had happened. If she didn't behave accordingly, she'd ruin everything.

She quietly said, "It was a difficult time for him."

Jennifer patted her hand. "Which is why we are so glad he found someone."

She smiled. "I'm glad he found me, too." She replied easily enough, but her brain began to scramble for answers. What kind of breakup hit a man so hard he didn't work for six months?

She told herself to stop. Told herself that if he wanted her to know, he'd tell her. She even told herself that she might not want to know because knowing might draw them closer, and she was already having trouble separating fact from fiction.

But nothing worked. Curiosity tightened her chest, filled her brain, wouldn't let her think of anything else.

Forty minutes later, the men ambled out of the den. Everyone had work the next morning. Apparently Ricky had a conference call with lawyers in Berlin, so he had to be up the earliest, which made them the first out the door.

He slid her black wool cape over her shoulders and directed her into the elevator.

Though part of her knew it was overstepping the boundaries of their deal, her curiosity and her genuine concern for him were too much to handle. As soon as she and Ricky were alone in the elevator, she intended to ask him what had happened.

But two seconds before the door closed, Dennis Margolis and his wife, Binnie, jumped in with them.

Dennis rubbed his hands together. "It's gonna feel even colder out there after sitting by that fire."

Binnie sighed dreamily. "I don't care. I hope it stays cold. We need snow for Christmas. The season is so much more fun when there's a coating of snow on the decorations. Don't you think, Eloise?"

"Um, yeah. I love snow. Especially for the holiday."

She smiled at Ricky, expecting him to smile back. He did, but it was a weak lift of his lips. Either he was really tired or "man time" in the den had not gone well.

As they walked through the lobby and into the frigid air and the limo, his phone rang again. She climbed into the car, but he shut the door and stood on the sidewalk talking. Twenty minutes later, Norman opened the door again. He slid in with a big smile.

"Good news?"

"More like major disaster averted. I thought I was going to have to go to war with a company in Europe, but turns out somebody just made a mistake. Once our R&D people went over the games in question with a fine-tooth comb, they realized we'd panicked prematurely."

She had no idea what he was talking about, but his company, his business, wasn't really her concern right now. "That's great."

"It's excellent. I expect a problem or two before every rollout, but it's nice when they resolve themselves so easily."

Glad he was in a better mood, she nonetheless waited a few minutes, until they were solidly in traffic, before she said, "Your friends' wives are really happy to see you dating."

"Um-hum."

Nerves filled her. How the hell did someone say, "So, what's the tragedy in your life?"

She licked her lips, gathering her courage. She couldn't handle the curiosity. But more than that, if his friends discovered she didn't know, it might ruin their charade. "They assume I know what happened to you."

He turned to her, his previously sleepy brown eyes suddenly cool and distant. "I'm sure they do."

She swallowed. Caught in the gaze she didn't recognize, dark, scary eyes of a stranger, she faltered. "So maybe you should tell me?"

He glanced out the window, then back at her. "One of the reasons I'm comfortable with you is that you don't know."

She frowned. "But wouldn't the charade make more sense if I knew?"

"Not if you pity me."

Pity him? What the hell had happened to him? "How about if I promise not to pity you?"

"You can't make that promise."

She glanced out the window. "What if somebody tells me? I mean, what if we get separated again and somebody just blurts it out?"

"I guess you and I will just have to stay close so that no one does."

She snapped her gaze to his. A combination of fear

and curiosity rumbled up from her chest. She was already fighting an attraction to this guy. Did she really want to be close to him? Every time they were out? Spend every minute together?

How had such a simple plan become so complicated?

After walking Eloise to her door, Ricky ran down the four flights of stairs and ambled to his limo. Once he was inside, Norman started the engine and headed out.

He'd been having a great time at the party, so great he'd actually enjoyed the ribbing he took from his friends about Eloise being too beautiful for a guy like him.

Then they'd gotten into the limo and she'd asked about Blake, and he felt as if he'd been hit by a train. He hadn't thought about his son in two days. He'd been so preoccupied with his work problems and pretend-dating that he'd forgotten his son. *His baby. His whole world for eighteen months.*

How could he forget him?

He tapped on the glass between himself and Norman. It slid open.

"Take me to the hospital."

Norman caught his gaze in the rearview mirror. "It's midnight."

"I have my key card and identification."

The glass closed. Ricky sat back, letting the air slowly leach out of his lungs. The pain that had been his constant companion reclaimed him. Thirty minutes later, the limo stopped. His door opened and he climbed out.

He used his card to get into the hospital. Even, determined steps took him through the silent lobby and up to the Intensive Care Unit for the children's ward.

He stopped in front of the wall of glass, staring at the sweet, innocent children struggling for life.

"Mr. Langley?"

He faced Regina Grant, night shift supervisor. "Good evening, Regina."

"Everything okay?"

"Everything's fine." But she knew why he was here. When they rededicated the wing, after his generous donation had renovated the floor and bought new equipment, she'd been the one who'd seen his distress. She'd cornered him in a room, and rather than extol him with platitudes, she'd told him to count his blessings. "If you can't think of any blessings…come here. Look through that window. Realize you do not have it as bad as some."

The memory made him shake his head. He missed his son. He missed him with a longing that lodged in his throat, tormented his soul. He wished he'd done a million things differently. And he hated that a work problem and a pretty girl had made him forget his little boy.

But so many people did have it so much worse.

"I'm just here reminding myself I don't have it as bad as some."

"You really don't. And life does go on."

Sadness rippled through him. Memories of his son's giggle, the warmth of his child's hug, that simple trust floated back. But along with it came an odd, unfamiliar fear. Life might go on, but he didn't want to forget his son. Never. Ever.

After a prolonged silence, Regina caught his forearm. "Here's a thought. Instead of visiting in the middle of the night, maybe what you need is a little interaction."

He faced her. "With the kids?"

"Yes."

"They're too sick." And he was too afraid.

"These are. But if you'd come at regular visiting hours and go to the left instead of the right when you get off the elevator, I'm sure the nurses could set it up so that you could read to the kids in their playroom."

He said nothing. She turned to go but stopped and faced

him again. "Cheering up some kids who need cheering would be better than staring at kids you can't help."

Sucking in his breath, he watched her go, wondering what the hell was wrong with him. He'd been preoccupied with business before and as soon as the crisis was over, memories of Blake had come in an avalanche. The difference this time was Eloise.

He couldn't let his fake date make him forget his son. Or his guilt. And if she did, he had to stop this.

CHAPTER FOUR

MONDAY MORNING ELOISE awoke to the real world. She dressed in work trousers and a thick sweater, then bundled herself in her quilted parka, a scarf and mittens. She rode the subway to Manhattan and an ordinary, crowded elevator to the twenty-ninth-floor law offices of Pearson, Pearson, Leventry and Downing.

She slipped off her mittens and scarf and hung her coat on the coat tree in the corner of the tiny space she shared with ten filing cabinets and the desk of Tina Horner.

Tina entered rubbing her hands together. "It should snow. Then even though it would still be cold, we'd at least have festive snow to make it feel Christmas-y."

"I was just talking about that with someone last night."

"So I'm not the only one who thinks we're being cheated by cold weather without snow."

Eloise sat at her desk, then hit the button to boot up her computer. "Nope, Binnie Margolis is right with you."

"Binnie Margolis?" Tina whistled. "Somebody's moved up in the world."

Eloise laughed. "Not hardly. I'm doing a favor for a friend, going to a few Christmas parties with him so he doesn't get hounded because he doesn't have a date."

Tina shrugged out of her coat. "So it's like going out with your cousin?"

Eloise winced. She absolutely did not have cousin-like feelings for Ricky Langley. But she wouldn't tell Tina that.

"Not exactly. But in exchange for me going out with him, he agreed to introduce me around in the hope that I'd make a connection and maybe find a real job."

Tina took her seat at the desk across from Eloise. "That sounds promising."

"It is. Or it would be—"

"Except?"

She bit her lower lip, wondering if she should come clean with Tina. She decided she needed to talk to someone. "Except I'm thinking I should end our deal."

"End a deal that might help you find a job? Are you nuts?"

"More like concerned. I thought he wanted a date because of a bad breakup, but the way the wives of his friends were talking last night I get the feeling something big happened to this guy."

"Big like what?"

"Something tragic. They said, 'after his tragedy' a couple of times."

Tina winced. "Sounds like maybe his last girlfriend died."

Oh. Wouldn't that make sense? "Could be."

"Too bad we're not allowed to use the internet here or we could look him up."

"I can always go to the library after work."

"Maybe you should."

Knowing she could investigate him later, she relaxed and got down to the business of typing legal briefs. Because she worked late that night, she couldn't go to the library. Disappointment and curiosity collided, making her too nervous to sleep.

As she lay in bed pondering Ricky, their deal and her life, it dawned on her that since she'd met him, she'd been immersed in helping him. All weekend long, she'd remade dresses, gone to parties and worked to make a good impression on his friends so he could be happy. And it had felt good. Really good. She'd been busy. Happy. Until his friends' wives talked about "his tragedy" she'd been enjoying this charade.

And thinking of someone else had made her stop dwelling on her own problems. She hadn't done that since her husband had died.

Maybe she shouldn't jeopardize their good rapport by looking him up.

Maybe helping a man with a tragedy in his past was exactly what she needed to get over her own grief.

Especially because he was a friend of a friend. Ricky Langley wouldn't be in Tucker Engle's circle of confidantes if there was something wrong with him.

He was a guy with a tragic past. A guy she could help. And in return she could forget about her own troubles.

Ricky trudged up Eloise's four flights of steps on Friday night, so sad he'd nearly canceled their evening together again. On Monday night, he'd gone to the hospital to read to the kids, as Regina had suggested, and it had been devastating. He hated seeing kids suffer. He couldn't believe Regina had suggested he read to children so weak they broke his heart, reminded him of Blake, reminded him of how stupid he'd been. His son was dead because he'd never asked Blake's mother to let him raise him. She was a party girl turned mother and he'd seen the difficulties she'd had fitting Blake into her life. She probably would have been happy to give him custody of Blake, as long as she got visitation, but he'd never asked.

Anger with himself had made his pulse race, and that night, he couldn't stay in the children's ward activity room. He'd bowed out before the kids even knew he'd come there to read, so there was no harm done to them. But as he'd struggled to get through his week without thinking of

Blake, without berating himself for not asking for custody, for not taking his son away from a woman who clearly wanted an out, he'd simply forgotten about Eloise Vaughn.

He almost laughed. Another man would think it impossible that he could forget a woman so beautiful she could be a princess. But that was his life.

When she opened her door to him, and he looked down at her dress, he blinked. The pale blue fabric complemented her pink skin tone and yellow hair, but it also glittered as if someone had woven tinsel into the material. She looked like a princess trapped in a snow globe.

His heart lifted a bit. "Wow."

She smiled. "You know, even if nothing else comes of fake dating you, I'm getting a real sense of satisfaction out of your compliments on my sewing."

He took her cape. When she turned for him to help her into it, he noticed this dress had a full back and sighed with relief. The gloom that hung over him like a dome loosened a bit. "You deserve to be complimented. I'd never guess you were taking old clothes and making them new."

They headed down the hall to the stairs. "It's not like I'm redoing things from the last century. Five years ago, my clothes were in style."

"Then you went to university and your money had to go for tuition."

She stopped at the top step and faced him. "Something like that."

"Hey, unless you're born into money, you're going to suffer through university."

A strange expression crossed her face. He wouldn't be this far in his business dealings if he couldn't read the look of someone who had something to say. The pinch of pain in her eyes told him it wasn't something good.

But instead of a confession, she said, "Or starve."

He smiled, but curiosity ruffled through him. She'd told him about her job problem, but it had never crossed his mind to think she might have had personal troubles in her past. Something that had broken her heart.

Still, he pushed it from his mind. He had problems of his own. And wondering about her wasn't part of their deal. Getting to know her wasn't even part of their deal. In fact, with as pretty as she was and as tempting, he might be wise not to ask questions.

In the limo, they talked generically about her job and his busy schedule as they drove to a hotel in the theater district. Lit for Christmas, Times Square took his breath away. So many lights. So much creativity in the Santa and sleigh that rode the tickertape around the jumbo video screens, and the Santa's workshop filled with elves in the toy store windows.

He shoved back the memory of bringing Blake here for a private tour of the toy store and focused on getting himself and Eloise out of the limo.

Again, the night was cold and, as they stepped out, Eloise shivered. His arm rose in a natural reaction to pull her close, but just before he would have touched her, he stopped himself.

Too many things happened naturally with this woman, and although that probably added to the success of their charade, it wasn't good for either of them personally. When they weren't actually at a party, he would keep his distance.

A small stairway took them to the hotel lobby, where they were directed to an elevator to the ballroom. Lively music blared at them as the doors opened.

Eloise turned to him. "Are we late?"

"No. We're right on time. Preston's a music promoter. Expect the unexpected. Including the fact that he might have started the party early just because he wanted to."

"Cool."

A laugh escaped, and he relaxed a little. Technically, he had to have fun and talk to her for the charade to work. "Cool? Maybe yes. Maybe no. But I'm betting on no."

She happily exited the elevator and nearly walked into

Preston Jenkins's arms. High as a kite, their host took their coats and handed them off to a huge, beefy man who looked like a bodyguard.

He hugged Eloise effusively. "You are as gorgeous as the gossip mills are reporting."

Her eyes grew round and shiny with what looked to be fear, and Ricky remembered how she hadn't liked getting her picture taken the week before. Now she appeared deathly afraid of gossip.

"Which is why," Preston slurred, "I'm thrilled that we are about ten feet away from mistletoe."

Her eyes grew even larger, and this time Ricky understood. No woman wanted to be slobbered over by a stranger, regardless of how much mistletoe hung over doorways. Protectiveness rose up in him. She was *his* date. She wouldn't be here if he hadn't brought her. He needed to get her out of this.

His brain scrambled for a way to save her, and eventually he simply opened his mouth and said, "Do you really think I'd let a schmoozer like you kiss my date?"

Preston slapped his arm. "Oh, such a kidder. I wasn't going to kiss her. I'm getting pictures of everybody kissing their *dates* under the mistletoe." He pointed to the huge bodyguard type, who displayed a camera.

His heart did something that felt like a samba. "You want me to kiss Eloise?"

Nudging Eloise and Ricky under the mistletoe, Preston grinned drunkenly. "Yeah. You kiss Eloise."

Happiness tumbled through him before he could stop it, before he could think of Blake, before he could think of the myriad reasons this was wrong. It was as if time froze and there was only him and Eloise and mistletoe. No crowd. No past. No future. Just a kiss.

Eloise blinked up at him. Her pretty blue eyes round and curious. The curls of her soft blond hair framing her face. Her pink lips parted.

His pulse scrambled. He hadn't kissed a woman in almost two years. And just touching the skin of Eloise's back had set his hormones dancing. What would happen when their lips met?

Fireworks probably.

His pulse kicked up again. He hadn't felt fireworks in forever.

Longing, swift and sharp, rose up in him.

He silenced it. They were only fake dating. Kissing took them to dangerous ground.

Except he hadn't kissed a woman in almost two years. Hadn't felt alive in almost two years—

He glanced back at Preston, who waved dramatically. "Go on! Camera's waiting!"

He caught Eloise's gaze again. Need prickled his skin. Desire swelled. And he had to admit he wanted this. He wanted to feel alive again, if only for a few seconds. It was foolish. But it was also only a kiss. One kiss when he'd been so long deprived hardly seemed earth-shattering, and he could go back to being miserable after that. Plus, if he didn't kiss her, he would ruin their charade.

He bent his head and barely touched his mouth to hers. Soft, smooth lips met his. She tasted like peppermint and felt like heaven, and his head spun. Had he said this wouldn't be earth-shattering? He'd been wrong.

His mouth pressed against hers, and simple need bubbled like a witch's brew in his gut. He knew he was flirting with disaster. But he couldn't stop himself. He'd never wanted anything as much as he wanted to simply lose himself in her. The softness, the sweetness he'd never found in another woman.

One kiss. Then he would walk away.

When Ricky's mouth shifted and he began to take, all the blood drained from Eloise's body, then returned in a grand whoosh of warm tingles. He'd touched his mouth to hers softly at first, in a kiss that felt almost experimental. Then his hands slid up her arms to her shoulders, and he pulled her just a little bit closer, pressed his lips a little bit harder and she melted.

She couldn't think. She couldn't breathe. Too many sensations bombarded her. The crisp scent of his aftershave. The power in the hands holding her shoulders. The softness of his mouth that pressed one second, then hesitated the next. He seemed to want this and fear it, and though she knew it was wrong, she opened her mouth and egged him on.

His hands tightened on her shoulders. Need crashed against need. The kiss deepened so fast, her knees might have buckled, but she wasn't paying any attention. She longed for the feeling of his tongue gliding along her tongue, his chest pressed against hers, his hands holding her shoulders.

He released her, and for two seconds they stared into each other's eyes. Then the music blaring from the ballroom registered, along with the sound of Preston laughing.

Standing by his bodyguard and studying the photo in the digital camera he said, "It's a great pic. You look fantastic. Young lovers. I adore you. Now move along."

Ricky gave a fake laugh and said something inane to Preston before he guided her into the ballroom. Her dress swooshed against her legs silkily and the scents of pine and vanilla permeating the room seemed strong and vibrant, as if kissing her fake date had brought all of her senses to life.

"Sorry about that."

"It's fine." She cleared her throat when her voice came out as a squeak. "Part of the deal."

But it wasn't fine. They'd taken that kiss too far, and it had been a mistake. She liked this guy. He was a good person with something sad enough in his past that his friends' wives called it a tragedy. They should keep their distance. Instead, they'd kissed and it had been amazing. Which was wrong. W…R…O…N…G. Because he didn't like her and she was going to get hurt.

They spent an uncomfortable half hour trying to make conversation as Ricky's friends, the people who would join them at their table, arrived. Her nerves continued as they ate dinner, danced and left the ballroom early, Ricky explaining to Preston that he had to rise before dawn for conference calls Sunday morning.

But in the limo on the way home, watching him sitting beside her, staring out the window, looking like a man lost, Eloise chastised herself. All night long, she'd held herself aloof, flummoxed by that kiss. This was a seriously unhappy guy and all he wanted was one nice Christmas, yet she couldn't stop thinking about herself. Her reactions to him. Her stupid hormones.

But that kiss had been one of the best of her life. If not *the* best. It was hard to stay objective after that.

She shook her head. What was she doing? She'd finally found a way to put some meaning in her life. She couldn't let one kiss distract her. Her back stiffened as she straightened on the limo seat. As God was her witness, she intended to give him what he really wanted. Christmas. A joyful, happy Christmas. No easing back into "the season," as he'd said the night they made their deal. No fake date. She would be someone who really cared about him and who gave him joy.

Ricky walked her to her apartment door and for a crazy second he thought about kissing her good-night. He couldn't get the mistletoe kiss out of his head. Or the expression of surprise on Eloise's face. He wanted to kiss her just to see it again.

What was he doing? He was too depressed, too wounded to bring a woman into his life.

At her door, she smiled politely. "The party was fun."

He sniffed in derision. "Preston's a freak."

"Or a guy who likes to have a good time." She straightened his bow tie, smoothed her hands down his top coat collar. "Maybe we should work a little harder to have some fun?"

He studied her face, her pretty blue eyes, warm pink mouth and sweet smile. She was serious. She wanted him to have fun.

Syrupy warmth flooded his blood. A strange feeling tightened his chest, and although it took him a few seconds, he realized it was affection.

He wasn't just attracted to her. He was beginning to like her.

But he knew that was wrong.

He stepped back. "Or maybe we should just put in an appearance at these things and leave early all the time?"

He turned and started down the stairs without waiting for Eloise to answer. No matter what happened at the rest of the parties, he wouldn't kiss her again.

The next morning, he called to tell Eloise she only needed to wear jeans and a sweater to that night's party, his fraternity reunion. The lilt of her voice tiptoed though him, reminding him of the kiss the day before, and he hung up as quickly as he could and lost himself in work.

That was the best way to deal with feelings—remorse over Blake, unwanted curiosity about Eloise. Work was the way to forget and give himself some peace.

When his phone rang a few hours later, he answered absently. "Yes?"

Tucker Engle laughed. "Is that any way to greet a friend?"

Tossing his pen to his desk, Ricky leaned back. "No." He laughed. "Sorry. How's Kentucky?"

"We're knee-deep in sledding and hot cocoa."

Ricky smirked. It was hard to imagine workaholic Tucker spending five or six weeks in the country. "Bored?"

"No. Actually, I'm enjoying it so much that I don't want to leave, but I've had an emergency crop up and I need your help."

Ricky sat up. After everything Tucker had done for him, he'd love a chance to do a favor in return. "What can I do?"

"I need to put in an appearance at a meeting for one of the companies I'm heavily invested in. I just need a presence. Somebody who can give my opinion."

"I'll be happy to go. Tell me the address and the date."

"It's today. I know it's Saturday, so if you can't go, it's okay."

"No. I'm happy to do it."

Tucker covered the details with Ricky, who made a few notes, but only a few, because there wasn't much for Ricky to do except make one brief statement.

Still, Tucker's reply showed he was grateful. "Thanks again."

"You're welcome. It's not a big deal. If it runs long, I'll just call Eloise and tell her we'll be late for my frat reunion."

Even as he said it, Ricky realized his mistake.

Tucker pounced. "So, you and Eloise hit it off on that ride home after the party?"

He winced. "You could say that."

"Good. You've been down too long, and Eloise could use a little pick-me-up, too. She's had some rough patches."

Ricky's eyes narrowed. Pretty, sweet Eloise had had some rough patches? Just from the tone of Tucker's voice, he could tell this was about more than her inability to get a job. He remembered the expression that flitted over her face when they'd talked about college. Obviously Tucker knew something Ricky didn't.

He opened his mouth to ask but couldn't. It didn't seem right or fair to ask questions about a woman who was only attending a few parties with him.

He wasn't supposed to care.

He *didn't* care.

He didn't need to know.

But even an hour after Ricky hung up the phone, as he dressed to go to Tucker's meeting, he couldn't get that odd look in Eloise's eyes out of his head. Curiosity overwhelmed him, so he typed her name into his computer's search engine.

Late Saturday afternoon, Eloise began getting dressed. That evening's party was Ricky's informal fraternity reunion, held in a pub in midtown. When he'd called that morning, he'd told her to just wear jeans and a sweater.

Still, knowing how men were about pride in front of fraternity brothers, and back to her mission of making sure he had a good time, Eloise dressed with care. She slid into an emerald green cashmere sweater that she'd been saving for a special occasion, fixed her hair in a long ponytail and applied just the right amount of makeup to look cheerful and festive.

She would get this guy out of his misery if it killed her.

He arrived, helped her into her parka and led her down the stairs.

"This might be like hell week."

She laughed. The fact that he hadn't mentioned putting in an appearance and leaving early encouraged her. "You think I can't handle a roomful of men and their dates?"

He paused at the door and looked back at her. "Some won't have dates."

"Oh."

He started walking again, and she stood rooted to her spot. He had to be in his midthirties. The people he went to school with would be about the same age, but they wouldn't have dates?

What did that mean?

When he reached the limo, Norman opened the door. Realizing she was standing in the lobby like a ninny, she scrambled to catch up. As soon as they were settled, Norman took off.

"So you're married."

Surprise kicked the air out of her lungs and made her forget all about the fact that some of his fraternity buddies wouldn't have dates. "What?"

He faced her, his eyes cool and direct. "You're married. I found your marriage license through a quick internet search and didn't find a divorce decree. Ergo, you're married."

Her heart galloped. Her nerve endings jumped. Every ounce of blood fell to her feet as every possible answer she could give him winged through her brain. But none of them would work. Shock and anger collided to create a horrible sourness in the pit of her stomach.

"For a guy who has his fair share of secrets, you're certainly not shy about uncovering mine."

"Believe it or not, I searched your name because I felt bad for you. I could tell from how you avoided the topic of college that something had happened and I wanted to know what."

His voice was soft, honest, but tinged with a bit of hurt. And why not? He thought he was going out with a married woman.

She sucked in a breath and said the words that didn't just pinch her heart; they filled her with shame. "My husband died."

The expression of concern that came over his face was totally unexpected. "Your husband died?"

She nodded.

He sighed in obvious disgust with himself. "I'm sorry. I was just so flabbergasted to find the marriage license and no divorce degree that I didn't look any further." He shook his head. "You're so young. I never in a million years thought to look for a death certificate." He shook his head again. "I am so sorry."

"If it made you so angry to find the marriage license

and no divorce decree, why didn't you just call and cancel?" But before he could answer, she figured it out on her own, and she gasped. "You hoped I had an explanation."

"I need you. I need this charade. Plus, you've been nothing but a nice person around me." He shrugged. "It was only fair that I give you a chance to explain."

Hope filled the black hole of shame that lived where her heart should have been. Laura Beth and Olivia accepted her, understood her. But she'd never had the courage to test another person's feelings about her. She wasn't supposed to care if Ricky Langley liked her. But it was suddenly, incomprehensibly important that he hear the story and understand.

"I fell for a guy with tattoos and a motorcycle and ran off with him. Although we loved each other, getting married was a huge mistake. It took only two months before I realized we were in trouble. He sat at home or in his buddy's garage, talking bikes and drinking beer all day."

His eyes sought hers, but he said nothing.

Shame and fear shivered through her, but she trudged on.

"I spent every day supporting him by waitressing." She glanced down at her hands, then back up at him. "This story makes me sound like I quit loving him when he refused to support me, but the truth was I never stopped loving him. I just knew we'd made a mistake getting married. I was about to leave him—"

"When he was killed on his bike and you were free."

A shard of pain sliced through her. For a guy who clearly hoped she'd redeem herself, he certainly was quick to find the dark cloud. "When he was diagnosed with cancer. I spent three months taking him to doctor's appointments, helping him through chemo, cleaning up messes, offering words of hope. That's when we started talking. It killed him that he couldn't find work, so he masked his pain by pretending not to care that I had to support him. I reacted by getting angrier and angrier with a guy who was already hurting, filled with shame." She stopped and closed her eyes. "Then he died, and I've spent the past years angry with myself." She opened her eyes. "Feeling guilty. Feeling desperately wrong. I hadn't left him, but I was about to and he would have died alone."

He studied her silently, then finally said, "I'm sorry."

This time she looked away. "It certainly wasn't your fault."

"No. But I shouldn't have probed into your private life."

The limo stopped. Norman opened the door and they stepped out.

Memories followed her up the sidewalk and beneath the portico, tormenting her with the knowledge that she'd been immature and foolish. Not in marrying Wayne, but in almost leaving. True, she'd stayed and nursed him until he'd died. But if he'd visited the doctor one week later, she would have been gone. The man she'd loved would have died alone.

When they walked into the pub, the noise of the crowd swelled over her, along with the scents of corned beef and cabbage. Ricky directed her to the room in the back, where round tables were partially filled with men his age. The pool table entertained six or eight tall, lean guys and two dartboards had the attention of another four or five.

Only about seven women, dates of the guys laughing and talking, were there. More than twenty guys but only seven women. And three of them she recognized—Jennifer, Muriel and Binnie. In spite of the trauma over telling her story, Eloise almost smiled. Ricky must have been in the geek fraternity.

"Hey, it's Ricky."

Everybody faced them. He shrugged out of his leather jacket and hung it on a hook on the wall before he turned and took her coat. She swallowed. Nice shoulders and a solid chest filled his warm amber sweater to perfection. His jeans all but caressed his perfect butt.

Before she could chastise herself for noticing, his mouth fell open slightly as his gaze rippled down her emerald green sweater to her tight jeans and tall black boots.

With her story out and his fear that she was a liar alleviated, she smiled in question. He'd brought her to the party to continue the charade for his own benefit, but he knew her now. And the confidence she could muster as a fake date suddenly seemed all wrong. Now, she was herself. Eloise Cummings Vaughn—not just struggling working girl, but also widow. She needed a word, something from him, that let her know things between them were okay.

He leaned in. "You look fantastic. But you always look fantastic. Thank you for doing this for me."

His warm breath tickled her ear. He smelled great. And his words told her what she needed to hear. They were back in good standing. She might be a real person to him now, but she was still a fake date.

A tall, thin guy wearing a sweater with a Santa face plastered across the front strolled over. Handing Ricky a pool cue, he said, "You beat me four games straight last year. This year I intend to win."

Ricky took the stick but glanced at Eloise.

This wasn't her party. It was his. Plus, telling him about her past hadn't changed her mission. If anything, it had strengthened it. She'd stayed too long in her self-pity. She'd lingered too long with her guilt. If the best way to get out was to help someone else, she would help him.

She smiled. "Hey, go. Enjoy yourself. I'll be fine."

She turned to walk over to the women, who had all gathered in a cluster but, on second thought, faced him. "Can I get you a beer?"

He smiled. Really smiled.

Their gazes caught and held, as one door of their relationship closed and another squeaked open. She was no longer a poor girl who needed his help. She was a woman who'd confided her past. He wasn't just a rich guy who wanted a date. He'd listened. He hadn't judged. He'd sympathized.

"Yeah. Thanks."

"Pitchers are all on a table in the back," the guy who'd challenged Ricky to the pool game said. "Help yourself pizza and wings, too. We don't stand on ceremony. It's self-serve."

She smiled at Ricky again. "I'll be right back."

She got him a beer and put two pieces of pizza on a paper plate for him. She took them to a table near the pool game, pointed them out for Ricky and walked over to the gaggle of women.

"All right. Spill. Who are you, and how the hell did you get Ricky to go out, especially at Christmas?"

Holding the glass of beer she'd poured for herself, she smiled at the dates of his fraternity brothers. "As I told Binnie, Muriel and Jennifer on Sunday, we met at the Christmas party of a mutual friend."

"Tucker Engle," a short, dark-haired woman supplied. "Jeremy and I were there and we saw you. That means you haven't known each other long." She stuck out her hand to shake Eloise's. "I'm Misty, by the way. I date the tall guy over there." She pointed at a true geek with glasses and a sweater vest. "Jeremy."

"Nice to meet you."

The remaining women introduced themselves, but as the conversation moved on, thoughts of Sunday's dinner party came back to her. Especially Muriel and Jennifer talking about his tragedy.

She glanced back at Ricky. When she'd told him about Wayne, she'd handed him the perfect opportunity to tell her his trauma and he hadn't taken it.

She tried to tell herself it didn't matter, that their relationship was only an arrangement, but tonight that argument didn't float. Not because she liked him or because the new feelings that had sprung up made the situation feel real. It was because she suddenly realized she might be fulfilling her end of their bargain, but he wasn't doing anything about his. He hadn't gotten her one interview. Not one.

She was doing everything he wanted, even confiding her secrets, but he wasn't doing anything for her.

It wasn't long before everyone had congregated together at a table. Soon, they pulled a second table over and then a third. As Ricky played game after game of pool, he watched Eloise kick back and chat, sip beer and eat a piece of pizza.

He was glad. He didn't know how his search had missed the death certificate of her husband, except that he hadn't been looking for a death certificate but a divorce decree. When he hadn't found one, he'd gotten angry and stopped searching.

He'd tried to rationalize her situation with the fact that every time he'd gone to her apartment, he'd only seen signs of two women living there. No man. No husband. And his internet search had confirmed that she worked as a temp in New York City, but she'd married in Kentucky. He'd assumed she'd left the bad marriage behind and was waiting until she could afford a divorce. Which wasn't a crime, but it was something she should have told him.

So her story in the limo had stopped him short. Especially the part about the guilt. Lord knows he understood guilt over someone dying. Most people understood the grief. He understood the guilt.

He started another game, but noticed that his fraternity brothers were ambling toward the tables with the women. They pulled chairs behind the chairs of their dates, but those without dates—and there were plenty—seemed to be congregating around Eloise.

As he played pool with Jonathan Hopewell, the laughter

from the now crowded tables rolled over to him. He glanced up and saw Kyle Banister, who was seated on a chair behind Eloise, lean in to say something to her. She smiled prettily and twisted to face him. Ricky missed his next shot.

Whatever she'd said made Kyle laugh. He reached across her, grabbed the pitcher of beer and refilled both their glasses.

"Your shot."

He spun to face Jonathan. "Sorry."

"I know it must be boring to never lose and have to play every challenger, but at least pretend it's hard to beat me."

He laughed and lined up his shot, but just as he slid the stick forward Eloise's laughter floated to him. He missed.

"Are you doing this on purpose?"

He ran his hand along the back of his neck. "No. I'm distracted."

Jonathan followed the line of his gaze and laughed. "You're not jealous, are you?"

"Of course not." They were in an arrangement. The fact that Kyle had outgrown his geekiness, fit into his sweater and had hair that could have been on an infomercial for workout videos meant nothing.

Jonathan put his next three balls into the pockets with ease. "I'm getting confidence from your jealousy."

"I'm not jealous."

Eloise's giggle reached him again. He nearly cursed. Not because he was jealous. He couldn't be jealous. Refused to be. He was worried about their charade.

He put his stick on the table. "You win, Jon. You play the next challenger."

"But everybody wants to beat you. Geez, you're no fun when you have a girlfriend."

Ricky heard Jon's words, but they barely penetrated. He was focused on his date, who was currently being chatted up by one of his friends.

"Hey, *sweetie*," he said as he ambled up to the table.

She looked up at him with bright, happy eyes and his stomach plummeted. He'd never been able to put that look in her eyes. But Kyle had.

"Hey!" She scooted her chair over and made room for a chair for him, which someone immediately provided. "Kyle was just telling me that his company is looking to hire a human resources director."

Ricky glanced at Kyle, who reddened guiltily. "Really? I thought you were just in start-up stages."

"We are," Kyle said defensively.

Which meant he didn't need an HR person for at least a year. He didn't have to say it. Kyle got the message.

"Think I'll go play pool with Jon."

Ricky found himself saying, "You do that," and then wondering why he had. He was not the type to get jealous. Ever. Eloise wasn't really his date. She was a cover. A symbol to let people know he was getting past his grief. So why was he behaving like a Neanderthal?

Eloise patted the chair beside her. "Have a seat."

Confusion buffeted him. The noise of the bar closed in on him, and the last thing he wanted was to be squeezed into a cluster of people.

"I want to go home."

He heard the words coming out of his mouth and almost couldn't believe he'd said them. He sounded like a petulant child.

But Eloise didn't argue. She smiled and rose.

He strode over to get their coats. He handed hers to her without looking at her.

As she slid into it, his fraternity brothers came over and said their goodbyes. When all his goodbyes were made, he waved good-naturedly at the women, who still sat at the table.

They waved back, but he knew what they were thinking. That he still couldn't handle being out. That he was defensive, a prima donna who wasn't even trying to get over his grief.

He and Eloise stepped out into the cool air and he stopped. "I forgot to call Norman."

She huddled into her coat. "Is he close enough to get here in a few minutes?"

"That's his job." He pulled out his cell phone, sent a text to Norman and shoved his hands into the pockets of his leather jacket. "You're supposed to like me. You shouldn't have been flirting with Kyle."

"The guy was talking about a job. Everybody at the table heard every word we were saying. Everybody could see we weren't flirting. He was offering me a job."

"A nonexistent job."

She huddled more deeply into her coat. "Well, I know that now that you embarrassed him."

He ran his hand over his face. Damn. He *had* embarrassed him. He'd made an ass of himself and embarrassed a friend.

He was definitely losing it. "You should still know better than to think a half-drunk guy at a party is legit."

"So in other words, I shouldn't believe the guys you'll be introducing me to at your other parties…oh, wait… the other people you've introduced me to haven't actually talked about jobs. They're only concerned with getting your attention."

Norman pulled up and she strode to the limo. She didn't wait for Norman to come around to the side, just opened the door herself.

Ricky raced up behind her. "It's the fact that they want my attention that may get you noticed."

She sniffed a laugh as she slid inside. Norman stood off to the right, waiting for Ricky to enter. Once he had, he closed the door.

"No one will ever notice me as long as you're around." She sighed, disgusted with herself for getting angry with him. But she was angry. She knew this relationship was fake, but after their discussion about Wayne, she felt he knew her. The real her. Plus, she'd promised herself she would help him enjoy the holiday.

Still, he was the one who had ruined this evening, not her. She shifted to the right. "Just forget it."

"No. If you have something to say, I want to hear it."

She sucked in a breath. As Christmas angels went, she was a failure. He was mad. She was mad. So maybe it was just time to end this thing.

"All right, you want the truth. You've already gotten a lot out of this deal. We've gone through almost half your parties, and I don't have anything to show for it. So I saw an opportunity with Kyle and I pounced."

He stared sullenly out the window. "You should have known what he told you was ridiculous."

"And I'm an idiot for falling for it. Great. Fine. Thanks. I get it."

She crossed her arms on her chest. They stayed silent until they reached her apartment building. When Norman opened the door, she slid out. He started to get out behind her, but she pushed him back inside.

"Norman heard our fight." She glanced at Ricky's driver. "Didn't you?"

The man in the dark suit and driver's hat winced.

"Which means he'll perfectly understand when I say I don't want your pigheaded behind walking me to my apartment."

Norman winced again.

She slammed the door on Ricky and ran into the building. Not slowing down at the steps, she took them two at a time, raced into her apartment and back to her bedroom.

The stress of the night had destroyed her. When she put her head on her pillow, tears slid off her eyelids and rolled down her cheeks.

It hadn't been easy remembering her marriage, Wayne

getting sick, his death. She'd bared her soul to Ricky, not expecting understanding, but in trust. And the way he thanked her was to tell her she was foolish.

Yeah. Duh. She already knew that.

CHAPTER FIVE

THE NEXT MORNING a series of sharp knocks woke Eloise and Laura Beth. Both ran to the door, shrugging into long fleece robes. Eloise got there first, looked through the peephole and saw a man holding flowers.

Without disengaging the chain lock, she opened the door a crack.

"Are you Eloise Vaughn?"

"Yes."

He set the tall vase on the hall floor. "These are for you." He turned to go.

Eloise fumbled with the chain lock. "Wait! I'll give you a tip."

The kid smiled. "Tip was included." With that he raced down the hall.

She cautiously opened the door and picked up the vase. Tissue paper covered the flowers to protect them from the cold. She ripped it off. A holiday bouquet—roses, white mums, tinsel and mistletoe—greeted her.

Laura Beth closed the door. "Wonder who they're from?"

She opened the card, smiled. "My fake date. He says our fight last night made everything look real."

Laura Beth huffed away. "And his billions of dollars make it possible for him to wake a florist at—" She squinted at the clock. "My God, it's not even five o'clock yet. And it's Sunday!"

"He also says I was right. He hasn't been fulfilling his end of the bargain. So he sent the flowers early to catch me before I planned my day. If I want him to, he'll send his driver to pick me up and take me to his condo, where we can redo my résumé and look over my options."

That stopped Laura Beth. "That's the most romantic thing I've ever heard a guy say."

Eloise laughed. Poverty certainly changed a woman's view of romance. "Yeah. Me too." But she shivered. She wasn't sure she was done being angry with him. And sometimes being with him made her feel like a selfish failure as a human being. He was hurting and he wouldn't even tell her why. But she needed a job—so desperately needed a job—that maybe it was time to forget being a Christmas angel and just go back to their original deal.

She texted the number he'd put on the card and told him to send Norman. Then she found a copy of her résumé and got dressed.

Forty minutes later the driver texted her that he was downstairs, and she raced out into the cold, cold morning.

Norman held open the door. "Good morning, ma'am."

Eloise smiled. "Good morning, Norman."

He closed the door, got behind the wheel and sped off.

Surprise made her frown when he stopped the limo at a respectable but far from plush condo building. She rode up the normal elevator to a very normal hallway and knocked on a simple door.

Ricky opened the door immediately, as if he'd been waiting for her. "I am so sorry."

She tried to smile, but being in his presence sent shivers down her spine. In a sweater and jeans, he looked gorgeous and approachable, making it difficult to remember they were from two different worlds. Worse, they didn't seem to get along. She shouldn't be attracted to him.

She shrugged out of her navy blue parka. "Your flowers said it, but helping me find a job would say it even better."

As he took her coat to a convenient closet, she glanced around. Dark wood cabinets dominated the kitchen of the small open-plan condo and matched the dark table and chairs that took up the space before the living room.

"Have you eaten?"

She faced him. "No. But I'm not hungry."

"You had one piece of pizza last night. Not enough to sustain you." He walked into the kitchen and pulled a griddle from a lower cabinet. "I'm making pancakes."

Himself? She almost smiled. "Where's your maid?"

"She went with the penthouse."

"You lost your penthouse and maid? Was it a bet? A poker game?"

"I *sold* the penthouse and she chose to stay with the new owner. Which is only right because there's not a whole hell of a lot of housecleaning to do around here. This condo's tiny."

She liked his apartment, but she wouldn't trade a penthouse for it. "Why did you sell your penthouse?"

He spared her a glance. "I didn't need that much space." He paused and pulled in a breath before he added, "I also wanted to be alone."

She didn't have to be a mind reader to conclude that he'd sold his penthouse and gotten rid of his maid after his tragedy. This was as close as he'd ever come to telling her something personal. So she appreciated the gesture, sort of a peace offering, and said, "Well, this is nice. Modern. Kind of bacheloresque."

"Bacheloresque?"

"I made it up. It's a word meaning like something a bachelor would own."

He laughed as he gathered milk and eggs from the stainless steel refrigerator.

"You're making pancakes from scratch?"

"No. I've got a box mix, but it allows me to add fresh ingredients so they taste better."

It made sense to her, and she totally agreed a short while later when she took her first bite. "These are great."

He smiled, and they ate their pancakes amid sporadic conversation about the food, the condo and the cold. She wanted to ask him so many things, especially because he knew so much about her. But now that they were back to being congenial acquaintances with a mission, she knew better than to breach boundaries, poke or prod. She wanted a job. He wanted to help her find one. And her Christmas mission? He seemed to like her best when she wasn't trying to make him happy. So maybe it was time to scrap that.

He cleaned up, rinsing the dirty dishes and putting them into the dishwasher. Then they took mugs of coffee into the room he called his den.

Obviously designed to be a second bedroom, the small space barely had room for the big table with the huge computer system with three oversize screens, two keyboards and three printers. "Wow."

"I design games and think up extraspecial search engines," he said as he hit the button that turned everything on. Lights blinked, screens flashed, small motors hummed. "Did you bring your résumé?"

She pulled the folded sheet out of her jeans pocket.

He frowned. "I hope you don't send it out like that?"

The implication that she wasn't smart enough to send a neat résumé sent anger rumbling through her again. But looking around and remembering some of his conversations with his peers, she finally realized he might be one of those guys who was so intelligent he didn't think before he spoke.

Still, she wasn't going to let him get away with dissing her. "I'm not a dingbat. I print a fresh one every time I answer a classified ad or get a lead."

He sat at the desk, scanned her résumé and brought it up on a screen. He read for a few seconds, then said, "I think your first mistake is that you emphasize the secretarial aspects of your temp jobs." He faced her. "You'd be better off to list the jobs without giving too much explanation of what you actually do. That way you're accounting for the time, proving that you're working and not a slacker, but taking the emphasis off those skills, so people realize you're looking for a job that uses your degree."

She nodded.

Without asking for input, he revised her résumé, making it incredibly short, but also focusing on the skills she'd acquired while earning her degree.

Then he wrote a generic email introducing her and sent the email off to four friends with a copy of her updated résumé attached.

"These guys all owe me a favor. Your résumé will go directly to them."

Blissful hope ricocheted through her. "That'll get me a job?"

"Trust me. Two of them owe me favors big enough that if they can find you a job in your field within their companies, you'll get it. Hiring a friend of someone you owe is an easy way to pay off big favors."

Her heart lifted. But in the room filled with technology, he looked alone. She studied his solemn eyes, wishing she could fulfill her private vow to make him happy. But ever since she'd decided to make his Christmas wonderful, they'd actually become tenser around each other. They'd even fought.

Of course, he'd also sent her flowers and made her pancakes. And now he was trying in earnest to get her a job. To fulfill his part of the bargain. Early in the morning, as if he'd been so upset with himself he hadn't slept.

Something prickled inside her heart. A nudge or a hint that she shouldn't give up. A nice guy was inside him somewhere, a guy who had obviously been hurt. A guy who deserved a happy Christmas.

Deciding it was smarter not to wreck their current peace, she rose from the chair beside his. "Thanks."

He stood, too. "You're welcome."

Ridiculous silence enveloped them again. They weren't really dating. Technically, they weren't even friends. Hell, if she was going to get technical, they didn't actually know each other. So a vacuum existed. A couple saying goodbye would kiss. Friends saying goodbye might hug. People who were nothing to each other had nothing to do but be awkward.

She picked up her mug, chugged the now-cold coffee and grimaced. "Ugh."

He sniffed a laugh. "Cold coffee is disgusting."

"I know, but I was looking for one last swallow of warmth before I went outside."

He frowned. "I have more coffee. Or if you want, I can make you a cup of cocoa before you go."

She'd turned to leave, but the offer surprised her so much that she stopped. She *knew* that deep down inside Ricky Langley was a nice guy. And maybe he'd offered her cocoa because he didn't want her to go. Maybe, if she stayed, he'd open up to her.

She faced him with a cautious smile. "I like cocoa."

"Good."

He led her to his compact kitchen and pressed a button. The appliance garage door rose and a shiny stainless steel one-cup coffeemaker appeared. She sighed with appreciation. "It's beautiful."

He laughed. "And I happen to have some of the very best cocoa." He glanced back. "From Switzerland."

She peered over his shoulder. "Yum."

The cocoa took seconds to brew. He handed her the mug, then made a cup for himself.

Drink in hand, he pointed toward the seating area in the living room. "No sense standing while we drink this."

As she followed him, nerves settled in. They'd been

going to parties for two weeks, barely speaking except in a crowd of his friends and only discussing general topics. Unless he decided to open up immediately, they had nothing to talk about. No small talk to ease him into confiding.

Sitting on the chair, she noticed that some of the casual sculptures on his end tables and mantel weren't exactly as "casual" as he displayed them. And most were works from some of Olivia's clients.

She smiled. Something for them to talk about.

"I'm guessing Olivia helped you choose some of your art."

"She's persistent."

"And good at her job."

He laughed. "Yes."

She sipped her cocoa. The chocolate flavor that burst on her tongue made her groan. "This is fantastic."

He nodded, then said, "You and Olivia must be very close."

"That's what happens when you share an apartment. We've been together since university."

"That's right. Olivia's from Kentucky, too."

"And so is Laura Beth."

"So you're like the Three Musketeers?"

She shrugged. "I guess. We've gotten each other through some tough times."

"Your husband's illness?"

She shook her head and looked down at her cocoa. Hoping he was using talking about her to ease himself into talking about his tragedy, she said, "No. I was alone for that. Although Laura Beth, Olivia and I grew up in the same small town, we ran in different circles. When I went back to university to finish my degree, we found each other." She peeked up. Not knowing how much of her story Olivia had shared, Eloise cautiously said, "Olivia had had something traumatic happen to her and my experiences seemed to help nurse her back to sanity."

"She identified with your loss?"

She shook her head. It was good for them to have something to talk about to ease him into sharing his story, but she wouldn't talk at the expense of Olivia's privacy. Carefully crafting her answer, she said, "She identified more with being persecuted and abandoned."

"You were persecuted and abandoned?"

She caught his gaze. If he was going to ease himself in, shouldn't he have done it by now? Still, he already knew about Wayne. What did it matter to go a step or two further?

"Sort of. My parents disowned me."

"What?"

"My parents have money. I had rebelled. Embarrassed them by marrying someone so far below their class. So they kicked me out."

"Oh."

Great. Now, to him, she wasn't just a stupid girl. She was a stupid girl who was alone.

Fury with herself rattled through her. She never should have accepted the cocoa.

But she had. And she'd started a story that made her look bad. Again. She was just plain tired of looking bad to him, especially because this part of her problem wasn't her fault; it was her parents'. And call her prideful, but once, just once, she'd like to look sane to him.

"Even though they'd disowned me, when Wayne died I went home with my tail between my legs, expecting a scolding and probably a time of penance but also expecting to be accepted back. And maybe getting some help with my grief. Some love. But my parents wouldn't let me in." She shook her head. "They didn't even come to the door. A maid told me to leave and never come back."

He stared at her. "You had told them your husband had died, right?"

"They could not have cared less." She sighed. "I lost

my family because I married a guy I loved when I was too young to realize all the consequences. And every year, especially at Christmas, I mourn the loss. Not just of my husband, but also of my family. Olivia and Laura Beth go home, and I have nowhere to go. No home. It hurt to be rejected. It hurt not having their emotional support. But it's the aftermath of my mistakes that are killer. Years of loneliness. Years of regret. Getting kicked out of my family means I have no family. I have no one. I am alone."

She combed her fingers through her hair. She'd gone too far. Said things she didn't even admit to herself. And he was silent. He wasn't going to confide, and he didn't sympathize. He made no move to comfort her. She'd finally vocalized the thing she hadn't even told Laura Beth and Olivia, and he sat there, saying nothing.

And it all started because she'd been stupid enough to think he would open up to her.

Man, she was a goof. Or she didn't know very much about men. Or she didn't know much about rich men. But this guy who so easily found all her secrets, and got her to confess the rest, wasn't about to tell her anything.

She bounced off her seat. "You know what? Sunday is our cleaning day. I've got to get back to the apartment."

He rose. "Sure."

He walked to his closet, extracted her coat and helped her into it. "Let me call Norman to drive you."

She faced him. "Yeah, thanks. I'd appreciate that."

He pulled his phone out of his jeans pocket and texted. "He'll be downstairs in a second."

"Thanks."

Horrible awkwardness once again enveloped them as they stood in his entryway, humiliation cascading from her head to her toes. Why would she think he would confide in her? And why did she think he should care about her troubles? He didn't like her. She was a fake date. He'd helped her with her job search because that was his part of the bargain. Not because he liked her.

And she was an adult. She might not have a family, but she had good friends in Laura Beth and Olivia. Soon she'd have a job. She wasn't really *alone.* She was just alone on Christmas.

She sent him her fake smile. "I really appreciate this."

"You're welcome…again."

She winced. "I already said thanks, didn't I?"

"Yeah. You did."

Again, the little foyer grew quiet, and she suddenly realized why this awkwardness felt different, stronger. She had no reason to be standing there.

She was such an idiot. Always an idiot.

She turned to the door and, a gentleman, he reached around her to open it.

She slipped outside and headed down the silent, empty hall to the elevator. When would she learn none of this was real?

Ricky stood in front of the closed door, filled with pain for her. As she'd told him her story, it had taken every ounce of restraint he had not to pull her into his arms and comfort her.

But to what end? He was wounded as badly, if not worse than she was. She needed someone strong, someone whole, to be whole for her, to fill her stocking at Christmas and tell her it didn't matter that her parents didn't want her… She had him.

Yearning rose in him. How he wanted to do that. Wanted to give her that. She'd cared for a husband with cancer. She'd nursed him. She'd probably watched him die. Her parents had abandoned her. Rejected her in her hour of need.

Then she'd moved to New York City and found nothing but failure and more rejection.

He understood what it was like to be alone. Still, even

in his darkest hours, he knew he could pick up the phone and call his mom and dad.

She had no one. Any scrap of consolation or comfort could fill her. But he didn't have anything to give. He couldn't be a boyfriend for real.

So he'd kept his hands at his sides, measured his words, hadn't given her false hope.

Now he ached for her.

The next day, he went to work carrying the ache, trying to console himself with the reminder that he'd done something good for her when he'd gone the extra mile, brought her to his home and sent out her résumé. But it didn't work. The ache stayed with him. It sometimes even nudged aside the guilt he felt over Blake's death.

Somebody, somewhere had to really help this woman. Not just be a roommate or listen to her troubles, but do something tangible. And finding her a job suddenly seemed like the salvation she needed and also the way for him to feel better.

His secretary came into his office with that day's mail. "Good morning, Mr. Langley."

"Just set the mail on my desk—"

He stopped himself. He knew he was upset about Eloise, but that had sounded gruff and rude.

"I'm sorry. I shouldn't have snapped at you."

Halfway to the door, Janey paused. Peered back at him. "It's fine."

"No. I shouldn't have snapped. It's just that I had a weird weekend."

She took the few paces that brought her to his desk. "Are you okay?"

"Yes. Why?"

She shook her head. "You've never said you were sorry before." She smiled. "Never mind. Not important."

She left the room, and he didn't think anything of it until his personal assistant forgot to ship his mother's Christmas gift and he exploded. "It's Christmas season! Holiday mail is a mess. It takes weeks to get a parcel delivered. You can't—"

Thoughts of Eloise rumbled through him. Her parents wouldn't even accept gifts from her. He had parents who loved him. They not only loved his presents; they sent him presents also. They wanted him home for Christmas. They wanted him home anytime. Any day. It was his own sadness and guilt that kept him away.

Why was he shouting over something so trivial?

He ran his hand along the back of his neck. "I'm sorry. I'm sure if you get it out today, it will be fine."

David, his gray-haired assistant, nodded. "Okay. I'll get right on it."

"Great."

David started toward the door but stopped and turned around. "You didn't need to apologize. I don't take it personally when you yell. I know that's how you are."

"How I am?"

"Sometimes you talk loud. I'm accustomed to it. It doesn't bother me."

David left his office. Ricky walked to the window and blew his breath out on a sigh.

Sometimes he talked loud?

Sheesh. Was he a grouch? A Grinch? Somebody who yelled so much people thought it abnormal when he didn't?

Thoughts of Eloise shamed him. She was alone, yet never once had he seen her bite anyone's head off. Even when they'd argued after his frat party, she'd been reasonable.

He sighed. He didn't like discovering he was a grouch. Especially because he wasn't. He was sad about his son. Lonely for his son. And everyone understood that.

He sat down and squeezed his eyes shut. He remembered Blake's one and only Christmas. He could hear the sound of his little boy's laugh. See wrapping paper strewn on the floor. Remember the way Blake loved cookies, chattered nonsensical baby words with Ricky's mom, sat on his dad's lap.

He swallowed.

If he was grouchy with his staff over missing Blake, over feeling guilty about Blake's death, he had a right. Even his staff knew that.

Feeling sorry for a woman he barely knew? It didn't make sense. Her making him feel bad for something he had no right to be guilty about? Well, that didn't make any sense either. Why should a woman he barely knew affect him like this?

He had to fix it. The best way would be to get his relationship with Eloise back to where it was supposed to be.

A deal.

Not a friendship, and certainly not a romance.

Simply a deal.

He didn't hear anything from the CEOs he'd sent her résumé to, and by Wednesday that bothered him. Once he got her a job, everything between them would balance out, and they could go back to being strangers pretending to date. So no response annoyed him. Still, his friends might not have called *him* because *she* was the one who wanted the job.

Given that it was Wednesday, the day before their next party—so he needed to call her with the information about that weekend's events—he picked up his phone. He wouldn't interrogate her, but if the subject of interviews came up, he wouldn't waste it.

"I wanted to let you know that Thursday's party is formal again."

"Oh. Okay. Good."

He winced, waiting for her to mention if she'd gotten calls from his friends, if she'd gotten interviews. When twenty seconds passed in silence, he sighed. "You didn't hear from my friends, did you?"

"No."

"Which means you didn't get a job."

"Nope."

Annoyance with his friends buffeted him. But sorrow for her sneaked in there too. This woman could not get a break. Still, he had troubles of his own. Guilt of his own. Shame of his own. A baby boy he missed so much sometimes his chest ached. He had enough trouble without getting involved with her and her problems. He had to help her find a job, but he couldn't get personally involved.

Needing to get them back to their deal and get himself out of this conversation, he said, "Even if someone hires you, the deal is twelve dates for a job. Not you get a job, then you quit." He grimaced, even more frustrated with himself. In trying to keep his distance, he'd made himself look like a grizzly bear. "I didn't mean that to sound as grouchy as it did."

She sighed. "I know."

He grimaced again. He almost told her how he'd noticed ten thousand times in the past three days how surly he was. How difficult he was to deal with. He knew it was the result of losing a child. And suddenly, he longed to tell someone. To share his pain. Or maybe he longed to tell her because he knew she'd understand?

But all he said was, "Good."

"So you want me to wear a gown."

"Yes." He paused. "Do you want me to make follow-up calls with the guys I sent your résumé to?"

"You can do that?"

"They are my friends. But they also owe me."

Silence greeted him. Finally she said, "Although I appreciate the offer, I still have some pride. I'd like to get a job based on my qualifications."

"You really don't have many."

"Thanks."

Damn it. He might not want to confide in her, but there

was no reason to hurt her. He slapped his desk. "See? There I go again. I have no filter on my tongue when it comes to business, and sometimes I'm just a little too honest."

"I think your honesty is your best quality."

He winced. "Tell my employees that."

"Why do you think your friends come to you for advice?"

"Because I tell them the truth?"

"Sometimes brutally."

He laughed, then marveled that he'd laughed even though he continually said the wrong thing. Even though he couldn't stop thinking about Blake. Even though he had guilt that swallowed him whole some days, she kept making him laugh and he kept making her miserable. "Let me call my friends."

"No. I don't want to be that girl in the office who only got her job because of her boyfriend. It's why I didn't want a job from you. I can't be the girl in the office who only got her job because her boyfriend pulled strings."

It wasn't so much what she said but how she said it that caused him to shake his head. "It's been a long time since anybody called me a boyfriend."

"Fake or not, that's what you are." She settled onto the wide sill of her living room window, wishing, like Binnie Margolis, for snow. Laura Beth was out. Olivia was in Kentucky. Christmas was getting close. Telling her story to Ricky on Sunday morning had pounded home the fact that she'd soon be facing another holiday by herself, without even a blanket of snow to make her feel cozy in her empty apartment with her eighteen-inch plastic tree and the cookies Olivia's mom would mail to her.

She swallowed. Desperate to get her mind off her troubles, she said the first thing that popped into her head. "So how was your day?"

He sniffed. "Same. Kinda boring."

"Really? Rich wheeler-dealer like you has boring days?"

He hesitated, as if he really didn't want to talk anymore, but he said, "It was fun when I started out. Now things are routine."

"Maybe you need a new venture."

"A new venture?"

"You know. Instead of writing new video games, invent a different kind of microwave popcorn. Try taking that to market. I'll bet you'll meet some challenges."

He laughed. "Microwave popcorn?"

"Hey, my dad loves the stuff…" Even as the words flipped out of her mouth, her heart tugged. Her stomach plummeted. As gruff and socially conscious as her parents were, they were her family and they didn't want her.

How could she miss people who didn't want her around?

Her eyes filled with tears. "I'm sorry. Someone's knocking on the door. I've gotta run. See you Thursday night. In a gown."

She didn't wait for his reply, just clicked off, tossed her phone to the sofa and laid her head on her knees. She refused to be pathetic, refused to let tears fall for the loss of people who didn't want her. She'd done that enough in her twenty-five years. All she wanted was a job, a way to support herself. And once she got it, she'd be fine.

She repeated that mantra as she went to bed, got up, showered, dressed for work, jumped on the subway, rode up in the average elevator to the law office and made coffee for the senior partners, none of whom even acknowledged her existence.

CHAPTER SIX

THURSDAY NIGHT RICKY walked up the four flights of stairs to Eloise's apartment, trepidation riding his blood. Every Christmas decoration reminded him of his son. Even the cold air reminded him of bundling Blake in a snowsuit, buying knit caps.

Wanting to roll up in a ball of misery and privately mourn Blake, he was tempted by thoughts of ending this charade. He could bow out of the rest of the parties. All he had to do was go to Jamaica or Monaco, and everybody would be jealous of his vacation. Nobody would wonder why he wasn't attending any more of the parties.

Except Eloise didn't have a job. Taking her to these events was his best way of keeping her in front of his friends who might want to hire her. Lord knows, sending emails hadn't worked.

Not sure what he'd find when she came to the door, he sucked in a breath before he knocked. When the door opened, she stood before him looking beautiful in a simple straight gown. Red and shiny, it complimented her hair, which she'd put in some curly creation on top of her head and spun thin tinsel through.

"You look great." The words popped out naturally, and he almost shook his head in wonder that just seeing her had him feeling better.

When she smiled, relief poured through him. It would

have been a long night if she'd been as depressed as she had been on Sunday morning and in their phone call. Instead, she'd pulled herself together. He admired that.

He returned her smile. "Every dress gets better."

She laughed as she handed him her black cape. "That's because the closer we get to the actual holiday, the more Christmas-y I feel. Just wait till you see what I'm pondering for Christmas Eve."

They walked to the limo and, when Norman opened the door, they slid in. With the advanced stage of the season, more and more shops and apartment windows were decorated for the holiday. Bright lights winked. Tinsel blew in the bitter breezes. Because it was cold, everything had a sparkly, icy look, but it wasn't quite as pretty as if there had been snow.

"I like snow too."

He spun to face her. Had he said that out loud? "I...um... grew up near the Finger Lakes." Damn. So much for trying not to be personal. "By now, they're probably knee-deep in the white stuff."

"Probably? You don't know?"

He peeked at her. "If there's snow?"

She nodded.

He winced. "I haven't talked to my parents in a while."

She said, "Oh. Okay," as if she understood. And he supposed if anybody understood complicated relationships with parents, it would be her.

But that only reminded him of how difficult her life was, and when she turned away from him, that ridiculous sadness for her filled him again. Fighting it, he squeezed his eyes shut. She would be fine. Once he helped her land a job, she'd be ecstatic. He did not have to feel sorry for her.

They walked into the hotel, and he dropped off their outerwear at the coat check. Just before they entered the ballroom, he saw her shift her face and change her countenance. She formed a smile big enough to remove the sad expression in her eyes, but he saw no light in them. Then she slid her hand in the crook of his elbow and they walked into the ballroom.

Guilt buffeted him. She was going the whole nine yards for him and he wasn't really doing anything for her.

Seated with another group of his friends, he held out her chair as he made quick introductions, and the discussion immediately zoomed to stock options.

This was why he'd never worried that anyone at any of the parties they attended would tell Eloise about Blake. His friends didn't talk about anything but business. And the wives who didn't join in on the discussion of stocks and strategies generally sat dutifully at the husbands' sides or chatted among themselves about inconsequential, party-worthy topics, not ridiculously sad things that would bring everybody down. He wasn't saying they were fake. They were more like courteous. Proper.

Still, with his mission in mind, he tried to work human resources into the conversation but couldn't. Frustration wound through him. No wonder Eloise couldn't find a job. No one seemed to care about the administration of their projects. All they cared about was the project itself.

When the dancing started, he and Eloise moved to the dance floor. He slid his hand across the smooth material covering her back. Attraction slithered through him. With every inch of his heart and soul, he longed to pull her to him and just give her what she needed. A little bit of affection. But although he might be able to hug her tonight, maybe kiss her, who knew what he'd be like tomorrow? And if he held her tonight, kissed her tonight and then couldn't get out of bed the next day because of debilitating grief... wouldn't he hurt her?

Yes. He would. And he refused to do that to her.

Needing to get his mind off how good she felt, he said, "So this is a pretty nice party."

She met his gaze and smiled. "They're all wonderful."

"I'm glad you enjoy them."

"I do."

His conscience tweaked again. While he took all this for granted, she was happy to get a good meal and a nice glass of wine, even though he basically ignored her. With the exception of dancing, he was generally occupied with his friends, and when he wasn't, his fear of getting too close kept him from really talking to her.

"Even with a grouch like me?"

She laughed lightly. "Oh, you're not so bad."

But he was. He knew he was. Ever since she'd told him about being alone and made him realize he had an abundance of things to be thankful for, he'd seen the signs. Short temper with his staff. Nothing but cool professionalism with Norman. Presents for his friends and his family bought by David. Hell, he didn't even know what he'd bought his own mother for Christmas. Since Blake's death, he'd insulated himself inside a bubble of sadness. He didn't think that was wrong, but he did see he was letting Eloise down. He'd made a promise that he couldn't seem to keep. And suddenly it became overwhelmingly important that he at least do something for her, even if it was only make her happy for one night.

"We should do tequila shots."

She laughed and pulled back so she could see his face. "What?"

He'd surprised himself as much as her with the suggestion. But now that he'd said it, it sort of made sense.

"Tequila shots. This party might be nice, but we've gone to six of these. They're getting boring. Tequila shots would liven up this place."

Another laugh spilled out of her, causing his heart to tug and his chest to tighten with something that felt very much like pride that *he'd* made *her* laugh for a change.

"I'm sure the hosts would be thrilled."

"Why not? Isn't the purpose of giving a party to make your friends happy?"

"Yes." She said the word slowly, as her eyes rose, and she met his gaze. Soft but curious, the light in her crystal blue orbs told him she was cautious about the shots, but the idea appealed to her.

Pleasure rolled through him. He spun her around, mentally thanking Tucker Engle for forcing him to take ballroom dancing classes so he wouldn't be awkward at these parties. Not only had it turned out that he loved to dance, but tonight he loved seeing that light in her eyes.

"So, if we asked the bartender to set up shots, maybe eighteen or twenty, we could probably get that many people to join us. I'll bet with every shot, our crew would grow."

"Our crew? Are you nuts?" She shook her head, but her eyes glowed.

He spun her around again. "Maybe. But I see at least three of my fraternity brothers. I'll bet we could have this place rocking in three shots."

She laughed gaily. "I'll bet you'd have a room full of drunks in three shots."

"But think of the pictures that would show up in tomorrow's society pages."

She laughed and shook her head. "It would probably be the newspaper's best issue ever."

The music stopped and, as always, one of his friends slid over. After introductions, he asked Ricky a question about a company he was considering partnering in and, as Ricky answered, his gaze slid to Eloise.

She stood at his side, smiling, playing the part. But they never touched. Aside from when they danced. Or when *she* put her hand in the crook of his elbow. Or when *she* fixed his bow tie.

He'd never touched her with affection. Never held her hand. Never put his arm around her. To a woman who lived her life without family, without affection, his lack of touch probably seared her.

He reached out and took her hand. Her gaze swung to his. He smiled. She smiled. He tugged her closer. And while they held hands, his conversation continued until the band began to play again.

This time when he pulled her into his arms, he felt her relax against him. He relaxed a little himself. He wasn't making this real. Just realistic. And, all right, he also wanted her to feel wanted. He might only need her to help him get through the holiday. But he *needed* her, which meant he *wanted* her around.

And she needed to know that somebody wanted her. Albeit for a little while.

When the band took a break, he walked her to their table, then excused himself. When he returned, he had two shots of tequila. She burst out laughing. Their table-mates frowned.

He nodded at the shots, as he sat by Eloise. "Private joke."

He picked up a shot and motioned for her to do the same. "Ready?"

"I think this is kinda nuts."

"It's been a long, hard couple of years for both of us. Maybe one night of I-don't-care is in order."

"One night of I-don't-care?"

"One night of forgetting everything and just having a good time."

She picked up her shot. "I could handle that."

They downed the tequila. She shuddered in distaste but laughed, and when the band began to play again, they were both more comfortable.

The music shifted to a quiet, mellow tune, and he pulled her into his arms for a slow dance. She melted against him. Loose from the tequila, he rested his chin on the top of her head and inhaled the fragrance of her hair. For the first time in eighteen months, he just let go.

When the band took a break, they took another shot and washed it down with a glass of champagne. Dancing took a lot of the sting out of the alcohol. Still, by the time they returned to her apartment, they were just tipsy enough to clamor up the stairs.

The "shh" she sent back to him from the step above his only made him laugh.

When they stopped in front of her apartment door, she said, "We're gonna get me kicked out of my building."

He put his hands on her shoulders. He wasn't one for medicating pain with alcohol, but tonight wasn't about getting rid of pain. It had been about acknowledging it and telling it to go to hell for a few hours.

"If I get you kicked out of your building, I'll find you another apartment."

She snorted a laugh. "Laura Beth and I can barely afford the one we have."

Her words slurred endearingly. He smiled stupidly. "I had a good time."

"So I'm guessing you're thinking we should have tequila shots at every party."

"Well, we wouldn't want to form any bad habits, but…" He glanced around, searching his alcohol-numbed brain for the words that should follow that *but*, and in the end he couldn't help stating the obvious. "It was good to loosen up a bit. I really had fun."

She put her hands on his chest. "Doesn't happen for you much, does it?"

He shook his head. "Doesn't happen at all."

"So, I'm good for you."

She was. When her life didn't make him feel like an ingrate, she was. Thinking of her, instead of himself, instead of his grief, instead of his guilt, was so much easier.

The urge to kiss her swam through his blood, making it

tingle. But it was the very fact that he was so tempted that stopped him. She was good for him. But he wasn't good for her. He was broken. She was broken, too. But that meant she needed someone strong, someone filled with love to shower her with affection. And that wasn't him.

He stepped back. "Good night, Eloise."

"Do you realize that's the first time you've said my name?"

"I say your name all the time."

"Yeah, when you introduce me." Her gazed locked with his. "But you've never said it to me."

The urge to kiss her shimmied through him again. She was so pretty, so perfect. So wonderful sometimes. And thanks to Preston he knew her lips were as soft as a cloud, the inside of her mouth like silk.

He took a step closer.

She put her hands on his lapels again and slid them up his chest.

Need surged. Not just from the intimacy of her touch, but from hope. He longed for her to put her hands around his neck, something she didn't do in their very proper dancing. He yearned for her to hold him. To hug him. To pull him close.

Instead, she straightened his tie and smiled up at him.

She wouldn't make the first move, but she clearly was telling him she wanted him to kiss her.

Desire pleaded with him. *Just do it. Just bend your head. Just kiss her.*

His breath faltered. Dear God, he wanted this.

But he knew himself. When the tequila wore off, he'd regret it. And even if he didn't, he'd leave her. Not in a big, splashy departure scene. But after these parties, he'd stop calling. He'd drift back to his own dark, quiet world because his guilt wouldn't let him handle the bright optimistic world she wanted. And he'd forget her.

He would hurt a woman who'd been hurt enough.

He closed his fingers around her hands and removed them from his lapel. "Good night, Eloise."

Then he turned and walked away, his mouth yearning for a kiss, his limbs longing to hold her, his heart telling him he was a fool.

Ten o'clock the next morning, Eloise's pride could no longer hold off the pounding in her head. She rose from her desk and walked into the employee break room, where she rifled through the cabinet above the sink until she found painkillers.

Getting water from the cooler beside the refrigerator, she glanced up sharply when Tina Horner walked in with her empty mug and ambled to the coffeemaker.

"What's up?"

"Nothing." She popped the two pills into her mouth, chugged her water and headed for the door and up the hall to her office. She and Tina weren't supposed to leave their cabinets full of confidential files unattended. A fact Tina frequently forgot...or ignored...because she was a full-time employee with little fear of being fired or replaced.

A few seconds later, Tina caught up with her. "Come on. You can't tell me nothing's wrong. I've worked beside you for weeks. You never need painkillers."

"Ricky and I went to a party last night."

Tina's face glowed with curiosity. "Another formal one?"

"Yep."

"On a Thursday?"

"Rich people don't need to keep the same schedule you and I do. I'm guessing if there's a party on Thursday, they don't work on Friday."

Tina took the left at the hall that led to their office. "So while you're here nursing a hangover, your date's probably still in bed?"

"Yep." But now that she thought about it, she doubted it. She'd never met anybody with the work ethic Ricky had.

Plus, he had enough technology in his den that he could work in his pajamas. The thought made her laugh.

Tina narrowed her eyes at her. "So add a hangover to a silly laugh, and I'm guessing you had a really good time last night."

She slipped into their office and over to her desk. "Yes. I had a good time."

Tina sat and eyed Eloise. "Let's see… What is it you aren't telling me?" She tapped her index fingers on her cheeks. "You drank too much. You probably also danced a lot." Her expression grew thoughtful. "But you've been doing that all along." She considered that for another second, then her mouth fell open. "He kissed you good-night."

Getting to work, Eloise examined the files list on her screen and said, "I wish."

Tina gasped. She bounced from her chair and over to Eloise's desk. "Your fake dating has turned into real dating!"

Eloise shook her head. "I said I wish. I didn't say it happened." And because of how happy dancing snuggled against him had made her feel, the realist in her had wept with sadness when he'd walked away from that kiss. A chance to bond. A chance to express that their feelings were changing. A chance to actually be themselves.

And he'd walked away from it.

"You really like him, don't you?"

Eloise squeezed her eyes shut. Memories from the night before flooded her. The joy of simple human contact had morphed into happiness, which had shifted into an acknowledgment that she more than liked this guy. "Sometimes I think I might be falling in love with him."

"Oh, honey!" Tina leaned her hip on Eloise's desk. "It's one thing to want to kiss and feel like you're living a fairy tale with a rich guy. It's another to start believing it's real."

"I know."

"You're going to get your heart broken. And this isn't

going to be like whatever heartbreak you had in college that drove you to New York City."

Eloise frowned. "What makes you think getting my heart broken drove me to New York City?"

Rising from Eloise's desk, Tina laughed. "The sad look that doesn't often leave your eyes."

"I have a sad look?"

"Sort of like a lost puppy."

Her head swam. All this time she'd thought she was a rock of sanity, when she was giving off a sad look. "I look like a dog?"

"You look like somebody who needs a hug. You're a sweet, wonderful person. If someone gets to know you and like you, it's hard not to want to help you."

"People want to help me?"

"Not everyone." Tina returned to her desk and put her attention on her computer screen. "But it's not easy to watch you struggle every day. It makes me want to do something nice for you. If only bring you a doughnut."

She remembered the once-a-week doughnut Tina bought her and then thought of the conversation she'd had with Ricky before he'd suggested the shots. "Or tequila."

Tina peered around her computer monitor at Eloise. "Tequila?"

She shook her head. "Never mind." But mortification filled her. Ricky Langley had been seeing her "sad face" for weeks. And last night she'd been particularly sad. So, like Tina, he'd wanted to cheer her up. He wasn't falling for her. That was why he hadn't kissed her. He didn't want to get romantic. He just wanted her to stop her sadness.

What an idiot she was! No wonder she couldn't get a job. Her ability to read people and their actions was nonexistent. And people looked at her and saw sadness. Not competence. Not reliability. *Sadness*.

She had to fix that.

* * *

Ricky got up late with no sign of a hangover. Smug, he showered, congratulating himself for remembering to hydrate before going to bed. But even as he had the thought, he wondered if Eloise had drunk enough water—

His heart stuttered. *Eloise.* He'd damn near kissed her the night before. Just the memory of that almost kiss put the need in his blood again, tightened his chest. He'd desperately wanted to kiss her, but he'd risen above it.

Thank God. Because he wasn't good for her. He lived in a world of guilt and sadness. He refused to bring her into that.

Norman arrived, and he got into the limo and tried to focus on that day's meetings, but he failed. Even thoughts of Blake drifted away when memories of laughing with Eloise filled his head. The noisy way they climbed up her stairway. Those thirty seconds he could have kissed her—

He frowned. He might have risen above the temptations of last night, but what about the next time?

The "next time" he'd be tempted wasn't a week away, time enough to shore up his defenses. Tonight they had another party. And he still had a tingle in his blood. A funny feeling that pressed into his heart every time he thought her name.

He groaned. She liked when he said her name. He liked saying her name. This was bad.

He entered the private elevator to his office suite.

He could handle the desire. That sweet need that nudged him to touch his lips to hers was a natural male urge. Especially with a woman as beautiful as Eloise. But that yearning to be held? The longing for connection that he'd nearly drowned in the night before? That was just wrong.

He didn't need connections. He didn't even *want* connections. Being alone was better for him. Then he didn't worry about snarling at his employees or insulting his friends.

Ever since he'd met Eloise, his entire life had kept getting confused. Even his work life.

He paused his thoughts. *That* was the real problem. She was drawing him back into the world again, as if he belonged there. She made him forget he had trouble in his life. But he did. He had troubles that wouldn't go away with a wave of a magic wand. He couldn't pretend they didn't exist.

He scrubbed his hand across his mouth. If he were smart, he'd have David call Eloise and tell her that her services were no longer needed. But they had made a deal, and he hadn't fulfilled his end of the bargain.

He couldn't back out. True leaders never reneged on deals. That was how otherwise-smart business professionals got bad names. He had to take her to the party that night. And every night until he found her a job.

Which meant holding her and talking to her.

He scrubbed his hand across his mouth again. If there was one thing he hadn't expected from this deal it was that he would like her. But, surely, he could get beyond that.

CHAPTER SEVEN

THAT NIGHT ELOISE wore a black gown paired with bright silver jewelry.

Feeling awkward and wishing he'd called and canceled, Ricky said, "As always, you look amazing."

She caught his gaze, her eyes searching his. He stood very still, very proper, under her scrutiny, hoping to make her believe it had been nothing but the tequila that had made him so affectionate the night before. That he didn't really want to kiss her. That he didn't really want anything from her except to finish their deal.

Eventually, she smiled slightly. "As always, you're good for my ego."

She handed him her cape, and, closing his eyes, he slid it on her shoulders, so relieved that she was handling this with grace and discretion that he couldn't even put the feeling into words.

But an unexpected urge hit him. His end of the deal was to help her find a job. Although that hadn't yet panned out, he would see to it that it did. And it would cost him nothing but a little time and effort.

But she spent every darned Friday and Saturday night with him. Not to mention a Thursday and some Sundays. Buying her an evening jacket, a fur, something better than her worn cape, wouldn't be out of line. To his bank account, it would be small token of appreciation. Just as going out with her had become difficult; going out with him couldn't be easy either. Yet she handled it like a trooper.

"I was actually thrilled to find a way to wear this jewelry."

Pulling himself out of his reverie, he realized they'd not only clattered down the four flights of stairs, but he'd missed a chunk of conversation. He opened the building door for her and she strolled outside.

"The jewelry looks nice with your dress."

She laughed. "Good evening, Norman."

He tipped his hat. "Ma'am."

They climbed inside. "You don't have to pretend you enjoy talking about jewelry."

"I don't mind." But he was clueless.

"I just sometimes get carried away." She sighed. "I love to dress up." She winced. "That makes me sound like a kid. I don't love to dress up as much as I love fashion. I love it when Olivia calls for advice." She paused, faced him. "You do know Olivia and Tucker will be at tonight's party."

That woke him up. "Really?"

"Yes. She called this morning, then texted pictures of two gowns. She almost wore something brown until I talked her into a beautiful red Vera Wang."

He struggled with a smile. He'd forgotten how goofy women could get about clothes. And tonight Eloise was particularly goofy, talking nonstop, as if she were trying to prove to him that she was fine. Happy. Not going to get hysterical on him because he wanted to pretend last night hadn't happened.

Appreciating that, he kept the conversation going. "That's a tragedy averted."

She playfully nudged his arm. "All right. All right. I get it. You think talking about clothes is silly."

Laughter bubbled through him. The kind he'd almost forgotten he existed. Teasing, we-don't-have-to-be-normal, merriment. "Tucker once called and asked for advice about his tux."

She laughed. "Stop."

"I said, 'Tucker, go with the bow tie.'"

She swatted him. "Stop!"

"He went with the regular tie and all night long everybody kept giving him funny looks."

"Stop!"

He laughed. "Sorry."

But to Eloise he didn't look sorry. He looked happy. The way he had when they were drinking tequila the night before. Three shots and some champagne hadn't nearly put him under the table as it had done to her. But it had certainly relaxed him. And it appeared his good mood wasn't gone.

She blanched remembering how she'd all but asked for a good-night kiss, and she was glad he'd not only walked away, but also seemed to have totally forgotten that she stood there wide-eyed, her lips parted, her brain chanting a litany hoping he'd telepathically get the message that he should kiss her.

Now that she knew he didn't like her—he only felt sorry for her—she absolutely wanted him to forget her begging for a kiss the night before. If it killed her, she intended to project happiness. No sad puppy-dog eyes, as Tina said. Just a normal woman at a party. With him still happy and with Olivia and Tucker around, that should be relatively easy.

As they got out of the limo at the Ritz, Ricky reached for her hand. His warm fingers wrapped around hers and her heart stumbled. All right, need-to-look-like-a-normal-woman aside, she desperately wanted to have another fun night. Another night when he was warm and natural. She would be alone on Christmas day. She needed good memories of these nights with him, nights when they laughed and had fun together, to think about when she played carols on her phone and tried not to remember she had no one in her life.

They met Tucker and Olivia in the lobby. Eloise hugged her pregnant friend, who, to a baby novice, felt extremely large around the middle. "I'm so glad you're home."

Tucker said, "We couldn't miss Fred Murphy's party."

His hand on the small of Olivia's back, Tucker headed for the elevator to the ballroom, and Ricky leaned down and whispered, "He was the first banker to give Tucker money."

She peeked up into his sleepy brown eyes, fighting the urge to believe his keeping her up-to-date with necessary information proved he liked her. Even though that might make her memories more interesting on Christmas Day, she didn't want to get carried away. As Tina had said, that was how women got their hearts broken. She just wanted to have a good time. Something to think about on Christmas morning.

"So all this fuss is about a loan?"

He shook his head. "An investment."

"Ah. Money he didn't have to pay back."

"Yes. But it was more the confidence he had in Tucker."

"I get it."

She and Ricky caught up to the Engles just as the elevator door opened. Eloise undid the buttons of her cape and Olivia gasped.

"So that's what you did with that big black ball gown?"

She laughed. "Hard to believe this used to have eight layers of tulle, isn't it?"

"It's stunning. I should be coming to you for my gowns."

"Oh, I don't know. That Vera Wang suits you very well."

Olivia glanced down at her red gown. "It is pretty."

"It's gorgeous."

Olivia shook her head. "Yeah, and I'm glad you talked me into it. You have such a talent for this stuff."

* * *

The discussion of gowns and sewing swirled around Ricky's head, and he almost laughed again at the silly conversation he and Eloise had had in the car. When he was with her, something about her always made him smile, and that wasn't good. When he was happy, he let his guard down and if he let his guard down too much, he'd kiss her. And if he started kissing her, he'd hurt her.

The opening of the elevator doors came as a grand relief, and they stepped out. Eloise handed Ricky her cape, and, as she turned, he saw the back of her dress.

Or lack thereof.

Walking to the coat check desk, he silently prayed for strength. She was making him laugh, forget himself and tease her. He was only human. With his attraction and sense of comfort with her, he kept inching closer and closer to the place where he wouldn't be able to resist kissing her. And tomorrow he'd regret it and pull back and probably hurt her.

He could not hurt her. No matter how hard he had to fight, he would do everything in his power to keep his distance.

Still, after dinner and the short, humorous awards ceremony Fred put on, he and Eloise were one of the first couples on the dance floor. Everyone knew he loved to dance, but, more than that, Tucker and Olivia were also here. As much as he wasn't the kind to fool his close friends, the charade was well under way. Despite fighting feelings for Eloise, he couldn't end their deal when he hadn't found her a job. And he couldn't tell his best friend that he wasn't really dating his wife's BFF, that it had been a bargain. They'd both look crazy.

So he pulled Eloise into his arms and she nestled against him. When her softness met his chest, he struggled with the desire to just close his eyes and enjoy.

He looked down. She looked up. Their gazes met in

acknowledgment of the fact that their tequila night had brought them closer. But he didn't want to be close. He wanted them to go back to being polite strangers who could pretend they liked each other.

So he pulled several inches away, putting enough space between them to retain his sanity. Still, every time they moved, his hand on the small of her back slid against her satiny skin. He remembered the sparkle in her eyes at her apartment door last night. How she'd wanted him to kiss her. How he'd longed to do just that.

But he also remembered that he was grieving his son, filled with guilt and remorse over his death. She had troubles of her own. Neither one was in a position to indulge an attraction that might end up hurting them both.

He held himself stiffly for the first set and was relieved when the band took a break. Eloise chatted with Olivia about her clients and art in general, and he and Tucker bounced around ideas about the stock market.

When the second set began, he was a little too tired to hold himself away from her. When she melted, his body tried to resist, but it was no use. Her breasts met his chest. Their thighs brushed as they moved to the music. His hormones awoke like a band of angels ready to sing the "Hallelujah Chorus."

"I don't think I've ever seen so many diamonds in my life."

Glad to get his mind off his hormones and also curious about where her mind had gone, he laughed. "Cumulatively or at this party?"

"It almost doesn't matter." She pulled back and looked at him. "Something odd has been striking me tonight."

With the feeling of the velvet skin of her back pressed against his hand, something had been striking him all night, too. He'd love to run his hand down her back just once. Just for the thrill of it.

But talking about that wouldn't do either one of them any good. So he smiled and politely said, "What's that?"

"My mom doesn't have a diamond necklace."

He bit out a laugh. "What?"

"Look at all these necklaces. Or just think about the one around Olivia's throat. Tucker adores his wife so he showers her with diamonds. That's how wealthy men show their love."

He smiled. "It is?"

"Sure. If you can't say the words, you buy a gift. A necklace. A bracelet. A fur."

His mouth twisted. He wanted to buy her a fur, but that didn't mean he loved her. "It's not always about love."

"True. It could be about respect or appreciation. You know, a thanks-for-putting-up-with-me gift."

He coughed. That was exactly why he wanted to buy her a fur. "You seem so sure."

"People are transparent. But none of this is actually my point."

"What's your point?"

"My mother doesn't have a diamond necklace."

"You think your dad doesn't love her or doesn't appreciate her?"

"I think he doesn't have hundreds of thousands to millions of dollars to spend on jewelry."

Ricky stopped dancing. Confused, he said, "Everybody here does."

"Which is the conclusion of my point." She nudged him to start dancing again. "My parents have lots of money. But they're not in this class."

He frowned, not quite understanding what she was getting at. "So?"

"So maybe that's why they were so mad that I embarrassed them."

He thought back to his beginnings in New York City society. He remembered renting a tux because he didn't own one and hiring a limo with a driver. He hadn't done it for the sake of impressing anyone. He simply wanted to fit in. Not look like an upstart. Not look like somebody who didn't belong. If Eloise's parents were image conscious, her embarrassing them might have shaken them more than normal people. That is, if they thought more of their station in society than their daughter. And it appeared they did.

"Maybe."

"The few times we came to New York City for Christmas events, they were extremely clear with me and my older brother that we shouldn't do anything to embarrass them."

He frowned, catching her gaze. "Where is all this coming from?"

She shrugged. "I did some thinking today. Came to some conclusions."

A happy thought filled him with hope. He might not have found her a job, but maybe being with him had caused her to see some things about her life, things that might help her stop being so sad.

"So the past couple of weeks with my friends has been good for you?"

She shook her head. "It doesn't matter."

He twirled them around. "Of course it matters. You miss your parents. You're trying to figure it out because you're trying to find an angle or reason to go home."

She glanced away. "I don't think so."

He desperately wanted her to be able to go home, to have the acceptance she needed. Not just to make sure she got something from their deal, but because no one should be alone for Christmas. Especially not somebody so pretty and so nice.

He waited a second, then said, "What would you have to do to be able to go home?"

She smiled devilishly. "Buy my mom a diamond necklace?"

He huffed out a sigh. "I'm being serious here."

"I don't think I can go home."

He glanced down. "Why not?"

She looked away for a few seconds, then caught his gaze again. "I've found more love and acceptance with Olivia and Laura Beth than I ever had with my parents. And with their acceptance I realized how dysfunctional my own family is."

He thought about how he hadn't been home in nearly two years. Didn't call. Didn't take his mother's calls. Because everything about his family reminded him of Blake.

"Everybody's family is dysfunctional to a degree."

"Not like this. My parents don't know how to love. Even though it hurts to have no one, sometimes a person is better off being alone than living around people who only use them."

Or sometimes a person is better off being alone than being with people who only revive their sorrow.

"Maybe."

"Okay, here's the best example. My parents would love to see me with you. They'd use that like a stepladder. They'd treat me like royalty to get to *you*. And then they'd use you for introductions or insider information or whatever they thought they could get. But when you and I stopped seeing each other, they'd put me back on a shelf again. Like something they pulled out when they needed it." She shook her head. "As a kid, when they'd put me back on the shelf, I'd jump through hoops to get their attention, their affection. I'd do well in school or volunteer to work for a very visible charity. Sometimes they'd pat me on the head, but most of the time they'd ignore me. Even in their home, at their dinner table, I was alone. Lonely. I don't want to go back to that."

He wouldn't either. No matter how much he stayed away, he knew the second he came home, his family would smother him with love.

Familiar sadness for her filled him, but he stopped it from totally taking over. She'd figured all this out on her own, clearly come to terms with it. She was a strong woman. A unique, wonderful person. No one needed to pity her. He might wish he could help her, but he would never, ever feel sorry for her.

The band took a break, and Ricky and Eloise walked back to the table. Tucker and Olivia leaned in together, as if they were telling secrets. But Olivia's face was pinched and Tucker's brow had furrowed.

Ricky tensed.

Eloise walked over and stooped beside Olivia's chair. "Wanna tell me what's going on here?"

Close enough to hear and not wanting to look overly interested in case it was a lover's quarrel, Ricky took his seat.

Tucker said, "We think Olivia might be in labor."

Eloise gasped. "And she flew? You let her get on an airplane this close to her due date?"

"She's not due for another month. Her doctor said it was fine."

Olivia panted out a breath. "Seriously. I'm not due for a month. This might not be labor. Everybody said it was fine for me to fly."

Eloise sighed. "It might have been fine for you to fly, but you're not fine now." She reached across the table, grabbed her small handbag, retrieved her phone and dialed 911. "This is Eloise Vaughn. I'm at the Ritz with a woman who is in labor."

Olivia said, "Really Eloise, that's not necessary…. Oh my God!"

Tucker stiffened. "What?"

Olivia caught Eloise's hand. "Tell them to hurry."

When Eloise finished the call, Olivia squeezed her fingers. "If it's possible, I want to get down to the lobby."

Eloise gaped at her. "The lobby?"

"I don't want to make a scene. Get me downstairs, hide

me somewhere. I don't want anybody to see if my water breaks or hear me if I scream."

There wasn't a woman in the world who wouldn't understand that and Eloise couldn't refuse. "Can you walk?"

Olivia nodded.

She motioned for Ricky to come over to them. "Tucker's going to help Olivia to the door. You and I are going to walk behind them just in case."

Ricky nodded, but memory after memory of Blake's birth tumbled through him. He hadn't been in love with Blake's mother. Basically, they'd been nightclub friends who'd slept together, and she ended up pregnant. He hadn't gone to birthing classes, didn't really want to be in the delivery room—and he hadn't been—but he'd gone to the hospital when Blake was born. The same hospital where his son had ultimately died. And that was probably the same hospital Tucker would direct Olivia to, if only because, like Ricky, he was on their board of directors.

Eloise caught his arm and pulled him in step behind Tucker and Olivia. "Get with the program, slick."

He shook himself out of his reverie. If this were anybody but Tucker and Olivia, the torrent of memories assaulting him right now would have frozen him solid.

But when Olivia's steps faltered, he was right behind her, ready to catch her.

Ricky's limo pulled onto the emergency entrance ramp behind the ambulance with Olivia and Tucker inside. Eloise leaped out the second the car stopped.

She was at the door of the ambulance as they pulled the gurney off and Tucker jumped down.

The pair, Olivia's best friend and her husband, hustled with Olivia into the emergency room.

Ricky held back. Everything inside him told him to leave. Too many bad memories were associated with this hospital. Yet he couldn't seem to get his mouth to form the words to tell Norman to go. His best friend's baby was coming early. Olivia's life could be in jeopardy.

And Eloise was upset. She might have taken control, but he'd felt her vibrating with fear through the entire drive over. He could not leave her.

He slid out of the limo, leaned inside his still open back door and sent Norman home. Blake had taken nineteen hours to make his appearance. Tucker and Olivia's child could take as long or longer.

He ambled into the emergency room, gave his name at the desk and flashed his ID as a member of the board. "I want to be apprised of Olivia Engle's condition every step of the way."

The receptionist shook her head. "I'm sorry, sir. But our privacy policy prevents that unless you're family." She gave him a hopeful look, clearly not wanting to get into a battle of wills with a hospital director.

Tucking his key card into his jacket pocket, he put her out of her misery. "Check with Mr. Engle. He'll tell you it's okay."

She walked away, and, a few minutes later, she returned and told him that Olivia had been taken upstairs to the maternity ward.

Haunted, afraid to go back to the part of the hospital that had the good memories, memories of Blake being born, of holding his son for the first time, of wrapping the tiny, squiggly bundle in a blanket before securing him in his car seat, Ricky took his time walking to the elevator and then down the long cool corridor to the waiting room of the maternity ward.

An hour went by. He sat. He paced. He sat some more, elbows on his knees, hands dropped between his legs. Eventually, he stood, untied his tie, undid the first two buttons of his shirt and walked to the intensive care unit in the children's ward, where he stood by the window and stared at the empty cribs.

If he closed his eyes, he could see his son bandaged and bruised, an IV locked into his hand, his little chest barely rising and falling as a ventilator did his breathing for him.

Tears filled his eyes, reviving his shame. Then he realized Tucker's baby might be too small, too weak, and the newest member of the happy Engle family might spend his or her first days or weeks or even a year in the same crib as Blake.

His shame morphed into fear. Real fear that Tucker and Olivia might face the devastation of losing a child. He could feel every bit of sorrow that would overwhelm them and cursed. That shouldn't happen to anyone. But Olivia and Tucker? They were special. They didn't deserve this.

The rustle of skirts interrupted the quiet, and he turned to see Eloise walking down the hall.

"Hey."

"Hey." He frowned. "This is a private ward. How'd you get in here?"

She showed him a key card. "Tucker gave me this and said to find you. How did *you* get in here?"

He pulled the key card just like Tucker's from his tuxedo jacket pocket.

"Wow. You two must be some big-time donors."

"We're on the board." He sucked in a breath. "How's Olivia?"

She winced. "Not in labor. The doctor's keeping her overnight just to be sure, but she's fine."

He breathed a sigh of relief, so glad Tucker and Olivia's baby would be okay that for several seconds he couldn't function. Finally, he ran his hand across the back of his neck and forced his muscles and brain to relax. "That's good."

She looked around. "It's so quiet here."

"That's normal in the children's ICU."

He expected a question or two. She'd earned the right

to ask them. He felt her curiosity like a living, breathing thing. Still, she said nothing.

His respect for her grew. He'd told her he didn't want her to know his past, his pain, because he didn't want her to treat him any differently—or, worse, to pity him. And if the casual way she behaved around him was anything to go by, she hadn't looked him up on the internet and hadn't asked his friends for information.

It boggled his mind that she hadn't investigated him. If the tables were turned, he would have been driven crazy until he gave in to his curiosity, but he would have given in. She'd been a rock. She was probably the most trustworthy person on the planet.

"Good evening, Mr. Langley." Regina walked up to them, giving Eloise a quick once-over. "And who is this?"

He looked from Regina to Eloise, who met his gaze with as much curiosity about how he'd answer as Regina had.

Their gazes locked. She'd gone to all his parties with him, always kept up the charade and always looked pretty for him, even though it probably meant working like a Christmas elf to get that party's dress altered. He'd refused to tell her his secrets and she'd accepted it.

He couldn't think of her as nothing but a fake date anymore. He might not be her real boyfriend, but she was more than a partner in a charade.

He caught her hand and squeezed it. "She's a friend."

Eloise smiled.

Regina said, "Well, it's quiet up here tonight. Stay as long as you like."

It didn't seem right to stand with Eloise at the window to the room where his son had died. He didn't want her to see his grief. Plus, with Olivia fine and the baby out of danger, there was no reason to stay.

"Actually, we were just on our way out."

"Good night then."

"Good night, Regina." He directed Eloise to the elevator. "I sent Norman home. We're going to have to get a taxi."

"A taxi! Do you know how expensive taxis are?"

He laughed, then realized that's exactly what she'd intended for him to do. But the sights and the sounds of the hospital kept him grounded in reality, and he suddenly felt guilty for those three seconds of happiness.

No matter how much Eloise lifted his spirits, in his heart he knew he didn't deserve to be whole.

CHAPTER EIGHT

ELOISE ROLLED OVER in bed the next morning, not able to get herself to crawl out and face the day.

She wasn't the kind to overthink things, but why would someone choose to wait in the intensive care unit of the children's ward instead of the maternity waiting room?

She let the obvious reasons flit through her brain. Maybe Ricky had spent time there himself as a child. Or maybe one of his siblings had. Or maybe he'd had a child who'd been there. Maybe a child born prematurely, as Tucker and Olivia's child had almost been the night before.

The last one made so much sense that new scenarios began rolling through her head. Scary scenarios. Things his friends' wives would call a tragedy. Things she had no basis to believe. Things that had no grounding in reality.

With a growl, she shoved off the covers, climbed out of bed and shuffled to the kitchen. Laura Beth already sat at the little round table, drinking tea.

"Hey."

"Hey. You're up early for someone who was at a party last night."

She walked to the counter and started making a pot of coffee. "We took Olivia to the hospital."

Laura Beth gasped. "Last night? Is she okay?"

"False labor. She's fine. Baby's fine."

"But…"

She faced Laura Beth. "But what?"

"There's but in your voice. Like there's a catch. She's fine but she's on bed rest or something. What's the catch?"

"There is none. It was just false labor. She's really fine." She bit her lower lip. "But my fake date did something that puzzled me."

"What?"

"He waited in the children's ICU instead of the maternity waiting room."

"Maybe he thought something would be wrong with the baby, so he waited there."

She gasped and closed her eyes. *Of course. That made so much more sense.* His choice of waiting place wasn't about him but Olivia's baby.

Unfortunately, by the time she walked to the table and sat, she'd poked a hole in that theory. "Isn't there a neonatal ICU? One just for newborns?"

Laura Beth shrugged. "I don't know. I don't know much about hospitals, but there may be a special ICU for newborns."

Confused again, Eloise sucked in a breath. "Well, he's also on the hospital board, so maybe he was just looking around, checking on things." She thought of the nurse who'd talked to him and grimaced. "No. That's not it either. A nurse came up to him. She acted as if she knows him."

"If he's on the board, of course she knows him."

She shook her head. "No. This was more like she knew him personally."

Laura Beth winced. "Was she young and pretty?"

"Middle-aged but very pretty. Still, it wasn't that. The way she reacted to him was more like she was accustomed to seeing him." She tried to remember their conversation. "She said stay as long as you like…as if he'd been in the ward before, staring into that ICU room."

Picking up her empty cup, Laura Beth rose from the table. "I think you're making more out of this than you should because you're trying to figure out the 'tragedy' those dinner party wives told you about." She shook her head. "Think it through. His friend's wife was in the hospital, maybe in early labor. That about stopped *my* heart. So I'm sure it scared him too. He might have simply gone to the children's ICU not remembering there'd be a NICU."

She frowned. "Maybe." Her brain could accept that, but her heart disagreed. There was something about the way he stood in front of that window, staring inside.

Her disappointment rattled through her. He'd called her his friend the night before. Yet, here she sat, trying to guess what had happened in his life because he didn't trust her enough to tell her.

"Bruce is taking me skating at Rockefeller Center today."

Not wanting to be thought of as that sad girl anymore, Eloise pasted a smile on her face for her roommate. "Cool."

"I might need to borrow that big navy blue parka of yours."

"Sure."

"You won't be using it?"

"No." She sighed. "We're going to another formal party tonight."

Laura Beth laughed. "Hey, I'd kill to go to even one of those parties. You've been to six or seven."

"Bruce hasn't asked you to one?"

Laura Beth's face reddened and she busied herself with tidying the area around the sink. "No."

Realizing her mistake, Eloise quickly said, "Well, be glad. They sort of get boring after a while. Repetitive." Plus, when they danced, she wanted to melt in Ricky's arms, but he held her two feet away.

She wouldn't tell Laura Beth that, though. She wouldn't be a "sad girl" with the puppy dog eyes anymore. "Usually, I'd spend the weekends before Christmas window shopping." With her subway pass, she could get anywhere in the city and see all the decorations. But what she liked best was Central Park. She'd go there to watch the white horses pulling gilded carriages and dream about someday taking a carriage ride. But that was another one of those silly things she didn't confide to her friends.

"This year, I'm so busy with Ricky and parties and making new gowns out of old ones that I haven't done any of the things I like to do."

And, today, the need to do something normal, to be herself, swelled in her like a tidal wave. She was losing herself in a man who didn't want her. When he was gone, and he would be, she'd be even more alone than she felt now.

Laura Beth shook her head. "Everybody in New York can do what you want to do. This year you get to go to parties. Enjoy it."

As Laura Beth left the room, Eloise squeezed her eyes shut as the truth bombarded her. The tidal wave that filled her with longing wasn't to do something normal alone. It was to do something normal with Ricky. To go window shopping with him. To go on that carriage ride with him. To see the tree at Rockefeller Center with him. She wanted to do something normal *with him* because she wanted him to be normal with her. At the big formal balls, he could dodge her questions. Hell, he could dodge actually spending time with her just by talking to his friends or dancing.

And she was tired of having dinner with people she didn't really know. Tired of not being allowed to let herself go when they danced. Tired of pretending to be happy.

But, most of all, she was tired of pretending it was okay that the whole world knew his past, his secrets, but she couldn't know because he didn't want it to affect how she treated him.

Didn't he know her well enough yet to understand that she'd always treat him with respect?

Why didn't he trust her?

That night when he arrived to pick her up, the insult

of being the only one in his social circle who didn't know his tragedy stiffened her muscles and put an icy tone in her voice.

He slid her cape on her shoulders, covering her silver dress. "You look great."

She faced him and smiled, but her cheeks rebelled at the attempt to lift her mouth, and her smile was barely a curve of her lips. "Thank you."

He opened the door. She led him into the hall and to the stairway. She said nothing as they walked down the steps, through the lobby and to the car. But she couldn't very well walk past Norman without a greeting.

"Good evening, Norman."

He touched the rim of his hat. "Evening, ma'am."

She slid into the car. Ricky slid in behind her. Neither said a word.

He cleared his throat. "So…difficult day today?"

She continued to look out the window. "No. It was a normal day. A little house cleaning. A little sewing."

"That's right. You work on your clothes the day of a party."

"Yes."

"Well, that silver thing you're wearing is really pretty."

She wanted to tell him that she'd struggled not to make it a dress with a low back. She loved that style. But in the end, she'd decided to give it a full back for him. She knew he didn't like having to touch her so much.

Her nerve endings caught fire. Two parties ago, he'd held her hand and brought her close, like somebody who liked her. They'd drunk tequila like silly friends, and he'd almost kissed her. Now they were back to being polite strangers.

Every time they took one step forward, he took two steps back. Tonight it cut through her like a knife, shredding her heart, bruising her soul. Even if he didn't want to love her, he should like her. She'd been nothing but nice to him.

The car stopped at another posh condo building. She faced him. "This is a private residence?"

"Yes. Binnie and Dennis are hosting a small gathering."

"I'm in a *gown*."

He looked at her. His big, beautiful brown eyes were totally clueless.

She threw her hands in the air. "I am not going to a private party in a gown!" Tears pushed behind her eyelids and threatened to show themselves. She'd been so upset with him all day that this little incident was toppling her over the edge. The last thing she wanted was for him to see it.

She glanced around. "Look, just go alone. You'll be fine. And I'll be fine. I can get myself home. I'm not sure where the subway is, but I can find it."

Before either Norman or Ricky could react, she shoved open her car door and jumped out.

He scrambled out after her. "Whoa! Whoa! Wait!"

"Forget it."

The whole situation closed in on her. Smiling for people she didn't know. Spending time with a guy who clearly didn't like her back. And missed opportunities. Obvious times he could have kissed her or been kind to her that he'd backed away from. She'd poured her heart out to him, not just because the conversation lent itself to her being honest, but because she wanted him to know her.

But he didn't want her to know him, and he certainly didn't want to know her. He'd listened to her story with bare minimum curiosity, and when she was done talking he hadn't consoled her. Leaving her empty. Feeling like no one. Nothing.

Who'd have thought going out with someone could make her so lonely?

Her arm suddenly jerked back and she was spun around.

"I made a mistake by not calling today to tell you what to wear. I'm sorry. We'll go home. You can change."

Her ridiculous tears spilled over. "It's too late now. By

the time we'd get back, they'd be halfway through dinner." She swiped at her tears. "Just go. Go see your friends. Have fun."

He tugged her arm to bring her closer. "At least let Norman take you home."

Fresh tears flooded her eyes. Somewhere deep inside her, she'd hoped *he'd* take her home. Ignore what she said about going to the party without her and comfort her instead.

But that was stupid. He didn't like her. He didn't want to like her. She was a hired date. It was okay to be upset that she was in the wrong outfit, but she couldn't be upset that he wasn't giving something that wasn't part of their deal.

Once again, she probably looked insane to him.

They walked to the car in silence, across the shiny rain-wet pavement. White Christmas lights adorned the trees lining the exclusive street. Huge evergreen wreaths with red and green plaid ribbons and shiny red Christmas balls decorated the double-door front entrance of Binnie and Dennis's building.

When they reached the car, Ricky opened the door for her. She slid inside and he closed the door behind her.

The sound was so final that her heart beat out a fearful tattoo. What had she done? By not going to this dinner party with him, she was proving he didn't need her anymore. He could go alone.

She groaned. She needed the job going out with him could provide. She needed his connections. And now she was throwing it all away because she'd worn the wrong dress?

She leaned back on the seat. That wasn't it. His not telling her about the party was a symptom of the bigger thing he wouldn't tell her. His tragedy.

He'd called her a friend.

But he didn't share his secrets.

And she liked him.

But most days he was only nice to her because he had to be. And he hadn't cared when she'd told him her secrets.

Yet she liked him.

A lot.

Felt some kind of soul connection that he obviously didn't feel.

That was the real humiliation. Longing for something that he didn't see.

The limo door suddenly opened. Ricky slid inside.

She sat up. "What are you doing?"

"I'm taking you home. I called Binnie and explained you weren't feeling well and bowed out."

"What?"

"I bowed out." He studied her face. "I can see something's really wrong."

And he cared?

She sniffed. Hope tried to nudge in, but she reminded herself of the truth and quashed it. If he didn't care that her husband had died and her parents had disowned her, he certainly wouldn't want to know that she felt left out, rejected, because he wouldn't confide in her. And she absolutely wouldn't tell him that she was falling for him. That would be the ultimate humiliation.

Wiping her eyes, she stuck with the convenient. "It's pretty bad to be the only woman in a gown at a dinner party. It would make me look stupid...clueless about social conventions."

He winced. "Sorry about that."

"It's fine."

Norman started the car and pulled out into the street.

Ricky settled back on the seat. "It feels weird to be going home."

It didn't to her. The sooner she got away from him, the sooner she could cry, call herself every kind of fool and splurge by drinking one of the precious cups of hot cocoa she'd squirreled away for nights like this.

"I mean, I'm dressed and you're dressed." He turned and caught her gaze. He smiled slightly. "Seems like a waste."

"I can wear this dress tomorrow." She glanced out the window, then faced him again. The crying might have been her fault. Might have been an overreaction. Might have made her look even more foolish than she already did to him. But forgetting to tell her how to dress? That was his fault. "Unless we're going to a dinner party tomorrow."

"I'll check the invitation when I get home and call you."

"I'd appreciate that."

He cleared his throat. "I still don't think we should just go home."

"The deal was twelve parties."

"I know. But missing one is sort of reneging on the deal." He glanced at her. "If you enjoy them."

She picked at her cape. "Sometimes I do." When he was himself. A normal guy. Which, lately, wasn't often.

"At least let me buy you dinner."

"I'm not hungry."

But even as she said the words her stomach growled.

"I think you are hungry."

"Stop feeling sorry for me!" The shout was out before she could stop it. "For Pete's sake! You hate people feeling sorry for you, so you should damn well understand I hate people feeling sorry for me!"

He grimaced. "Got it."

Shame filled her again. She didn't know why she was so emotional tonight, but she was. And she needed to get away from him.

She turned to the window and looked out at the city decorated for the holidays, the festive lights that seemed to be mocking her.

"So if you could go anywhere you wanted to tonight, where would it be?"

She squeezed her eyes shut. "You're not going to drop this, are you?"

"I always try to make up for my mistakes."

So now she was a mistake? "Terrific."

"Where would you want to go…if you could go any-where you wanted?"

She was halfway tempted to tell him Paris just to shut him up. But what if he actually took her there? She wasn't risking that. Imagine how much she could embarrass her-self across the pond? No, thanks. Enough New Yorkers thought she was a sad girl with puppy dog eyes. She didn't need to add Europeans to the list.

She scoured her brain for somewhere reasonable to tell him but somewhere he'd nonetheless refuse.

When it came to her, she smiled.

"What I'd really like is a carriage ride in Central Park."

He sniffed. "It's raining."

"I know. Drat. Stupid suggestion." She sighed. "Might as well just go home."

He pulled out his cell phone. "Now, hold on. Let's not get ahead of ourselves." He hit a button. "David? Can you do me a favor and arrange a carriage ride?" He paused, then laughed. "Right now, actually." He paused again, waiting a minute or two before he said, "South entrance? Great. Thanks."

"So it looks like we have a carriage."

She gaped at him. "It's raining!"

"It's also what you want."

She sighed. The one time she really and truly didn't want him to be nice to her, when she wanted him to be his usual self-absorbed self so she could just go home and wallow in her own misery, he decided to be nice.

"I want the carriage ride on a sunny day or a warm night." Now she sounded like a spoiled child. "Not a night when it's raining."

"We got a carriage with a roof. And they have blankets."

He seemed so happily proud of himself that she had to fight not to roll her eyes. She wouldn't talk him out of this, and she had always wanted to go for a carriage ride through Central Park. Might as well just enjoy it. She'd have plenty of time to wallow in misery on Christmas day.

"Thank you."

"You're welcome." He tapped the window to give Norman instructions. In ten minutes, the limo stopped.

The entire street sparkled with raindrops. Although there were no stars, the moon hung overhead, a bright round ball. White clouds rolled by, sometimes hiding it, but eventually it would appear again, as if smiling at her, telling her to relax, everything would be okay.

After a short chat with Norman, Ricky helped her onto the red seat of a white carriage, sat beside her and tucked the covers around her.

"You're going to be cold in that cape."

"I don't care." And suddenly she didn't. She'd wanted one of these rides since she was a little girl. She would listen to the moon and not miss a minute of it.

As the horse-driven carriage clomped its way into Central Park, she huddled tightly under the blanket.

"So of all the places to go, things to do, why this?"

"Once when we drove past as kids, I almost had my dad talked into a ride. But my mother vetoed it at the last minute."

"Oh. Sorry about that."

"Not your fault." She laughed. The brisk air filled her lungs. The shiny wet path sparkled like the road to a fairytale castle. "Besides, I'm here now." She cuddled into the covers, leaned back and took a long drink of the fresh air again.

He pulled a bit of the blanket onto his lap. It wasn't cold enough to snow, but it was wet, the kind of damp cold that seeped into bones. She didn't blame him for wanting to cover up.

"I've never done this either."

She peeked at him. The steady clip-clop of the horse's hooves filled the dark, wet air. "Really?"

"Though I did bring my son here...to Central Park."

Ricky's tongue tripped over the awkward words. He shouldn't have mentioned Blake. All that did was open floodgates for questions. But tonight's mistake had been big enough that she'd cried. She'd tried to hide it or stop it, but she'd lost the battle and he'd lost all control. He'd have given her every cent of his fortune to get her to stop.

A carriage ride was a small price to pay.

Before she could ask questions that would lead to answers he wasn't ready to give, he added, "Blake loved it. It was summer." He huddled more deeply under the blanket, bringing them closer together as they passed bare trees, shiny with cold rain that might turn to ice. "I took him to the carousel, but there are a bunch of baseball fields near there, and he went nuts when he saw them." He laughed and shook his head. "It's hard to tell an eighteen-month-old that he can't play with the big kids."

Her gaze stayed on his face, her expression curious but tempered. She'd wanted to know about his circumstances and he'd refused to tell her. She would recognize this was a huge concession.

He cleared his throat. "Anyway, I'd thought about taking him on a carriage ride, but, luckily, he got tired and we went home."

"You have a son?"

He shrugged, not able to tell her Blake had died, if only because he knew he couldn't handle the pain remembering his son's death would bring.

But he also felt oddly free that he'd spoken about his little boy. Because everyone was so silent about him, sometimes it felt as if he'd never existed. "Yeah."

She caught his gaze, examined his face and said, "You and his mother aren't together?"

He shook his head. "No. We were essentially strangers

who created a child." He winced. "We sound like terrible people. We weren't."

She put her hand on his sleeve. "I get it. No need to explain."

He suddenly wished with all his heart that he could explain, that he could talk about his son, his *baby*. He longed to reminisce about good times. To remember his little boy fondly. To laugh.

But all those things did was remind him that, in the end, he hadn't had what it took to be a father.

He shook that off. He'd have plenty of time for guilt on Christmas morning. "So, anyway, she's part of the reason the search engine I created is so thorough. The system was already in beta testing when she told me she was pregnant. Her pregnancy caused me to add a few more rules to an already elaborate algorithm."

Confusion flitted through her blue eyes. "Why?"

He shrugged. "She was a single woman living alone in an expensive condo in New York City."

"She must have had a great job."

"She had no job."

"Rich parents?"

"Nope."

"Oh."

"Exactly. She'd gotten the condo from the last guy she dated. After she told me she was pregnant, I ended up picking up the tab for her utilities, groceries…all her monthly expenses."

"Yikes."

"Not that I minded, but I knew I had been bamboozled." Needing to change the subject quickly, before she started asking questions, he said, "What about you? Any bad dates in your history?"

She cuddled closer, wrapped her hands around his arm and closed her eyes. Their breaths misted on the chilled air.

He knew she'd nestled into him for warmth, but his chest loosened. His nerves settled. She wasn't upset anymore.

"In high school, I only dated boys my parents approved of. In college…" She shrugged. "You know that story."

"Yeah."

They lapsed into comfortable silence. The horse's hooves clip-clopped. The freezing night air bought them closer under the blanket. Everything inside him stilled. For the first time in eighteen months, he was calm. Totally calm.

After a few minutes, he realized she'd fallen asleep. Her crying must have worn her out. He tucked the covers more tightly around her and leaned back, closing his eyes and enjoying the fact that he wasn't working or thinking about work or at a party talking about work.

After a while, the driver turned the carriage around and headed back. The air became colder and colder and they nestled tighter and tighter under the blanket, sharing their warmth.

A contented smile framed Eloise's beautiful face. He studied her perfect complexion, her small nose, the fan of black eyelashes that rested on her pale skin. He'd never met a woman so physically perfect. A princess.

His brow furrowed. An abandoned princess. Somebody nobody wanted.

When the carriage stopped, he shook her gently. "Time to get up."

Her eyes popped open. "I fell asleep?"

He laughed. "Only for a little while." The longing to kiss her bubbled up again. If anyone deserved love, it was her. Their gazes locked. A spray of rain tumbled from the branch of a nearby tree and drummed against the carriage roof. Seconds ticked off the clock, as they gazed into each other's eyes and desire warred with common sense. He had nothing to offer her but money…and himself. A broken, guilt-ridden man, who might end up hurting her more than her parents had.

The driver appeared at the side of the carriage, breaking the mood and taking the decision to kiss her out of his hands.

"Ride's been paid for, including tip." He grinned. "For which I add a hearty thank-zyou."

Not wanting Eloise to know he'd paid double for the ride to assure a happy driver, Ricky shoved the covers away. "Come on."

He helped her down from the carriage and directed her across the street to the waiting limo.

Norman pushed off the front bumper and opened the door as Ricky and Eloise approached.

"Nice ride?" he asked Eloise as she got closer to the car. She smiled. "Very nice."

Ricky got into the limo behind her. With the heater blasting, they had no need to huddle together. And he missed it. Settling onto the supple leather seat a few feet away from her, he missed her warmth. He missed comforting her. Nothing made him feel normal the way pleasing her had. But there was more to it than that. He always felt a connection, a yearning when he was with her that went beyond simple bonding. It was like they belonged together.

But he knew in his heart that had to be wrong. He didn't belong with anybody. Not only was he so broken he didn't have anything to give, but he hurt the people who got closest to him and he absolutely refused to hurt Eloise.

In front of her apartment door, she smiled slightly. "Thank you. I had a great time."

"You feel better then?"

"Yes, though I'm sorry I got all hysterical."

"Believe it or not, I'm not." He paused. "It was nice to do something out of the ordinary. To talk about things other than work."

Her hopeful gaze met his. "You should do it more often."

He glanced away. "Maybe."

"Well, it was fun and I appreciate it."

He caught her gaze again. Saw the smile in her eyes. Felt the ice around his heart melt.

A need to be worthy of her raced through him, heating his blood. A wish that he could love her rose from the very bottom of his broken, battered soul. His whole body vibrated with the desire to be whole. To be ready. To be everything she needed him to be.

She reached out and wrapped her arms around his waist, hugging him to her.

He knew she meant it as a thanks, but sensation after sensation rippled through him. Trust. Need. Yearning. They were so strong he couldn't resist the urge to raise his arms and settle them around her shoulders. When her arms tightened in response, his arms tightened too.

He closed his eyes, fighting the longing to kiss her that swelled in him. He reminded himself he was broken. Told himself she deserved better. But the carriage ride, the look of contentment on her face, the way she had listened to him without asking unwanted questions, without judgment, all formed like bright pictures in his head, blocking out the negative, until he couldn't fight instinct anymore. He opened his eyes, bent down and put his lips on hers.

At first he didn't think she would respond, but her lips came alive slowly, tentatively, as if she were every bit as afraid of their feelings for each other as he was.

Something dark and possessive rose up in him. He deepened the kiss, and she followed, again slowly, again tentatively. Their tongues twined, and his heart overflowed with something so intense it took his breath away.

This was right. He knew it was right.

When he could stop thinking about Blake, about his mistakes, about his stupidity, all he felt was rightness with her. A click.

But even that scared him. When he was with her, nothing else in the world mattered. But maybe that was the scariest thing of all. Could he love someone so much that he'd forget his son? Was it even right to love someone so much that he forgot his son? His baby. His heart.

He pulled back, knowing every bit of his turmoil, every bit of his need was in his eyes.

She smiled tentatively. "Good night."

"Good night."

He tried to turn away, but his feet felt rooted to the spot. Her warmth drew him. He wanted to stay close to it. But he also didn't want to hurt her.

He started down the hall before he lost his conviction. The aftereffects of the kiss hummed through him. Part pleasure, part yearning, they drove him to race down the steps without faltering.

As good as this felt right now, he knew getting involved with her—with anyone—could be the biggest mistake of his life.

Or hers.

CHAPTER NINE

ELOISE STEPPED INTO her apartment, closed the door and leaned against it.

He kissed me.

They hadn't just had a private evening in the carriage ride she'd longed for since childhood, but he'd kissed her. Not forced by mistletoe. Not a little tipsy from tequila. But with real emotion.

She walked into the cold, silent apartment, wishing Laura Beth wasn't dating Tucker's vice president. The late-night coffeehouse meeting hadn't turned into a job for Laura Beth. It had become a romance. And now Ricky had kissed her and she just wanted to share the news, but there was no one to share it with.

The sound of the key in the lock of their apartment door clicked into the silent room. She spun around to see Laura Beth and Bruce stumbling into the apartment.

When they saw her, they both froze. "Eloise? What are you doing here?"

She smiled, hoping her entire face wasn't glowing with joy. "I live here."

Laura Beth gave a fake laugh. "Right. I just thought your party would last longer." She faced her boyfriend. "You remember Bruce?"

She stepped forward and shook his hand. "We weren't actually introduced."

He smiled politely. "It's a pleasure to meet you."

The air tingled with awkwardness. She normally didn't dislike someone on sight, but Bruce's slick good looks gave her an odd feeling. His blond hair was too yellow. His tanning booth tan too dark. It was as if he was trying to look like a surfer king. But he didn't live in the tropics. He lived in bitter cold New York City, where it rained when it should be snowing and snowed when it was least convenient.

His gaze slid to Laura Beth's and he nudged his head in the direction of the bedrooms.

Eloise's skin actually felt like little bugs were crawling on it.

Laura Beth pointed down the hall. "I'm just going to get some things from my room, then Bruce and I will be off again."

"Okay."

Laura Beth scooted away.

She found herself alone with Bruce, who looked her up and down, as if he were judging her or comparing her to Laura Beth…or just being plain sleazy.

She thought of the mother of Ricky's son. A woman who'd taken a condo from her first boyfriend and used her pregnancy to get living expenses from Ricky. And suddenly everything Ricky had done in the past weeks, his hesitancy, his fears, made perfect sense.

Laura Beth raced into the living area again. With a small overnight bag in her hands, she grinned at Eloise. "I'll see you in the morning."

Eloise nodded and the pair left.

Considering sleazy Bruce, and perhaps making incorrect comparisons to Ricky's child's mother, she walked down the hall to her bedroom, understanding why Ricky was taking his time with this romance. Not everybody in this world was trustworthy. He'd been burned. Obviously badly. He would not want to be burned again. That's why it took him so long to trust her.

Some of her joy returned. Ricky was a good, honest guy.

And he liked her. If that kiss was anything to go by, he *really* liked her.

Plus, she'd rushed into things with Wayne.

If anybody understood the reasoning behind taking things slowly and valuing every step, it should be her.

So if she understood, why did thinking about Bruce suddenly make her feel trouble was on the horizon?

Barefoot and wearing only a fleece robe, Ricky trudged to his silent kitchen the next morning. At the counter, he pressed the button to reveal his coffeemaker. He pulled a single-serve container from the fancy holder, tossed it inside and set his coffee to brewing, remembering how Eloise still missed her stolen coffeemaker.

He laughed, then squeezed his eyes shut. Something about her always made him laugh. Made him forget. Made him feel normal.

Dear God he liked her. But in the light of day, he wasn't sure starting a real relationship was a good idea. He had more dark days than light. True, being with her helped him forget Blake, but he wasn't sure that was appropriate. And he did not want to hurt her.

Yet it seemed so right.

Determined not to think about it and to let nature take its course, he reached for the week's accumulated mail and rifled through it. A shiny brochure slid through his fingers. The hospital's annual Christmas plea.

He pulled it out, curious not just because he was a director, but also because he wanted the hospital to get donations. A collage of pictures of the kids who'd been through the hospital for various reasons populated the cover page. He liked it. Simple but effective, it told the story of how the hospital saved lives. Many lives. Especially the lives of children.

But when he saw the picture of Blake, a tiny photo tucked among all the others, his heart stopped.

What the hell?

Not only had they not gotten permission to use that photograph, but who would have been stupid enough to think he'd want his deceased son's picture on a brochure?

He grabbed his cell phone, hit speed dial for his assistant and waited two rings before David answered.

"Who authorized Blake's picture to be in the collage on the front of the hospital brochure?"

"Blake's picture is in that collage?" Horror rippled through David's voice. "That has to be a mistake."

"Call hospital PR. Have the remaining brochures destroyed. And find out who gave them permission to use that picture."

"Absolutely."

Conversation ended, Ricky grabbed the brochure and tore it to shreds. Of all the damned stupid mistakes!

He raked his fingers through his hair and reached for his phone again, only to realize he was about to call Eloise.

Eloise.

Why did he automatically want to call her? What would he say? That his son was dead? That some idiot screwed up and put Blake's picture on a million brochures? That his heart was broken? That everything he'd felt while watching his son struggle for life had come storming back in living color?

He squeezed his eyes shut as misery reminded him this was his life. *This* was what he had to offer Eloise. Sharp shards of pain that pierced his heart at unexpected moments of memory. Deep depressions that dragged him down so far he couldn't speak some days.

How foolish was it to believe she would want this? How selfish was it?

He sucked in a breath, tossed the phone to the counter, grabbed his coffee and strode to his office.

He considered calling her to tell her they wouldn't be seeing each other anymore. No matter how much hurt he heard in her voice, he would endure it, simply because he knew a little sting now saved her real pain later. But he hadn't fulfilled his end of their deal. He couldn't stop seeing her until he found her a job.

His resolve sharpened. He had to protect her. That meant he had to get her a job. Then he could tell her he'd changed his mind about going to the rest of his parties and wish her well with her future employer, and she would be out of his life.

When Ricky's knock sounded on her door that night, Eloise drew in a deep breath. The night before he'd talked about his personal life, his son, and he'd kissed her. He liked her. No matter what feelings creepy Bruce instilled, she knew Ricky liked her. She wasn't going to screw this up by being afraid or overeager. He needed time to trust her, and she would give him time. After all, they still had plenty of parties to attend, and she'd be dancing with a man who had kissed her like a guy falling. These next few weeks might be the happiest of her life.

Her heart shivered with anticipation. She drew another breath, subdued the bright smile that might scare him silly, and opened the door.

"Hey."

"Hey."

If the dull expression in his dark eyes wasn't clue enough, his slow entry into her apartment told her he regretted kissing her. The urge to squeeze her eyes shut surged, but she stopped it, reminding herself he had a child with a woman who wasn't exactly scrupulous. He hadn't said much beyond the fact that he supported her at one time, but what if they'd had a disagreement and she'd taken his child away from him? What if she hadn't just moved to another city or state? What if she'd disappeared? What if the tragedy in his life was that he had a little boy he adored but he couldn't see him or be part of his life?

She hadn't seen any sign that a child had ever been in his apartment. No one at any of the parties ever asked him about his child, proving that was his sore spot. What worse could an unscrupulous mother do than take away a beloved child from a doting father?

If Eloise wanted him to open up to her, she had to prove herself to be trustworthy. She couldn't overreact when he pulled back. She should respect it and show him he could trust her not to probe but to let him come around in his own time.

"You look very nice."

He glanced down at his tux and black topcoat. "I look the same as I always do."

She laughed. "I know. You wear it well."

He sniffed a sound that was almost a chuckle—almost.

Her heart picked up a bit. Rome was not built in a day. Neither was trust.

She handed him her cape. He slid it on her shoulders. "You look nice tonight. But you always look nice, too."

"Thanks." The soft pink dress she'd altered hadn't been much of a task. The quietly elegant strapless gown hugged every curve and accented her pale skin, but it wasn't fancy. She'd deliberately not gone flashy or fancy, but stuck with her own taste rather than fashion. Up to now, she'd worked to make herself look like the perfect sparkly date for a rich guy. Tonight, she wanted to be herself, to give him a taste of the real her.

Which, now that she added it to everything else, was probably the smart thing to do. From here on out, she wasn't Eloise Vaughn, fake date. She was the real Eloise Vaughn, the woman she wanted Ricky Langley to fall in love with.

He opened the door and she walked out. "So how was your day?"

He wouldn't meet her gaze. "My day was very long."

"How so?"

"Special project."

She stopped at the top of the steps, not really wanting to push, but seeing this as an opportunity they could connect as real people. "Yeah? Anything you can talk about?"

"I'd prefer not to, but suffice to say I'm having trouble figuring out an angle for a problem I have to solve as soon as possible."

"You're sure it's nothing I can help you with?"

He hesitated but eventually said, "Yes."

They walked down the steps and out into the frigid night. "We need snow."

He sniffed again, an acknowledgment of her comment but not quite a reply. Still, she wasn't daunted. The man had kissed her because he'd wanted to. She'd even tried to dissuade him by not kissing him back, but he hadn't stopped. He'd deepened the kiss. He might be afraid to trust, but he was falling. She could feel it. And if she wanted him, then she had to give him time.

As they walked under the portico of the entryway of Santana Lawson's Montauk beach house, an itch formed under Ricky's collar. In her gorgeous pink dress, Eloise looked amazing. Even more amazing than she looked in the fancy, sparkly dresses she typically wore. The feeling of rightness with her had risen at least three times in the limo. He fought them all, not for himself, but to protect her. Still, this would be a long night.

He guided her into the entryway where Santana stood greeting guests. Wearing a black tux, a black shirt and a black tie, with his shoulder-length hair pulled into a tight ponytail at his nape, Santana played the part of unconventional investor to the hilt.

"So, somebody finally got this guy out into the circuit again."

Eloise laughed lightly. "It wasn't so difficult."

Santana kissed her hand. "Not for somebody as beautiful as you, I'm sure."

Jealousy licked in Ricky's stomach like the strike of a match, but he shook it off. He couldn't like her. Didn't have anything to offer her but years of misery. Jealousy had no place in this deal.

Grasping Santana's hand, he said, "Thank you for inviting us."

Santana's eyes sparked with curiosity. Ricky could see he wanted to ask a million questions, but he only said, "It's my pleasure." He pointed down the hall. "Ballroom's the first door on the left."

Eloise's shoes clicked softly on the Italian marble floors. She sucked in a breath to compose herself, the way she always did before they entered a party. At the beginning of their arrangement, she hadn't known most of his friends. She'd had to alter dresses to fit in. Yet, she'd never groused. Never complained. She just did what she had to do.

Admiration for her rattled through him, and he suddenly realized how intensely he would miss her. When he found her a job and they stopped seeing each other, he would sit in his quiet office and think of these nights…and miss her.

She placed her hand in the crook of his elbow. "Ready?"

Their gazes met. He reminded himself that what he felt didn't matter. He had to think about her. Her future. Her happiness.

"Yes. I'm ready."

But the reminders didn't make him feel any better. The sadness that flashed through him wasn't the red-hot searing pain of missing Blake. It was softer. More like remorse than regret.

He walked them to their assigned table and was surprised to find world-renowned clothes designer Bob Barbie was headed there too. He only recognized Bob because the designer had hit a rough patch the year before and Ricky had lent him money.

"I'm not sure how I got to sit with you business geeks," Bob said, laughing as he held out a chair for his date.

"We're glad to have you, Bob," Ricky said, turning to Eloise. "This is Eloise Vaughn." He smiled. "Eloise, this is Bob Barbie."

Her eyes widened. "*The* Bob Barbie?"

Bob smiled as if bored. "Yes."

"Oh my gosh! It's such a pleasure to meet you. I loved your fall collection."

"Everyone did." His eyes narrowed as he studied Eloise. He said, "Humph," then he turned to his date, effectively closing the conversation.

Eloise leaned into Ricky and whispered, "I don't think he liked my dress."

He frowned. His gaze automatically fell to the strapless pink gown. Cleavage peeked at him and he licked his dry lips. Nothing about her was imperfect. Everything was touchable. Tempting. His fingers itched to touch her as his brain tingled with the longing to think about what it could be like for them.

He swallowed, fighting needs that struggled to overcome common sense.

Eloise tapped her fingers on the table. "Pink's not a Christmas color. Maybe he doesn't like people wearing un-holiday colors during the holidays."

He cleared his throat. "Don't be silly."

She laughed. "I guess that is pretty silly."

"All right. I give up." Bob's angry comment rolled across the table. "Who are you wearing?"

"Excuse me?"

"Whose gown? I've run through everybody I know and I can't figure it out. So just tell me."

Eloise laughed. "You can't guess because I made this gown."

Bob's eyes narrowed. "Yourself?"

She winced. "Yes."

"But you bought someone's pattern…"

She shook her head. "No. I made it myself."

He propped his hand on his waist. "You're lying."

Anger stiffened Ricky's spine. "I hope you didn't just call my date a liar, Bob."

He waved a hand. "I'm just saying the dress is too good to have been made willy-nilly."

"It wasn't made willy-nilly." Eloise said with a smile. "I made it from an old dress."

"Well, now you're just poking fun at me and my whole profession."

Eloise might be laughing at snarky Bob, but Ricky's defenses roared again.

As if sensing that, she put her hand on his arm and calmed him as she faced Bob. "I'm going to take that as a compliment."

"And you should. Good grief, woman, you've got some talent there." He sucked in a breath. "I hope I'm not having dinner with my competition for next year."

Eloise laughed again, but Ricky looked from Bob to Eloise. He glanced at her gown, then back at Bob. His mouth fell open slightly. She might not be good enough to be Bob's competition, but something flashed through his brain. An insight. An intuition.

Maybe he should be introducing her to designers instead of CEOs. She might not have any human resources experience, but he'd seen her remake at least eight dresses. And she could sew. She was perfect intern material for a designer. In fact, he already knew the changes he'd make to her résumé. He could see himself selling her, getting her a job—a job she could not only do, but also probably like better than being stuck in a stuffy office.

His heart lightened but only for a second, then it dipped

with sorrow. The sooner he found her a job, the sooner he'd stop seeing her.

But she needed a job. And she needed to be away from him. He might be incredibly sad to lose their last few dates, but walking out of her life was the right thing to do.

He spent the first hour of dancing looking for designers he could waltz her in front of and failing miserably. He knew CEOs. He didn't know designers, except the one he'd lent money to.

Plus, he'd assumed she wanted to work with a designer. What if she didn't? He'd easily come to the conclusion this was what she should want, but until *she* realized it, he couldn't really change her résumé or send her on interviews.

Preoccupation with his mission kept him too busy to remember their attraction, too busy to regret that he couldn't have anything to do with her. But as they walked up the steps to her apartment at the end of the night, his chest tightened.

The closer they got to the spot where he'd kissed her, the more he remembered. The softness of her lips and the feeling that loving her was right closed in on him, stealing his breath.

He stopped after only two flights. "You know what?"

She faced him with a smile.

He worked up enough energy to return her smile but just barely. "I'm going to skip the second two flights of stairs tonight."

"Oh." He watched myriad emotions flutter through her soft blue eyes, but she said only, "Okay."

Still, when he turned to walk away, he knew he hadn't fooled her. She realized he was dodging a kiss. A kiss she wanted. A kiss he wanted.

The urge to pivot again and yank her into his arms spiked. He could kiss her senseless in thirty seconds. He could take command, take control, love her the way she deserved to be loved—and ultimately hurt her.

He kept walking.

Eloise stepped into her dark apartment, once again regretting that she didn't have anyone to talk to. He'd pulled back so far it was as if their kiss hadn't happened, and she wondered about the wisdom of not calling him on it, demanding he explain how he could be so affectionate one night and so distant the next.

She ambled to her room, her dress swishing, her spirits struggling to remember that she'd said she would give him time and that she had a job to do too.

She had to prove herself trustworthy. But how could a person prove herself trustworthy in a sea of people having fun? She couldn't. And when their dates were done, she would lose him.

The following Saturday night when Ricky picked her up for yet another formal party, his heart stumbled in his chest. He didn't know the proper name for the style of her dress and could only describe it as something he'd seen worn by ancient Greek goddesses in history books. Her hair piled on top of her head, with curls tickling her nape, also reminded him of a goddess.

If he'd thought he'd had trouble keeping his distance before, the way she looked tonight blew every other night out of the water.

He'd think himself in deep trouble, except her being beautiful in an exquisite dress actually worked for his plan. Instead of trying to search out designers, he'd stacked the deck. And he'd gotten the idea from Bob being seated with them accidentally the week before. This week, he'd called their hosts, the Connors, and asked for a favor.

He helped her up the few steps to the hotel. They smiled at the doorman and eased their way into the elevator. They'd taken only three steps into the ballroom when Jason Grogin caught his arm. "Hey! Ricky! Good to see you."

He shook Jason's hand, not quite as happy to see Jason as Jason seemed to be to see him. Jason was one of the people Ricky had originally sent Eloise's résumé to. And neither one of them had heard a word from him—in spite of the fact that he owed Ricky a huge favor.

Instead of, "Good to see you, too," Ricky merely said, "Jason."

Jason faced Eloise. "And this must be Eloise Vaughn."

"Yes." She shot Ricky a questioning look as Jason shook her hand.

"Your résumé landed in my in-box a few weeks ago, but I have to apologize for being out of town."

Her face lit. "You've been out of town?"

"Yes. So I didn't see Ricky's email until yesterday." He smiled. "I'd hoped we'd run into each other tonight." He caught Ricky's gaze. "We do have a job for you."

Eloise all but jumped for joy. "You do!"

He handed her a business card. "I spoke with my human resources person today, and she penciled you in for an interview after the holidays. It's just a formality, mostly about having the correct paperwork for our files. As far as I'm concerned, you're our newest employee. Assistant to the director. Who, I might add, is in her sixties and will probably be looking to retire in four or five years."

Eloise's mouth fell open. "Oh, my God! Thank you."

Jason smiled. "You're welcome." He slapped Ricky's back. "Enjoy the party."

Ricky said, "Thanks," but the muscle in his jaw twitched. "It's just like him to waltz up to us weeks later and offer you a job."

Eloise blinked. "I don't care if he was late." She caught his arm. "You did it! You got me a job!"

He should have been happy. His debt was paid. Instead, annoyance rattled through him. He'd finally seen what was right before his eyes all along—that Eloise had chosen the wrong career—but before he could get her in front of a designer who would realize her talents, Jason's offer would spoil it.

He found their table and pulled out her chair just as Artie Best pulled out the chair across the table for his date, a pouting redhead, undoubtedly a model.

Ricky smiled. The Connors had come through. This battle wasn't over yet.

As he sat, he motioned to Artie. "Eloise, I'd like you to meet Artie Best."

Her eyes grew, as he'd hoped they would. "Artie Best of Artie Best Dresses?"

Artie laughed. "The same. Still trying to get as popular as Jimmy Choo of Jimmy Choo shoes. But my name doesn't have quite the ring."

"Oh, your name rings fine with me." She sighed dreamily. "Your fall collection knocked me out."

His eyes narrowed unhappily. "Then why are you wearing someone else's gown?"

Eloise glanced down at her royal blue dress.

Glad he'd reacted the same way jealous Bob Barbie had, Ricky jumped in. "She's not wearing someone else. She's a designer herself. She's wearing her own dress."

"No kidding?" More businessman than Bob, Artie stood and motioned for her to do the same. "Let me take a look."

With a quick glance at Ricky, she rose cautiously.

Ricky slid his chair back so Artie could get a full view. But he hadn't needed to. Artie wasn't shy about pulling her away from the table and turning her around so he could examine all sides of her gown.

"I have to admit I've noticed you before."

She blinked at him. "You have?"

"Yes. You wore two dresses that were almost identical." He smiled. "The ones with no back."

She laughed. "The style is kind of a crowd favorite."

Artie said, "With your behind I have no doubt."

Ricky rose. "You know, Eloise is looking for a job."

"Really?"

"She has a degree in human resources, and though that probably doesn't translate into design, I think it's pretty clear she has talent."

Eloise faced him, her eyes round and questioning. "And no experience in fashion or design!"

Artie batted a hand. "Oh, please. Did you sew this?"

"Yes."

"Then you have experience." He turned her around for one more look at the blue gown. "I'm going to the Bahamas for the holidays, but I'd love to talk to you about coming to work for me when I get back."

"That'll be too late," Ricky said, helping Eloise to sit again as Artie walked back to his chair. "She has an interview with a company for an HR job and her rent is due."

Eloise's mouth fell open and her eyes flashed fire, but Artie laughed. "Working girls, right, sweetie?" He squeezed the shoulders of his beautiful red-haired date who looked totally bored with the conversation. "I remember the days when rent was a problem." He sighed, pulled out a card and wrote on the back. He handed it to Eloise. "That's my office. I'm leaving for the Bahamas tomorrow afternoon, but if you get there by eight tomorrow morning, I can run you through some paces."

Eloise blinked at him. "I…I…"

"She'll be there," Ricky said. "I'll have Norman drive her."

"Great."

Eloise didn't know whether to laugh or groan. She'd spent two years all but starving, desperate for a job, and finally she had a job, and Ricky didn't seem to want her to take it.

As soon as they got on the dance floor, away from the

table full of designers they'd been seated with, she pounced. "What are you doing?"

Looking smug and handsome, he said, "What am I doing about what?"

"I got a job and you totally disregarded that and got me an interview."

"An interview for a job I think you're much better qualified for."

"Designing?"

"Or learning the ropes in a low-level position that'll get your foot in the door of the industry where your talents really lie."

She gaped at him. "Life isn't about talent. It's about skill."

"And you have the skills." He glanced down at her. "What are you afraid of?"

With her gaze holding his, her pulse stuttered. *I'm afraid of you. I'm so in love with you my heart hurts. But you want me to prove myself and I don't know how. And we're just about out of time. That's what I'm afraid of.*

Instead, she looked away and said, "I went off on my own once before, remember? Followed my heart. Married a guy I loved. And it ended abysmally."

"Yeah, it did."

"Yet you want me to follow my heart again?"

"Yeah, I do."

"Did you ever stop to think that you don't get a vote?"

"Of course I don't. But I know you. And I think of you like a friend."

Her gaze met his again. That was what he'd said the night at the hospital. *Friendship. Not love—*

Oh, Lord. Had she made too much out of that kiss? She knew he'd felt something. She'd thought she only needed to prove herself, but what if he really did just think of her as a friend?

"You have more energy and enthusiasm than my staff

all put together. But not for business…" He winced. "For your clothes. I don't mean to insult you or trivialize it, but I think you'd have more fun in fashion."

She glanced away. What had she expected? That he'd say, "I love you. That's why I want you to be in the job where you're more suited? That's why I want you to be happy?" The man was wounded. He'd trusted a woman who didn't deserve trusting. He might have kissed her with real emotion, but after that he'd shut down. She'd thought all she had to do was prove herself, but what if he'd shut down because he simply didn't want her?

Or what if that kiss hadn't been as good to him as it had been to her? What if that was why he was back to calling her his friend?

Disappointment choked her, but her pride surfaced to save her. She would not make a fool of herself in front of him again.

Although every fiber in her being wanted to weep, she took a long, slow breath to compose herself and quietly said, "I probably would have more fun in fashion." She glanced at him again. "But would I be able to eat?"

"Eventually."

She laughed. Dear God, the man was honest. Here she was ready to fall into a black pit of despair and he didn't sugarcoat her situation. Of course, he probably didn't realize she was drowning. That she had fallen in love and he hadn't.

"If there's one thing I like about you, it's that you speak your mind."

"I do. My guess is you'd have a year as a gopher of some sort and years of apprenticing, but at least this time your sacrifices would have a goal. And someday you might make it big. Maybe start your own line."

"My own line? Isn't that a little ambitious?"

"Not if you have an investor behind you. Someone who knows your work and likes you."

Her eyes sought his again. His gaze didn't waver.

OMG. Had he just admitted he liked her? That he wanted to stay in her life? With their Christmas deal ending, was he looking for a way to continue to see her?

"You'd do that?"

"We'd have to see how you progress under Artie's tutelage, but, yeah, I'd do that."

She stared at him, her eyes drowning in fresh tears. Her chest swelled with hope. Designing her own line was a dream come true, but the hope came from staying in his life. He wasn't leaving her. He was making a place for her so that he could take his time.

They had time.

"Look. Go to the interview tomorrow or don't. It's your choice. But at least know you have a choice."

She licked her suddenly dry lips. "Yes. I do."

The music stopped and the couple next to them walked over. Ricky shook the man's hand and introduced him to Eloise as Steve Grant, a Wall Street guy, and his wife, Amanda, a lawyer. She smiled politely and nodded and agreed when it seemed appropriate, but her head was swimming.

In the space of an hour, her entire life—all her goals— had changed, but all she could focus on was the fact that she'd see him again. He was making room for her in his life, a reason for them to see each other for however long he invested in her.

Her brain froze. *For as long as he invested in her?*

Had he turned their relationship into another business deal?

CHAPTER TEN

THEY RODE HOME in absolute silence. On the one hand, she didn't want to lose him, and staying connected meant they'd continue to see each other. On the other, if his offer was only a business deal, she might have already lost him.

At her apartment door, he said, "So, you're okay with everything?"

Okay? She wasn't even sure she understood it. But she did want the interview. And she did understand that even if Ricky didn't love her, he'd done more than provide job opportunities for her. He'd gone the extra mile and helped her find what she really wanted to do with the rest of her life.

She couldn't dismiss that or belittle it.

"I'm ecstatic. I wouldn't have even attempted getting an apprentice job with someone like Artie Best." She caught his gaze. "Thanks. Really."

He smiled. "I'll send Norman tomorrow morning to drive you to the interview."

Confusion poured through her. He'd almost kissed her on their tequila night. He'd kissed her with unbearable emotion the night of their carriage ride. He'd understood something about her and her career that she hadn't even realized herself. Yet he was so distant she had no choice but to believe that sending his car for her was only an extension of their deal.

"You don't have to do that. I'll take the subway."

He stopped her by putting his hand on her shoulder. "It's Norman's job to know how to get places. He'll do the research tonight to find Artie's offices. That way you can relax and spend your mental energy preparing for the interview."

Because that made sense, she nodded. "Thanks."

Although his hand was on her shoulder, he didn't try to bring her close for a kiss. Hell, he didn't look one bit like a man who wanted to kiss her. He just squeezed lightly, turned and started down the hall. "Good night."

She swallowed. Emptiness tightened her chest. Even if she got a position with Artie Best, and—years down the road—Ricky decided to invest in her designs, he could pass her off to assistants. This might be the last time she ever saw him, and she was looking at his back as he walked away.

Her voice a confused whisper, she said, "Good night."

"I'll see you tomorrow afternoon."

Her breath stumbled. "Tomorrow afternoon?"

He faced her again. "For my office party."

She blinked.

"You can tell me how the interview went then. In fact, why don't we just have Norman bring you to my office after the interview, save some time?"

Her heart fell. He just wanted to hear about her morning with Artie Best. "But I'll be dressed for an interview, not a party."

He shrugged. "My employees are coming to the office on an afternoon they don't have to, so it's informal. Jeans. Sweaters. You'll be fine."

He headed for the stairs, and she walked into her apartment. They might be going to another party, but he hadn't wanted to kiss her and he had gotten her a job. Even if he continued their deal, they only had one more party and one wedding.

How the heck was she supposed to prove herself in two events? Especially when it was clear he was distancing himself.

As promised, bright and early Sunday morning, Norman texted her that he was outside her apartment building. In skinny jeans, tall black boots and her beloved green cashmere sweater, she slid into her parka and scrambled down the stairs.

Norman awaited her at the door to the limo.

"Good morning."

He smiled. "Good morning."

She slid inside and he got behind the steering wheel. When the car began to move, he opened the glass that separated them.

"I'm hoping you have good luck on your interview."

She laughed. "Yeah. Me too. There's only so long a person can live on noodles before they start feeling like a big bowl of chicken soup."

Catching her gaze in the mirror, he grinned. "I like you. You're not Mr. Langley's typical date."

"He likes them richer?"

"He used to like them poutier."

"Used to?"

"He hasn't dated in a long time. But when he dated, the women he chose were rich and spoiled, or models or starlets, women accustomed to attention." He smiled in the mirror again. "You're their opposite."

She didn't have the heart to tell him Ricky dating her had been a ruse. Her soul was so sad that the only thing keeping her going this morning was the knowledge that she might get a job in the fashion industry. Not in a stuffy office, but at a place where she'd help design the clothes the rest of the world would wear.

It wasn't quite a magical end to her dating a man she

accidentally fell in love with, but it was heady stuff, and she would appreciate it.

So she pasted on a smile for Norman and said, "Thank you."

"No. Thank you. And good luck."

Although his thank you puzzled her, through the rest of the ride she focused her attention on what she'd say to Artie Best. For once, she wasn't going to an interview hoping for rent money. She *wanted* this job. *Wanted* this career. She would have to be sharp to get it.

Artie Best's office was the top floor of an old factory. Quirky and fun, it was filled with fabric and dress molds, sewing machines and drafting tables. Racks of dresses lined the entire side wall.

"This place is great."

He ushered her to a small room in the back. "We like it."

As he sat on the chair behind a big metal desk, he motioned for her to take the seat in front of it. "So you haven't been to design school?"

She shook her head. "No. Sorry."

He inclined his head. "I didn't go either."

Her spirits rose a bit. "You didn't?"

"No, but I apprenticed." He sat back. "Your boyfriend's a very wealthy, influential man."

The heat of embarrassment filled her. She had to struggle not to tell Artie Best that Ricky wasn't her boyfriend. If he was only hiring her to get in good with Ricky, it wouldn't get him very far. But if she admitted the truth to Artie Best, then she'd be betraying Ricky.

Still, she couldn't quite hold her tongue, couldn't deceive him into thinking he'd be getting something he wasn't. "I'm only here because you want to get in good with Ricky?"

"No. You're here because you have talent. What I'm telling you is that I don't do favors for rich guys. If you think dating Ricky Langley will get you special treatment, then this interview can be over. If you think dating Ricky Langley means you don't have to apprentice, you know the way to the door. But if you want a real career in this industry, if you don't mind hard work and a learning curve…then I really do want to talk."

Four hours later, she all but skipped out of Artie's building onto the street to Norman, who held open the limo door.

"You got it?"

She beamed. "Yes!"

"Very good."

He closed the door and slid onto the front seat, started the engine and drove off.

She leaned back on the soft leather, her heart pounding, her spirits lifted in a way they hadn't been in five years. She didn't have a goal anymore. She had a vision. She could see herself working for Artie, learning, squirreling away information and experience until one day she could be her own boss. Have her own line.

Her own line.

Even the thought stole her breath.

Norman pulled the limo up to the curb in front of a tall white office building. She danced inside, pushed the button for the floor listed for Ricky's suite in the building directory and rode the elevator, trying to school her face so Ricky's employees wouldn't think she was drunk or high or just plain crazy.

The doors opened on a reception area. A black marble security station looped around in a huge semicircle. A pleasant security guard greeted her.

"Can I help you, miss?"

"I'm Eloise Vaughn, Mr. Langley's friend. I'm here for the Christmas party."

He studied a list on a tablet screen and frowned. "I'm sorry. I don't see your name."

A week ago that would have thrown her for a loop. Her

pride would have taken a direct hit. Knowing Ricky had forgotten her, she would have slunk away.

Today? Nothing could stop her. The hurts of the last five years had been tidily tucked away. She was a new person now. A woman with a job and a vision. A woman who wasn't afraid to stand up for herself.

A woman who wasn't letting the love of her life go without a fight.

She struggled not to gasp. When had that happened? And when had she gotten her boldness back?

She didn't know. Maybe the excitement of finally finding her way had filled her with strength. But whatever it was, it felt right.

Wayne might have been a love in her life, but Ricky was *the* great love of her life. She wasn't losing him.

She smiled at the security guard. "Give him a call. Tell him Eloise is here and I'm not on your list."

He hesitated.

"Don't be afraid. He really did invite me."

Skeptical, the security guard picked up the receiver of the black phone on the desk. He pressed a button.

"Mr. Langley, I'm sorry to bother you, but there's a woman at the desk…an Eloise…" He grimaced. "Yes. Thank you." He hung up the phone and smiled at Eloise. "You can go back."

She headed to the glass doors that led to a cubicle canyon, but she stopped. "What about you?"

The guard faced her. "Excuse me?"

"What about you? Don't you get to go to the party?"

"The guards take turns manning the security desk. We go into the party in shifts."

From his place in the back of the huge one-room main office of his company, Ricky watched Eloise open the door, then pause and talk to the security guard. Concern for the young man was written all over her face.

He shook his head. She was such a sweet, considerate person that the thought of losing her rocketed sadness through him. She was different from any woman he'd dated, any woman he knew—except Olivia. But wouldn't it make sense that friends like Olivia and Eloise would share the same traits? Honesty. Integrity. Kindness.

Or maybe, knowing her and Olivia, he was finally coming to realize all women weren't like his ex. He'd never date another party girl again, but there were plenty of good women in the world. Eloise being one of the best.

Still, the fact that Eloise was so good, so wonderful, made it imperative that he not drag her into his depressing life. So this would be their last day together. Their last party. If she'd gotten the job, there was no reason to prolong the agony. If he wanted to remember her, he would have to drink in every detail today because he'd never see her again.

She walked past gray cubicle walls draped with tinsel, under the big red holiday ornament that hung from the center of the ceiling and by the ledges of windows that held evergreen branches sprayed with fake snow.

He knew the second she saw him because she smiled and waved. His heart flip-flopped as he motioned for her to join him.

She all but skipped over to the copy machine where he stood. Adding that skip to the light in her eyes told the whole story. She'd gotten the job.

Not wanting to spoil her moment, he said, "Well?"

"I got it!"

"I knew it."

She unexpectedly rose to her tiptoes and hugged him tightly.

His heart tripped over itself in his chest. He longed to take her face in his hands and kiss her. Hard. But that would only confuse things. Or make him pine for things he couldn't have. He squeezed his eyes shut and for a few seconds enjoyed the feeling of her arms around him. Then he stepped back.

"What are we going to do about your gifts?"

He glanced up to see David giving him a curious look. And why not? This time last year, he couldn't even attend this party. This year, he'd doubled bonuses, come to the party and had just been hugged by a pretty girl.

Still, none of his assistants had mentioned gifts. "What gifts?"

Tall, gray-haired David shifted uneasily. "Well, because this is a party, I thought it might be cute to put the bonus envelopes into little gift boxes. That kind of morphed into buying everybody a watch."

He frowned, but Eloise tugged on his arm. "It *is* cute."

That was one of the reasons he liked her. He thought like a guy. Logical. Straightforward. She was more of a people person. Now that she'd had approved it, he supposed tucking bonuses into watch boxes was cute.

"Okay."

David smiled at Eloise and she smiled back, as if they shared some great secret.

"I think everybody will love it."

"So I just have to hand out gifts?"

David winced. "Well, there is one teeny tiny other thing you could do to make this party really fun."

He sighed. "What?"

David glanced at Eloise, then quickly back at Ricky before he said, "Would you mind putting on the Santa suit?"

His face fell. His heart stuttered. The one and only time he'd worn the Santa suit he'd had Blake at this party.

Eloise touched his arm again. "I think that would be cute, too."

He swallowed.

Obviously reading his reaction, David shook his head. "Don't worry about it. I just got carried away."

Ricky caught Eloise's gaze again. She tilted her head and smiled at him, encouraging him.

He wasn't ready. But something about the way she looked at him emboldened him. At some point, he had to get back into life—or at least pretend to get back into life so his employees could stop worrying. After he gave out the gifts, the party would be over. His employees would go to the bar down the street. It wasn't like he had to be Santa for hours. Just twenty minutes.

Surely, he could do that?

"Okay." He looked Eloise again. "But she has to be the elf."

"Elf?" She laughed.

David beamed at Eloise. "Love it! Follow me."

They walked back to David's office and he pulled two big boxes from a closet. He smiled broadly as he handed Eloise the top box. "You can change in the ladies' room just down the hall." He handed the fatter box to Ricky. "You can just change here."

With that he left the office. Eloise followed on his heels.

Ten minutes later, Ricky was in his fat suit when Eloise returned from the ladies' room dressed in green tights, a short red dress and a long green hat that had a jingle bell that bounced off her shoulder when she walked.

"This is weird."

She looked cute. Happy. Like Christmas spirit personified. Everything in him filled with joy, reminding him of the incredible happiness that swirled through his parents' house at the holidays.

He jerked himself back to reality. Where had that memory come from? Why had looking at Eloise made him think of his parents?

"You should be me." He adjusted the fat pack at his belly. "I feel like a couch pillow."

She laughed.

And his heart lifted again. She obviously loved Christmas, and making her laugh suddenly felt like it should be his life's mission.

He sucked in a breath, confused by his jumbled thoughts. Especially because that last one was just wrong. It couldn't be his mission to make anyone happy. He was too depressed.

He picked up the sack of presents David had left behind. "I can't believe I agreed to do this again."

"You've done it before?"

He took a long breath, wondering why he always spoke before he thought with her. "Once." He shook his head, again dislodging unwanted memories that flooded his brain. Memories of Blake this time. Christmas in his penthouse. Sneaking into the living room to plug in the tree lights so that when he carried Blake into the room everything would be perfect.

Everything had been perfect.

His breath stuttered out. His feeling of sadness returned. "It's not important. The important thing is you've got a job."

"A career," she interjected. "As I was explaining to Artie why he should hire me, I realized that even though I'm probably still going to starve for a few years, it will be sacrifice with a purpose. Exactly what you'd told me." She caught his gaze. "How'd you get so smart?"

He quickly looked away and hefted the heavy sack over his shoulder. "Part of being a leader is knowing where people fit. I'm amazed it took me so long to figure you out."

He pointed at the door. "Let's go. When the punch runs out, everybody goes to a little bar down the street. We need to give them their gifts before they desert us."

She opened the glass door of David's office and directed him down the hall.

"Ho! Ho! Ho!"

At Ricky's joyful call, the seventy or so employees scattered about in the cubicles stopped talking.

"Has everybody been a good employee?"

Eloise laughed gaily. The little bell at the end of her hat tinkled.

"This is my elf, Eloise." He paused and faced her. "Eloise Elf…it has a nice ring to it."

She rang her bell. "I think so."

Everybody laughed.

That strange feeling floated through Ricky again. This time he recognized it. Happiness. He told himself he didn't deserve it, but it didn't go away. Plus, it felt different. Strong. Weirdly strong. As if the earth had shifted and everything in his past was gone.

He shook his head. Everything in his past gone? He didn't *want* his past gone. He didn't want to forget his son. That was absurd.

He got himself back to the business at hand, distributing the bonuses hidden in gifts wrapped in bright red, green, blue, silver and gold foil paper.

Eloise handed him the first box. He read the name, and when the employee opened his gift—a watch—he also found an envelope. He ripped open the envelope, did a small dance of joy, raced over to his cubicle where he grabbed his coat and ran out.

Seeing the confused look on Eloise's face, Ricky leaned in. "Employee bonuses, remember?"

She turned to him and he realized he'd leaned in so far their faces were only inches apart.

"Oh?"

The temptation to kiss her stormed through him, knitting itself to that odd sensation that everything had shifted. But it couldn't have shifted. He couldn't change the past. He might love having her around, but she was better off without him.

He pulled away. "Some of the junior employees, people learning the ropes, earn just enough for their keep. This year, thanks to you, I realized they needed a better bonus."

She smiled. "You're a good guy."

Happiness fluttered through him, not because he thought himself good, but because he knew she genuinely believed it. It had been so long since anyone had thought of him as good—since *he* had thought of himself as good—that even stranger feelings rose up in him.

If they had been alone, he might have told her about Blake. Everything inside him longed to tell her, even though he could see no point to it. In a few hours, he'd never see her again. So maybe it was lucky this was the wrong place, the wrong time.

He handed out the gifts, and the reaction that rippled through the group made him laugh. Everyone came up and shook his hand. Some people told him what they intended to do with the unexpected extra money. Others just hugged him.

Christmas spirit warmed his heart, and he finally identified the odd feeling swimming through him. It wasn't happiness. After eighteen long months, he felt normal. He hadn't changed. The world hadn't shifted. He was simply coming back to the land of the living.

But he had also been correct. Once the punch ran out, his employees jetted off. A few suggested he join them at the pub. He politely declined.

With everyone gone, he walked through the room, gathering wayward wrapping paper and empty punch glasses.

Out of her elf suit and back in her jeans and sexy black boots, Eloise sat on a desk, watching him. "So now you clean up?"

"My mom always taught me to pick up empty glasses." He shook his head with a laugh. The memory of his happy childhood was so strong he couldn't banish it, and longing to be home filled his chest. "Old habits die hard."

"Oh, I don't know. It seems to me your mom taught you well. She sounds like a good person."

He hesitated. "She is." That funny feeling—the sense that he was reentering the land of the living—rattled through him again. He could see his mom and dad by the big Christmas tree in the great room of their log home. He could see his sisters with their kids and spouses. He could see the empty place in the crowd, by the mantel, where he should be standing.

Her laugh penetrated his haze. "Hey! Earth to Ricky."

He glanced up sharply. She sat on the desk, one leg tucked under her. A glass of punch in her hand. The gleam of success in her eyes.

He knew that he had Eloise to thank for the normal feeling that kept creeping up on him. And, although she was happy right now, she had no one. He might have gotten her a job, but she'd be alone on Christmas. It just wasn't right.

He ran his hand along the back of his neck. "Give me ten minutes to change out of this suit."

"Sure."

He raced down the hall. As he slipped out of his red flannel Santa clothes, he grabbed his cell phone and called David.

The noise of the pub poured through the phone when his assistant answered.

"I know you're celebrating, but I have a major mission for you." After the promise of another bonus, Ricky outlined his plan.

David laughed, but Ricky said, "Don't take this too lightly. This mission comes with a deadline. You have just a little more than one hour."

Norman drove them back to her apartment, and even to Eloise, who hoped to stall her time with Ricky, it seemed as if he took his time.

But eventually the silent ride came to an end. She wasn't surprised that Ricky shifted nervously as they climbed the several flights of stairs to her apartment. He hadn't made any mention of the Christmas Eve wedding she'd been expecting to attend with him. And she suspected this was it. Their last few minutes together.

When they finally reached her apartment door, he put his hand on her shoulder. "Mind if I come in?"

She met his gaze slowly, not sure why he wanted to come in. Would she get a kiss? An explanation? A sad goodbye? Or did he want a few minutes to remind her that in a few years, when she had some experience, he would fund her?

Her spirit of boldness rose up in her again. She was not letting him go without a fight. If he was giving her five minutes of private time, she would use them.

"I'd love for you to come in." She had no idea what she would do, but she wasn't going to just stand there, letting him go, letting him pretend there was nothing between them.

She turned, unlocked her door, opened it and stopped dead in her tracks.

Surrounding her pitiful eighteen-inch plastic tree were several boxes.

He leaned in, over her shoulder. "I think Santa's been here."

"*You're* Santa."

"Exactly."

He gave her a nudge into the apartment. "Go. Open them."

Not sure what was going on, she hesitantly walked over to the little tree. Sitting on the window seat, surrounded by cotton pretending to be snow, the plastic tree was dwarfed by one tall box, one huge box and three smaller ones.

Her chest tightened. All this time she'd been thinking she had to make a move to keep him. But maybe these gifts meant he was trying to keep her?

"Open the little ones first."

Confused, she slowly picked up the small square box to find a pink cashmere sweater. *Pink.* The color he'd liked her in the best.

Her gaze flew to his. "I love it."

He smiled. "I knew you would. Open the next small one."

She ripped the wrapping paper off a box that had clearly come from a jewelry store. "A diamond watch?"

Before she could say anything, he directed her to the last small box. "Keep going."

She opened the gift to find a book: *How to Get the Most Out of Your Intern Experience*.

She laughed. "I'll need this much more than a diamond watch."

He pointed at one of the two bigger boxes. Steeped in bewilderment, she opened this one a little slower. It contained a satin evening cape.

"Not a fur," he said, explaining his choice. "Something I think you'll be comfortable in. And look," he said, pointing out the quilted material beneath the shiny cape. "It has a lining for really cold nights."

She caught his gaze. He beamed at her. She'd never seen him so happy. As much as she wanted to ask him what the hell was going on, she couldn't spoil his fun. "It's perfect."

He pointed at the final box. "Now, the last one."

She ripped off the paper to reveal a shiny new coffee-maker. Her gaze swung to his.

"There's a year's supply of coffee too."

She said, "Thanks," but her voice choked. He'd gotten her coffee? Only a person who truly knew her, who paid attention to her, would know how much she'd missed her coffee. How could that possibly mean anything except that he loved her? Her eyes filled with tears.

"You don't like it?"

So why didn't he just say he loved her?

"Everything is perfect."

"Over the past few weeks you've given me lots of gifts. The biggest one was happiness."

She looked at him, her eyes blurry with tears. *Just let him say it. Please let him say it!*

"You changed me. I was stuck. I couldn't even see a speck of light at the end of any tunnel. All I saw was darkness until you. Then gradually I started seeing things differently again, and today I realized I felt normal."

Her confusion returned. "You feel normal?"

"Yes. Not perfect, certainly not good, but normal."

"So you bought me a bunch of gifts?"

"Important gifts. Things I know you'll need."

Confusion and pain collided to create an indescribable tightness in her chest. She was expecting him to tell her he loved her and instead he'd bought her gifts to show his appreciation.

But they were important gifts.

Gifts that proved he knew her and cared enough about her that he bought the things she really needed. He *had to* love her. Nothing else made sense.

She slowly met his gaze. "You have to help me out here." She lifted the new evening coat. "What does this mean?"

"It means you no longer have to wear your wool cape."

She shook her head fiercely. "No. Don't cop out. The real bottom line to all these gifts is that you know me. You *like* me."

He nodded. "I do."

"So do these gifts mean we're dating for real?"

"Oh, Eloise." He shook his head. "You wouldn't want that."

Her heart kicked with fear. After everything they'd shared, how could he not see they were made for each other? How could he believe she wouldn't want him?

"I would! I *do*!"

"You don't."

She set the coffeemaker on the sofa and scrambled over to stand beside him. When he turned to walk way, she caught his arm, forced him to face her.

"Tell me why. After all these weeks of dating, getting close, why are you pushing me away?"

He didn't even try to deny that he was pushing her away. "Because I'm no good for you."

"That's another cop-out. Another vague reason that explains nothing!"

"Be glad I'm not letting you in." He pivoted, motioning with his arms to the gifts and wrapping paper. "Christmas kills me."

"Hey, it's not exactly a walk in the park for me either. I'm alone. I lost a husband and have no family. You can't tell me not seeing your son is worse."

He stared at her, his mouth slightly open. "How can you say that?"

"I know it's painful. I think it's unconscionable that your ex took him away—"

He gaped at her. "My ex didn't take him away."

"She didn't?"

He squeezed his eyes shut, then popped them open again. "No, Eloise. He died. My son, Blake, died."

Her brain froze. Her breathing stalled. Incomprehension stopped her heart. "Your son is *dead.*"

He said nothing.

White-hot anger fueled the pain that roared through her. "Your son is *dead*…and you didn't tell me?"

"I didn't want your pity."

"Pity?"

"I always told you that. I wanted you to behave normally at those parties. To make it look like we were beyond my tragedy. And it worked. I could even play Santa today."

The shock and pain that filled her nearly burst her chest. She fell to the sofa, feeling like a hundred different kinds of fool. But most of all, she just felt sad. He hadn't trusted her enough to tell her the most important fact of his life.

He didn't love her.

She loved him, but he clearly didn't love her.

He scrubbed his hand across his mouth. "Look, I'm sorry. But I needed this. I really, really needed a few weeks of pretending I was okay."

She said nothing. The pain of knowing he didn't love her, that he probably didn't feel anything for her, was too intense.

"Blake was eighteen months old. He and his mother had been at a barbecue. She wrecked her car, a convertible. She hit a pole...and Blake was thrown from her car. He lived for only forty-eight more hours."

She went from upset to horror so quickly her breath caught.

"You want to know the worst of it? Had Blake been buckled into his car seat properly, he would have been fine." He took a breath and turned to Eloise. "His mother had been drinking. She wasn't sloshed, but her blood alcohol was over the legal limit. And she hadn't buckled him in right."

"She didn't want him. Never had. She wanted eighteen years' worth of child support. I have no doubt that she loved Blake. But she wasn't a mother. I saw the signs." He squeezed his eyes shut. "I saw a hundred signs. And I wanted Blake. I had a weekend nanny I could have hired permanently. I had the big penthouse. I had the money. But I always thought I'd talk to her about my taking custody the next weekend or the next or the next." He faced her sad Christmas tree again. "Now Blake is dead and his mother is serving out a manslaughter sentence."

Eloise caught his gaze as a bit of understanding crept in. His story wasn't just a story of loss. It was a story of failure. And guilt. Pain. Shame. Torment. He believed his son's death was his fault.

Her anger dissolved in the face of her love for him. Not quite sure what to say, she slowly rose from the sofa. "You can't change the past. But that doesn't mean you should stop living."

He spun to face her. "It doesn't?" He laughed harshly. "Really? Because there are some days I think stopping living would be easier. My son is dead. It *is* my fault. I deal with that every day."

"Of course, you do. But you just told me I gave you eleven dates of happiness. You're on the right track."

"I'm on no track. I take one day at a time, bury myself in work. It's all I have. All I deserve."

Her fight returned. Something inside told her if she didn't reach him now, she wouldn't get another chance. "I know it's hard to see right now, but you deserve more. A lot more."

His voice softened. She could almost see defeat settle on his shoulders. "No. I don't."

She sucked in a breath. The do-or-die feeling flooded her, urging her forward. "It doesn't matter what you think you deserve because I already love you."

"Then you're a fool." He walked over and slid his hands up her arms, as if comforting her. "You are a wonderful, beautiful woman who deserves to be pampered and loved. Getting involved with me would be nothing but sorrow for you."

Before she could stop him, he scooped his jacket off her sofa and walked out. Eloise raced after him, but he was so much faster than she was that by the time she reached the lobby, Norman was already pulling away from the curb.

He wasn't ever coming back. She'd never see him again.

Her chest stung. Her eyes filled with tears.

As always with him, she didn't feel her own pain. She felt his. Only this time it was stronger, like a coal from the burning pits of hell. His son was dead. He felt responsible for the imprisonment of a woman he shouldn't feel sorry for. He took too much on his shoulders.

It was no wonder he didn't want another wounded person in his life.

CHAPTER ELEVEN

THAT NIGHT RICKY couldn't settle. He had a bottle of Scotch, a glass and some ice, but he didn't feel like drinking. He didn't want to pace. He couldn't sit and mope. He had too much energy.

Energy.

He shook his head, lifted the Scotch and poured himself two fingers.

But though he brought the glass to his lips, he didn't drink it.

Everything felt off, wrong.

He walked to the back wall of the main room of his condo and stared at the decorated windows in the middle-class building across the street. He thought about his parents' huge log house, how good it looked decorated for the holidays. He closed his eyes, remembering the feeling he'd had that afternoon at the Christmas party. Eloise had been a perfect elf. His employees had been so happy that it fed something in him. And he'd remembered things about Christmases past. Things before Blake. Things that felt right. Good.

He thought about Eloise, sad at her apartment, and shook his head. It was for her benefit that he'd left her. This time next year she'd probably be so happy she wouldn't even remember he existed.

His chest tightened a bit at the thought, but he knew she deserved better, and he forced his mind off her.

His gaze landed on the pretty decorations in the windows of the building across the street again and he suddenly, overwhelmingly missed his parents. He might have to let Eloise go, but his parents were stuck with him. They had to let him into their lives.

He chuckled a bit. That was how he'd thought before Blake.

Maybe Eloise was right. Maybe she had been good for him. He might not be able to have a love in his life, a commitment, but it was time to let his parents in again.

He picked up his phone and called his mother.

After a short conversation, he called his pilot and arranged to fly home. Twenty minutes later, he reached into his closet for his leather jacket. But remembering the temperatures by the lakes in December, he changed his mind and took out his old navy blue parka. It should have reminded him of his last trip home, of taking Blake down a snowy slope on a saucer sled. Instead, he thought of Eloise. She'd worn a parka like this one to his fraternity reunion. As old and beat-up as the coat he pulled from the closet, her parka was undoubtedly as warm as this one.

And if there was one thing he knew about Eloise, it was that she was nothing if not practical.

He cursed as he shrugged into the coat, telling himself to forget about Eloise. About the pain that sliced through him at the thought of never seeing her again. About the emptiness that had filled his chest as he'd walked away from her. The unmet needs he knew she could fill. He would not saddle her with his life.

In his plane, he tucked earphones in his ears, put his seat back and listened to the soothing sounds of the ocean for only about ten minutes before the rhythm of the plane put him to sleep. He slept the full hour-long flight.

He wished his crew happy holidays and they thanked

him for the generous bonuses he'd given them for flying so close to Christmas. As he walked down the three steps to the tarmac, he saw his dad's old beat-up SUV sitting by the hangar of the private airstrip.

Wearing a brown work coat and boots, his dad leaned on the front fender, huddled against the howling wind that blew snow around him. He waved and joy stuttered through Ricky. He jogged down the steps, duffel bag in hand and walked over. His dad enveloped him in a hug.

"Your mom is so happy you're coming home that you better not tell us this is a two-hour visit."

He laughed and clasped his dad's shoulder. "Nope. I took two weeks. The staff has Christmas week off, but I decided I needed a rest."

His dad took a step back, studied his face. "You don't look tired. I expected you to look tired."

"I slept on the plane."

"Yeah, yeah, yeah," Jim Langley said as he rounded the hood of his SUV. "I get that you slept. But I'm not talking about sleepy tired. You've been away so long, I expected you to look worn down."

He opened the SUV door, tossed his duffel bag into the back and slid onto the passenger's side seat. "I've been coming around. Getting my energy back. Feeling a little better about things."

"So your mother said." He started the vehicle. "Time heals all wounds."

"This wound won't ever heal."

His father was quiet for a minute, then he said, "Maybe you don't want it to heal. You lost your son. Your first child. One of our precious grandchildren. We'll always remember him." His dad took his eyes off the road for a second to spear Ricky with a look over his glasses. "But life has to go on."

"Yeah. It might take me awhile to get there." If he ever got there at all, but he wouldn't burden his dad with that.

"Well, we're glad you're home."

They finished the drive to the house talking about the price of grapes and competition from a new vineyard. Ricky's eyes misted when he saw the huge log ranch house. Colorful Christmas lights blinked from evergreens that lined the lane and rimmed the wide front porch.

His dad grabbed his bag before Ricky was even out of his seat belt. By the time he came around to the side of the SUV facing the house, his mom was on the porch. She met him on the steps, hugged him so tightly he lost his breath, then pushed him away.

"Let me look at you."

His dad said, "He doesn't look tired."

"No. He doesn't." She studied his face again, then hooked her arm through his to walk him into the house.

Memories of Eloise hooking her arm through his before they entered a ballroom flooded him. He could see her take a breath, put a smile on her face and walk into the room as if she owned it.

"So? Coffee? Tea?"

Snapped out of his thoughts, Ricky faced his mom.

"Your dad's taken your bag upstairs." She grinned. "I made snickerdoodles, and your sisters should be here any minute with their kids."

He shrugged out of his coat. "I thought they didn't come over until Christmas morning."

His mom batted a hand. "Are you kidding? They couldn't wait. They're dying to see you." She leaned over and kissed his cheek. "You're the best gift we're all getting this Christmas."

He thought of Eloise again. If she dared go to her parents' house, she stood a good chance of getting rejected. Yet here he was, being told his visit was his family's best gift.

His mother tapped his arm. "You say you're getting better, but you keep leaving me."

He smiled. "Thinking about something."

"That's what worries me."

"It's not what you suspect." He glanced around the updated house that still retained its rustic log cabin feel. A huge tree stood in front of the window. Garland looped across the fireplace mantel. Candy canes lined the rim of a bowl full of nuts and chocolates. Eloise would love this.

"I have a friend." He cleared his throat. "Actually a friend of Olivia's who needed help finding a job. We spent time together to...well, fix her résumé among other things, and while we did she told me about her family."

Her mother tilted her head in question.

He shook his head, trying to dislodge thoughts of Eloise, especially because he couldn't explain her.

"Did she help you feel better?"

"Yes." This he could answer. "Assisting her was a big part of why I feel better."

"And did she tell you about her good family Christmases and how you needed family? Is that why you suddenly decided to come home?"

He winced. "Just the opposite. Her family sounds abysmal." He cleared his throat again. "I guess she made me realize how lucky I have it."

"And you gave her a job?"

"No." He laughed. "She said she wouldn't take a job with me because she didn't want everybody at the office thinking she'd only gotten her job because we'd gone out."

His mother fell to the chair behind her. "You went out?"

From the stairs, his dad incredulously said, "On a date?"

Seeing they were getting the wrong idea, he said, "On eleven dates. But not like you think. I needed someone to go with me to my events so everybody would think I was fine—not grieving anymore—and stop worrying about me. We traded. She went to my parties, and I worked with her to find her a job."

Walking over to the sofa, his dad laughed. "You went out with the same woman eleven times?"

What was so weird about that? "Yes." He looked from his mother to his father. "She's very pretty and very nice and we got along very well."

His mother said, "Huh."

"She had a tragedy in her life, too. She'd married young and her husband died." He winced. "From cancer. She nursed him through his last months."

His dad shook his head. "She sounds like a very nice woman."

"She is. Losing her husband really hurt her, but to make matters worse, her family deserted her because her marriage had embarrassed them."

His dad's face contorted with disbelief. "What kind of family does that?"

"Like I said—a bad one."

His mother straightened on her chair. "So what's she doing for Christmas?"

He swallowed. "I'm not sure."

His dad frowned. "Let me get this straight. You went out with a woman eleven times. Because she had as difficult of a past as yours, you talked enough that she helped you get your bearings about Blake. Yet she told you she had a bad family, probably nowhere to go for Christmas and…" He caught Ricky's gaze. "You left alone?"

"It's complicated."

His mother rose. "No. It's not." She walked over to his chair and stooped in front of him. "Do you think just anybody can bring you around?"

He frowned.

His dad shook his head. "Son, you love this woman."

"I don't. I mean, yes, we were good together. We talked. She talked me through a lot."

"What did she say when you told her about Blake?"

He swallowed. "That she loved me."

His mother slapped his arm. "Well, you fool! She told you that she loves you. You talked to her about something you've never spoken about with us, and you don't think you love her?"

He licked his suddenly dry lips. He could see Eloise's face, the pain in her eyes when he walked away. But he could also see the happiness in her eyes on tequila night. The way she looked standing at that door, begging him for a kiss...the feelings that tumbled through him as he fought not to kiss her. The desire to be held by her. To belong to her.

Oh, my God.

"I—"

The door opened and his two sisters, their husbands and four kids poured in. After coats were removed and hung, he was enveloped in hugs. And the whole time his mouth stayed open as one truth blinked over and over and over in his brain like a Christmas light stuck in blink mode.

He loved her.

He pulled away from a particularly emotional hug from his sister. It all made sense now. That's why he had wanted to tell her about Blake. Why telling her hadn't broken his heart.

She had opened the door for him to move on.

The question was...could he?

Eloise awakened to the ring of her cell phone. She bounced up in bed, realized it was Christmas, and the deathly silence of her apartment closed in on her.

She was alone.

Ricky didn't want her.

The pain in her heart became like a great, throbbing weight.

The phone rang again.

Maybe Ricky had changed his mind? She'd made her case. She'd seen the sadness in his eyes when he'd left—

She grabbed the phone.

But Tucker and Olivia's engagement picture appeared on her screen.

Her heart swelled from disappointment. But she chastised herself. These were friends who truly loved her. If nothing else, she'd always have Tucker and Olivia. And Laura Beth would call.

She might not have the person she loved, but she really wasn't *alone*.

She cleared her throat, then swallowed back her tears before she clicked the button. "Hey, Merry Christmas!"

"Merry Christmas!"

The chorus that rang out to her was from Olivia's entire family. Her chest shivered from the desire to cry.

"Did you get the Christmas cookies?" Olivia's mom called.

"Yes!" She squeezed her eyes shut and swallowed back tears. She'd been in Olivia's parents' house enough that she could picture the cozy living room, stockings on the fireplace mantel, a fat awkward tree in the corner brimming with blinking lights and an odd assortment of ornaments collected over the years, each with a story.

That was tradition. That was love—when you cared enough about someone that you wanted to remember everything they gave you.

"They're wonderful." She tried to keep the wobble out of her voice, but her efforts were in vain. Still, she trudged on. "I'm going to have two for breakfast with my coffee."

"Oh, sweetie! Are you crying?"

Eloise blinked back her tears. "I just woke up. My voice is a bit hoarse."

She heard a click, then Olivia's voice came through the phone clearly. She'd taken her off speaker.

"Are you sure you're okay?"

"Yes." She sucked in a breath. "I love the sweater you

bought me. But I wish you hadn't. Laura Beth and I can't afford to exchange gifts. We feel awkward."

"Gifts are gifts, not obligations."

She squeezed her eyes shut, so happy for Olivia that it was hard not to appreciate her gestures. "I know."

"Tucker sent his plane back to New York. He said to get yourself to the airport so you can have Christmas dinner with us."

Eloise pressed her lips together. "Thanks. But I have to work tomorrow, remember? Besides, I'm fine. I'm going to find some Christmas movies on TV and just relax with your mom's cookies."

"Oh, Eloise, come to Kentucky. I can't stand to hear you so sad."

She almost told Olivia that being alone for Christmas wasn't her problem. She almost told her that her heart had finally found a place to rest, but Ricky didn't want her. And that no amount of turkey dinner, Christmas cookies and good friends could make her feel better today.

Instead, she swallowed and said, "I'm fine. I have a new job the first of the year. Just like I told you when you called yesterday, I'm someday going to be a designer."

Olivia's voice brightened. "Yes, you are."

"I'm going to be somebody."

"Yes, you are! Next year you're making all my gowns for the holiday."

"And in a few years, you can help me buy all the art for my penthouse."

Olivia laughed. Eloise smiled. That was what she wanted. To hear Olivia laugh and know she hadn't ruined her Christmas. "Go. Celebrate. I'll be fine."

"Okay. Merry Christmas."

"Merry Christmas."

She clicked off the call and fell back on her pillow. Maybe she could sleep through the day.

Even as the thought crossed her mind, a knock sounded

at her door. Knowing it was probably somebody looking for one of her neighbors, she sighed. Eventually, they'd look at the number on her door, realize their mistake and move on.

They knocked again.

She almost called, "Read the number on my door," but knew they wouldn't hear her from her bedroom. After the third series of knocks, she also realized they weren't going away.

She flipped off her covers, grabbed her fleece robe and scurried to the door, fixing a smile on her face because she truly didn't want to ruin anyone's Christmas. Especially with a scowl over a missed apartment door.

She sucked in a breath, broadened her fake smile and looked through the peephole.

Standing in front of her door and holding a Christmas tree was Norman.

Norman?

She opened the door. "Don't you have family?"

He laughed. "Yes, but I got an entire year's salary to bring this tree to you."

She stepped aside. "That's just crazy."

Ricky walked in behind him. After a quick kiss on her cheek, he said, "I know."

Her heart somersaulted. "What are you doing here?"

He set two bags of ornaments on her sofa. The scent of fresh pine filled the air. He pulled out his cell phone, tapped a few buttons and the music of a carol filled her tiny apartment.

"I'm making your Christmas merry and bright."

Norman tipped his cap. "Unless there's anything else, I'll be going."

Ricky said, "Thanks, Norman."

The driver said, "Merry Christmas," and left.

And then they were alone. Confusion sang through her veins, but so did a sting of pride. No woman wanted to be the charity case of the man she loved. She'd rather be alone than pitied.

She picked up a strand of tinsel. "You didn't have to do this."

"I know."

Pride rose in a fierce roar. "I don't want your charity."

"I know that too."

Frustrated, she made a strangled sound.

"Don't get so huffy. Help me decorate the tree so I can explain."

He held out a shiny blue ball.

With a sigh, she took it.

"Okay, so I went home for the first time in a year and a half."

Although she wanted to be angry, her heart squeezed for him.

"My parents were thrilled to see me. My sisters brought their kids over. My younger brother hugged me."

"Oh. That's so sweet."

"It was."

He said nothing else, just wrapped a strand of lights from the top of the tree, along the branches in circle after circle until he reached the bottom. Then he plugged them in. The tree glowed.

She sighed. "It's beautiful."

"And we're just getting started."

Her heart singing with happiness that would soon become sorrow when he left, she caught his hand. "I can't do this. I can't pretend nothing is wrong. I told you that I loved you and you told me you couldn't love. I accepted that. If you stay, my heart will be broken all over again."

"Even if I tell you that I love you too?"

Her breath froze.

"That's why I'm here." He reached for tinsel and looped it around the fat tree. "I thought I was finally ready to go home. I knew being with you had started to heal me. And

I believed the logical next step was to be with my family." He faced her and caught her gaze. "Turns out you *had* helped me heal. Enough, though, that it wasn't my family I needed. It was you."

"Oh." Her chest had tightened so much that was all she could say.

He opened his arms. "Come here."

She stepped into them.

"I'm so sorry I hurt you. But I had to go home to realize it was you I needed."

She pulled back. "Say the part about loving me again and just kiss me."

He laughed. "I love you. Seriously. I fell like a rock."

She smiled, and he kissed her. His lips met hers unerringly, as if they'd found home, and every cell in her being rejoiced.

Just then his cell phone blasted the "Hallelujah Chorus."

She would have laughed, except the kiss was too delicious. His lips skimmed across hers, nipped and sipped, stirring her blood. Her arms lifted slowly, almost as if unsure this was real. Her hands walked up his sweater-covered chest and finally linked behind his neck.

His arms wrapped around her, tightly, securely, as if he'd never let her go. For the first time in her life, she knew what it was to be genuinely wanted.

They broke apart slowly, their gazes connected. He smiled. She smiled.

His whispered words broke the silence. "I never thought I'd get over my son's death. Then you taught me that you never get over it, you go on."

She nodded. "It was what I had done with Wayne."

His hand skimmed down her hair. "Have I told you lately that you're beautiful?"

She laughed. "I don't think you've ever told me I was beautiful. Your friends have, but you always focused on my clothes. A nice, safe way to compliment me."

He sniffed a laugh. "No more playing it safe. I want to be in this for everything. The good times and bad."

"That's the way it's supposed to be."

"You agree?"

She nodded.

"Well, since you basically just accepted my marriage proposal—" he took a step back, rummaged through one of the bags "—I guess you'll need this."

He produced a black velvet ring box. Her gaze flew to his. "This is it?"

"This is it."

He got down on one knee, opened the ring box and displayed a huge diamond solitaire. "Will you marry me?"

Her eyes filled with tears. He was the answer to a thousand prayers said on long lonely nights, most of them on Christmases. "Yes!"

He rose and kissed her again. This time she melted. He was the kindest, most wonderful man in the world and now he was hers. She gave herself over to the kiss, opened her mouth, let their tongues twine and dance. As they should because it was the happiest day of her life.

When they finally broke apart, he shifted away. "And there's one more thing."

Through happy tears, Eloise glanced at the second black jeweler's box he handed her. She caught his gaze. "What's this?"

He nudged the box at her. "Open it."

She lifted the lid and an array of diamonds winked at her. She glanced up sharply. "It's a diamond necklace."

"For your mom."

Her brow furrowed. "For my mom?"

"You said the only way you'd ever be accepted into your family would be if you bought your mom a diamond necklace."

She gasped. "I was kidding."

"I thought it through. I think you're right. We need to make a grand gesture to get back into your family."

"If you remember that conversation correctly, I also told you I didn't want to be back with my family."

"Everybody needs family. You'll just go back with new rules. You'll accept what they can give you because you'll have *my* love. You won't ever go without love again. In fact, I'll give you so much you'll have enough left over to give your parents. And eventually, maybe they'll come around. Or maybe they won't. But it won't matter."

She blinked back tears and slid her arms around his neck again. "That's sweet."

"No. That's real love. No family left behind."

She smiled. "*Nobody* left behind."

"Exactly."

This time she kissed him. Long and deep and sweet. And he finally got the chance to do what he'd longed to do for their entire courtship. He let his hand slide from her shoulders, down her long sleek spine, to the swell of her bottom, then back up again.

She was his.

And he was hers.

Neither one of them would ever be alone again on Christmas.

All the dark places in Ricky's heart suddenly lit with glorious light. He'd always miss his son. Always regret his mistakes. But he knew in his heart of hearts, even someone as young as Blake would know everyone deserved a second chance.

He broke the kiss and glanced at the window. Big, fluffy flakes billowed behind the glass. He smiled. "It's snowing."

EPILOGUE

THEY MARRIED A few months later, on a sunny spring day in New York City. Crisp air filled Eloise's lungs as she and Ricky ran out the door of St. Patrick's Cathedral into a sea of bubbles being blown by their guests.

Standing to the right, her mother dabbed tears as her dad straightened to his full six-foot-three, as proud as any father she'd ever seen. Her older brother grinned at her, happy as a clam to be an entrepreneur himself, thanks to an investment by Ricky.

No family left behind.

She still wasn't convinced her parents were as glad to have her back as they were that she was marrying someone with more money than most banks, but as Ricky said, they wouldn't care. Family was family.

With Ricky two steps ahead of her, holding her fingers, she navigated the stairs to the sidewalk in the slim satin gown designed by her boss, Artie Best.

Ricky kissed her knuckles and they ran to the limo, where Norman, in dress blues, awaited them.

He grinned as he opened the door. "I can take you to a hotel for a few hours before the reception."

"Or we can go get the pictures," Eloise said with a laugh.

"Yes, ma'am."

They slid inside, Norman closed the door and Ricky reached for her, giving her a long, slow kiss.

"So, Mrs. Langley, how's it going?"

She laughed. "You just wanted to be the first to call me that."

"I like the sound of it."

"I do too."

"And we're going to be happy together."

"Yes."

She knew it was true because she'd been down this road before. She was smarter now. She hadn't given away her heart willy-nilly, and Ricky hadn't accepted it without thought. This passion would last forever.

Hours later, at the end of the reception, she prepared to toss her bouquet into a throng of hopeful single women. Two seconds before she threw it, she noticed Laura Beth wasn't in the group. She sat at a chair at one of the round tables beside the dance floor.

Seeing this, Eloise was a bit confused as she threw her bouquet, and the bundle of flowers didn't just go too high, it also went too far...

And fell in Laura Beth Matthews's lap.

* * * * *

FROZEN HEART, MELTING KISS

ELLIE DARKINS

For Betty

CHAPTER ONE

'YOU ARE GOING to try this one.'

Maya Hartney forced the corners of her mouth up into a professional smile while she waited for Will Thomas to bite. Behind her back she clasped her hands to stop herself chewing at a nail.

She'd tried dozens of combinations of dishes for this tasting, even though squeezing in an extra job next month was pushing her business to its limits. But it had been impossible to say no when Rachel, Will's assistant, had pleaded with her so earnestly to consider catering for an Appleby and Associates gala dinner.

These moments, waiting for a client to try one of her dishes, were nerve-racking but necessary. Once they'd taken a bite her nerves gave way to sheer pleasure. She loved to watch people enjoy her food. Ever since the first time it had happened, years ago, when she'd first cooked for her university housemates, it had given her a physical thrill. The joy that her food brought showed in the small smile people gave as they closed their eyes and savoured the taste for a moment. Now, ten years later, she lived and worked for that moment.

And she'd never had reason to doubt her food's capacity for bringing joy. Until now.

Will Thomas had already refused to try her starter, and

her flutter of nerves congealed into a lump of dejection as she realised he probably wouldn't try this course either.

Maya swallowed awkwardly, thinking hard, wondering where she had gone wrong. Her late night last night had seemed worth it, if it meant she had this dish just right, but there must be something that she'd misjudged. She bit her lip for a second as she ran through the possibilities in her mind and her pulse picked up speed as she considered improvements she could make. Maybe the dressing *was* a little too acidic? But then he hadn't even tried it, so he wouldn't know that. It must be the presentation that needed more work. The rest of the meal would have to be perfect to get this pitch back on track.

It had nothing to do with the fact that her mouth had watered the first second she'd seen Will Thomas and he'd met her gaze with steel-grey eyes. It was because she'd felt the chill of his presence since the second he'd arrived, and her whole body had wanted her to resist it. To fill the room with light and colour so that the cold couldn't take hold of her. She'd fought too hard against it to let it in now.

There wasn't a splash of colour anywhere in the office: grey walls, grey carpet, glass table and black leather chairs. She'd not experienced a chill like this for ten years, and would be a happy woman if she never felt it again. There was colour in every part of her life these days, displacing cold grey memories; now this room threatened to undo a decade's positive thinking.

When Will Thomas had walked in the room had suddenly made perfect sense. Charcoal suit, crisp white shirt, black hair with just a few flecks of silver at the temples. Grey eyes that bore an expression as clinical as their surroundings. Despite all this attraction had prickled at her skin, along with a warning, and she'd had to take a breath to steady herself.

His gaze had left his smartphone only briefly, dropped

from her face to trace the contours of her curves and finally she'd seen a brief spark of heat in his eyes. The light had been there for just a fraction of a second before he'd caught it, extinguished it, and taken a step away from her, his eyes snapping back to his phone.

She'd crossed her ankles to stop herself taking a step forward, sensing that he wanted space, trying to respect that. Her eyes, though, had seemed desperate to pursue Will Thomas, to roam over the lines and planes of his face, down to where his shirt, crisp and starched and white, was open at the collar.

She'd introduced her starter: a salad of hand-harvested scallops, pan-fried and served with rocket and prosciutto, finished with a dressing it had taken two full evenings to perfect. He'd given it a derisive look and asked her to move on, his fingers twitching on the screen of his phone. Email withdrawal, she assumed. She'd catered for enough business dinners to recognise the symptoms. But the knowledge that he was choosing to check his emails over trying her food made her restless. Her food always spoke for her—what was she meant to do with someone who refused to listen?

On this man those chiselled cheekbones and intriguing silver eyes were entirely resistible.

She closed her mouth and bit the inside of her cheek to stop herself from a very unprofessional outburst.

He *had* to try this dish. She was certain that it would fix their impasse. If he would just give the food a chance *she* could still win him over. She'd sourced tender duck from a nearby farm and selected only the most beautiful vegetables from her local supplier. The herbs had come from the garden of her cottage in the Cotswolds and the sauce, a delicate balance of wine, red berries and orange, was—as of last night's final run-though—perfect.

She wanted it to be right, needed it to be perfect, because if she could no longer rely on her food what else did she have to offer?

Taking a step towards him, she brandished the fork.

'You *are* going to try this one,' she repeated with renewed determination.

She tried to paste the smile onto her face again to soften the blow, but there was no disguising the fact that this was an instruction, not a request, and her frustration had made her words short and sharp.

Will met her gaze and seemed to study her; his eyes narrowed while he inspected her features, as if weighing up his opponent. He slipped the smartphone into his pocket and took the fork from her.

'Do I have a choice?'

Maya couldn't be certain but a ghost of a smile had seemed to flicker at the corner of his mouth. His eyes left her face only briefly as he forked a mouthful of the meat and dipped it into the sauce. She grew warm under his relentless scrutiny and thought again of that moment when she'd first seen him. His eyes had widened when he'd noticed her standing in the conference room, as if he couldn't quite take her in, as if he didn't understand her. She didn't want to be difficult to understand. She had no interest in being enigmatic. What she needed was for him to like this dish, to restore her belief in her food—in herself.

For a moment as he chewed she thought she'd done it, that her food had broken this man's icy resolve. He closed his eyes for a moment, and she was sure he was savouring the flavours she'd worked so hard to blend and perfect. His body stilled, his breathing was slow, his fingers were at rest on his phone. The muscles of his face hinted at a smile. But then in an instant it was gone; his eyes snapped open and she saw only indifference.

'That's fine.'

Fine? *Fine?* Perhaps she'd imagined it, she thought. That

moment when it had seemed, however briefly, that he had been won round. Or maybe she hadn't, and he was just determined for some reason *not* to enjoy her food, whatever she put in front of him. Anger at his uninterest prickled—how could he be so determined not to enjoy something she had poured her joy and happiness into?

This wasn't going to get any better, she realised then. She just had to find a way to get through this. To protect herself from the barbs of his coldness until she could get out of there. She relaxed her hold on her anger, bringing it to the fore, letting it protect her from his cold indifference.

'Dessert?' she asked, dreading the response, dreading the rejection, but wanting to get it over with.

'I'm sure you've got that under control.'

'Blackberry fool?' Why not show him how his dismissal hurt? she thought. It wasn't as if he would even care or notice. And it might make her feel a little better.

His eyes held hers and she felt the heat in her face sink to her belly when he continued to stare at her. She shifted under his scrutiny, trying not to wonder what he was thinking, why he was studying her irises. It seemed that her anger could reach him where her food hadn't.

Will raised an eyebrow. 'It sounds like you've got the measure of things, Miss…'

'Maya's fine,' she said, her words still terse.

'Maya,' he repeated, his voice a little less steady than it had been.

He took a deep breath and she saw a blank mask descend over his face, shutting out whatever it was that had flashed between them in the past few seconds. It was a pattern, she realised. A few seconds when his features flickered with emotion, some pleasure or enjoyment. And then he chased it away, locked his face down hard. His voice too, when he spoke next, was the model of professionalism, his words hard and steady.

'Thank you for coming, Maya. Leave your quote with my assistant and someone will be in touch.'

Anger fought for room with sorrow and the pain that had haunted her since her childhood. Will had shut her out in a fraction of a second. It had taken him the space of a blink to forget whatever it was that had made him pause and consider her the moment before. And she couldn't help but remember how her parents had so easily done the same.

He'd reduced everything that she'd created to a string of numbers on a spreadsheet. A simple calculation that took no account of love and passion. She couldn't meet his eye—didn't know if he was even trying to as she shook his hand. As he walked out she let her frustration loose as she tossed cutlery and crockery back into bags and boxes and then packed away the barely touched food.

She tried rationalising what had happened to make herself feel a little better. It wasn't that he wasn't interested in her food, it was just that he only cared about the numbers. Perhaps she should have guessed the moment he'd walked into the room that this was just another business meeting for him.

She'd never been so infuriated by anyone in her life, she thought as she headed out to her car. It wasn't just his lack of enthusiasm for her food, it was the way that he'd seemed completely unwilling to let himself enjoy it, his determination to see life in columns and cells. He'd only tried one course out of three: her food had never stood a chance of impressing him because he had never been prepared to let it.

That thought drained her anger, sapped the tension from her muscles, as she remembered the last time her passion been faced with pure indifference.

Even if she was offered the job she knew she wouldn't be seeing him again. She knew that to cook, and cook well,

for that man after today's disaster would be impossible—
a complete waste of good food and time, and too close to
too many bad memories. She couldn't do it.

Will glanced at his watch and then back over his shoulder
as he waited for Maya to come to the door. He shouldn't
be here. He'd tried to convince Rachel to do it for him, but
she had told him that going against Sir Cuthbert Appleby
was more than her job was worth, that he'd have to suck it
up and do it himself. So he'd spent his evening crawling
through Cotswold villages—time away from the office
that he really couldn't afford—in order to ask for something he desperately didn't want.

He looked up at the front of the cottage as he waited
and cringed. Just like Maya, the house was a riot of colour.
Roses crept up the warm sandstone, over the door and up
towards the thatch, and window boxes overflowed with
bright-coloured flowers.

When she'd walked out of his office two days ago he'd
thought—hoped—that he would never have to see her
again. Even the thought of it had made his skin prickle.
There was something about her that disturbed him, something that he couldn't ignore no matter how much he might
want to. In those moments when he'd dared to look her
straight in the eye he'd seen her every emotion flash across
her face. She'd worn her love for her food openly and ex-
travagantly. He'd flinched away from it, intimidated in the
face of such an outpouring of emotion, fearful of its effect
on his iron self-control.

If he'd had any other choice he'd have stayed as far away
from Maya Hartney as he could. What did he care who
they hired anyway? He wouldn't even have been doing the
tastings if Rachel hadn't sneaked them into his calendar.
But then Sir Cuthbert—the senior partner in his firm, the
man who held Will's career in his hands—had spotted

Maya as she'd been on her way out of the building and Will had been forced into a corner.

Sir Cuthbert had arrived unannounced in Will's office.

'What have you done to Maya Hartney?'

No greetings, no small talk.

'What have I done to her?' Will had asked carefully. 'Nothing. Why? What did she say?'

By the time Will had admitted he hadn't tried even half the dishes Maya had brought with her he'd known that he was in trouble. Sir Cuthbert had had that look in his eye. The one that told Will he wouldn't want to hear what was coming next.

'I'm worried about you, Will.'

Not what he'd expected. And his concern wasn't necessary in the slightest.

'There's no need, Sir Cuthbert,' he'd said, relieved that he wasn't about to lose his job. 'I admit I was a little preoccupied in that meeting, and I'll make amends with Maya Hartney if I need to.' He made a mental note to have Rachel send her something.

'It's more than that, Will,' Sir Cuthbert had persisted. 'You don't take your holiday. You're always the last to leave the office. Some mornings I wonder whether you've been home at all.' He glanced down to the smartphone in Will's hand. 'You can't be parted from that thing for more than a minute. There's more to life and to *business* than the numbers, Will. It's about people too. You need to take some time off or you're going to burn out.'

Will had suppressed a groan, impatient to get back to work, not interested in cod psychology from his boss. 'I'm grateful for your concern, Sir Cuthbert, really. But there isn't a problem. I don't need time off.'

'This isn't a request, Will.'

The older man crossed his arms and widened his stance, and for the first time Will realised he was serious. The man had no reason to question his commitment to his job. He put in twelve-, fourteen-, eighteen-hour days. Whatever it took to get the job done. He was more at home in his office than he was…well…at home. When he was there he was focussed. He tuned the world out, saw only his projects, the numbers. And now he was being reprimanded for spending *too much* time here.

'I mean it. If you don't take some time off I'm going to have some difficult choices to make about your role here. The pro bono work you're taking on, for example.'

'You can't make me drop the Julia House project, Cuthbert.' A swift shot of panic hit Will in the belly, but he pushed it away, determined to think this through logically, rationally. He smoothed back the sharp emotion until he couldn't feel it any longer; he didn't want to examine it or need to understand it. He just knew that ensuring the success of Julia House was an imperative. He had to make this work, so he focussed on fixing the problem.

'I don't want to, Will. I know it's a good cause, and I know it means a lot to you. But you're stressed and you're tired and today you took it out on Maya Hartney. Make it up to her. Fix the problem and take a few days to recharge, get some perspective. Or I'll have no choice but to cut back your non-essential work.'

How could he tell Sir Cuthbert that he hadn't been rude because he was stressed, or tired? He felt neither of those things. Throughout his life he'd trained himself to feel nothing. To manage his emotions—keep them at bay. He'd been rude to Maya because she had unsettled him, scared him, and putting distance between them had seemed the safest thing to do. Now he found himself standing on her doorstep, half hoping she wouldn't answer the door, worried about what it could lead to if she did.

Will wasn't sure what it was about her that had heated his blood and demanded his attention, but he'd had to force his eyes to his smartphone for the whole of their meeting just to keep any semblance of peace in his head. It had been years—more than a decade—since he'd last had to fight so hard to keep his cool.

He was used to meeting beautiful women. He was even used to taking beautiful women to bed. But he'd been blindsided by Maya's bright colours, her wild hair and the vulnerable anger in her eyes. He didn't want her in his head, and the gnawing feeling in his belly that had started when they met was disturbing. He was used to control. To taking what he wanted, giving what was desired and walking away with no one getting hurt. There was no reason to cede control here. She was just a little unusual. That was all. It was taking his brain a little longer to learn how to keep her at the same distance it did everything else.

Finally Maya came to the door. Back in the office he hadn't let himself really notice her appearance. But there it had been easier to stop himself, to pull his eyes back to his smartphone or the safe grey of the walls. Now he truly opened his eyes to appreciate her. The first thing he noticed, of course, were the colours. She was wearing *all* of them. He was far from an expert in these things, but was it normal to wear orange and pink together? Did one normally add yellow to that mix?

There was more to see than colour, though. His eyes followed the curves of her body, noticing the way her skirt spilt over her generous hips, swinging gently as she shifted her weight to one leg and waited for his gaze to reach her eyes. He knew that he should be looking away, shouldn't be indulging himself, allowing his guard to slip. But she fascinated him. Her very presence brought light and heat and energy. And, as much as he wanted those sensations gone, he couldn't help but pander to his curiosity.

When his gaze reached her face she raised an eyebrow.

His appraisal hadn't gone unnoticed. And it seemed that the attention was not appreciated. *Good.* He dragged his mind back to his work, back to Julia House. This was business and nothing else. There was no way that he could let Cuthbert pull his project. He had given his word that he would secure funding without fail, and if that meant persuading an errant chef to get back onside, regardless of the unsettling effect that she had on him, then that was what he would do.

He firmed his stance and squared his shoulders. He would make this right.

Maya opened the door wide, and as soon as she clocked him her face dropped into a scowl. Her hands rested on her hips, one of them wrapped tight around a wooden spoon. She was not expecting his visit, and he wasn't a welcome surprise. Well, good. He wasn't exactly thrilled to be here either.

Will braced himself. He had the horrible feeling that this was going to get messy. And he didn't *do* messy. Ever. He did cold and rational and detached, and he did it better than anyone else in the city. It was the only way to find any sense of peace. Looked as if she was going to make him grovel. And if he didn't he would have to deal with Rachel's disapproving silence in the office tomorrow. When she'd heard Sir Cuthbert demand that he take time off she'd appeared in the doorway of his office with a flyer and a plan.

'Mr Thomas, I wasn't expecting you.' Maya brushed a smudge of flour from her cheek as she spoke.

'You wouldn't answer my emails, and we need to talk.' He knew that he sounded brusque—terse, even—but he wanted to stay focussed. Regardless of the constant threat of distraction, he needed to think strictly business to get this deal done.

Maya squared her shoulders, mirroring his confronta-

tional stance, but then a beeping sound came from inside
the cottage. She hesitated for a second, still eyeballing him,
before turning and walking across the hallway.

'We can talk, if you insist,' she called over her shoulder,
'but I'm not going to change my mind and I'm not going to
stop. I've got a sauce on the stove that won't wait.'

'Fine, fine.'

This hostile reaction had him on the back foot. He'd not
expected this—not after her polite smiles in his office. But
perhaps he'd underestimated the impact of his detachment.
Perhaps she'd found those smiles harder to fake than he'd
realised. He almost smiled himself—it would be so much
easier to keep her at a distance when she was obviously
keen to do the same. But he didn't like the thought that
he might have hurt her. That he was the cause of that fine
line of distress between her eyebrows.

He hated that she had him concerned, and thought that
he might have exposed a vulnerability. A chink in her
bright flowered armour. Because that would mean a connection between them—something they shared. Something
that couldn't be undone or ignored.

He followed her through to the kitchen, his eyes drawn
again to the shift of her skirt over her hips, the fabric clinging slightly to the curves of supple skin. He shook his head
to clear his thoughts—again. This wasn't him. He was in
his suit, working, and normally that was a guarantee that
nothing distracted him. But this attraction was more than
just an unwelcome distraction; it was a threat to his control and to the detachment that allowed him to function.

He dragged his eyes away just before she turned around.

'So, what can I help you with, Mr Thomas?'

Her tone was cool, and her manner no more friendly
now that they were indoors. He was glad. It gave him
every reason to respond with equal coolness. It kept her
at a safe distance.

He spoke with cold, clipped tones the words that he'd rehearsed in the car. 'I understand from Rachel that you won't cater our function next month.'

'I won't.'

She turned away from the stove to face him head-on. The slight tremble in her clenched fists gave away her nerves, but her shoulders remained firm and he could see that she wouldn't back down from him easily. He'd had no idea at the time that his words, his actions, had had such an impact. But he could see no other reason that she would be so hostile towards him now.

'Can I ask why?' He ground the words out through clenched teeth and suspected even as he was saying them that he would regret doing so. A niggle of guilt had been eating away at him and he was starting to see why. He'd offended her—which was something he'd never intended. His standoffishness has been purely a defence mechanism.

Maya sighed, and from the way her shoulders tightened and she turned away from him to stir the sauce on the stove he guessed that she didn't enjoy conflict. Part of him was glad to have that insight; he saw a way to get what he wanted. If he pushed hard enough she'd back down just to avoid a fight.

She took a deep breath and then spoke. 'As I explained to Rachel, I don't think my food is right for your dinner. I think you will find another caterer who will better meet your needs.'

Her words sounded rehearsed, and though he was sure that she'd meant them to sound indifferent the edge to her voice and her vigorous beating of the sauce gave her away. Another twinge of guilt and a pang of fear fought for space in his belly. He'd had no idea that he'd hurt her feelings so much, and no real sense of how in jeopardy his project was until now.

He took a deep breath and tried to swallow the dry lump

in his throat. 'I'm aware that I didn't give your food the attention it deserved when you came to the office, and I'm sorry that I was distracted during our meeting. We'd very much like to work with you.' He had to get this back on track, he thought, rubbing the back of his neck.

'Well, thank you for your apology,' she said, still refusing to look at him, 'but I'm afraid the answer's still no.'

'Why?' he persisted, his voice growing softer, though he hadn't intended it to. He was just changing tack, he told himself, just trying another way to get what he wanted. It didn't mean he wouldn't push her if he really needed to.

'Like I said, I don't think we're well suited. I don't think we'd work well together.'

She was still turned determinedly against him, her voice hard.

Will ran a hand through his hair, testing scenarios in his mind, trying to think objectively. Trying to find a rational, sensible business argument with which he could persuade her. 'Your food was fine,' he said, 'and I'm not asking you to work with me. I'm asking you to cater a dinner.'

'That proves my point exactly.' She whipped around and met his eye, brandishing her wooden spoon like a knife. Her voice and the colour in her face rose. 'Fine,' she said. 'You thought my food was *fine*.'

Partly he was pleased. Glad to have a reaction from her at last, thrilled that she was turning to face him. But mainly he was concerned about what this flash of anger meant for Julia House. He'd crafted a business argument that he was sure would put things right. And it had made things worse.

Maya turned back and continued to thrash at the sauce, hypnotising him with the way her skirt swung with every movement. It took a few seconds for his brain to catch up with his ears and eyes. What was wrong with *fine*? Nothing. There was no reason for him not to hire her, and no reason he could see for her to object to him. But though she'd pulled herself together he had seen hurt and anger cross her face. He didn't understand it, didn't understand why she had so much invested in this food of hers, but he didn't like that he'd upset her.

'Maya?' He wanted to leave. He didn't want to involve himself in whatever it was that made this woman turn down business because he'd described her food as 'fine'. But without her onside Sir Cuthbert could withdraw the company's support for the charity. He stayed put.

Maya took a breath and turned around, pasting on the smile that he recognised from his office.

'I'm sorry, but I can't cook for people who think my food is "fine". If I know you won't enjoy the food, I won't enjoy cooking it. If I don't enjoy cooking it, what's the point? The food won't be any good and I won't be happy.'

'Is this a general rule?' he asked. He forced a note of humour into his voice, hoping to lighten the mood.

The atmosphere in here was intense, and he could see from her tight muscles and hunched shoulders that Maya was a few wrong words away from an outburst that would put a permanent end to his project. Even putting that aside, he didn't want to see that happen. Being so close to such a volume of emotion made him uneasy; he could feel his own emotions welling up in response, weighing heavily against the door that kept them shut away.

'Do you always turn down business from people who don't gush over your food?' He tried to inject a little laughter, but his voice cracked and that door shifted when he saw the distress in her features.

'I don't know about a rule,' she said, her voice weaker now, flat, as she stared down at the floor. 'It's never happened before.'

Will took a minute to think about this. He knew that he was the problem, and that the solution had to come from him. But he was trying desperately to see a way out of the plan that Rachel and Cuthbert had pincered him into. There had to be something. Because the thought of having to go through with it tightened his chest until he struggled to breathe.

'Look, Maya. I know we don't exactly see eye to eye on this; I don't appreciate food like you do.' He took a deep breath, tried to steady his voice. 'But what if I was prepared to learn?'

He regretted the words immediately. He knew that as much as he would try to fight off the memories being back in a kitchen, oohing and aahing over delicious treats, would be close to torture.

'What do you mean?' She turned around and looked at him, surprise in her voice and on her face.

'Back at the office you told Rachel that you're running a cookery course next week, and that there was a space free. If I take the course, try to connect with your food, will you reconsider?' He controlled his fear and his voice, but if he'd had any other choice, if this was any other project, he'd be running from here—from her—as fast as he could.

She eyed him carefully, her head tilted to one side. 'I'm not sure.'

She turned to face him. The anger and the tension had left her stance, and instead she studied his face. The tightness in his chest lightened.

'And that space is gone anyway. The client called me—they managed to find someone to fill it.'

'Well, can't you run it with one extra?'

Maya shook her head and went back to her sauce, stirring more gently now. But Will didn't make a move to leave. He had to get her to agree, somehow, and she looked as if she might be thinking it over, reconsidering. Eventually, she spoke.

'I can't. There's not enough space in the kitchen and it

wouldn't be fair on the other students. If you're serious, though—if you really want to learn—I have some time the following week. I'll have to fit in some development and planning work, but if you're happy to work around that I can run another course.'

He gulped. 'One on one?'

'One on one.'

CHAPTER TWO

MAYA FIDDLED WITH her necklace as the car door slammed and forced her feet to the floor, determined not to be waiting for him at the door. This was a bad idea. The hurt she'd felt in his office was something she'd thought she was long past. The feeling of rejection was something she'd not felt since she'd last seen her parents. But after an hour in this man's company self-doubt had been needling her non-stop.

If it hadn't been for the flash of fear and hurt she'd recognised in his eyes—well hidden, but still just visible—she'd have turned him down again. But in the face of his desperation, and her curiosity, she'd known she had to think of some way to help him. And perhaps if she could get him here, get him to enjoy her food, those doubts would fade. Her faith in the joy she could bring with her food could blossom again.

She tidied away the last of her lunch dishes and surveyed the kitchen. It was always spotless, of course, but this morning, with summer in the air, it seemed to glow more than usual. It had been carefully designed to balance the charmingly old and the strikingly modern—the stainless steel of a professional grill with rich, warm Cotswold stone and aged oak beams. Perhaps the charm of the old cottage would mellow him, she pondered nervously.

Nervous anticipation spread through her body at the

thought of being alone in the house with the man who had so riled and frustrated her. Their last two meetings had left her unsettled, and she knew that she was gambling with her emotions, with the happy life and the confidence that she had built for herself, and couldn't quite recall why she had suggested this.

Because when he had come to her, asking her to reconsider, she'd seen a glimpse of something in his eyes that had made her pause—just for a second he'd seemed vulnerable. So different from the coolness she'd felt in his office—and she was curious. She had also seen what he'd been trying so hard to hide—he needed her. He was desperate for her help. And she'd found that she couldn't say no, whatever it might cost her.

And then she remembered how he had looked at her, his wide eyes skimming her, almost in disbelief…how her mouth had watered and her lips had tingled at the sight of him…and she suspected she might have had an ulterior motive.

She hadn't been able to stop thinking about him in the days since they'd met. To start with it had been easy to ignore her attraction, to concentrate instead on her hurt and her anger at the way he had completely rejected her food—and, by extension, her. But since he'd come to her door, begged her to reconsider, she hadn't been able to get those silver eyes out of her mind, trying to work out what was beneath.

The doorbell rang and she knew that it was too late for doubts and worries. She would make this work.

Smoothing back her hair, she forced her shoulders down and went to answer the door.

'Will, welcome to Rose Cottage.' He flinched as she said the words, and she had to school her features not to reflect it back to him. Acting on instinct, she reached out and placed a hand on his arm to reassure him. She hated to see anyone distressed, ached to make things right. But he pulled away from her abruptly, shock and annoyance on his face. She cringed; she'd only been trying to help and he'd rejected her. Again.

Now, of course, she was questioning the wisdom of having him here more than ever. But she had a chance to make this cold, indifferent man fall in love with food, to make his world a brighter, more joyful place, and she couldn't resist it.

And the plan had one other redeeming feature, she supposed: Will was pretty easy on the eye. He wore another grey suit today—Maya doubted he owned any other colour—and a crisp white shirt, open at the neck. She guessed that he'd come straight from the office, no matter that it was a Sunday, and he had the look of a man who spent too many hours staring at a computer screen. But the austerity of his clothes highlighted the sharp steel of his eyes and the hint of shadow below his cheekbones. A calculating look came over those grey eyes then, and she could practically see the cogs turning as he tried to turn the situation to his advantage.

She looked over the evidence of his apprehension: set shoulders, grim face, flat voice. She realised that she was never going to convince him of the joys of her cuisine if they were both approaching the week like this. One of them would have to make the effort to brighten the mood in here. She'd pasted on a happy face often enough before; she could do it now.

There was no getting away from it: he was gorgeous. She'd noticed it the first time she'd set eyes on him. But even with those sharply defined cheekbones, the hint of stubble, the lips she was dying to taste, there was one flaw she couldn't overlook. He just wasn't quite...*there*. Any time she'd sensed she might be getting a look at the real Will Thomas, every time a conversation took a turn away from the strictly rational and objective, he'd disappeared into himself in an instant.

Sometimes the shutters just slammed down. At other times they wavered long enough for her to see something lingering—a tiny suggestion of past hurts, perhaps, that had made him the way he was. Whatever it was that she'd glimpsed, it was enough for her to know that getting involved would be bad news

She'd spent the first eighteen years of her life devoid of affection, lacking warmth and love. She'd been an unwelcome surprise to older parents, shunted from nannies to boarding school and back again, and she had never stopped trying to impress them, never stopped hoping that one day she'd make them proud.

Even when she'd gone to a prestigious university, as they had, and completed her history degree, as she'd thought they'd wanted, it hadn't been enough for them. Her whole life she'd been a disappointment to them. But when she'd discovered her passion for food, the joy that she could bring to her housemates and friends with her cooking, she'd also found the warm glow she could create in a room. She wanted, *needed*, to live her life among people who were happy and contented, and she'd do everything she could to make those around her feel that way. So she'd used the money her parents had given her—she would have swapped it in a heartbeat for genuine affection, but that was the one thing they'd never offered—to start her culinary training and then her business.

She couldn't, *wouldn't*, allow herself to develop feelings for someone who was never going to be able to return them.

'So, are you ready for this?'

Maya eyed the knives laid out on the scrubbed oak countertop and wondered if this had been the wisest move.

It looked as if she had some sort of medieval torture lined up for them, and from the resigned, stoic set of Will's face she could see that he was expecting nothing less. She didn't like the thought of hurting him, and wondered again whether she was doing the right thing? But he had come to her wanting to learn, and she was determined to help, to bring him happiness.

'I thought we'd start with something simple. So we're going to cut a fillet from this fish—' she gestured, smiling tentatively, to where she'd laid two gleaming fresh fish in a bowl of ice '—and then make a herb butter. It'll be delicious.'

She'd hoped that some of her enthusiasm might rub off, but Will didn't look convinced. His fingers were curled into tight fists and she could see the tension all the way up his arms to his shoulders. His eyes darted around the kitchen, before fixing on a spot in mid-air.

She looked up at Will's face, trying to see how he had reacted to her suggestion. So far, no change. But she'd no choice but to plough on and hope that her gamble would pay off.

'Here.' She handed him the fish and the filleting knife and showed him how to clean and gut it. 'What you need to do next...'

She started to explain, and caught Will's eye as she looked up. He was watching her intently. Well, he might not be connecting with the food, she thought, but he did look determined to get this right. That was a start at least.

'What you need to do next is feel for the spine through the flesh and just let the blade glide along that line.'

The look on his face told her that he was determined to follow her instructions, but the way he was gripping the knife made her nervous.

'Just relax your hand,' she said. 'The knife is sharp, so you just need to guide it and let it do the work.'

He grimaced as he forced the point of the knife into the fish. He was overthinking it, trying to push the knife where he thought it should be going rather than responding to the feel of it in his hand.

'Wait,' Maya cautioned him gently, taking in his fierce expression and white knuckles; she didn't want him to slip and cut himself. 'You just need to be patient with it. Don't rush.' She moved closer to his side and laid her hand over his, easing his fingers back from where they were gripping the knife. 'Loosen your hand.'

Will did as he was told, and suddenly Maya was aware of how much closer she'd moved. The whole of the left side of her body was pressed against him, and her right arm, reaching across her body to help Will hold the knife, was doing something outrageous to her cleavage. She looked up and saw that Will had just made the same realisation. The red flush spreading over her face and chest added another colour to that day's collection.

She tried to step away from him, hoping that she hadn't given away evidence of her attraction. The last thing she needed was him guessing about the feelings she was trying to chase away. She didn't want them—knew that acting on her attraction was bound to lead to hurt.

As she moved away she felt the knife slip, and knew before it happened that it was heading straight for her index finger.

'Ouch!' she yelped as the blade nicked her skin. She tried to draw her hand away, but sliced deeper into her knuckle in the process.

Concern clouded Will's face as he reached for her hand. 'Are you okay?'

Maya tried to pull back; being close to him was too tempting, too good to be safe. But he took a gentle hold of her wrist as he examined the cut.

'I'm fine, really.'

She pulled her hand from his, wanting to clear her head. He was making it impossible to think clearly. All she wanted was a little space, a little distance between them. But he kept moving closer. His face still screamed grim determination, only this time *she* was the subject. He would help her whether she wanted it or not. When he was standing so close to her, showing such concern for a little cut, she had to remind herself of what she'd realised out in the hallway. Indulging that flutter in her belly and the racing in her pulse when she looked at Will Thomas was a very bad idea. Nothing was guaranteed to hurt her like indifference did. And she knew first-hand Will Thomas's capacity for that.

She headed for the first aid box she kept by the sink.

'At least I didn't bleed on the fish.' There was a little shake in her voice as she realised the strength of her feelings and the depth of her vulnerability. 'It'll still be okay for dinner. And you were doing a great job before I slipped.'

'*You* were doing great,' Will corrected her.

She turned to look at him, taken aback by the gravelly tone of his voice. His face showed more distress than ever, and she wondered why.

'You were fine; you just need to loosen up a little.' She spoke guardedly, protecting her feelings and his. With one hand under the tap, she tried to open the catch on the first aid box.

'Let me do that,' Will said, walking over to her.

She tried to insist that she could manage, but he washed his hands and then pulled the box from out of her reach. When he turned back he had gauze, blue plasters and a bandage in his hands and a determined look back on his face.

'Will, I think just the plaster will probably do it.' Maya risked a chuckle, hoping that it would break the tension in the air, but Will ignored her and stepped closer.

'Stop, Maya. Why is it so hard to let me help you? You don't have to do it all yourself.'

What other way was there? She'd done everything for herself all her life. And then spent most of her adult life doing whatever she could for other people. No one had ever tried to take care of *her* before.

She looked up at him and forgot everything she had told herself about not letting him close. Lost every self-protective instinct she had nurtured since stepping into his office. He just walked straight through every barrier she'd erected, every promise she'd made to herself since they'd met. Instead of getting away, she wondered how she'd not noticed before how tall he was—another inch closer and he'd be able to rest his chin on her head—and explored the structure of his face from this new, sharper angle.

His eyes didn't leave her face, though they darted between her eyes and her mouth as he reached across and turned off the tap. His forehead wrinkled and his eyes were serious as he wrapped gauze around her finger, applying pressure as he pulled her hand between them, and then reached for a paper towel. He scrutinised the cut, watching the red beads bloom from her skin, and then clamped the gauze down. Maya gave a little gasp of discomfort.

'Sorry,' Will said, and she saw that his concern was genuine. 'But the pressure will stop it bleeding.'

She knew that, of course, but she couldn't help wondering whether that was really why he was standing so close, why neither of them had taken a step back. She told herself that he was only so close because he was helping her. But she knew that she was kidding herself. She'd been drawn to him from the first time she'd met him, and it was only her rigid determination to protect herself that had stopped her imagining this intimacy before. She wasn't sure that she had the strength to pull away now that she was here.

She took a deep breath to steady the swimming sensation that threatened to make her sway.

When Will was satisfied the cut had stopped bleeding he carefully unwrapped a plaster and pressed it around her finger, catching her eye as he did so and watching her expression. Smoothing the edges down, he inspected the digit from several angles, ensuring that the plaster held firm, and then held it up for her approval.

'Thanks.' The word came out breathy, unsure, and as she heard her voice she knew that she had to act. She had to do something—and now—if she was going to stop herself getting hurt. This had gone more than far enough already. Maya looked up from her finger to Will's face. 'It's fine now,' she said, trying to pull her hand away.

But Will kept a firm hold on it, using it to pull her fractionally closer until her chest was pressed against him.

And then he froze. Maya watched reality crash through his face as he realised what he was doing. He dropped her hand and turned away from her, and she glimpsed his hard, set expression twist into a grimace.

Relief and disappointment flooded Maya and she leant back against the sink, trying to remember that space was what she had wanted. But his rejection stung her nonetheless. She kept her eyes on the floor until she could look up at him with an indifferent expression.

'Let's carry on,' she managed eventually.

Will proceeded to hack the remains of the fillet from the fish. She briefly considered trying to help, but her last attempt had ended in a sliced finger. By the look of the way he was handling the knife this time around, if she tried to interfere now she was likely to lose a hand. For the first time she could remember she wished she wasn't in her kitchen. She wished she could escape upstairs, hide away from this man and the dangerous effect he had on her. But she'd committed to help him and she wouldn't go back on her word.

Things didn't improve when she tried to explain the sauce. She'd hoped that a simple herb butter would be a good way for him to become familiar with the flavours of the different herbs from the kitchen garden behind the house. But his response when she suggested that he smelt and tasted each one was 'nice' or 'fine'. And the increasing detachment in his gaze showed him retreating further from her with every prompt, shutting her out just a little bit tighter.

In the end, with her finger and her feelings hurting more than she wanted to admit, she decided she just wanted the day over with and gave up any pretence of trying to reach him. The sooner it was ready, the sooner they could eat, and then she could escape this stifling atmosphere that had invaded her home.

This wasn't what her kitchen was for. She loved to share her passion with other people. Help them to discover a new talent, or develop a skill, or just eat chocolate pudding until they couldn't move if that was what brought them pleasure. This room existed to make people happy, created the bliss that she needed to fend off the memories of her childhood. Or it had until this man had walked in here, all taciturn and cold, and brought her decades-old insecurities with him.

With a final addition of salt and pepper she decided that the food was as good as it was going to get, considering the mood of the chefs, and set it on warm plates. She and Will carried the food and a bottle of chilled white wine to the table outside, and Maya wondered how they were going to get through this dinner. Will had said barely five words since they'd left the sink, and if she allowed it to the silence would become unbearable.

But what could they talk about?

Maya wished that she'd thought this through before she'd agreed to run the course for him. She loved to talk about food. When people found out that she was a cook they always asked about her work, and she was happy to talk shop for as long as they would put up with her. But she suspected that food would not be high on Will's list of favourite topics of conversation. In fact she wondered if he had ever had a conversation about food that hadn't involved a consideration of gross profit.

Silence. It was definitely not golden. It was bad-tempered and it was awkward and it was the final insult for a much-abused meal.

She gazed out over the meadow beyond the garden, hoping that the view, which never normally failed to cheer her, would have its usual soothing effect. The shadows of the clouds chased over the ground, causing the colours of the wildflowers to shift and change, and the corners of her lips twitched upwards. She encouraged it into a full-blown smile as she let the beauty and serenity of her home topple her bad temper.

She'd fallen in love with the view, and this house, the moment that she'd first seen them. It was exactly what she'd needed: somewhere to escape from the slick city kitchens she had been working in until then, to get away from the constant client pitches, the networking events. And so she'd created a haven here—somewhere she could experience the intense colours and fresh scents of the natural world, could be completely creative. And she'd made herself part of the community. Here she understood what she needed to do, how to make people happy.

She'd thought she'd known what she was getting when she'd paid for the old stone house and its beautiful garden. And then the place had sprung a surprise on her.

The first cookery class she'd run had been a complete accident: she'd invited faithful clients to come for the weekend and sample her new menu, not long after having her professional kitchen installed. She'd been sure no one else would feel quite the same thrill she did at the sight of her new oven, but she'd wanted to show it off anyway.

Except once her guests had arrived they hadn't been content just to sit and watch her cook for them. They had all wanted to muck in, despite the fact that not one of them had known how to chop an onion. They'd pushed her to let them help, and she'd realised that cooking wasn't the only thing that could make her glow. Teaching was another way of sharing her food, and her love of food, with others. Before the weekend was over they'd practically written her business plan for her, and she'd found herself with a teaching business alongside her cooking.

And now Will was threatening that thrill as well. Every time he turned his nose up at her food he impugned her teaching as well as her cooking.

But the beautiful view boosted her. She'd bloomed when she'd come here from the city, when her world had shrunk and she'd finally found a place for herself. Maybe Will just needed a little of that magic. He'd charged her with teaching him, and she wasn't going to give up just because of his bad temper.

As she gazed off into the distance she realised that putting space between her and Will, constantly pulling away from him, was going to doom their experiment from the start. How could she expect him to open up and appreciate what was around him if she was sitting there trying to pretend that he *wasn't* there?

She drew her gaze back from the meadow and fixed it on Will's face. The expression in his eyes was serious, focussed, and it intrigued her. She wondered what thoughts lay behind those silver-grey eyes, where he went when he retreated like this. Tracing her gaze over his features, she followed the line of his straight, narrow nose to lips that looked almost too full, too sumptuous, with his slim face and sharp features.

He slid his knife through the fish in neat, straight lines, carving it methodically. She watched, intrigued, his precise, emotionless approach, and fought down her instinct to look for approval. Her feelings when she served someone her food were always the same. Did they like it? Of course Will's face gave her no hint. She had to force down the disappointment that he showed no pleasure in it. Tell herself that this was still early days. But she couldn't stop herself hoping. Just a few small genuine words from him would soothe her fears, show her that they were on the right track. Ease the pain that the rejection of their first meeting had caused.

Will seemed to sense her staring at him, because he glanced up and held her gaze for a moment, before remembering what manners required of him.

'This is nice, thank you.'

Maya sighed; they still had a lot of work to do—not least on thickening her skin. But they had to start somewhere, and if she wanted him to be open with her, to open himself to the joy that she hoped her food would bring, she would have to show him the way. She should see each barb as an opportunity—he had come to her for help, and each sting would tell her how much work they still had to do.

She glanced across at the meadow, letting the colours and the glory of the sunset sink into her skin and smooth away this latest hurt. Eventually she turned to Will, trying to reflect those rays of evening sun back to him.

'So, Will, why don't you tell me more about your work?'

He met her eyes again, and she watched his face for clues, signs that he was making progress. But all she saw was him bracing himself, hardening his eyes and fixing a neutral expression. All that for small talk, she thought, and wondered what pain lingered behind the façade to make it such a frightening prospect.

'My company offers a range of financial services,' he said, his voice flat and clipped. 'At the moment I'm working on a project to raise funds for a health sector construction scheme.' A frown creased his brow and he looked troubled...tired. 'But I won't bore you with the details.'

'I'm not bored,' she said. 'I wouldn't have asked if I wasn't interested. I'd like to understand more about your work. It's a charity fundraiser, the dinner you want me to cater, isn't it? Do you do a lot of work with charities?'

'No.'

As she watched she could see him trying to distance himself further. He looked away, past her shoulder, and plucked his phone from his jacket pocket. She suspected he didn't even realise that he'd done it. One-sided small talk was its own particular form of torture, and without his help she had no idea how to steer this conversation onto safer ground. She stumbled for words, not wanting them to end the evening on an awkward silence, hoping for even the tiniest breakthrough. She decided to stick with business questions—maybe if they could get comfortable talking about that, they could progress from there.

'So, is it interesting, working with a charity? What type of charity is it? How did you get involved?'

Perhaps if she just kept throwing questions out there one of them would stick. But at the last one Will dropped his fork, placed his elbow on the table and rested his head in his hand.

Will looked...broken. More pain than she'd seen one person bear weighed heavy in his eyes and on his shoulders, and she hated that she'd caused that. Regret curled in her belly at the knowledge that she'd brought someone so much grief. This week was meant to be about pleasure, about learning to appreciate flavour and beauty and art.

But from the way that his elbows had come up onto the table to turn him in on himself, shield his body, she knew that she'd made a huge error.

Her instincts told her to move closer, but his body language screamed *Keep Out*. She rested her hands flat on the table to stop herself reaching across to him. Seeing Will like this threw everything that she'd thought she knew about him into new light. She'd seen hints of something haunting him, but had never imagined that he was carrying such raw pain.

'Will…?' She didn't want to make this worse; she only wanted to help.

'It's a hospice,' he said quietly. 'I have a…a family connection to it.'

'Oh.'

She knew that the response was inadequate. His few words, forced out through gritted teeth, had carried a great weight of buried hurt. There was so much she didn't know about him, but with those words she'd started to understand him a little more. No wonder he was distant, if *this* was what threatened when he opened up. No wonder he eyed her with distrust and trepidation when she wanted emotion from him.

'I'm sorry,' she said, caving in to her instincts and touching his hand. 'It's none of my business.'

'It's fine.' Will picked up his fork, shrugging off her touch, and his face was smoothed over.

Maya guessed that he was fighting against memories, and winning this time.

'Julia, my foster mother, died fifteen years ago. One of her nurses started a hospice charity and asked me to provide financial advice.' He spoke with an angry edge to his voice, apparently still fighting for control.

'Oh,' she said again. It was still inadequate.

'I don't want to talk about it,' Will said, solving her dilemma. 'Not now. Not ever.'

* * *

Maya lay in bed and checked the clock on her bedside table. Still only five o'clock. A little early to be crashing around when she had a guest in the house, especially one who'd seemed so annoyed with her by the time they'd gone upstairs last night. After her disastrous attempt at small talk Will had swept up the dishes from the table and clattered around in the kitchen, tidying up. She'd followed him, wanting to help—with the dishes, with his pain—but he'd scowled at her when she'd walked through the door and told her that he could manage. She'd started to argue, to insist that he didn't need to, but the glare that he'd sent in her direction had had her retracing her steps out through the door. She'd watched through the window as she picked up the last few things from the table, had seen the blank look in his eyes. He'd scrubbed at the counters, cleaning them in long straight strokes, and she guessed that he'd found some comfort in those actions.

She'd known beyond doubt that her presence in the kitchen would upset him further. It didn't matter how much she wanted to apologise, to put things right, he'd needed her to stay away.

When he'd finally gone upstairs she'd wished him goodnight and told him she'd see him back down here in the morning; then she'd sorted through the last few things in the kitchen before following him up. As she'd reached the landing she'd heard frantic typing, fingers being hammered into a keyboard, and had let out a long sigh. This week was already proving to be so much harder than she'd ever dreamt, and this was only day one. Will had asked her to teach him, but she was worried that he would fight the temptation to learn with his last breath.

Lying in bed was doing her no good this morning. She'd woken so many times through the night, thinking about the disastrous evening in the kitchen and on the terrace—she couldn't have slept for more than an hour at a time.

Making this week a success had never seemed less likely than it did this morning. But Will had laid down the gauntlet, challenged her to teach him, and she was determined to see it through. He was here, and there was something in that simple fact that made Maya want to persevere. This man needed happiness in his life, something to balance the grief she had glimpsed last night, and the only thing she knew that could deliver joy of that magnitude was food.

She wouldn't push. She couldn't force something that he didn't feel. All she could do was make her food so irresistible that he couldn't help but enjoy it. And her sleepless night had given her plenty of time to think about how to go about it. This morning she wouldn't ask Will to cook. She would just surround him with delicious smells and tastes, lighten his mood and help him feel relaxed in the kitchen.

She dragged her tired body out of bed and into the shower, making plans in her head for something that would reach out and bring Will a little relief. Perhaps something with fresh fruit? That way it would introduce him to more of her garden. Or something spiced that would appeal to the nose as well as the palate?

After blasting her hair with the dryer she selected her pinkest, floweriest, summeriest dress from the wardrobe. For someone with as much red hair as she had it was not an obvious choice of colour, but she was going to exude sunshine and pleasure today. Will had been in her house a day, and seemed even less happy than he had when he'd arrived. She couldn't allow herself to take a step back; if she was going to make this work she had to throw everything she could at it.

She hunted frantically for ingredients, looking for inspiration in the walk-in fridge, grabbing fruit and butter, eggs and milk. She whipped and beat and whisked and folded, and every time she slid another tray into the oven she reached for a mixing bowl again. The familiar actions chased last night's shadows out of the kitchen and she breathed more easily as she saw the results of her work piling up on the countertops. This would work. This had to work. There had to be *something* here that would get through to him.

She threw the switch on her food mixer, adjusted the oven temperature, turned cakes out onto racks. A simple sponge, shortbread, scones, pizza bases. She found spiced cream, home-made jams and fresh berries. Perfect for building layers of flavours.

She picked at the fruit and munched on biscuits as she went. With her recent late nights, and the stress of a student who didn't want to learn, she was asking for a migraine. Lucky for her, keeping her blood sugar up and cooking out her stress were the best ways to fend one off.

And when at last the huge container of flour was empty she leaned back against the counter and surveyed her work. Spoons, spatulas and whisks were stacked up by the sink. Her supply of mixing bowls was exhausted and every inch of counter space was covered with the evidence or the fruits of her labour.

Some of it she barely remembered making. She hadn't been thinking. She'd just let her hands and her heart take over her body.

She thought of Will's fingers stroking the screen of his phone, hammering on his laptop last night, and couldn't help but recognise the similarities. She'd reached for comfort this morning, as she'd seen him do.

There was more food here than she and Will could eat in a month, never mind a week. It could go in the freezer once it cooled, she thought, mentally flicking through her diary for the next couple of weeks. She had a couple of afternoon teas booked that the cakes and biscuits would be perfect for.

She glanced at the clock. It was gone ten o'clock already and she'd seen no sign of Will yet. Oh, well, he wouldn't be the first hardened workaholic to succumb to the effects of country air. She'd plan for elevenses and if there was no sign of him by then she'd knock on his door, just to make sure everything was okay. *Unless he's not in his room*, she thought to herself, and her spoon dropped to the counter with a clatter.

What if he had left already? Decided that whatever she was trying to teach him wasn't worth sticking around for?

A stab of pain slid through her belly as memories of being just not good enough surfaced. Weekends spent in an empty house because her parents had had more important things to do, or long summer holidays spent at school because she wasn't wanted at home. She'd thought that those feelings were long gone. Until she'd met Will Thomas she'd not thought of those times for years, but now… He had rejected her once. It would be so easy for him to do it again.

The hollow feeling of fear curled in her stomach and she rushed to the front door, relieved to see Will's car still parked on the drive. He was still here. That had to count for something. She still had a chance.

She couldn't quite rationalise her relief, given how frustrating yesterday had been. But, however difficult it was proving to be, she needed to help him. She couldn't look at someone in pain, someone who needed help, and simply do nothing. And then there was the spark that she'd felt between them when he'd bandaged her finger. The tender concern he'd shown her. The way that he'd started to pull her close before getting spooked. The fact that he'd pushed her away almost immediately should have been enough to tell her that she would have been better off if he'd gone.

'Everything all right?' Will appeared at the top of the

stairs dressed in grey trousers and another crisp white shirt, phone in hand.

'Everything's fine,' Maya said, not wanting him to guess what she'd been thinking. 'I thought I heard the doorbell.'

She gestured widely with her arm towards the front door from where she stood at the bottom of the stairs. Turning her body towards him, she rested her hands on her hips and smiled up at him.

'Did the country air knock you out?'

'No, no. I've been up for a while. I was going to come and find you, actually,' Will said.

He was looking for her? Warmth spread through her body at that thought, chasing away the cold she'd felt a second ago when she'd thought he might have left. She was so overwhelmed with relief that he hadn't walked away, hadn't rejected her as she'd thought, that she didn't step back from the stairs as he descended. Even when he reached the bottom and was standing just a few inches away. Instead she enjoyed the feeling of being close to him, the way the air between them almost hummed. Like yesterday, those few good moments in a sea of disaster, when he'd shown such concern for the little cut on her finger.

The memory of the cold that had followed as he'd walked away was not, apparently, enough to make her body stop wanting him.

'You were?'

'Yes, my battery's about to die and I've forgotten my charger.' He poked at the screen of his phone and then gave a long sigh. 'I have a conference call in ten minutes. I don't suppose there's a spare one around here anywhere?'

Maya gulped, trying not to show her anger. He was working. He'd probably been up at the crack of dawn, as she had. But whereas she'd spent hours in the kitchen, try-ing to figure out how they were going to make this experiment of theirs work, he'd been happily ensconced in his room, getting on with business as normal. He hadn't even bothered to tell her what he was doing that morning. He'd just got on with his day without giving her a single thought.

Maya felt a chill sink through her as the implications hit home. She had spent all morning trying to make his day better in a small way, even if all she had to offer him was cake. She knew that it couldn't possibly fix his pain. But she'd tried. She'd thrown everything at helping him the only way she knew how. And he'd not thought of her at all. He couldn't have made it any clearer how little she, her food or her time meant to him.

She took a step back as her shoulders slumped, and her arms came across her body, protecting her from further blows.

'That's not a problem, is it?' Will ran a hand through his hair and it came to rest of the back of his neck.

Maya picked up on the tension in his body, the sharper edge to his voice. He'd sensed he'd upset her, she guessed, and was looking for an escape route.

'I'm sorry; I didn't think you'd need me in the kitchen until this evening. You didn't mention last night…'

Actually, she had mentioned it last night, but he clearly hadn't been listening. And she shouldn't have to force him. His attendance on the course had been *his* idea. He was the one who had said that he wanted to learn—or that he was prepared to try, at least. And if that was the case then he had to be proactive. He had to make an effort—not just show up when he thought it was unavoidable.

She clenched her fist against the anger building in her—at herself as well as at him. All morning. She'd spent all morning trying to make this idea of his work, and he hadn't even bothered to turn up.

This thought, heaped on top of disappointment, sparked anger—at Will, at her parents, at herself—and she knew that they couldn't continue like this. Every day that she was around Will she was reminded that she'd never been enough. When her food wasn't working for her she felt unworthy of his, *anyone's* attention. She wasn't helping him; all she was doing was hurting them both. He would be better off leaving.

Maya tried to keep the heartbreak from her voice, reminding herself that really this was just business. 'I think we need to talk. I'll be waiting for you in the kitchen.' She didn't bother looking to see Will's reaction but stalked through the door and let it slam behind her. She knew that she hadn't succeeded. Her words had been sharp, clipped, forced out so that her voice wouldn't waver. But she knew that she hadn't fooled him into thinking they were detached.

When Will walked into the kitchen she recognised the determination on his face—he was obviously worried that he had blown his chance with her, and with good reason. She couldn't take any more of his cutting insults, whether he knew that he was making them or not.

'Oh, I didn't realise you'd started already. You should have shouted if you needed my help.' He ran a hand through his hair as he took in the array of baked goods cooling on the counter.

A flush of colour crept up Maya's neck as she tried to rein in her frustration and embarrassment—her every feeling was laid bare on the worktops of her kitchen. Hours of love and hope had been poured into cake tins, lined up carefully on baking trays, and there was no hiding from the passion that was displayed on every side.

'I didn't need your help, Will,' she snapped. As if it wasn't bad enough that she was wearing her heart on her sleeve, showing him how important he was to her—something she hadn't quite realised herself before this moment—he'd completely missed the point. 'I'm perfectly capable of doing it myself. But why weren't you here? This week was *your* idea.

You committed to doing it. But all I'm getting from you is half-measures. You're wasting my time as well as yours, and I think you should pack your bags and go.'

She watched as her words registered and knew that she had shocked him. For a minute he actually relaxed and leaned back against the counter, his eyes wide as he watched her. She could understand why. She almost wished she could see herself from the outside right now, because she didn't recognise the person who had just spoken. Maya was always nice. It was who she was—what she did every day. Making people happy. She wasn't sure that she'd *ever* lost her temper and spoken to someone the way she'd just hissed at him.

She was surprised at how good it felt—it was exhilarating. There was a freedom in it that she'd never felt before. If her food meant nothing to him, then she had nothing else to offer. He couldn't make her feel any worse than he had just now, so what did she have to lose?

She held her ground, refusing to look away as he continued to stare at her, and she guessed that he was weighing up his options. She felt sure that he wanted to go, that he was here under duress of some sort, because he surely wasn't enjoying it. Watching him, she could tell that it was complicated. There was more to his insistence on her catering for him, more to him being here, than he'd told her, but would that reason outweigh his desire to get away?

'I'm sorry,' he said eventually. 'I'm here to learn; I'm committed to this.'

Apparently it would. But if he thought that was a decent apology, he was mistaken. She crossed her arms a little harder across her chest and tilted her head, waiting for him to continue.

'I didn't sleep,' he said at last, 'after what we talked about last night. But I shouldn't have taken that out on you. This is very important to me.'

There was no faking that sort of sincerity, she thought, noting the way his voice was carefully controlled—presumably to stop it breaking. She might be angry. She was *definitely* angry. But that didn't make her insensible to his feelings. Will was hurting.

'I'd need you to make a real effort,' she told him. 'You need to decide right now whether you're going to take this seriously. If not, I'll pack your bags for you.'

Will eyed her warily but she stopped herself from taking her words back, from apologising. Instead she waited. Waited to see what effect her words would have when she didn't care what the listener thought of her. When she had nothing to lose.

'I didn't expect things to get so...personal, but from now on no half-measures,' he said. 'I *will* do this. Properly.'

Apparently brutal honesty got her what she wanted.

She watched him force a smile onto his face. She would have preferred to see a genuine one, but she liked that he was trying. And she thought that maybe there was still a chance that she could help him, as he'd asked.

'Okay. We'll try again. But you might want to lose the suit—change into something that doesn't need dry cleaning,' she added. If he was willing to try she would give him another chance. If nothing else it would be an interesting challenge to try and teach someone so different from her usual clients. At least that was what she could tell herself. It was nothing to do with the spark she felt between them; nothing to do with exploring this new-found bravado and honesty. Nothing to do with the way her body craved being close to his.

CHAPTER THREE

THREE MINUTES LATER Will appeared in the doorway dressed in jeans and a black T-shirt.

Definitely an improvement, Maya decided, her eyes lingering on the contours of his upper arms. She was determined to start afresh, to put all thoughts of their argument and her hurt aside. His hands were in his pockets, but his arms appeared stiff, belying his façade of calm. His jaw was tense, his mouth pulled into a hard line. But Maya forced herself to look away, to paint a smile on her own face and hope that soon she would see it reflected in his.

'Ready to get started?' she asked, in a sunny, breezy voice. She wondered whether her own attempt to cover up her feelings was any more successful than his.

'Sure,' Will replied, not quite keeping the apprehension out of his voice, but she appreciated the effort.

Maya forced another smile and loaded cakes and biscuits onto a tray. 'I thought we'd sit outside as it's such a lovely day.'

She headed out to the terrace, where the sunlight broke through the leaves of the trees, throwing mottled patches of light onto the tablecloth and making the sugar atop her biscuits glisten. She set the tray on the table, beside a pot of tea and bowls of fruit. Finally, with all her tools in place, she took a seat opposite Will.

'Right, this is elevenses…' She checked her watch. 'Or

near enough. You'll probably be pleased to hear that this doesn't involve actual cooking.' She'd rehearsed the words in her head when he'd disappeared upstairs to change, but now she stopped, taking in the blank look in his eyes and realising she'd lost him already.

'Elevenses?'

'Elevenses. Tea and cake taken around eleven in the morning.' She said. 'The preserve of grandmothers everywhere.'

'But you're not a grandmother,' Will pointed out, and she was surprised to see him relax a little, perhaps even a hint of amusement in his eyes as they met hers and wouldn't look away.

She smiled in return, relieved that the tension between them was lifting, and couldn't help wondering whether there was anything else to see in those eyes. Whether maybe some of the attraction she'd been fighting off since she'd met him was reflected there too. Her heart lurched at that thought; it had been hard enough keeping her own feelings at bay—knowing that he might feel the same would make it so much worse, so much more dangerous.

'You're right. I don't even *have* a grandmother. But I do love tea and cake. So here we are.'

'Fine. Good. Elevenses,' Will said, like a child learning a lesson by rote.

'So this morning there's no cooking, just eating,' she continued, keeping her voice light, knowing that their truce, this new lighter mood, could be swept aside with one wrong word. But she breathed a little easier, smiled a little more as he stayed with her rather than retreating. She finally broke their eye contact and reached for the teapot, wanting something to do with her hands to help her resist the foolish urge to reach out and touch him.

'So I just have to eat? You didn't trust me with a knife this time?'

The smile spread from Maya's lips to her eyes at Will's attempt at a joke. From white knuckles to this was quite an achievement, though the slight tension in his shoulders told her he was still a long way from comfortable.

'I'm not letting you get off quite that easy,' Maya replied, and then took a deep breath.

This was a risk, but there was no point them working together, no point them trying, if all they could do was speak pleasantries. They had to be able to use this bond she could feel forming between them to get the job done, get Will thinking, *feeling* about food.

'We're going to eat and talk.' Maya could have sworn she saw him pale at the thought. This was the reaction she'd expected to fish guts, not to talking about tea and cakes. 'We'll start with something easy. I promise.'

She tried to think tactics while she poured the tea. Should she push when he was so uncomfortable? She knew already that there was more to Will's aversion to food than she had first realised, that there was a painful connection she could only guess at. But he was the one who had asked her to do this, to help him appreciate food. He had asked to come; he had asked to stay. She could be sensitive, but she wasn't going to give up.

She passed him the bowl of raspberries. 'Try one of these.'

Will took one of the berries, stuck it into his mouth and swallowed it whole.

Maya rolled her eyes, laughing. 'Why don't you try that again? And give yourself a chance to taste it this time.'

Will did as he was told, and held her gaze seriously as he took another berry from the bowl and chewed slowly, deliberately, before swallowing.

'How did it taste?'

'Nice.'

He said the word confidently, and she guessed he wasn't

being deliberately exasperating. He just didn't let himself feel anything more than that. He'd had so much practice at blocking it all out that 'nice' seemed like a perfectly reasonable answer. Well, it wasn't, and he had to know it.

'You said you were going to *try*,' she reminded him. 'From now on the word "nice" has been excised from your vocabulary. I want you to *think*. I want to learn the flavours and textures you like. I want you to learn those things too. Neither of us can do that if everything is *nice*.' She waited for a response, but the silence between them grew heavier. She was the first to crack. 'You said you were going to try,' she said again, more gently this time.

She wouldn't cave, she decided, fighting against every instinct that told her to help him. Because all her efforts, all her tiptoeing and pushing and careful planning, would mean nothing if he wasn't prepared to commit to this. If he wanted to sit in silence—fine. If he wanted to get up and leave—fine. But she would not be the first to speak. She leaned back in her chair, crossing her arms across her body and fixing Will with a stare, willing him to try, to give her a chance.

'Sour.'

So much time had passed she'd almost forgotten why they were sitting there, but at the sound of his voice a smile spread across her face.

'Perfect!' she declared, as if this were the most insightful comment ever to be made about a raspberry. Well, she was willing to bet it was the most insightful thing Will had ever said about a raspberry—or any other food for that matter. And it was more than that, it was proof he was trying. 'And the texture...?'

She didn't have to wait this time.

'Soft,' he said, his voice quiet and even.

'Great.' Her arms spread wide in delight and her smile spread further as she spooned some cream onto a shortbread biscuit and sprinkled some of the chopped berries on top.

'Try this.' She wanted to tempt him with something delicious, something that would make 'nice' impossible. He was doing so well, she was finally getting through to him, and she didn't want him to lose this momentum.

He took the biscuit from her and bit into it. She could see the cogs working in his brain as he tried to think of something to say. She tried sitting there, watching him struggle—his eyebrows drawn together, one hand rubbing at the back of his neck—but she longed to step in. Now he had got started, and looked willing to learn, a few pointers and a little help seemed only fair.

'So…' she started, leaning towards him, giving him a chance to come up with something. Anything.

'The biscuit was sweet,' he said decisively. 'Crunchy.'

She thrilled inside at this first evidence that they were winning. She didn't even know what it was that they were fighting, but that didn't make it any less of a victory. He was finally giving her a chance to show him the pleasure that could be found in food—in her food, in *her*. She lifted a hand to her forehead at that thought and shook it away. *That's not what this is about,* she told herself. *This is about Will.*

About helping him—because he'd asked her; because he needed it.

'And with the raspberry?' she prompted, keen for him to pursue his line of thought and build on the bond she could feel strengthening between them. The trust that was implicit in his simple statement.

He took another bite of the biscuit, chewed slowly, and then caught a drop of cream from his lower lip. Maya caught her breath. Her attraction to him had been simmering away in the background, but the swipe of his tongue on his lower lip brought it to a steady boil. She leaned back in her chair, hoping that the extra inches of space between them would cool her off, get her mind back on the food, where it should be.

She watched him as he swallowed, closed his eyes, apparently deep in thought. He leant forward as he opened his eyes and spoke precise, considered words.

'I like the contrast.'

He liked the contrast. He *liked* the *contrast*. He had eaten her food, thought about the different tastes, and then expressed how the food had made him feel. This was hope. Light at the end of the tunnel. She'd been so hurt by his rejection of her food, of *her*, that this reversal stole her breath and her control. Perhaps her growing feelings for him weren't something to hide from. Perhaps they were something to nurture, to explore. If he was opening up about food, then what else in his heart was changing?

'That's brilliant,' she said, leaning closer.

A grin had spread over Maya's face and Will couldn't help reciprocating. *This shouldn't be so hard,* he told himself, enjoying the sight of the smile spreading across peachy pink lips and bright green eyes sparkling with encouragement. But what she was asking of him was even more difficult than he had imagined. He'd known that being in a kitchen with all the memories of happy times he could never recover would be painful. But he hadn't imagined that his every sense would be assaulted. That a scent could summon a memory, that a taste would bring him pain, a texture remind him of all his losses. And he couldn't flinch away from them. Not if he wanted to succeed.

It felt as if every word this morning was another step along a tightrope. If he was to fall, and Maya pulled out of their deal, then his job would be gone and the Julia House project along with it—and that wasn't an option. He wished they'd not given the hospice her name. He might not be here if they hadn't. But failing the project was failing *her*, and after everything she had done for him he didn't want to let her down.

But Maya was making life hard. She wasn't doing it on purpose. She couldn't know why something so simple was so difficult for him—couldn't know that for him thinking about food meant thinking about Sunday dinners around a scrubbed oak table in a steamy, fragrant kitchen. It meant thinking about illicit fish finger sandwiches with Julia before Neil, his foster father, got home from work, and it meant thinking about a creamy, sticky gateau with thirteen candles.

If he let go now, lost his focus even just a little, he knew he would never again find the calm that he'd spent years perfecting. Maya was asking him to open his senses, to enjoy food, enjoy life, and it seemed such a reasonable thing for her to expect. But impossible for him to deliver.

He reached for another of the shortbread biscuits and took a bite. Maya looked at him again, expectant, waiting. He wanted to be able to do this. Wanted her to see that he was trying, taking this seriously. He needed her to see that if he was going to get her to stick to their deal. And—much as he didn't want to think about why—he liked it when she smiled. It seemed as if the expression jumped from her face to his, as if her happiness spread from her body to his. Every time it happened he longed to do it again. He tried to force the feeling away, to box it up somewhere safe, somewhere he wouldn't have to think about it. Feelings like that—feelings that might one day lead to affection, to desire, to love—brought pain.

'Describe the biscuit,' she said, breaking into his thoughts, as if it was the simplest thing in the world. 'Give me the first word that comes into your head.'

Just one simple word. His elbows were leaning on the

table, and this thought dropped his forehead into his hand. Breaking eye contact, breaking *any* contact. He closed his eyes against the torrent of memories. *Home*. The last place that he remembered eating freshly baked shortbread. Not his expensive apartment, with its view of the city skyline, but a modest semi in the suburbs. That was the only place he had ever called home, and he couldn't go back.

'Don't let yourself think about it,' she said.

Maybe she thought he had nothing to say. Maybe she thought that he was scrabbling for ideas, not for sanity.

'Just say whatever pops into your head.'

He glanced up and met her eyes. Was she doing this on purpose? Had she found a weakness and decided to pick away at it? But her smile, though faltering now, when he looked up at her, showed no guile. She thought she was helping. She was just doing what he'd asked of her after all.

But Julia had baked that first day he'd gone home with them, and he couldn't fight away the memory of it. He'd installed himself at the kitchen table, with earphones in and his maths homework in front of him, hiding in plain sight. Julia hadn't tried to talk to him, to coax him out of his self-imposed isolation. She'd just got on with what she was doing. And when she'd placed the plate of still-warm cookies on the table and pulled out the seat beside him he'd taken out his earphones and smiled cautiously.

'Don't tell me if you like it,' Maya persisted, her voice encouraging. 'Don't tell me if it's good or bad. Just tell me something about the biscuit.'

'Is there a point to this, Maya?' he asked, crossing his arms over his body, knowing that his tone was harsh, that he was being cruel. But he couldn't take this any more.

There was only so much pain he could bear, only so many memories he could keep at bay. Around Maya it felt as if he was constantly at saturation point. As if her colours and her joy and her enthusiasm took so much energy to fend off that he had no reserves to fight off the memories too. It wasn't her fault—she wasn't doing it consciously—but the effect was the same. He hated the look on Maya's face as he spoke—a guilt-producing blend of shock, disappointment, pain. But he'd had to do *something*. Maya's gentle words threatened to undo fifteen years of determined effort, and he couldn't let that happen.

'Because it doesn't seem like we're doing anything useful here. All you're asking me to do is describe a biscuit. It's not like it's rocket science.'

'No,' Maya replied, sitting back in her seat and crossing her arms to match his.

The shock had faded from her features and now she looked hard, angry. With good reason, he knew.

'It's *not* rocket science. A few weeks ago I couldn't imagine a grown man unable to offer such simple observations. But then I strolled into your office and you lowered my expectations considerably.'

The words tumbled from Maya's mouth, and he couldn't help but be impressed by this display of grit even as he regretted the hurt that he knew powered it. But as he managed to distance himself from the emotions that had caused his outburst, the implications of what he'd done started to filter into his brain. If she kicked him out, refused to cater the fundraiser, his career would be in serious trouble and so would Julia House. He needed to backtrack—and fast.

'I'm sorry,' he said, keeping his arms tight to his body, his voice level, trying to keep a tight hold on his emotions. He couldn't afford another outburst, another wrong word. 'I shouldn't have said that.'

From the angry set of her shoulders and the hurt etched on her face he knew his apology hadn't been enough. Dread churned his belly as he realised that he had to go further. That if she was to forgive him, if he wanted to keep his job and the charity afloat, then he had to explain his behaviour properly.

'Maya, talking about stuff like this. I find it…hard.'

'No kidding it's hard.'

Neither her voice nor her body language had softened. She kept her arms crossed tight across her front, and her eyebrows were drawn into a hard, distressed line.

'I feel like I'm banging my head against a brick wall. The minute I think we're making some progress you go and say something like that and I wonder why we're both here. You said you were going to take this seriously, and— stupidly—I believed you. What are you even doing here, Will? You have no interest in learning. You don't think that anything I'm doing here is important.'

Will shook his head, trying to think, to plan. 'It's not that. I know it's important to you. But I can't…' His voice trailed off, and when he looked up pain and disappointment were so clear on her face that he knew he'd gone way too far. He'd crossed a line, insulted her and her work. It was clear from the joy that she radiated when she talked about her food how much feeling she invested in it.

His words had cut her deep. If an apology wouldn't set things right, he knew that there was one thing that would— but it would cost him more than anything else to give it to her. The only chance he had was to tell her the truth.

He rubbed his hand against the back of his neck, taking a moment to try and compose himself, to try and think about how he was going to get through this, how he'd get the words out without revealing his vulnerability. Eventually he looked up and started speaking.

'When I was a kid,' he started, trying to distance himself from his words, trying to pretend it was someone else's painful life he was describing, 'I used to spend a lot of time in the kitchen with Julia, my foster mother, and being here—well, it's bringing back a lot of memories. Ones I'd rather forget.'

Maya opened her mouth to speak and the hardness in her face started to shift, falling into compassion. He took a moment to wonder at her—that she could so easily set aside her own hurts at the sight of someone else's pain. Then he stiffened, thinking that she was about to reach out to him. But perhaps she saw the movement, or guessed what he was thinking, and she stayed back, giving him the space he needed.

'Will, I—'

The chime of the doorbell broke her words, and Will felt tension leach from his muscles as he realised he had been granted a reprieve…a few moments alone.

Maya rose from the table and, after a quick glance back at him, walked away.

CHAPTER FOUR

WHEN MAYA HAD seen the look of relief on Will's face she'd been grateful for the interruption. It seemed that a few moments alone was what he needed, and she was also selfishly grateful to have been saved from having to think of an appropriate response.

As she opened the door she wondered whether they had imagined the bell—wishful thinking, perhaps—but then she looked down and saw a head of angelic golden curls.

'Carys, what are you doing here? Where's your mum?'

The three-year-old reached up for a cuddle, and as Maya lifted her she saw her mother appear from behind the people-carrier parked in the lane, holding hands with Dylan, Carys's four-year-old brother.

'Maya, I'm sorry to just throw them on your doorstep like this,' said Gwen, her neighbour, 'but there's a total emergency at the office and they need me to come in. I was wondering if there was any chance you could watch the kids for a couple of hours?'

Maya hesitated for a second. She wanted to help; the lines on Gwen's forehead told her that her neighbour really needed her, and Maya felt a shiver of dread at the thought of having to turn someone away who needed her help.

But she had promised to help Will first, and springing someone else's kids on him wasn't exactly fair. Perhaps she could help Will *and* Gwen—and not risk censure from either of them. If Will would give it a chance then perhaps having the kids around would help. Keep their minds busy until they could think and speak a little more clearly. Will had looked grateful enough for the interruption a moment ago: maybe he'd welcome its extension.

'Just give me a minute,' she told Gwen. 'I really want to help but I have a client taking a course this week. If he doesn't mind then of course the kids can join us.'

She bit at a nail as she walked out to the terrace, unsure what would greet her there. Will was sitting staring out over the fields, his brow slightly furrowed.

'Will?' He jumped as she spoke his name, and his gaze whipped to her face.

'Problem?' he asked.

'No, not exactly.' She squared her shoulders and forced her voice to be level. 'My neighbour's got a bit of a crisis and wants me to watch her kids. I can take care of them without it affecting the course, but I just wanted to check if it's okay with you.'

'You've said yes?' His tone was a little sharp, and she could see wariness in his eyes.

'Not yet. But she's really stuck and I want to help her.'

'Why?'

His question, his softer tone, and the genuine curiosity on his face threw her.

'Why…?'

He just nodded, watching her carefully. Her body heated under his gaze and she felt aware of her every movement. The rise and fall of her chest against the neckline of her dress…the slight breeze catching her hair.

'I want to,' she said. He waited for her to continue, and the question niggled at her. She'd never even considered that she *wouldn't* want to help. 'The normal reasons, I suppose. Being a good neighbour, a good friend. Helping someone who needs it.'

He nodded slowly, but his scrutiny didn't let up.

'Okay,' he said eventually, slowly, as if he were already regretting it. 'Fine.'

She walked back to the hallway, unable to shake the feeling that she'd just misstepped somehow—as if Will had seen something she hadn't wanted him to. But when she spotted Carys and Dylan her face broke into a smile. Carys reached up her arms and Maya hitched her onto her hip, turning to talk to Gwen.

'All sorted. I'd love to have them,' Maya said. 'Do they need lunch?'

'Oh, that would be great. They've not eaten. I can't believe I didn't think about that. Are you sure you don't mind?' Gwen asked, though she was already walking back through the front door. 'Thanks, Maya, you're such a star. I promise I'll be as quick as I can.'

Maya wished she had a camera when she walked out onto the terrace with a toddler on one hip and a child clinging to her other hand. Will was standing by the table, his hands planted firmly in his pockets and his face grave. *He looks like he's heading for the electric chair*, Maya thought, suddenly doubting the wisdom of this move. This might push him too far, ensure that the whole endeavour was ruined. He stood there silently, not moving, and Dylan took another half-step behind her, his hand digging into the flesh of her thigh for security.

'Carys, Dylan—can you say hello to Mr Thomas?' She tried to make her voice cheery and welcoming, hoping it would break the stand-off between Will and the kids, but neither seemed fooled by it.

She widened her eyes at Will, pleading with him to make an effort. He could have just said no. He'd agreed to the kids being here—he couldn't carry on like this. With her gaze fixed on his, she realised he wasn't being difficult or rude. Not on purpose, anyway. It was as if he'd been frozen. His lips were even slightly parted, as if he'd meant to speak.

She ached to help him, could feel fear and pain radiating from his body. But she'd heard Gwen's car disappear down the lane so they were all stuck with each other for the time being.

'Will?' she said gently, not sure if he would even be able to hear her wherever his mind had taken him. 'If you want to go back inside…back upstairs?'

It was as if her voice had brought him back, snapped him into the present, and he pulled his hands from his pockets. One went to rub the back of his neck and Maya breathed a sigh of relief.

'No. I'll stay,' he said with grim determination. 'Hi, Dylan. Hi, Carys.'

Maya could just about hear the responses mumbled into her hair and hip. She'd never seen the children so shy before, and knew that they must be picking up on the tension between her and Will.

She'd resolved in the hallway to try and put Will's harsh words behind them. They had hurt. The direct insult had hit her where she was most vulnerable, and she wasn't sorry that she'd lashed out and stood her ground, that she'd shown him that she wasn't prepared to let him make her feel like that. The honesty and openness he'd shown when he'd told her the truth weren't a free pass. It didn't mean he could get away with speaking to her like that again. But it was the surest sign she'd had that this was working. That she and her food were getting through to him. And she didn't want to lose that progress.

When the afternoon was over they'd both have a decision to make: where was their relationship, such as it was, to go from here? Will needed to come to terms with the fact that if he wanted the course to work it was going to get emotional. And she had to learn his boundaries—when to push, when to give him space. If they couldn't do that, then he'd have to go.

'Now, I don't know about you three,' she said, trying to be bright, 'but I'm hungry. Who wants pizza?'

She didn't get the rapturous response that she'd been hoping for, but at least Dylan came out from hiding behind her skirts. She bustled the children back into the kitchen and set about finding aprons for them. Will walked through too, carrying their plates from earlier, and stood watching as Maya tied aprons, rolled sleeves and washed hands.

She left the children drying their hands by the sink and went over to him.

'Thanks for agreeing to this,' Maya said. 'And for sticking with us. The lesson won't be exactly as planned but I'll keep to it as closely as I can.'

'No problem,' he said.

The emotion that had leaked into his voice stilled her, and she dropped the tea towel she was using to dry her hands. He was standing close, just a foot or so away, and she looked up at him. He looked sincere, and for a second she said nothing, did nothing. She couldn't break her gaze away from his, and he didn't look away either. The urge to reach out to him almost overwhelmed her, but she knew it would spook him, knew it wasn't what he wanted. She wasn't sure it was what she wanted either. He'd proved today how easily he could hurt her.

She nodded. 'Let's forget about it for now. Are you okay with these two for a second?' she asked, knowing that she was pushing her luck but hustling off to the pantry.

With the door closed, she leant back against one of the shelves and took a deep breath, trying to slow her heartbeat before she went back outside.

She didn't know quite what to make of Will's revelations. It wasn't her he was fighting, it was his past, his memories. She should feel pleased, but knowing everything that stood between Will and happiness made him feel further away. He'd opened up, but he'd hurt her too, and her feelings for him had never been so conflicted. How could she imagine that anything might happen with a man who could cut her so effortlessly? But how could she ever walk away from the bond she felt strengthening with every conversation?

Finally, feeling somewhat calmer, she grabbed the pizza bases and toppings she'd prepped earlier and shuffled her way back into the kitchen. Will greeted her with a look of relief. Once she'd separated the squabbling children and installed them on high stools Maya started handing out the ingredients and ladling sauce into the middle of each pizza. She was grateful for the noise, the chaos, the distraction, and watched, amused, as Will observed Dylan and Carys attacking the pizzas with zeal. She'd made pizza with them once before—it wasn't the first time Gwen had dropped them off in a hurry—and they'd both started spreading the sauce around the base. Carys with a spoon and Dylan, somewhat unconventionally, with his hands.

Maya spoke across Dylan's head. 'I hope this is okay? It is what I'd planned for us, but not exactly under these circumstances.'

'It's fine, but—pizza? It doesn't really feel like cooking. I didn't even make the base.'

'It's about the ingredients,' Maya explained, glancing at the bowls on the counter, all of which appeared to have acquired tomatoey handprints. 'I thought we could try a few different things, talk about the different flavours…'

Her voice trailed off as she realised what she'd said. She didn't want to push him further—not just now. She looked up and found his gaze on her, his expression thoughtful.

Did he feel it too?

A connection flared between them. Something holding them together even when they both fought hard against it.

She'd caught him looking at her, and she couldn't help but wonder if he liked what he saw. And then there were moments when everything stilled, when she saw, heard, felt only him. Heat crept up her cheeks as she remembered how he'd pulled her close after bandaging her finger, how much she'd wanted him.

A red slimy hand slapping onto her arm snapped her back to the present.

'I've finished!' Dylan shouted.

Maya forced her thoughts about Will away, hoping she'd been able to keep them from her face, and looked down at the three pizzas on the counter. Two were loaded with sauce and cheese and toppings. The one at the end had just a perfect circle of rich red sauce.

'Dylan, Carys, why don't you tell Will which are your favourite toppings. I don't think he can decide which ones he wants best.' It seemed like a good idea, enrolling the children to help teach Will. She sensed that they'd pushed each other as far as they could today. Using the kids as her proxy would give them both a little space.

When Dylan and Carys declared the pizzas finished she slid them into the oven and started mopping up tomato sauce—the children had got it everywhere, including all over themselves. She handed a clean cloth to Will—the handprints up his arms and across the front of his T-shirt testified to the fact that Dylan had overcome his initial shyness.

Twenty minutes later Maya watched Will as she placed the pizzas in the middle of the table. They'd all agreed to share, and Will gamely reached for one of Dylan's slices, an unusual anchovy-egg-pineapple combination. She wondered if he knew how gross it was going to taste. Probably, she reasoned, but likely he just didn't care. He took a bite of the pizza and Maya couldn't help laughing at the look of disgust on his face—maybe they were getting somewhere after all. This morning they'd covered good flavour contrasts; this afternoon they'd covered bad.

Will saw that Dylan was watching him and faked a grin. 'Mmm, delicious,' he declared, taking another bite.

When the pizzas were finished, Maya's question, 'Who wants pudding?' was greeted with shrieks from the children.

Will helped Maya to carry the plates into the kitchen and tried to avoid tripping over Carys, who had followed them. Their fingers brushed as he passed her the stack of plates and Maya waited for him to flinch. Although he tensed he stayed close; it was she who pulled away. This was dangerous, she told herself. Indulging these feelings would lead to hurt and heartbreak. She almost wished they were arguing again; it made it so much easier to keep this attraction of hers at bay. *Get a grip,* she told herself as she turned away and concentrated on dessert.

She loaded up a couple of trays with the leftovers from elevenses and they carried them back out to the table.

'Okay…' Maya slipped back into teaching mode. The children were giving her the perfect excuse to keep things simple. 'We're all going to make the nicest biscuit or cake that we can with the ingredients on the table. Then we'll all try some of everything. How does that sound?'

She decided that there was no point shying away from the fact that Will had come here to learn, but she could keep the lesson gentle, knowing he didn't need pushing further after this morning.

Thankfully there was not much room for disaster here. She wondered how Will was going to handle this—would their difficult start to the day have had any impact? He reached for the shortbread and she worried that he was going to repeat what she'd made for him this morning. Repetition wasn't a bad way to learn, but it wouldn't exactly inspire confidence that he was making progress.

But he veered away from the shortbread and picked another biscuit instead. He took a spoon and tested some of the whipped cream, the spiced cream, a few of the different types of fruit. Without saying a word he took a spoonful of the spiced cream, spread it deliberately and evenly over the biscuit, and finished it off with neat rows of pineapple.

Will presented the biscuit to her and then leaned in close to the table, watching her face. He looked nervous and she felt a shock of excitement at the knowledge that he was making such an effort for her food, for *her*.

She picked the biscuit from the plate and took a bite. The tang and the sugar from the pineapple worked perfectly with the spiced cream, and the crack of the biscuit between her teeth contrasted beautifully with the smoothness. Delicious. Of course it could be a fluke, but she preferred to believe that maybe this was another baby step in the right direction. At this rate they might even make a proper, grown-up-sized step by the end of their week together. And where would that leave her? If he could do this, start to feel, rather than fight off his emotions, what did that mean for the spark between them?

'Are you okay with Dylan for a few minutes?' Maya asked when they'd finished clearing up. 'I think Carys is ready for a nap.' And *she* was ready for a few minutes away from Will, she admitted to herself.

'What am I meant to do?' he asked, apprehension clear on his face.

'Just have some fun,' she said. Did it always have to be so hard? 'Read a book, I think there are some in the bag Gwen dropped off. Build a tower out of something, or play football in the garden. I'll only be ten minutes.'

She headed upstairs with Carys, drowsy on her shoulder; then tucked her into her bed and gave her blonde curls a stroke. As she watched the little girl fall asleep, enjoying the calm and quiet her mind could find when she was away from Will, shouts erupted from the garden. Maya hurried to the window, worried about Dylan, but when she looked down she saw that two of her plant pots had been requisitioned as goalposts, and that the noise was just part of Dylan's elaborate goal celebrations. She glanced towards the bed, making sure that Carys hadn't been disturbed, and then leant against the window frame, watching the boys playing in the garden.

Will was running with the ball, a grin on his face and his body loose and relaxed. He gave an exaggerated dummy, but then deliberately lost the ball to Dylan, who ran determinedly towards the goal. With only a metre or two to go, and Will fake running dad-style behind him, Dylan's foot landed on top of the ball and started to slip. Maya raced to the door, knowing that he was about to fall and wanting to get to the garden before the inevitable tears and bruises.

When she reached the hallway downstairs she realised she couldn't hear any shouts, any tears, and then panic really kicked in. With a hurt child, quiet was always bad.

Maya ran through the kitchen and out through the back door, full of dread. Red-faced and breathless, she reached the garden, but Dylan was running about without a mark on him. Will, on the other hand, sported an impressive grass stain down his left arm and his jeans and his elbow oozed blood.

'Is everything okay?' Maya gasped. 'I saw Dylan trip and—'

'Will caught me!' Dylan shouted. 'But then he fell over too.'

Will shrugged. 'It was nothing; we're fine. But we need a goalie. Are you game?' His voice was a little tentative, as if he was as unsure as she about where they stood with one another this afternoon.

She gave him a long, considered look, trying to assimilate this fun, fearless man playing games in the garden with the one who had snapped and snarled at her this morning. Impossible. But she saw his words as what she hoped they were: an olive branch.

'Go in goal, Maya!'

After another glance at Will she kicked off her sandals and took up position between the plant pots as the boys kicked the ball between them.

Will laughed at something Dylan said and she found herself fascinated by the carefree happiness on his face. She'd never seen him look like that before, and it threw into stark contrast the expression he usually wore. In it she saw the extent of his grief, the control he must constantly exert in order to keep his emotions at bay. A few hours ago she'd been ready to pack his bags for him and show him the door. But this glimpse of the man Will could be, if only he allowed himself to be happy, changed her mind.

'Thanks so much again, Maya,' Gwen said as she steered the children towards the door late that afternoon.

'It's no trouble,' Maya said, trying not to sound as weary as she felt.

It had been no trouble since she was a teenager, stepping in to help in a crisis. It was hard to say no, especially when someone just turned up on your doorstep with an emergency. Occasionally, when she was reorganising her day in order to accommodate an urgent favour that just couldn't wait, she wondered what it would be like to say no. But then why *shouldn't* she help her neighbours and friends? Certainly not just because of a little inconvenience.

Will walked up behind her as she was saying goodbye at the door and Gwen looked at him with obvious admiration. Maya blushed and rushed to introduce him. 'Gwen, this is Will Thomas—he's on the cookery course this week.'

Will reached past Maya to shake Gwen's hand, and

stayed close, though he never let their bodies touch. Maya craved the feel of his solid bulk against her, but knew she mustn't lean in to him.

'Pleasure to meet you,' Gwen said. 'I'm so sorry; I didn't realise that Maya had a course this week. I hope the children didn't get in the way?'

'It's fine—we had fun,' Will reassured her.

Maya stayed at the door to wave at the children, who were shouting goodbye from the back of the car. She had to step back a little to close the door and for a fraction of a second Will's body pressed up against her. Maya held her breath, wondering when she was going to make herself move away. When he would move. But neither of them did. Not until she felt herself relax just a fraction.

Will stepped back from her and Maya looked out of the door one last time, desperate to hide the blush she was certain was rising on her cheeks. She was furious with herself, with him, and so very hurt. She hadn't *meant* to step into him like that—she'd just needed to get out the way of the door. But in that moment when they were touching she'd wondered what it might mean…if it meant anything at all. With one decisive step backwards Will had told her everything she needed to know—a banner couldn't have been clearer: *Not Interested. Off Limits. Back Off.*

'So, peace at last,' she said, trying to cover the pain of his rejection with false cheer as she walked back to the kitchen and started tidying. 'You don't have to do that,' she said, when Will followed her into the room and started to help.

'It's fine. About this morning…'

The last thing Maya wanted was to rehash this morning's harsh words. They'd tried so hard to get back on track, and it had worked—right up until that moment at the door.

She held up a hand to stop him. 'Look, I think we both

said things we didn't mean. I think that, if we can, we should just forget about it and try and move on. If you still want to stay, that is?'

'I do,' he said. 'And I will try. I *am* trying.'

'I'm glad.' She fell silent for a long moment; she *was* glad—whether that was a good idea or not. 'Right, I'd scheduled a couple of free hours before dinner, so feel free to go for a walk, or...' he was already reaching for his phone '...do some work. I'll meet you back here at six.'

'Sure.' The look of relief on his face at the prospect of a couple of hours away from her stung, but she stored the feeling away for when she needed a reminder of why developing feelings for Will was a seriously bad idea.

At six o'clock Maya walked back into the kitchen, not feeling quite as refreshed as she'd hoped. She'd planned to have a quick shower and change her clothes, but the menus she'd been developing for a garden party later in the month had absorbed her so much that time had slipped past unnoticed.

As she reached the kitchen door she realised how much she wanted to look her best around Will. Of course he might not notice—or care; that was why he was here, right? Because he didn't appreciate the sensory aspects of life. But surely he knew enough about women to know what he liked? Maybe it was better like this, she reasoned. Keeping him at bay with a crumpled skirt and frizzy hair. It seemed easier than trying to keep her own feelings in check.

When she walked through the door into the kitchen Will was ready and waiting, a chef's apron tied around his waist. He was still trying. She broke into a smile despite herself.

'So, Will, what do you do when you're not working?'

It was a brave conversational gambit, Maya acknowledged as she took a bite of pastry, given his usual reaction when she asked him to talk about himself. But small talk had to start somewhere. They couldn't eat *every* meal in silence.

'I work a lot,' he replied, looking a little uncomfortable but not yet running for the hills. 'It doesn't leave time for anything else.'

No mixed signals there, she thought, her mind drifting back to the moment when he had stepped away from her earlier. She stored the thought away again: protection against future weakness on her part.

'But what about you?' he added, skilfully turning the conversation away from himself—a trick Maya guessed he'd performed more than once. 'How long have you been running your business?'

'Me?' She knew that he was deflecting her questions, but she grinned anyway. Just the thought of the business that she'd built always had that effect on her. It delighted her, thinking of how many people she'd cooked for and taught over the past few years. And talking about her was still talking. An infinite improvement on last night. 'I've been going for four years now.'

'You've built quite a reputation in such a short time,' Will said. 'And I know new catering businesses often struggle in the early years.'

He looked impressed, and she guessed that his business brain was busy calculating her turnover, gross profit and costs per head. He probably couldn't help but think of her business as an accumulation of figures. She almost felt insulted, but knew that wouldn't be rational. She couldn't change the way he saw the world—all she could do was try and make a little room in it for the things he wanted to learn. But perhaps by the end of the week he'd be able to see the parts of her business that she really loved—the relief on a client's face when she pulled off a perfect béarnaise sauce in thirty-degree heat, the sigh of pleasure when a customer took a bite of a duck breast cooked to the perfect shade of pink, the sparkle in someone's eyes when their runny poached egg oozed over delicately smoked salmon.

'And this place?' he asked, gesturing towards the cottage with his arm and looking—to Maya's delight—genuinely interested. 'Have you been here since you started?'

'No. I used to have a kitchen in London, to be close to my clients. But I bought this place because I needed somewhere to get away from it all. I find London so…cold. So unfriendly. I wanted somewhere I could relax and feel part of a community.'

'And how's that working out for you? Babysitting aside?'

She looked up to find his gaze on her, an astute look in his eye. She couldn't shake the feeling that he was criticising her, even though she couldn't exactly figure out why.

'I like it.' She spoke slowly, treading carefully. 'It makes such a difference, living somewhere you can get to know people. Big cities are so anonymous. So lonely.'

'So many people to meet,' Will countered.

'I prefer it here. The sense of community. It's…'

'Familiar?' Will suggested.

Maya shook her head, as if dislodging a troubling thought. 'What's wrong with that?'

'Nothing, I suppose. I think I'd miss the variety, though. In a city there's always someone new to meet.'

Always someone new to disappoint, Maya thought. Another person to try and please, wondering the whole time if she'd figured them out right. No, it was better here, where she knew her neighbours, knew her community, and clients found her through word of mouth.

'Maybe you should try it more often?' Maya suggested. 'Taking a break in the country.'

She watched the start of a smile form at the corners of Will's mouth, saw the fine lines around his eyes that told her it was starting to spread. And then as quickly as it had begun it was gone. Replaced by a look of complete professional calm.

'I don't think that'll be possible,' he said. 'So, have you always cooked?' Once again he steered conversation away from himself.

'No,' Maya said, trying to decide whether she was more disappointed or relieved that Will hadn't taken her words as an invitation to come and stay with her again. She hadn't meant them that way. The words had just slipped out before she'd had a chance to think about the damage they might do. 'The kitchen was always my mother's domain at home.'

'And you didn't cook together?' His blank face held for a beat and then, for a brief moment, Maya saw the shadow of profound pain cross his features.

'No. I would have just been in the way.' She tried, but she couldn't keep the sadness out of her voice. She'd been so close to that chill in recent days, to the iciness that only memories of her parents could bring. She'd spent the last ten years trying to banish it, to force it from her life by creating colour and happiness wherever she could, but it seemed that tonight it was determined to follow her.

'So what made you decide to set up your business?' Will asked.

She imagined he had spotted her distress and thought he was steering the conversation back onto safer ground. But she couldn't let him run like that. Eventually he was going to have to face some of those emotions he seemed so scared of. You couldn't divide life into business and feelings, and she couldn't disconnect her business from the money that had started it. She shouldn't—couldn't—expect him to face his pain and not do the same, encourage him to stay while running away herself.

'My parents gave me the money to start the business. It arrived one day out of the blue and it was enough for my culinary training and to start the business I'd been thinking about.'

Will looked uncomfortable—no doubt because the conversation had taken another turn into the personal. 'I'm sure they're very proud,' he said, almost as if by rote.

Maya gave an involuntary snort at the thought of her parents being proud of anything she'd done. The look on Will's face told her it hadn't gone unnoticed.

'You're not close to your parents?' he asked.

Maya let out a long sigh. 'I've only seen them a handful of times in the last decade,' she said. 'They live abroad—the Caribbean, the last time I heard. They send money occasionally, but that's all they do.' The heaviness in her chest seemed to drag at her shoulders, closing her in on herself. 'I wanted so much to make them proud, but they aren't. It doesn't matter what I do, how hard I work.'

She fought against the pressure in her chest, pushing her shoulders back, painting on a smile, determined not to let her parents spoil this evening. But they'd both dropped into a thoughtful silence.

'Anyway,' Maya declared eventually, determined the night wouldn't continue in that sombre mood, 'enough about that. Do you want to check on dessert or shall I?'

Will gave a small sigh—of relief, she guessed—and even managed a smile.

He disappeared into the kitchen with their empty plates in his hands and a grim expression on his face. Maya listened as the oven door opened and then closed, glad to have a few moments to gather her thoughts. She never spoke to anyone about her parents, and the wrench she'd felt at her heart as she recounted their sad relationship had made her realise how hard Will must be finding his time here. She felt a stab of sympathy.

Will returned a couple of minutes later with two bowls of perfectly golden pie and steaming custard. Maya breathed out a sigh of relief. She'd have eaten it whatever it looked like, but this was even better than she'd hoped for.

'Okay?' Will asked as he placed the bowls on the table.

'Perfect.'

The rest of the evening passed pleasantly enough, and the easiness that was creeping into their conversation helped her shake off the memory of her parents' rejection. But it was strange, Maya thought as she got ready for bed later than night, that she still knew so little about this man who was sharing her house. Even though they'd talked all through dinner, he was still a stranger to her.

CHAPTER FIVE

'A FARMERS' MARKET. That sounds great. And we're going there because…?'

Maya smiled. Fake and forced his enthusiasm might be, but at least Will was trying. She'd been prepared for terse Will this morning, after she'd heard him tapping away on his laptop after she'd gone upstairs last night, and again when she'd headed down this morning, but despite the black bags under his eyes he was making an effort.

Even exhausted he looked delicious, she thought, trying not to lick her lips. A little ruffled, not quite the composed, serene man she was used to. He looked altogether more human, and harder to resist.

'No one reason in particular.' She reached for the coffee pot to distract herself and poured them both a second cup. 'Let's just go, try and enjoy it, and see at the end of the day what we both got out of it.'

'But it's a market,' Will persisted.

Maya could see him trying to understand.

'So we'll be buying food—is that not the point?'

Maya took a sip of coffee and started a slow, deliberate count to ten.

'We have more than enough food for the week already, actually. I want you to try and go into this without any preconceptions. A shopping trip doesn't *have* to be about filling the cupboards.'

He nodded slowly, and Maya was worried by the look
of intense concentration on his face. He was overthinking this already, and they hadn't even left the house. But
she told herself to stay positive. They'd had plenty of set-
backs, but Will was making progress, learning. She looked
up again from her coffee, and found Will watching her intently. A blush rose to her cheeks, but she couldn't make
herself look away.

For days now she felt as if she'd been running from this,
but sitting here, sharing breakfast with this man, suddenly
felt overwhelmingly intimate.

She knew all too well the effect that one's company
could have on your mood. Her lonely childhood had led
to a miserable adolescence, and she knew now, but hadn't
been able to see then, that unhappiness bred unhappiness.
It was only after the magical day when she'd cooked that
first meal for her university housemates that she'd realised
that a smile was contagious too.

So she fixed hers back in place: today she would project nothing but delight. Even if it killed her.

Her mind wandered as they drank their coffee and she
found herself wondering what Will must think of her. He'd
made it abundantly clear that he didn't understand her, that
he had never come across anyone like her before. But did
he *like* her? That first day in his office his eyes had swept
her, up and down. No doubt he'd been comparing her to
the glossy women who worked for him. She'd spied them
through the glass walls and partitions and met the perfect
example in Rachel, Will's elegant assistant.

But since then there had been those moments when
she'd felt his eyes following her as she moved about the
kitchen, or he would look startled when she turned to him,
as if he had been caught doing something he shouldn't.

And now, with his eyes on her face as they shared
breakfast for two, she considered that he might like what

he saw. She panicked. How could she not panic when faced with those eyes—grey, the colour of a winter sky, but somehow not as cold, not as hard as they had once seemed? One of them should speak. One of them had to break this silence. Her mug slipped from her fingers and shattered on the cool, tiled floor of the terrace. She hadn't realised her grip on it had loosened to such an extent.

She dropped to her knees and started gathering pieces of the mug—until the sudden appearance of Will's hand on her wrist stopped her dead.

'Let me,' he said in a conspiratorial tone. 'Your hands have suffered enough.'

He took a piece of china from her and Maya sat back on her heels, still too stunned to do anything useful. She shook her head, trying to dislodge the cloudy feeling that her shared look with Will had caused, and went to find the dustpan and brush. Perhaps it was just a strange manifestation of cabin fever, she told herself. But she was frightened of what that look might mean. It had been easy to write off her developing feelings for him, not allowing herself to indulge her crush when she knew that a relationship would be impossible. But what if that was changing? What if he *was* capable of more? She would never know what might happen without showing him how she felt, but if he knew and knocked her back she wasn't sure she could bear the rejection.

Will barely hid a snigger when he saw her battered old four-wheel drive, painted a joyful shade of magenta, and she half expected him to insist on driving his car—even though, from the look of the paintwork, this was the first time his sports car had been outside the M25. But he said nothing and climbed into the front seat without a word of protest. She smiled at this lack of pride.

As they stepped out of the car at the farmers' market

she saw Will take in the scene and carefully watched his face for a reaction. Some slight tension around the eyes showed her that he was feeling uneasy, but he was here, and at the moment that was all that mattered. She, on the other hand, could not stop herself from beaming, taking a deep breath, trying to catch the smells of the stalls nearest to her.

To her surprise, Will's face broke into the hint of a smile. She'd seen his smile so rarely she'd almost forgotten how it transformed his face and lit up his eyes; it felt like a gift—another delicacy to add to the ones she knew were waiting for her on the market stalls.

'You look happy to be here,' he commented, and she was thrilled that his voice sounded light, untroubled.

'How can I not be? I know what's in store for us once we get started.'

'And what's that?' He looked suspicious.

'Well, I don't know about you, but I'm thinking cheese, fruit, bread—maybe some cured meat. That'll be lunch sorted. And then cake.' At the sight of apprehension creeping into Will's face she reached out and brushed her hand against his arm. 'Don't look so worried.'

As she withdrew she could hear the thudding of her heartbeat in her ears, and wondered whether she'd given herself away, made her attraction too obvious. But he didn't seem to have noticed. Instead the corners of his mouth lifted in a small grin.

'This market is like a theme park for you,' he said. 'You look like Dylan did yesterday when you brought out the pudding.'

'I can't help it,' she said, laughing, relieved that he'd not read anything into her gesture. 'I mean, just *smell* it. It's incredible.'

Her jaw dropped slightly in surprise when he laughed along with her.

'So,' Maya said, 'do you want to stick together or separate?' She guessed that being surrounded by food like this might be a little intense for him, that he might want some space while he eased into it.

'Let's stick together,' he said, and she felt a warm glow starting to spread in her chest. 'I can learn more that way,' he added, and she crashed back down to earth. *Right*. He was here to learn—that was all. Because he wanted something from her, not because he wanted *her*.

They drifted from stall to stall, tasting and snacking, and Maya had never been more aware of another person's presence. When they stopped she had to school her hips to prevent them from leaning into him. Had to consciously stop herself trying to breathe in his scent. When her hand brushed against his as they were both reaching for the same cracker to sample a rich, spicy chutney, she let out a small gasp and had to feign a fierce competitiveness for the last unbroken cracker to hide her spontaneous reaction. She couldn't show him how she felt, couldn't even hint at it, because if he were to know and to reject her again it might just break her.

'Have you been to a market like this before?' Maya asked as they wandered on, making small talk, trying to distract herself.

A sudden look of pain on Will's face warned her that she'd wandered into dangerous territory. *Again*. Maya floundered. She hated herself for a moment for causing him anguish, but knew that such moments were necessary—were part of what Will had asked her for. It seemed every time she tried to speak to him she managed to hit a nerve, touch on some subject that brought those shutters behind his eyes crashing down.

'Once.'

And they were back to monosyllables. 'Did you enjoy it?' She couldn't keep tiptoeing around these questions.

Will had asked her to teach him to appreciate food, and these questions, this pain she was causing him, were all part of it. To her surprise he stopped walking and looked at her intently.

'Yes,' he said eventually, slowly. 'I'd completely forgotten. I went with my family when I was thirteen...fourteen. Just before—' He stopped. 'I ate so much cheese I was nearly sick.' The distress on his face was replaced with a melancholy smile. 'I've not thought about that day for years.'

She had to force down a smile. She knew how sad he seemed, but this revelation was another little sign of their progress, that her teaching was working.

They turned and strolled on, and Will gave her another small smile as they came upon a stall selling cheese.

'Should I ration you?' Maya joked as he tried a couple of the samples, keeping her hands well away from him this time.

'Julia tried, but I didn't listen. She had no sympathy when I felt ill.'

'I don't blame her. She sounds like a sensible sort of woman.' She kept her voice light, tried not to show how thrilled she was that he was talking about his past, about food, about himself.

'She was,' Will replied, still smiling. 'But Neil was a soft touch. He brought me tea and toast and let me watch telly all afternoon.' Will's face fell then, and he turned purposefully away.

More pain there, she thought. More that she didn't understand.

'What's next on your list?' he asked, his voice harder, almost terse.

Maya blinked, taken aback by this sudden change in mood. 'I'm heading for the bakery.'

'Right. I'll meet you there,' Will replied. 'I left my phone in the car. Can I have your keys to go get it?'

She handed them over, and with that he stalked away towards the car park. She stood and watched him go, feeling an ache in her chest at how easily he could walk away, how easily he rejected her company.

'So who's your date?'

Maya turned at the abrupt question to find Gwen behind her.

'Oh, no. That's Will,' Maya reminded her, pulling herself together. 'He's on my course—he was at the cottage, remember?'

Gwen nodded, but her eyes were still following Will as he walked towards the car.

'Hmm… The way he keeps looking over here at you, I'm not sure I believe that.'

'Really?' The question sneaked out before Maya could stop it. 'He keeps looking over?'

'See for yourself.'

Maya risked a quick glance over her shoulder and found Gwen was right. Will was looking back at her. She gave a small sigh, because what if he *was* attracted to her? She'd lived the best part of twenty years with people who were cold and unavailable, and they had made her miserable. And no two words better described the man who had pitched up on her doorstep on Sunday. There was no man on earth attractive enough to make her want to repeat the experience.

But she'd seen Will change over the past few days, seen a light at the end of the tunnel that suggested that his frostiness wasn't permanent. But without that to hide behind she was frightened. Because if Will was open to a relationship the question changed. It wasn't whether he wanted a relationship; it was whether he wanted *her*.

'So he likes you—and I'm guessing from the colour of your cheeks that you like him too. What's stopping you both?'

'Gwen.' Maya tried to speak firmly, knowing that she had to stop this train of thought in Gwen's mind as well as her own. 'There's absolutely nothing going on with Will. How are the kids?'

'Oh, they're fine. Actually, the kids are the reason I came over to talk to you. You remember it's Dylan's birthday party this weekend? Well, I was so sure that I had everything sorted, and I thought I had ordered the fairy cakes, but I've just been to see Elaine—you know, from the bakery—and she says I never placed the order. She has a wedding this weekend and no time to do them. I'm a complete dud in the kitchen and I wondered if there was any chance that you—?'

Gwen was getting a little frantic, her voice rising and her hands gesticulating more and more widely. Maya reached out to catch one of her hands; she hated to see anyone upset, especially when she was able to help. She knew the question was coming, and even though she had no idea how she was going to manage it she knew that she was going to say yes. What else could she do? If she wanted to keep Gwen as a friend she'd have to find a way to do this for her.

'Of course I can bake some cakes, Gwen, if that's what you're asking.'

'Oh, Maya, thank you so much. The kids love your baking and I know that they'll be so pleased. You're a lifesaver. I don't know what we'd all do without you.'

Maya didn't let her smile drop until Gwen had breezed away towards the car park and tried not to think about what whipping up a hundred iced fairy cakes would do to her schedule. It was already tight, with prep and planning to do for the private functions booked in next week, and Will's dinner to prepare for if he got through the course. But what was she meant to do—say no? She cringed at the thought.

'Anything the matter?'

Will appeared behind her, wearing a calmer expression than when he'd walked away. Maya suppressed a sigh of disappointment. Once again when he was faced with something he didn't want to think about, something he didn't want to feel, instead of sharing it with her he'd taken himself off and come back smoothed over and closed off.

'Nothing,' Maya said, her mind returning to her schedule, still trying to work out how to rearrange it to fit the baking in.

'Dylan and Carys's mum—did she upset you?'

He sounded genuinely concerned, she thought, and the touch of his hand on her arm shocked her into looking up at him. How did he do this? Going to automaton and back, constantly cycling. It was dizzying, trying to keep up, never knowing which Will she was going to get.

'I'm not upset,' she said, wondering at the way sensation seemed to spread from his fingertips throughout her body in swirling streams of warmth.

'Then why did you look so serious?' he asked, and his words snapped her back to the present.

She looked down at where he touched her arm and was surprised when her skin looked normal. She had half expected to be able to see ripples and waves dancing like light on her skin.

'She just wants me to make the fairy cakes for Dylan's birthday on Saturday.' There was no hiding the breathiness in her voice and she wondered if Will would notice it, if he would understand it.

He looked surprised. 'Surely you can't have time for that? You told me what your schedule's like at the moment. I take it you said no.'

'Oh, well, I hate to say no if I can help.'

'You said no to me.'

His words surprised her, and she looked up into his

eyes. He'd said the words softly, quietly, without heat or anger, but she sensed hurt behind them.

'That was different.' Because he'd already hurt her so much by then what had she had to lose? She couldn't have felt any lower than the moment he'd refused to try her food; refused to give it—*her*—a chance.

He looked at her for a long moment before he spoke, seeming to absorb her words. 'Right.'

She felt his scrutiny in her mind, her character.

'And this happens a lot, I'm guessing? Crises. Emergencies. Cakes. Babysitting. And you never say no?'

She crossed her arms, uncomfortable with the turn this conversation had taken. Of course she didn't say no. Why would she want to be lonely her whole life? Accommodating emergencies, helping people out when they needed it—it was worth it to have friends in her life. People who cared about her. And this week was about him, not her, anyway. She didn't need to be judged.

'It's nothing, Will. I just help out my friends if I can.'

But that wasn't enough—not for him, it seemed—because he took a half-step closer to her, kept his gaze on her face as he ran his hand through his hair and rested it at the nape of his neck. 'She's taking advantage,' he said.

Of course she wasn't. She just needed some help. Maya wondered what had Will so riled up. 'It won't impact on the course, if that's what you're worried ab—'

'It's you I'm worried about.'

He stepped forward again, his hands reaching for hers, but this time Maya took a step back, shocked at the strength of feeling in his voice.

'I'm just trying to be a good friend.' But his words had shaken her, and her voice wobbled as she tried to understand what he'd said, as she thought back over her friendship with Gwen, looking for evidence she could use to refute him.

He dropped his hands and crossed his arms after she flinched away. 'This isn't about her at all. It's about you. About you wanting to please her—please everyone. Is she a good friend to you?' he asked, stepping closer again. 'Or does she take advantage because she knows you can't say no?'

Maya raced through memories, looking for something, anything she could throw at him to prove him wrong. Gwen wasn't taking advantage, was she? Maya had never thought of it that way, never questioned whether there was anything wrong with a neighbour asking a favour. She assumed any of her friends would do the same for her if she asked. It was just that she never had—never wanted to be a nuisance, to put people out.

'It's not like that,' she said, but her voice was small, full of the doubt she was feeling. Why would he turn her doing something nice into something bad? Why did he even care? 'Don't try to make it sound as if she's doing something wrong.'

'I'm not saying *she's* doing anything wrong.' His voice was low and vaguely threatening. 'I'm saying *you* are.'

'That's ridiculous.' She bristled at his words, his accusation, and threw her hands in the air. 'How can you possibly twist it like that?'

'I don't think what you're doing is the problem, Maya. I think the reason you're doing it is. So prove me wrong. Why is it so impossible to say no? Why are you so desperate to keep your neighbour happy?'

My parents— She shut down the thought before it could fully take form. How could her making cakes be about her parents? Other than the odd Christmas card and a couple of cheques, she'd not spoken to them in years. She barely thought about them. And yet she'd never stopped trying to impress them, trying to make them love her.

Will's calm expression belied the raw, ripping pain his questioning had caused.

'That's enough.' She spat out the words as she plucked the car keys from his hand and turned towards the car park. She ignored him calling after her. Tears pricked behind her eyes and she fought to keep them there, to stop them running down her cheeks. Tears wouldn't solve anything, she knew. The only thing that kept the sadness away was acting relentlessly happy. It was what she had to do, what she'd been doing for years to chase away the shadows of her childhood—and Will had seen straight through it.

Will stood in the middle of the market and watched Maya walk away from him. Torn between chasing after her and giving her space, he just stood for a few moments, struggling with indecision. The twist of guilt in his stomach reminded him that he'd taken things way too far. There was no hiding from the pain that he'd seen in Maya's face, and the knowledge that he'd done that to her—again—was devastating.

He hadn't set out to criticise her, to hurt her. He'd been genuinely worried when he'd seen how anxious Gwen had left her and had wanted to make her see that she didn't have to do this—didn't have to say yes every time someone asked a favour. But as he'd been speaking he'd started to realise where he fitted into this pattern too. She wasn't bothered about teaching him anything; she just couldn't bear that he hadn't liked her food and was determined to change his mind.

He thought back to the look on her face that day he'd first met her, when he hadn't given her food his full attention. Back then he hadn't known her well enough to recognise how hurt she'd been that he hadn't liked her food—or hadn't said that he did. But he could see now how much other people's opinions mattered to her. And not the way it did with the people he normally came into contact with, who either wanted the approval of their boss or a newspaper column.

When Maya felt the disapproval or disappointment of others it caused her real pain. He flinched at the thought of it. There was no point trying to please people all the time. He had discovered that long ago. Through a series of foster parents and children's homes he had learned that it didn't matter how well he behaved, how charming he tried to be—it didn't matter whether the people he lived with loved him or not—because he always got hurt.

And it wasn't even as if she had to *try* to please him. Just the sight of her, the smell of her, brought a smile to his face whether he wanted it or not.

But even if he'd judged her right, guilt over the way he had spoken to her gnawed at his gut, and he set off towards the car at a slow walk. He knew that the pain his memories of the market had thrown up had coloured his words. That he'd been striking out against Julia and Neil as much as he had against Maya. He breathed a sigh of relief when he saw the bright pink vehicle still parked where they had left it. He knocked on the window and Maya lifted her face from her hands and opened the door.

'I'm sorry. That was out of line.'

Maya nodded slowly.

Will climbed in the passenger seat before she could change her mind, and then turned to look at her, not knowing what sort of welcome to expect.

'Out of line,' she mumbled, 'but maybe a little true.'

He'd wanted to help, pointing out that she didn't have to constantly try to accommodate everyone, that a friendship should go two ways, but it had backfired, and he'd hurt her. He felt a strange ache in his arms, and knew the only thing that would cure it would be to pull her to him, try and soothe the pain that he'd caused. But he couldn't do it—because where might it lead? It could never be just one touch, he knew. The passion that he'd felt the few times their skin had brushed told him how much he had to fear from her. That if he ever got her in his arms he'd never want to let go. And that was too big a risk.

He opened his mouth to speak but she shook her head slowly, thoughtfully. 'Not now, Will. Let's just get home.'

They arrived back at the cottage and Maya went straight to the kitchen with the few bags of food they'd bought. Will followed behind at a distance. He knew that he should leave, that he'd said too much, felt too much already, but he didn't want to. And somehow the fear he felt of confronting his memories was rivalled by the fear that Maya might make him go and he would never see her again.

He gave a small shudder. He had sworn fifteen years ago that he would never let anyone close enough that losing them would hurt, but somehow over the past days Maya had crept beneath his defences.

He tried to imagine the life he would be going back to—his dull, grey, cold life. And he realised that all the things that had terrified him when he'd met her, and that still terrified him—her passion, her joy, her colour—he couldn't imagine life without any more. He didn't want his life as it had been before her. Yet he couldn't risk contemplating a life *with* her.

Eventually she returned from the pantry and found him leaning against the counter.

'So what now?' she asked.

'I'm sorry,' he said again. 'I shouldn't have said what I did.' His eyes fell on the kettle. 'Should I make some tea?'

Maya laughed—a brittle chuckle that sounded as if it had travelled through tears. Tea? It did seem a little ridiculous. But it was what Julia would have done, and he didn't know what else to suggest.

'So…tea? Is that what Julia would have recommended?'

He knew that her use of his foster mother's name was a challenge. If he wanted to stay they couldn't keep dodging this—he couldn't keep dodging *her*. Eventually they'd have to talk. And he was the one who had led them here; he'd decided to get personal. He'd brought up *her* parents. She didn't seem to want to talk about them any more than he wanted to talk about his. But if they were going to see this week through then he had to stop running.

'Probably,' he said. 'She thought there was little that couldn't be fixed with a pot of tea.'

'Like I said, she sounds like a sensible woman.' Maya took a deep breath. 'Tell me about her.'

At every mention of Julia Will's heart gave an involuntary clench. He fought hard against the feeling, pushed it out of his chest as he had learned to at the age of fifteen, had been practising ever since. But what could he do other than what Maya asked? If he didn't she'd ask him to go, give up on him. And if he went back to the office without her on board it would be a disaster for his career *and* Julia House. At least he tried to convince himself that that was the reason why he was about to do this—why he was sorting through words and memories to find the best place to start his story. That this was why he was so desperate to stay, couldn't contemplate walking away from her yet.

'I was in care from when I was a toddler.'

He sat down at the table as he started speaking and nudged the handles of the mugs and teapot with his fingers, focusing on them, not brave enough yet to look up and meet Maya's gaze. But then she reached across the table and her fingertips brushed against his. He wondered if it was an accident, if she was aiming for the teapot, but then her fingers twined with his and she gave his hand a gentle squeeze.

'I've never known the full reasons why I was taken in by Social Services, but a family couldn't be found to adopt me and I lived the next few years in group homes. I guess the longer I was there, living without a real family, the harder it was to find someone who would take me. When I was about twelve Julia and her husband, Neil, visited the home. They were registering as foster parents and wanted to meet some of the children who might be placed with them. I don't know what Julia saw in me...'

When Maya laced her fingers with his a little tighter, brushed her thumb across his, he almost drowned in the sensations it provoked. Her touch offered support, courage, sympathy, strength. Finally he looked up and met her gaze. In her face he saw nothing of their angry words, no trace of the hurt that he'd inflicted on her. Her eyes were sad, but somehow he knew that it was *his* sadness that was reflected there. She had encouraged him from the moment they met to open up, to engage with her, to show her what he was feeling. And now that he was doing it she didn't shy away. Instead she anchored him with her fingers and listened.

'I didn't go out of my way to be friendly to Julia. By that time all I could think about was keeping my head down and counting down the hours till I could leave the home, leave school, get on with being independent. She came over and chatted to me, and I thought nothing much of it. A few months later I was told they'd like to foster me.'

He took a breath and squeezed Maya's hand, borrowing some of her strength. He knew that he had to lay out all the faults and insecurities and fears that had led to his hurtful words, and just hope that Maya could forgive him.

'I wish I knew what it was about them that made me give it another shot. Maybe I could see it was my last chance to have a family. I was with them for two years before Julia started to get sick. It had taken a long time for us to start to feel like a family, but eventually—somehow—it started to work. There were kick-abouts in the park with Neil, and helping Julia in the kitchen. Sunday lunches and trips to the shops—all the everyday stuff that had baffled me for years.'

When the Wilsons had taken him in he had thought that was it. He had finally found somewhere he could be loved, be safe. He had even dared to start loving them back.

And that had been his biggest mistake.

'When she first got sick none of us realised how bad it was going to get. They'd caught it early, they said, the lump, and so her prognosis was good. In the end it just meant a long, drawn-out year of suffering—for her, for all of us.'

First he had watched as his foster mother had grown thinner and paler. He'd held her hand when her hair fell out. And then, after he had said goodbye to her for the last time, he'd realised his foster father was gone as well—to a dark, lonely, scary place where there was no room for a foster son. So it had been back to the group home.

On the day he'd returned Will had decided two things. One: his memories could do nothing but hurt him, so he would lock them away. Two: he would never let anyone he loved leave him again. And the only way to guarantee that was never to love.

The first of those promises was well and truly broken now, and he couldn't see any way to fix it. But the second…? Maybe he could still salvage that one. He needed to find some limits again, keep Maya at a safe distance. Once he knew that he could see out the week, that she would cater the fundraiser, he would never have to see her again.

'Will, I'm so sorry,' Maya said, and he could see from the tears brimming in her eyes that she was feeling every moment of his pain as he was. 'So your foster dad…' she said eventually. 'Neil?'

'Neil's another story,' Will said, wanting this to be over

now, hoping that he'd explained enough for her to forgive him. 'Can we leave it for another time? Today's been—'

'A lot. I understand.'

'So, did you have anything planned for us this afternoon?' Will asked, briskly untangling his fingers from hers and locking them tightly around a mug. Even the burning heat of the porcelain couldn't mask how empty his hand felt without Maya's palm safely enclosed.

'Er…we were meant to be baking.'

She looked flustered, as if she hadn't realised that she'd reached out for him until he'd broken the connection. He forced himself not to notice the blush that rose on her cheeks.

'Baking's fine.'

'I thought we could try a few different breads,' she said, and he nodded at her vaguely. 'I had a few ideas when we were at the market that I'd love to try out.'

'Fine.' He gripped the mug harder and spotted the way her gaze lingered on his knuckles. She couldn't have failed to notice the shift in the atmosphere, but he refused to dwell on it. This was what he had to do to survive.

She talked him through different types of bread, her voice faltering and unsure, her gaze sneaking sideways at him when she thought he wouldn't notice. He pushed her further and further away from him in his mind with every word. And, as he'd known it would, his world grew duller and colder. But he knew how to live with this bleakness. If he didn't do this now—didn't protect himself—if he fell for her, he wouldn't survive in that world.

By the time he had all his ingredients formed into a smooth dough he thought that he might have found some sort of equilibrium.

'Now you can pretty much pummel it,' Maya announced.

Her blunt words had him snapping up his head to look

her in the eye. She'd watched his retreat, he gathered, and was fighting back.

'You need to knead the dough, but I don't mind how you do it. Fold it, roll it, stretch it, throw it on the counter. It's up to you.'

That he could do. He methodically folded and then pressed the dough with the heel of his hand, exactly as she was, and with each movement he shut out the world a little more until there was nothing left of his memories or the pain. No room for Maya in his new mantra: *Fold, press, turn. Fold, press, turn.*

Eventually, she spoke.

'Will, that'll do.' Her words were sharp, terse.

He wouldn't care.

He looked up at her. 'We're done?'

'We're done. It just needs to go somewhere to prove.'

They were done. That was all he needed to know.

'Will!' she called, just before he disappeared up the stairs, her voice full of trepidation. 'Don't forget we're booked in at the pub for dinner.'

Dinner tonight. There had been something in the paperwork she'd sent over about this. Something to do with palette and identifying flavours and supporting local businesses too. It was an integral part of her week-long cookery course. He sat down on the bed and leaned forward, his elbows resting on his knees. He didn't know if he could do this. It had taken ten minutes of unbroken concentration and repetitive kneading to achieve any semblance of calm and peace.

And then, with one sentence, she'd undone all his solid, unrelenting effort.

He rubbed his forehead with the heel of one hand and reached for his phone with the other. Stroking the smooth glass with his thumb, he scrolled through his emails. He dashed off a couple of replies and then re-read the one from a Julia House board member, passing on Neil's contact details and telling Will that he'd love to be in touch again.

Will's thumb hovered over the 'delete' icon, as it had a dozen times in the past weeks, before he closed the message. He replied to a few more urgent business emails and waited for the familiar action to ease the tension from his shoulders and the ache from his insides. But relief did not come. Even after he'd fired up his laptop and spent an hour going through the Julia House financials he still couldn't shake Maya and the disappointment on her face before he'd come upstairs from his mind.

He stepped into the shower and turned on the taps. It was only when the icy water hit his shoulders that he realised he'd instinctively set the temperature to cold. Even that realisation caused an unwelcome flood of images. The light in Maya's face as she bit into a pastry; the way his skin had scorched when she'd laced her fingers through his, offering silent support; the delight in her eyes as he'd enjoyed her shortbread.

He stepped further under the water and allowed it to pound on his head and drive out the flame of desire the memories had provoked. With his hand resting against the tiles he leant into the spray, letting the heavy stream of water beat at the tension in his muscles. He washed quickly, letting every drop of cold water draw the emotions of the day from him. He would not leave the shower until he could think of the look of hurt on Maya's face without it hurting him. Not until he was sure he could think of her dispassionately. And only when his neck and shoulders felt numb from the cold did he allow himself to turn off the taps and reach for his towel.

He pulled on his charcoal suit and a black shirt and smoothed his hair. When he looked in the mirror he was satisfied with the result. There was nothing on his face to show his struggle. To test his defences, he allowed an image of Maya entry to his mind. Her face that day when he'd answered emails rather than eat her salad. His shoulders tensed, and he had to push hard on the door that kept his guilt out—but it did shut. This was going to be okay, he told himself. He could get through this. But he was under no illusion that tonight was going to be easy. Maya didn't batter her way through his defences; she smiled and laughed and charmed and listened until he threw open the doors and invited her in. He had to be more careful.

CHAPTER SIX

As MAYA WAITED in the kitchen for the sound of Will's steps on the stairs she shifted the waistband of her dress—a bright flowery tea number—and wondered if there was time for her to change. The dress was one of her favourites, and she'd thought that tonight she'd need the cheering effect of the turquoise flowers and the full fifties-style skirt. But now it felt like too much. She had watched Will mentally retreat this afternoon, leaving her with a bland automaton, and somehow turquoise, pink and orange didn't seem quite appropriate any more.

She always took her students to the local pub; it was good to see whether they could identify flavours and techniques, and sample a style of cooking other than her own. It was normally a lively, boisterous evening, with plenty of good food, good wine and good conversation. Well, two of those should be manageable—as long as there wasn't some sort of crisis at the pub—but the last seemed almost impossible. After what had seemed like a major breakthrough earlier, when Will had told her about his childhood, his later silence had seemed like a quid pro quo.

Will fixed his eyes on the dessert menu, determined not to look up until he had found something resembling control. He'd been searching for it all through the meal, but every time he'd thought he had it, every time he'd thought she was safely shut out, he saw something, smelt something, tasted something that brought everything crashing back. When they'd been back at the cottage getting through this evening had seemed simple, if not necessarily easy. All he had to do was keep a safe distance between himself and Maya; shut her out in exactly the same way he'd shut everyone else out over the past fifteen years. It was the only way to stop himself from falling.

'What are you thinking? Dessert?'

And there was the problem. Every time he thought he'd found control she found another way back in, and it didn't seem to him as if she was even trying. It wasn't as if she was pushing, or looking for his weak spots. It was just something about her, the way she overwhelmed all his senses, that made her impossible to ignore.

This time it was a simple question about dessert; last time it had been the sight of pink nail varnish against fiery red hair; the time before that the way the soft cotton of her skirt had brushed against his leg when she'd turned suddenly.

He lowered his menu and looked up to see her watching him. Frustration was etched into her features.

'Fine, if that's what you want,' he replied, keeping his voice carefully neutral.

Her sigh, not quite as supressed as he guessed it was meant to be, cracked his control a little further. He looked up at her again—and wished he hadn't. She was leaning forward on her elbows, examining the menu, and the button at the gently curving neckline of her dress strained and then escaped.

When looking away didn't work he took a long sip of his red wine, hoping it might bring him some measure of calm. But the taste, the flavour, was so *voluptuous* it kept his mind in the one place he shouldn't, *couldn't* allow it to rest.

It was so tempting just to give in. To open his eyes wide and drink in the sight of her, to stop fighting it and let her gravity pull him in. But what happened when he crashed to the ground? He wouldn't endure another loss—had no intention of rebuilding his life again. This time when Maya asked the question he kept his eyes determinedly neck up. They rested on the plump curve of her bottom lip.

No help at all.

'Chocolate pudding,' he declared, surprising himself. Because that was just what this situation needed: rich, gooey, decadent chocolate pudding.

When Maya's tongue darted out to moisten her lip he knew he had to do something drastic.

He drew his mind away from Maya, away from the pub, away from his thoughts. Concentrating all his effort on protecting himself, he ran through columns of numbers in his head. Mentally scrolled through the spreadsheets sitting on his laptop. He calculated gross profits, net profits, tax liabilities and risk exposures. And when he let himself back into the room he could look at Maya without needing to reach across and touch her. Success—for now.

He glanced down at the chocolate pudding—he hadn't even noticed it arrive—with trepidation.

Maya let go of a sigh of relief as the waiter placed her dessert in front of her. She was so tempted just to give up. To tell Will to leave, that she would cater his dinner—anything to end this torturous week. But every time she thought back to everything he had told her, to the way he had gripped her hand when he'd spilled the secrets of his past, she knew that she had come too far to walk away from him now. She just had to get through this cheesecake and then she could go home. No more half-finished sentences, no more monosyllabic answers, no more staring at the tablecloth rather than meeting her eye. She could get home, get out of this dress and go to sleep. A few hours' hiatus from the heartbreak of seeing him give up.

To test her guess as much as anything, she asked, 'How's the chocolate pudding?'

'Fine.'

She flinched. But then held out her spoon, half wondering if she was mad to do it. 'May I?' she asked.

She was about to reach across when Will's spoon, laden with chocolate pudding, appeared in front of her nose. He caught her eye at last and held her gaze in a challenge. She didn't back down. Still Will didn't look away.

The pudding was divine. Rich, moist, decadent. But— and she couldn't resist a small smile of satisfaction—still not as good as hers. She licked her lips, not wanting to waste any of the rich chocolate sauce, or the opportunity to get a reaction from Will. This was the closest he'd felt to her since they'd finished their tea and tackled bread-making earlier. A few hours ago she'd watched stone-cold Will shut the other Will—the one with the beating heart and human emotions—out. She had even seen the physical change as his shoulders and jaw had tensed and his eyes had become unfocussed, as if he were looking through her, not *at* her.

It had hurt so much, knowing that it was deliberate. He'd let her in, let her close, and then regretted it. Had forced himself back out into the cold and left her alone. It had cracked her heart, knowing that even with the bond that had been forged between them over tea and secrets he could walk away from her so easily.

But right now, in this second, he was definitely *here*. His eyes drifted up from her lips to meet her gaze.

Desire was written plainly in his eyes, clear and un-guarded. The knowledge went straight to her belly and then dropped lower, heating, awakening. She couldn't forget all the times that he'd hurt her in the past few days, but she couldn't hide from the intensity of his expression either. Couldn't hide from the fact that he was fighting demons— and perhaps could only win if she stuck with him. If she stuck around, put her heart on the line, she might get hurt. If she walked away without knowing, she definitely would.

And then—*bang*. The shutters slammed hard and she gasped, as if her fingers, her heart, her whole body had been caught by them and crushed. The only consolation she had to temper the pain was that it had seemed harder for him this time—almost as if the battle playing out in his mind was growing fiercer. But whether it was hard or not to shut her out it didn't matter. All she knew for sure was that he kept doing it.

Maya forked cheesecake into her mouth as she tried to soothe the pain in her chest. Perhaps she should take a leaf out of Will's book? She closed her eyes. She would take herself away from here, just for a moment, find some peace. She tried to guess the ingredients of the cake: the usual of course—ricotta, cream, vanilla, a hint of lemon— but there was something else there too. Something unexpected. She kept her eyes closed, not wanting anything from the outside world to distract her, wanting to focus her whole mind on this simple task.

'Maya?'

Her eyes flew open at the sound of his voice. And she cursed her body for its lack of caution.

'Where did you go?' he asked.

'Nowhere.' She didn't bother hiding the hurt from her voice. Why should she spare his feelings when he had no regard for hers? 'I'll get the bill.'

She breathed a sigh of relief as they walked back through the front door, thankful that this night was nearly over. Not even the sight of Will's gorgeous face across the table had made the dinner pleasant.

For some women she supposed it might be the cheekbones that made him so attractive, or the hint of muscles beneath his shirt. For her it was the fine lines that appeared during those rare moments when he smiled, the reminder that he was still human underneath, however hard he fought against it.

He'd barely spoken over dinner. Every time it had looked as if he might, every time she'd seen that light in his eye that told her that he was there, the moment had passed. But perhaps, after how close they had felt this afternoon, tonight was the wake-up call that she needed—a reminder of how disastrous getting involved with Will would be. Because she couldn't live her life waiting for those moments, looking for those lines, waiting for a hint of something more than cold tolerance.

She'd been there before—constantly trying to get some reaction from the people who were meant to love her—and she wouldn't do it again. She knew that she liked making people happy. With Will's input she was starting to see that she liked it a little too much. But that didn't mean she should be looking to spend time with someone she could never please.

'Well, goodnight,' Maya said at the bottom of the stairs.

'You're not coming up?' Will's words were gruff as he crossed his arms.

'No. I need to get back in the kitchen.' She'd never spoken a truer statement. She needed her kitchen; she needed space. She needed distance from him and the pleasure that only her art could bring.

'You look tired,' Will blurted out, and Maya sensed he hadn't meant to say it.

She bit her lip. She wasn't going to let it get to her—wasn't going to let his words hurt her. She knew that he hadn't meant them to cut. He'd not given them—*her*—any thought at all. They'd just spilled from him on the spur of the moment.

And she didn't care that he thought she looked tired, she told herself. She did look tired. She *was* tired. But to have him stand there in his immaculate suit and shirt, with his perfect bone structure only improved by the hint of tomorrow's stubble, and remind her that she didn't quite match up hurt. It was further proof, if she needed it, that even if Will was interested in a relationship she'd be crazy to think he'd be looking for one with her.

'Well, great—thanks for that. I'll see you in the morning,' she said, turning and walking into the kitchen.

She heard the kitchen door open and knew that he'd followed her in. She wished he hadn't. Wished she could have some time to patch up the grazes she'd accumulated that evening from his glancing blows. And she didn't want him to see how much he had hurt her. Somehow that seemed like protection. If he saw her feelings for him then he would feel as if he had to say something. Let her know that he didn't return them. Showing him what she felt would be opening the door to rejection, and she didn't think she'd be able to stand that.

'Maya, I only wanted you to see—'

She whipped around and stared at him, stopping his words with a raised hand. What right did he have to make her try and see anything? He was the one who had her feeling like this: confused, overwhelmed, unsure of herself. With his constant advances and retreats, the unending shifts between them. And now he'd decided to *worry*?

She looked up and met his eyes, and his expression made her gasp. She had never seen him wear a look so intense. Not even when he was talking about his past. And she understood it instantly. Any chef recognised hunger when she saw it.

He took another step closer to her and she took half a one back, trying to preserve the space between them. Trying to protect her heart.

'It's okay, Will.' Her voice shook. She had suspected that he was attracted to her, had seen flashes of interest in his eyes, felt the chemistry between them. But nothing like this. Nothing so raw, so unguarded. 'I *am* tired, but there are a couple of things I need to do tonight.'

The words felt insubstantial, weightless compared to the energy thrumming between them, the intensity with which he held her gaze, the anger, hunger, fear that simmered in the air.

'You're only in here because of the extra job you took on. The cakes for the kids' party.'

That was what he wanted to talk about? Why he was looking at her as if she was a cold glass of water on a hot day? Why his voice had turned rough and low.

'Yes, and I need to get on. So, goodnight.' She couldn't take much more of this. One minute she was drawing small talk from him as if she was extracting a tooth; the next he was marching into her kitchen and picking a fight over her schedule. He'd changed his mood more times than she could count in the last few days…hours. How was she meant to keep up? How was she meant to know what *she* was feeling when one minute he was acting as if she wasn't even in the room and the next was looking at her as if she was everything he needed?

'It's late, you're tired, and you're about to pull an all-nighter because you're afraid of upsetting a neighbour. Why *is* that?'

What the hell did that have to do with anything?

At least it made it easier to know what she was feeling—anger. That was enough. Her face grew hot as she battled to keep her temper. She didn't know why he was pushing this, but it stopped now.

'It's none of your business, Will. I think you should go up.'

'But I think it is my business,' he said, raising his voice.

'Because why ever you're doing this is the same reason I'm here. The same reason you won't cook for someone who doesn't like your food. I'm not here to learn. I'm here so that you can convince me to like you.'

Tears rose behind her eyes, but she used her anger to fight them down. She would *not* let this man drive her to tears. His words were cruel, and felt more so because she knew that he was right. He had taken one look at her life and seen exactly what drove her. Exactly what caused her heart to ache every time she thought of her parents. Exactly what made her so desperate to make everyone around her love her.

But what else was she supposed to do? Go back to her life before, with no love, no affection, not even any warmth? She'd found a way to enrich her life, a way to be around people that made her happy. Was she supposed to turn her back on it because it involved a few late nights and reorganised days?

But part of what Will had said struck home. Perhaps this *wasn't* the way things were supposed to work. All one-way, giving all she had just to get a shaky friendship in return.

Will was wrong about one thing, though. 'You make it sound like I tricked you into this—like I forced you to be here.' She ground the words out through gritted teeth and a tense jaw, not wanting to get drawn into a discussion, wanting to be left alone. But she had to correct him if this was what he thought had led them here.

'You think I'm doing this out of choice?'

'That's exactly what I think,' she said, furious enough to forget her resolve and argue. 'I walked away and you came running after me. Don't turn this around.' She spat the words, flinging her arms wide for effect.

'I had *no* choice,' he said, his face showing his fight for control.

'Really? What was so important that you couldn't find

someone else to cook? We both know you don't care what you eat, so why do this? Why put *me* through this?' Her voice had started to shake with the last words.

'Because Sir Cuthbert Appleby threatened my job and Julia House if I didn't. *That's* why.' His voice broke as he threw the words at her, one hand coming up to rub his forehead and his neck, as if the admission had been painful to expel.

Maya's hand flew to her mouth as she took a step backwards, reeling. *That* was why he had come? Because he'd been threatened? Nothing to do with her. Nothing to do with food or feelings, or anything that he had led her to believe. The shock curdled into hurt as the implications hit home. All this time she'd thought that it was his past that was keeping him from engaging with her. His memories that made him run. But it wasn't that at all. He just didn't want to be here. Didn't want *her*. He never had. Of *course* this was about money. She'd been kidding herself that he was in any way interested in learning anything.

'Maya, listen to me—'

'Just go!' she shouted across his angry words. She didn't want excuses, or even an apology. What she wanted from him had never been on offer. She'd had enough. Enough of his ups and downs, his steps forward and back. She'd watched him change direction so many times now her head was spinning. She just wanted quiet. Wanted her kitchen and her peace. 'I've had enough, Will.' She hoped that careful, reasoned words would make him go. 'I know being here is proving difficult for you, but that's not my fault. I never asked you to come.'

She turned her back to him and started washing her hands. Maybe he'd take the hint and leave her in peace.

'You didn't,' he said, his voice coming from close by her ear, so near that she could feel his warm breath on her skin. 'But I'm here.'

She jumped as two strong hands settled heavily on her waist, and she fought against her body's impulse to enjoy it, to beg for more. She longed for it. For his arms around her, his lips on hers. But she couldn't shake her doubts. What would it do to her if he disappeared again?

'I don't know what this is, Maya,' Will said, turning her to face him.

She couldn't look up and meet his eyes. It would be too much, too intimate. She knew that if she did it she'd give in. But he lifted a hand to her face and cupped her jaw gently, tipping face up towards him. She closed her eyes.

'I don't understand it. If I had a choice I'm not sure I'd even want it. But you came along and—'

'I didn't do *anything*,' she said, opening her eyes, her flash of anger giving her the courage to face him down.

'You did something,' he said, his voice low, gravelly, outrageously sexy, his thumb stroking her jaw. His expression carried a hint of accusation. 'I don't know what, or how. But I never expected this. Never realised I'd have to fight so hard...'

His words tailed off as his gaze dropped to her lips. His desire was written in every line of his face. Her hands skimmed up his arms, still unsure whether to push away or pull closer, and with every one of her pounding heartbeats resisting grew harder.

If her lips met his there'd be no turning back. No more hiding from the desire that flickered between them,

His hands slid further round her waist, pulling her tight to him, and with one long sigh she knew that she was lost. She stretched up on her tiptoes and met him in a searing kiss.

She'd fought against this as hard as he had. It had been difficult enough when Will was being surly and taciturn. When he was pressing up against her, solid and hungry, his hands worshipping her, it was impossible. And yet as the shock of that first taste of his lips receded, rational thought fought its way back in. She moaned, thinking that she might never find pleasure like this again and knowing with absolute certainty it had to stop.

Will mistook her moan, though, for as it escaped her lips he backed her up against the kitchen counter, his hands gripping her waist, lifting her.

She had to act now, because if she waited another minute, another second, she knew she'd change her mind. She lifted her hands to his chest, allowed herself just the briefest, lightest of caresses before pushing him away.

They both stood for a moment, as unmoving as statues, and the only sound was the rapid gasp of their breath. When Maya eventually looked up at him she bit her lip as relief and regret warred within her.

'I—' he started, but she didn't want to hear that. Didn't want to hear that he was sorry for their kiss—not even if she knew herself that it had been a terrible idea. Hearing him say it would tear at her heart.

'Let's…'

She started speaking without knowing what she was even thinking, never mind what she wanted to say. Surely they had said enough already? Nothing had changed. This wasn't magically going to be easy. There was no 'easy' where Will was concerned. There was too much to think about tonight. And she knew that there were only two words that could keep the rest of this evening from getting any more complicated.

'Goodnight, Will.'

Will leant back against the kitchen counter, heart racing, breath ragged, feeling desperately empty. What had just happened? He hadn't meant to touch her: he just hadn't been able to bear her turning away from him like that, upset. And then once he had brushed his fingers against her he hadn't been able to let go. Electricity had crackled between them; resisting had become impossible. He'd had to kiss her, had to pull her closer. Every thought he'd had in his mind, every memory, every fear, every doubt, had been chased away by her hands in his hair, her soft lips, her hot body. He'd been lost. All he'd known was what he'd wanted. Maya. More. Everything.

Their kiss had assaulted all of his senses, and part of him was desperate to follow her and kiss her again.

When she'd pushed him away it had been as if part of his body had been torn away with her.

But now he was starting to remember all the reasons it shouldn't happen again; one kiss had his head rushing and his heart dangerously unprotected.

Instinct told him to run. The last few days with Maya had caused him more pain than he had experienced since he was a teenager. But she'd brought him more delight too. That one brief kiss had been packed with more pure pleasure than he could remember feeling before.

Slowly, he uncurled his fingers from the edge of the worktop. He had to fight this—as she was. He had to get these feelings back under control and be practical. Whatever his feelings for Maya, he had to consider Julia House too.

He hadn't wanted to get involved with the project initially, but one of the nurses involved in the project had helped to care for Julia and had seen Will's picture in the *Financial Times*. She'd persuaded him to become a trustee on the board, and Sir Cuthbert had agreed that the company would provide pro bono financial advice. He would treat it like any other project, Will had reasoned, just another spreadsheet.

But he could no longer think of Julia House as columns and rows and cells. Because he was constantly being reminded of those last weeks of Julia's life and of the people who had cared for her. Surely that care had a value that couldn't be entered on a spreadsheet? Which was why the thought of Sir Cuthbert pulling the project from him was terrifying. It wasn't just money or business on the line here; it was people's lives, their families, their memories. And after these last few days with Maya it had never been clearer how important those things could be.

CHAPTER SEVEN

MAYA'S ALARM BLEEPED on the nightstand beside her and she reached a hand across to turn it off. Six o'clock. She'd not got to bed until the early hours and had spent the rest of the night tossing and turning, trying to decide what to do this morning. Would she ask Will to leave? She knew that she should. Last night had proved to her that she couldn't trust herself to make the right decisions in the heat of the moment. That the strength of her attraction could and would overpower any sense of reason if given just half a chance. She should tell him this morning. Tell him anything he wanted to hear just so long as he would leave. Because he had to leave some time, she knew. And better that she sent him away than waited for him to disappear.

Or perhaps she wouldn't have to ask, she thought with a jolt. Perhaps he'd come downstairs with his bag packed and be out of the door before breakfast. Her treacherous heart lurched at the thought.

Being with Will, even when it was terrible, was always exhilarating. She said things to him she wouldn't dream of saying to anyone else. She could speak to him without double-checking every word, without worrying whether he was going to judge her. The first time they'd met she'd been overwhelmed with hurt at his rejection. But what had come after—the honesty and straightforwardness—

it was refreshing. She felt like herself in a way she hadn't for years.

So he was the one person in her life she felt she could be truly honest with. Could tell him to get lost if that was what she wanted. But she didn't want to. Not yet. Not with that kiss still burning in her mind.

She decided to go downstairs early, stake her place in the kitchen, be waiting for him when he emerged.

Downstairs, she turned the radio on and then walked into the store room in search of fruit and yoghurt for her breakfast. She had to do something; she hated the idea that he would walk in and catch her staring into space like a dolt, know that she was thinking about him. She turned the volume up a little higher—the music would stop her straining her ears, trying to hear if he'd come downstairs, or for the sound of his car on the driveway.

When she walked back into the kitchen to find him sitting at the table, fake nonchalantly leafing through a newspaper, she nearly dropped the bowls she was carrying. Bright summer sunshine played in his hair, and she couldn't help but remember the way it had felt under her fingers last night—how she'd run a fingertip over that spot, just there, where light gathered on his forehead. Before he even looked up she could feel the rush of blood to her face.

'Morning,' she said, her voice wavering.

'Good morning,' Will replied in false surprise.

Maya was gratified to see him fidgeting with the corner of the newspaper. She couldn't resist a smile at this proof that he was not immune to her after all. That, as much as he might sit and pretend normality, he remembered how he had lost himself with her last night. From the look of his tousled hair and the dark shadows under his eyes, she wasn't the only one who'd had trouble sleeping last night.

She picked up a bag of granola mix and carried everything to the table, still wondering as she did so what she should do—whether to make him leave. By the time she'd left her room this morning she'd made up her mind to tell him to go, but this doubt and indecision on his face, this vulnerability that mirrored her own, made her doubt herself. And just because they weren't talking about this kiss it didn't mean that the memory of it wasn't there in the room with them. It was almost physical, its presence was so strong, and it marked her every movement.

Will stood, a careful, controlled smile on his face, as she approached and he reached out to take one of the bowls. His hand brushed against her as she passed it to him and she looked up and caught his eye when she felt heat radiating through her skin. They both stood still, their eyes locked together. Attraction and hesitation fought within her breast, pushing her towards him and back in equal measure. Her body appeared still, belying the struggle she felt.

Maya searched his eyes, trying to judge which Will she had with her this morning. She saw neither stone-cold barricades nor the hot, passionate temper she knew was hiding in there somewhere. She saw only doubt and confusion. She looked away, hoping it would stop this pull she felt towards him. But it was there; it was constantly there now. And she wondered for the first time whether it would *always* be there, humming in the air. Even if she sent him away, even if he went, would they ever be able to break this or would it haunt her for ever?

She sat down opposite Will and spooned yoghurt, fruit and granola into her bowl. When she looked up Will was watching her thoughtfully. She looked away quickly again, embarrassed. Were they just going to carry on as if nothing had happened? They only had two days left on the course. Perhaps they *could* just ignore it? Who was she kidding? She could no more ignore this feeling in her chest than she could give up cooking.

As she lowered her spoon a sudden bright spot in her vision made her freeze in panic. *Oh, no. Not now.* Her body couldn't do this to her now—not with Will in the house. Not today of all days. But the second bright light confirmed it, and the churning of her belly told her she couldn't waste time sitting here. Her migraines weren't pretty, and they definitely didn't require an audience. She knew she had a few minutes to get herself to the bathroom, and that once she'd finished throwing up she'd need a dark, quiet room until the headache gave up its hold on her.

She dropped her spoon and pushed to her feet.

'Maya? What's wrong?'

From the concern flickering at the corner of Will's eyes she knew she looked as bad as she felt.

Trying to get away from the table, she stumbled. Making a dignified exit really would have been so much easier if her eyes would just co-operate and focus. But she whacked her hip into the corner and squealed in pain, curling her body in on itself.

'Maya, tell me what's happening.'

Will came to stand beside her and his palm, huge and warm, rubbed her injured leg. His other hand came up to cup her jaw, as it had last night, and the memory brought fresh tears to her eyes. He smoothed her hair from her face and tucked it behind her ear, then tilted her face so she had no choice but to look at him. She groaned. Why, of all days, did this have to happen now?

Because she'd spent all night trying to convince herself that what she felt for Will could be forgotten, ignored, destroyed, instead of sleeping.

'It's nothing,' she told him. 'Just a migraine.' *Just* a migraine. A migraine that would have her with her head down the toilet just as soon as she could get there, and then feeling that her brain was being skewered by a red-hot poker for at least the rest of the morning and probably the afternoon. Just a migraine.

'What do you need?' Will asked, and even through her disturbed vision she could see the worry in his face.

'Nothing. Just to get upstairs. I can manage,' she said, her stomach roiling. 'But I can't see…'

She tried to push away from him, but his arm came around her waist and he propelled her towards the stairs. She half thought about pushing him away, assuring him she could manage on her own. But she needed to get upstairs *now*, and this way did seem quicker.

She directed him to her bedroom and, with her queasy stomach warning her she was on a deadline, let him guide her. By the time they made it to her en-suite bathroom he was practically carrying her.

She sat on the side of the bath and leant against the washbasin for balance.

'Thanks for that,' she said. 'But I'll be—'

She was interrupted by the first wave of sickness and dropped to her knees, reaching for the toilet. She groaned when she realised that Will was right behind her.

'I'll be fine.' She managed to get the words out this time, but still he stayed.

He stayed through the noise and the tears. When her nausea abated long enough for her to catch her breath he ran a flannel under the cold tap and then pressed it to her forehead. She leaned back against the bathroom wall, eyes closed, trying not to read too much into this. But she couldn't help it. She couldn't quite truly believe that he was here with her. She knew what it must be costing him…the price he must be paying in memories. With the kiss last night, and now this, she realised that she couldn't trust anything she'd thought about him before today.

'Will, you really don't need to stay.'

'Maya, I'm only going to say this one more time. I'm

not leaving you alone like this. I know you don't want to inconvenience me, because I know that's how your mind works, but let me help you.'

She risked opening her eyes for a second, but winced at the bright light. Will reached up for the pull cord and turned it off, leaving them in darkness.

I know how your mind works. The words repeated themselves in her head. He really did seem to. No one had ever been close enough to her to do that. No one had ever taken her at more than face value. No one else had seen the loneliness and the pain that fuelled everything she did. Every failed friendship and frustrated relationship. But he was here, helping her, out of choice. Not out of obligation—she'd given him every opportunity to bail, and she couldn't have been more of an inconvenience, and he was still here for her.

'Thank you,' she said eventually.

'It's nothing. What do you need?'

She couldn't remember ever hearing his voice like that: soft, gentle, caring. What did she need? Him…like this… for ever.

And failing that? She wrinkled her nose and took a second to think, to consider the state of her stomach. The poker had started its steady push into the left side of her brain.

'I need to go to bed.'

Will took the flannel from her forehead and ran it under the tap, and then, despite her feeble protests, washed away the tears and grime. He handed her a toothbrush and a glass of water, and then one solid muscled arm slipped beneath her knees and another snaked around her back.

'It's fine, Will. I can manage.'

He shushed her protest and carried her back through to the bedroom. Looping her arms tight around him, she turned her face into his shirt as the door opened and light streamed in. His neck hid her from the light, and his skin was warm and smooth, and it also smelt delicious. Not even a migraine could dull the pleasure of being so surrounded by him, and from the thud of his heart he was no more immune than she. He deposited her gently on the bed, untangling his arms from around her, and went to close the blinds and the curtains.

'Can I get you anything?' he asked again, coming to sit beside her.

She tried to be practical, sensible, and directed him to the various medications she needed from her dresser drawer. But what she really wanted was his arms around her again.

A sharp stab of pain forced her eyes shut and she knew that only sleep could make this better now. But she resisted for a few seconds, not wanting to break this spell Will had cast, before fatigue finally dragged her under.

When she woke she took a second to assess the damage. The nausea was gone, and her head seemed fine—until it was hit by a screeching sound. It took a good few seconds of agony before she realised that the sound was coming from *outside* her brain. The smoke alarm.

She jumped from the bed and swayed slightly, which reminded her she needed to take things easy for the evening. But the screeching didn't let up.

'Don't get up! It's all under control!' Will shouted over the din—from the kitchen, by the sound of it.

Maya hesitated and the noise stopped. What was she meant to do, though? Just lie here all day? No, she had too much to do. What was he doing down there? she wondered as she threw on clean clothes and headed for the door. Realisation struck when she realised what the smell was, and she actually faltered on the stairs, not quite believing it.

As she pushed open the kitchen door Will was depositing a slice of charcoal into the bin and the kettle was whistling fiercely on the stove. She pulled it from the hob, and a second slice of charcoal from under the grill, as Will fought with the foot pedal on the bin.

'You didn't have to come down,' he said, distracted. 'You've had nothing to eat or drink all day, and I read...' He glanced over to his laptop, and she could see the NHS website still open in his browser.

'It's fine. I wanted to see if there was anything left of my kitchen.' She laughed quietly, testing its effect on her head. So far, so good. But she dropped into a chair at the table, not wanting to push too much too soon. Her feeble-feeling knees had *nothing* to do with the sight of Will Thomas making toast for her, she told herself, though she knew it was a lie. She could still feel the air humming with the imprint of last night's kiss, though it felt different...warmer, somehow...less threatening.

'I had it under control,' Will said, cutting into her thoughts as he sliced another slab of bread from the loaf. 'I just turned my back for a second to get the kettle on, and then the alarm started.'

Maya went to stand beside him, testing herself in proximity to him. 'Honestly, it's fine. I've been asleep for hours. I needed to get up.'

And she could hardly expect him to wait on her hand and foot after everything he'd already done. Everything felt different this afternoon. She tried to kid herself that it was Will's effect on the kitchen that was making it so— crumbs and bread knives and tea-making everywhere— but it was more than that. *She* was different; *they* were different.

'You need to rest,' Will said gently, dropping the bread knife and turning to face her. He reached out and stilled her hand as she went to open the tea caddy.

'You don't have to run around after anyone today. Can't you let me do this?'

His voice was warm and gentle, no fear or tension in it, but it wasn't the drained, empty voice of last night either. It was full and plump, rounded with…with what? Happiness? Contentment, perhaps? With Will's fingertips still brushing against her arm it was hard to argue with him.

His other hand dropped to her waist and turned her slowly around. 'Go back to bed; I'll bring this up in a minute.' He brushed her hair away from her face before pushing her gently towards the door.

She could hardly believe that one person could alter so much in such a short time. But he had. There wasn't the panic of the man who had run, scared, if he thought she was getting close to him. Nor was there the unguarded passion of the man who had kissed her in her kitchen. The man in her kitchen today was solid and sweet. Considerate. Kind. But she knew that the painful memories from Will's past weren't going to be solved by a chocolate pudding and a kiss.

And solid and sweet was lovely—really—but thinking that the passion between them last night might have been replaced with something cosier was not a welcome thought either. Solid and sweet was generally at its best right after something a little hotter and stickier.

But then she was changing too. Before all this—before Will—she wouldn't have been able to sit and wait while someone made her food; she'd have been down there in the kitchen, insisting on doing it herself, terrified that being a nuisance would drive him away.

All last night she'd told herself that this couldn't work. That she would never kiss Will again because he wasn't capable of giving himself to the kind of relationship she wanted. But he had been here for her today. Yes, she'd seen shadows cross his eyes, had seen sadness in his face, but he was here. He hadn't run away—neither in body nor in spirit.

Maybe he *was* capable of more. But that didn't mean he wanted it. Or that he wanted *her*.

CHAPTER EIGHT

Maya yawned as she climbed back into bed and sank into the pillows, letting her eyes drift closed. Her body felt loose, limp, and she felt herself melting into the mattress, the light summer quilt lying softly on her skin. She'd opened the curtains now that her light sensitivity was gone, but was too sleepy to enjoy the view. Migraines sapped her strength, but she was used to managing on her own. She'd been doing it for so long that she'd never realised there was another way.

Will appeared in the doorway with a tray in his hands, and looked around for space to put it. There wasn't a lot to spare. Her room had been described as 'bijoux' by the estate agent, and even that was generous. It should have been a box room, really, but when she'd launched her cookery school she'd taken the smallest room for herself so she could offer the more generously proportioned ones to paying guests. She cleared a couple of magazines off her bedside table and Will plonked the tray there and then stood beside her, looking awkward.

'Oh,' Maya said, shifting over a little, making space on the bed. She looked up at him, suddenly shy. 'It's really the only space in here.' *It's just the offer of a seat*, she thought. *He can't read anything into that*. Harder still to see double meanings when she wasn't even sure if there were any. Did she want to invite him into her bed? Did she even know?

After another pounding beat of her heart Will sat a little stiffly beside her and then reached for the tray. When he turned back he presented her with builder's tea and burnt toast with a grin on his face that suggested he had prepared a feast.

She smiled at him in return. It might as well be a feast: it was probably the only thing she could manage to eat after this morning's events. The novelty of being cared for gave everything a rosy glow and an added shine. It was startlingly easy, she was realising, to accept his help. And he showed her every time he smiled that her needing him was bringing them closer, not driving him away.

Will sat beside her and watched as she bit into the first slice. 'Are you not having anything?' she asked, fiddling with the handle of her teacup.

'I don't know if we can risk me making any more just yet.'

'I can make you something,' Maya said reflexively.

She was halfway out the bed when Will gently grabbed her hand; she realised what she was doing and hesitantly lay back down. His warm hand anchored her to the bed, soothing her insecurities, her fears. She didn't have to do this with Will. Didn't have to try all the time to deserve his company. He wanted her to just *be*. A warm glow started in her belly and spread through her chest until it lit up her face.

'At least have a slice of mine,' she said, feeling her way around this new world, not sure what to do if she wasn't doing everything herself. 'I'll let you make us both some more afterwards if it will make you happy.'

'Fine,' Will agreed with a smile and took one of the slices. He bit into the charred bread and pulled a face. 'This is horrible.' His face dropped into a grimace as he spoke. 'Why are you eating it?'

'No, it's fine,' Maya lied, stifling her laugh and forcing down the rest of the slice when she saw Will's downcast expression. She took a large glug of tea, wincing slightly at the bitterness. 'Here,' she said when she realised he didn't have a drink either. 'Have some of this. It'll help.'

'Thanks.' He took the cup from her, letting his fingers brush against hers as he did so.

As he took a sip of the tea Maya was surprised by how that intimate gesture sent a spark of desire through her belly. She had thought that they might be able to avoid facing what had happened last night. Not for ever—maybe just for a few hours. A little time to catch their breath, just to enjoy one another, but maybe it couldn't be that simple.

'This view's incredible,' Will said, shifting himself further down the bed, stretching out long legs and looking out of the window.

Or maybe it could be that simple…just for now. Immediately beyond the cottage's garden a meadow of wildflowers stretched for nearly half a mile. And beyond that evening sunlight glinted on the river that meandered through the valley. She walked down there most days, thinking over recipes, breathing in the smell of the countryside, taking snapshots with her camera for future inspiration.

'It's beautiful,' Maya said with a grin on her face. 'I much prefer it here to my old London life. I could never have run my own residential cookery school in the city.'

'It *is* beautiful here,' Will agreed gently, carefully. 'And you should be proud of your business. But is this what you really want? Don't you feel you're missing out on everything the city has to offer? The energy? The vibrancy? I think you can love this place and love the city too—your cottage is a beautiful retreat, but don't make it a prison.'

His eyes were firmly fixed on the window, giving her space. She examined his features, wondering how it was he saw her so clearly, how he could make her see herself so clearly.

'Was it always difficult with your parents?' he asked eventually.

Maya sighed—he was going to keep picking away at this. And then she realised—this was what he'd been trying to do all along: help her to talk about the things that pained her the same way she'd helped him. He'd not always been subtle, and he'd not always been right, but he'd always been trying to help. And of course it all came down to this—to her past. Will had helped her see how her need to prove herself to her parents had infected every friendship, every relationship she had ever had.

She took a couple of slow, calming breaths before she answered his question. 'It was never really *difficult*. Not for them, at least.'

'What do you mean?'

'Well, they didn't want me around, so I never was. I had nannies. I was sent away to school. They bought me a house when I went to university so I wouldn't have to come home in the holidays.' She looked up and caught his fractionally raised eyebrow. 'I know how it sounds,' she said quietly. 'I know I had lots of material privileges. I was lucky I could use their money to start my business. But I would have traded it in if I could.'

'I know,' he said with a sympathetic smile and a squeeze to her hand. 'And what about your cooking?'

He really *did* understand her, she thought, touched that he knew exactly the right question to ask to get to the heart of the matter. The part of her story that had always hurt her most.

'I tried to talk to them about it once.'

Her voice was quiet as she remembered that night—how she'd prepared what she wanted to say, rehearsed it over and over in the car on the drive home. Arguments and counter-arguments and curveballs, all ready to fight her case.

'I wasn't enjoying university, and I was only getting by

because I worked non-stop. I wanted to quit, to go to college and study culinary arts. I had this whole plan laid out, and I went to them and told them what I wanted to do. If they'd even told me that I wasn't to do it that would have been better, I think.'

'What *did* they say?'

'They said that I should do what I thought best. And would I be gone by seven because they were going out for dinner.'

He found her hand with his and squeezed. But Maya didn't feel the sadness and despair that this memory usually caused. Saying it aloud like that for the first time, she suddenly saw how outrageous her parents' behaviour had been. It occurred to her that their lack of interest was not because of anything she'd done, or hadn't done. They were just two very selfish people wrapped up in their own lives.

'And you stayed on the course?'

With a resigned sigh, she finished the story. 'I worked every minute for the next two years to get my first. They didn't even come to my graduation.'

'You know what?' he said. 'I wish I could say that deep down they're proud of what you've achieved here. But I don't know them, and I can't guess at how they feel. What I *do* know is that *you* should be proud of you. It's up to you what you're going to do with the rest of your life; whether you can leave their cruelty behind and start trying to please yourself.'

He was right. It wouldn't matter what she did, what she achieved. If she measured her success by what her parents thought of it she'd never be happy. She looked up at him, surprised and touched both by what he was saying and the fact he was saying it. She'd told herself that she wasn't going to think about what was happening between them until she was recovered from this migraine, but she couldn't help marvelling at this change and wondering what it would mean for them.

'It doesn't matter what they think,' he went on. 'It matters what *you* think.'

She stifled a yawn as she thought over his words, and looked out of the window at her little slice of English countryside. She thought of all the people she had taught and cooked for over the years. All the happiness she had brought people and how much happiness they'd inspired in her. She felt a warm glow of satisfaction and knew she couldn't be bitter, or angry, or sad about anything that had led her here.

'Actually, I think I'm doing okay. What about you?'

What about *him*? What did she mean? Did he think *she* was doing okay or *he* was doing okay? He pondered the question—the questions. If he'd known a month ago where he'd find himself sitting now he would have considered his present situation very *not* okay. He didn't get close to people. He didn't talk about his family. He didn't think about his family. It was a very small, but very firm set of principles that kept his life in check. And he had broken every one of them in the last week.

It had hurt. There had been times when he'd known he hadn't experienced pain like it since Julia died. But when he tried to think of anything that had happened in the last year—the last ten years—that came close to how good kissing Maya had felt, he came up with nothing.

He opened his mouth to answer her, but she gave a little snuffle. She'd fallen asleep. And as he turned to look at her her head dropped and rested against his arm. He tried to extract his hand from hers without waking her, but then she rolled, trapping both their hands beneath her. He sat back, unsure what to do.

It wouldn't be right to stay like this, but it was so very

tempting. For a start, after his sleepless night and draining day, the sight of any bed—even one without Maya in it—would tempt him almost beyond reason. With this bed, this woman, it would be nigh on impossible to walk away. She looked contented, though, and he smiled. He'd been worried that she would be upset, talking about her parents, but she seemed lighter, more relaxed. *Too* relaxed, he thought, watching her sleep and missing her company.

But getting into bed with an unconscious woman wasn't exactly his style. He pulled his hand out from under her slowly, trying not to disturb her. But her eyes drifted open and she seemed surprised to see him there.

'I was just going,' he said softly.

'Don't,' Maya whispered as her eyes drifted shut again, and threaded her fingers with his. 'Stay.'

Sagging back against the pillows, Will couldn't help but enjoy the feel of her body against his side. In five minutes…ten…when she was in a deeper sleep, he'd go.

But half an hour passed and he made no move to leave, too contented and peaceful to drag himself away. He'd thought he'd known peace before—before Maya. But now he could see that feeling for what it was: emptiness. He'd got through his days without feeling sad or angry, but the cost was never feeling joy or elation or love. This peace filled him, made his every cell feel alive. Eventually his eyes started to drift shut.

He woke briefly in the night, to find Maya curled tightly against him, an arm thrown across his belly; an ankle hooked around his, and he wrapped his arms around her waist, desperate to hold her close. As the sun slanted through the open window in the early hours Maya woke too.

He watched her as she drifted out of sleep, a small smile on her lips. Eventually she looked up.

She pulled back slightly and tilted her head, a sleepy,

sensual smile teasing the corners of her mouth. He met her gaze head-on and his hand left her waist to drift slowly up her arm.

He wanted her. She looked beautiful. Crumpled and sleepy, but so candid. She wasn't playing games. Her joy at finding him there radiated from her face, and he was desperate to kiss her. But he couldn't do anything about it—not unless he knew it was really what she wanted. He knew what *he* wanted—her. All of her. All of the time. He had never imagined before that he could feel like that—that he could be overjoyed to realise it was what he wanted. He couldn't walk away from this. He couldn't sacrifice this joy because he was afraid.

'Are you awake?' he asked in a whisper, his breath disturbing the hair that had fallen across her face. He brushed it gently away.

'Yes,' she breathed, lifting her hand to his chest and closing her fingers around his shirt. Will's eyes dropped to her hand, and then moved back to her face. He thought he must be dreaming, that such a perfect moment couldn't possibly be real.

His hand drifted higher, brushing over her arm, her shoulder, until it rested on her jaw, where his thumb gently caressed her. As he brought her face towards him his gaze flickered from her lips up to her eyes, until Maya moaned softly, and he kissed her.

His lips moved slowly, tentative and gentle, and the kiss stayed sweet as they tested and explored. But even through the torrent of sensation assaulting his body he could feel Maya slipping away from him. Sleep was pulling at her, and he knew he had to let her go—for now. Only the thought that they would wake again in a few hours—here, together—and pick up where they left off soothed him.

'You're tired,' he said. A statement, not a question. 'Go

back to sleep.' He kissed her gently on the forehead and tucked her head under his chin, and then locked both arms firmly around her waist.

Her bed was screaming.

Maya opened her eyes in a panic, trying to work out where the noise was coming from. Darkness surrounded her and she realised that her face was pressed up against something warm and solid; she pushed at it with her hands but it fought back, pulling her down on the bed, refusing to let go. Suddenly claustrophobic, she struggled harder and sat up; it was only when she looked down that realisation struck. It was Will—in her bed. What the…?

'Morning,' she said hesitantly.

'Good morning,' Will replied, his face losing its sleepy, dreamy quality as he saw her. He look startled, awkward. 'Sorry, I forgot my alarm was set,' he said, jabbing at the screen of his phone until the noise stopped. 'You look much better today,' Will said, his voice a little brusque. 'How do you feel?'

'Honestly?' she replied, leaning back against the pillow. 'A little confused.'

His face fell, but as her gaze dropped to his lips she remembered—remembered every second of the kiss they had shared that morning…or last night…whenever it had been. But she couldn't think of what to say, and before she could find the right words her belly rumbled.

'You're hungry,' Will said shortly as he stood up.

She sat forward and rubbed the sleep from her eyes, trying to keep up. 'Just give me a minute to wake up properly and I'll make us some breakfast.'

'You will not.'

She tensed at his overbearing tone.

'It's fine,' she countered. 'You go ahead and I'll be down in a second.' She ran a hand through her hair and tried to sound calm, as if waking up with a man she was falling for was something that happened every day.

'Maya, *I'll* make a start on breakfast. No arguments. Come down when you're ready.'

He walked out of her bedroom before she had a chance to argue.

As soon as the door closed behind him Maya dropped her head into her hands. She couldn't be more mortified. She'd woken up wrapped around him like some crazy clingy woman, and now he had run at the first possible moment. It just didn't make sense. Her memories of that kiss were suffused with warmth, pleasure, delight. But she hadn't seen that Will in the man she'd woken up with this morning.

Well, no wonder, she told herself as she remembered the way she'd acted when she had first woken. She'd practically beaten her fists on his chest to get him to let her go. As if being sick in front of the man hadn't been bad enough.

She let out a groan, threw on some clean clothes and headed for the kitchen.

Will had found cereal and fruit and had laid the table for breakfast. A pot of tea sat on the countertop with a couple of mugs, and he'd even managed to find the milk jug. The boy learned fast. He emerged from the pantry and she gave him a cautious smile, uncertain whether to mention their kiss. Where would she start? She hadn't even had a chance to think about how *she* felt about it yet, never mind what she might want to say to *him* about it.

'This is nice,' she said lamely.

'It's nothing,' he replied. 'Sit. Eat.'

She did as she was told, trying to enjoy the novel experience of being fussed over, but Will's brusqueness was making her tense, nervous.

'So what are we doing today?' Will asked her, and a warm glow chased away her doubts.

He was staying. It was amazing, she thought, how the

landscape of their relationship had changed so much that there wasn't even any question of him leaving before the week was up.

'I'm actually not sure,' Maya replied, relaxing slightly, hoping that a smile would improve his mood as well as hers. 'Yesterday threw me a bit. Let me check my notes for what we're meant to be cooking.'

'I didn't mean what are you going to teach me. I meant what are you going to do to recuperate?'

She looked up, and although his tone was sharp she saw concern, not anger in his features. She smiled wider: he was still trying to protect her.

'I'm done recuperating,' she said decisively, excited to embark on the day now that she knew that Will was staying. 'What I'm going to do is teach you to make coq au vin!' she said as her plans came back to her. 'And then I'm going to bake and ice a hundred fairy cakes.'

She could see him trying to decide whether to lecture her. But eventually his concerned expression cracked into a hint of a smile and she knew he was going to agree. *Good choice*, she thought. There was no way she could be kept out of the kitchen for two days in a row, and she loved that he understood that.

'Or you could teach *me* to bake and ice a fairy cake? By number ninety-nine I might have got the hang of it.'

'Do I have a choice in this?' she asked good-naturedly.

'Not really.'

He smiled, and it reached the pit of her stomach. She thought about everything he'd done for her yesterday— everything he'd seen and heard, the memories she must have stirred up. And he'd done it all for her. Agreeing with him now was the least she could do.

Will must have sensed her wavering: he spoke with a grin. 'I can pretend you do if it makes you feel better.'

CHAPTER NINE

Why was he offering to make fairy cakes? Why was he here, full-stop?

The answer was simple: Maya.

A few days ago his brain had been screaming at him to leave. But now, even knowing that there was a risk that one day he might get hurt, it wasn't. Not when the rewards of staying were so vast.

Being around Maya made him happy—happier than he'd ever felt before, he suspected. But that wasn't quite enough to quiet the voices. They were no longer screaming, and he was no longer going to obey unquestioningly, but that didn't mean that he could block them out completely.

And they had plenty to say this morning: about how scared he'd been yesterday when he'd thought Maya might be seriously ill. How painful it had been to sit in that bathroom with her and not be able to make her better.

The pain of losing Julia suddenly felt fresh in his heart, and he was terrified of going through it again. Terrified that one day he might have to face the pain of losing Maya. And the closer she got, the worse it would be.

She'd lost him again. Maya eyed Will carefully, trying to squash her feelings of disappointment until she was sure. But there was no denying it: she hadn't noticed when it had happened, or what she'd said to cause it, but as she watched

him methodically and purposefully cream butter and sugar
she could tell he wasn't really there. She was determined
not to panic; maybe he just needed space—time to adjust
to everything that had happened last night, this morning.

He'd been withdrawing more and more all day, but even
though he wasn't talking he was telling her more than he
realised. She'd given him a list with the quantities of ingredients to weigh out, but after he'd done that he'd been
the one to add the butter and sugar to the mixing bowl and
pluck a wooden spoon from the jar of utensils.

She didn't say a word. Didn't even offer him the electric beaters for fear of disturbing whatever he was working through in his mind.

He'd looked up and met her eyes more than once, and
she'd held her breath, wondering if this was the moment
when he would come back to her, when he would open up
and give them...whatever this was...a chance. But he'd
always looked away, his jaw tense and his eyes regretful.

Everything that had tumbled into the open from the
time his lips had met hers had been washed away from
them, and she was frustrated and sad in equal measure.
She couldn't begin to imagine the pain that Will must have
felt at losing his family, but he wasn't the only one to have
pain in his past. He couldn't just decide to disappear from
the world because sometimes it was *hard*.

He had a choice here; if he really wanted to he could
be happy. They could be happy together, she was sure.
But not if he was going to keep running like this. He just
needed the courage to try.

When he added a spoonful of flour with the first egg,
to stop the mixture from splitting, the words escaped her
before she could stop them.

'You've done this before.'

Will looked up suddenly, with a look on his face that
told her he knew he'd been caught out.

'Neil had a sweet tooth,' he said, and then looked away.

She chanced a small smile. Her words had been a challenge and he'd not let her down. He could have ignored the question, he could have lied, but instead he'd told her the truth.

His eyes returned to the bowl and didn't leave it again as he gently folded in the flour. Maya resisted the urge to speak, not wanting to push her luck. After everything he'd told her about Julia, the pain that he'd faced, she couldn't imagine what more there was in his life that could hurt him. Neil had 'had' a sweet tooth, Will had said, and she wondered with a pang of sadness whether he'd lost his foster father too.

Later she watched as he iced perfect swirls on to the tops of the cakes. Neither of them had said a word for close to an hour. Maya had kept deliberately quiet: she knew him well enough now to judge when to push and when to give him space. She knew something else too: he'd come back to her. They'd been taking two steps forward and one step back since the minute that they'd met. Frustrating—yes, but going in the right direction.

She wished she could put her hand over his, soothe him, but she knew he needed to do this, needed to think. A week ago she'd have been convinced she'd done something wrong, that she wasn't enough for him. Now she knew that wasn't true. It was his problems he was fighting, not her. But eventually she saw the fight leave his face, and she knew he was on his way back to her.

'I haven't seen him for fifteen years.'

She searched his face for clues, listened carefully to his tone, trying to work out what he wanted, whether he wanted her to ask more.

She chose her words thoughtfully, wanting to help and encourage, but not to pressure him.

'Was that what you wanted?'

'No.' His face was filled with raw emotion as he took a breath and then fixed her with his gaze. She knew why— knew how much stronger she felt when they were together, and that he must feel it too. 'He sent me back to the home. I didn't have a choice.'

Her arms ached with the need to pull him close, but she knew she couldn't do that. Will needed space, and to do this in his own time. He had just shown her that they weren't clear of the woods or their past yet.

He'd gone back to his icing, and the look on his face was so unlike anything she'd seen before. He was entirely focussed on making each one perfect. But not in the tense, white-knuckled way he had been when he'd first arrived.

She glanced around the kitchen, taking in the sight of boxed and iced fairy cakes covering almost every surface. There must be almost a hundred, she thought.

She was just about to ask Will if he wanted to call it a day when there was a knock at the front door.

'Gwen!' Maya exclaimed, surprised to find her neighbour on her doorstep—again.

'Maya, I'm *so* pleased you're home,' Gwen said, pushing past her through the doorway. 'I've got an emergency on my hands, again, I know—I'm sorry.'

She started to explain, but stopped when she saw Will emerge from the kitchen.

'Oh, you're still here,' she said, with a transparent smile at Maya. 'I heard you were both in the pub on Tuesday night.' She bumped Maya with her hip.

'You wanted to ask me something?' Maya prompted, wanting to deflect her attention. Whatever was there between her and Will today it was too young, too fragile, to be scrutinised like that.

'Oh, yes. Well, I absolutely *have* to get to the office this afternoon and it will be a nightmare if I have to take the children. Could you watch them for me?'

Maya fixed a smile on her face, trying to think through her plans for the rest of the day. They *had* practically finished the cakes—there were only a handful left to ice—and she hadn't firmly decided on anything else for that evening.

'Um…'

She really didn't want to watch the children though. And she knew that this was her chance—her opportunity to make a stand. She had every reason to say no to Gwen. Her head might be just about back to normal, but her whole body felt exhausted. Definitely not up to the challenge of two under-fives. And she wanted space for her and Will too—space to see what might happen.

'They're just outside in the car,' Gwen went on. 'I told them to wait until I'd checked with you, but I'll go and get them now. Thanks, Maya. You're a life-saver.'

Maya squirmed. She knew she should say something. Will was right: this wasn't fair. But as her brain raced through what would happen if she said no she felt a gnawing anxiety in her gut. Would Gwen disappear from her life if she let her down? Would all her friends, if word spread? The spectre of that lonely existence hovered beside her as she shifted her feet, willing herself to speak.

Will cleared his throat and gave Maya a pointed look. Gwen turned back around at the sound, leaving Maya with no choice but to say something.

'Actually, Gwen…' she started, but didn't know how to continue. Will placed a warm, firm hand in the small of her back and pushed her forward half a step. She took a deep breath. 'Um…I don't think I can help today,' she said, her eyes fixed to the floor. 'I had a migraine, you see, and I'm still not quite recovered. I'm sorry.'

'Oh!' Gwen said, looking mildly embarrassed. 'I hadn't thought… Are you okay?'

Maya nodded quickly, knowing a blush was rising on her cheeks. 'Better than yesterday.'

'Well, don't worry about it at all,' Gwen said. 'You look after yourself. And call me if you need anything.'

'Wait,' Maya called as Gwen reached the door. 'We've almost finished the cakes, if you want to take them with you now?'

'You've finished them already?' Gwen asked. 'Maya, you're an angel.'

'See—not so hard,' Will said as Gwen drove away and they both stepped back to close the door.

Maya turned sharply to face him, her hands planted on her hips, furious.

'You didn't have to do that, you know. I'm perfectly capable of making up my own mind.' She'd been giving him space all afternoon, not pushing more than she thought he could take, and then he just blundered in and practically forced her to tell Gwen no when she'd not even had a chance to think it through.

'Did you *want* to look after her children?' Will's voice was infuriatingly reasonable as he leant back against the door and watched her.

'I wouldn't have minded,' she lied.

'Really? After yesterday, did you really want to watch someone else's children? Again?'

That was hardly the point, Maya thought, though she wasn't sure who she was trying to convince. It was exactly the point. It was everything Will had been trying to show her since she'd arrived. Everything she'd come to see was true about the way she was living her life. But she would have got there on her own; she'd have told Gwen no eventually. Probably.

'Maya, I'm not sure why you're angry,' Will said, his voice irritatingly calm.

Anger prickled under her skin and she knew it should be aimed at herself. That she'd fallen at this first opportunity to stand up for herself. But Will stood there looking so smug, as if it was the easiest thing in the world to change, when he'd been fighting against it since the moment they'd met.

'I only wanted to remind you what we'd talked about,' he said. 'You were going to say yes when you wanted to say no.'

How did he see through her like that? Through everything she did to the decade-old heartache beneath? How could he hit so quickly on her fears, make her so vulnerable? Her heart pounded and she could feel the adrenaline coursing through her veins as she threw her anger at him, desperately trying to direct it away from herself.

'And what gives you the right to interfere?' she demanded. 'What gives you the right to tell me anything about how to live my life?'

'You know exactly why.'

He raised his voice to compete with hers, his shoulders tensing now. He was surprised, she guessed, at the turn the conversation had taken.

'Because... Because I—' He stopped abruptly.

Maya waited for a beat—waited for him to finish that sentence. When he didn't, she couldn't resist. 'Because you *what*?'

Suddenly Will's expression softened and he smiled at her, shrugging.

'Because I care, okay? Because when I see someone hurting you reason flies out of the window and I can't stop myself from caring. Is that what you want to hear?'

Maya stared at him, shocked into silence; her anger dissipated in an instant.

'Are you going to say anything?' Will asked.

'Thank you for being honest,' Maya said carefully,

knowing it wasn't really enough—not after the way he'd laid himself bare.

She couldn't even begin to think what to say back. That she cared about him too? Well, of course she did; he must know that. But one thought above all others won her attention, and she knew she couldn't ignore what had happened any longer. She had been so certain it was real when those memories had flooded back. But maybe they hadn't—maybe it was fantasy. Either way, she had to know.

'Will, about last night…'

He looked at her intently, but didn't rush to fill any blanks.

'I woke up and you were there…and…' She took a deep breath, thought back to those magical few minutes in the small hours of that morning—how right it had felt to be in his arms, how perfectly they'd understood each other. It *was* real—it had to be. 'I know I didn't imagine it.'

A smile crept up from the corners of Will's mouth as he took a step towards her. 'You didn't imagine it,' he said, and the smile finally reached his eyes. 'It was real. Very real.'

He leaned in close and brushed his lips against hers. Even this, the briefest of caresses, set off sparks that lit her up from the soles of her feet to her hair.

'I was worried you didn't remember. That you weren't really awake,' he said.

'It took me a minute to wake up. Mornings aren't my best time.'

'I'll have to remember that,' Will murmured.

The suggestive glint in his eye made her blush, but his implication that there would be more mornings to come—the first hint that this could be something real, something lasting—glowed in her heart.

'So what shall we do this evening?' she asked, still finding it wondrous that he was really here, *present*, with her.

'I'm going to make you dinner while you take it easy.'

The easy confidence of his voice told Maya she'd no choice in the matter. But instead of instantly dismissing the idea of being waited on she sat with the thought for a moment, tried to imagine what that would feel like.

'Am I just meant to watch you slave over a hot stove? I'm not allowed to help at all?'

'You're not allowed to do anything,' he told her. 'When was the last time anyone made you dinner?'

She knew the look on her face told him everything he needed to know.

'Precisely,' he said, a little smug. 'No arguments.'

'Okaaay…' she replied hesitantly.

She'd let him have his way. She'd give his idea a try as he had trusted her so often this week. It was impossible to deny this happy, easy-going Will just about anything. It delighted her to see him like this, so close to carefree.

But she knew being in the kitchen was hard for him, and they'd already spent hours there. 'It's still early. How about a walk first?'

They wandered through the garden and out across the meadow, heading for the river. Will stayed close by her side, and the occasional brush of his arm against hers, the touch of his hand under her elbow, created layer upon layer of awareness in her body.

Her skin tingled with anticipation, almost as if there was some sort of charge between them—some energy that was only satisfied when they were touching, when it could explode. Their gazes met occasionally, and the looks that passed between them seemed to travel from his eyes directly to her chest, constricting her lungs, making her gasp for air, until he looked away and she could breathe again.

Eventually they reached the path between a leafy avenue of trees and Maya paused, as she always did there, to look back at her cottage. The bright afternoon sun played on the walls, soaking life into the old stones, and the sea of colour in the meadow shifted and changed with every breath of the light summer wind. She let out a deep sigh of contentment and closed her eyes, tipping her face up to the warmth of the sun. She thought, as she did every day, how lucky she was to have found a place that had brought her such happiness and peace. But Will was right. Just because she was happy here it didn't mean it was the *only* place she could be happy.

He moved behind her, and when he settled his hands on her shoulders she relaxed into them, revelling in the knowledge that she could do this. That he was offering her all he had to give, was hers for the taking. His hands slid round her waist and pulled her back tightly; he pressed a kiss to the side of her neck.

'It really is beautiful here,' he murmured.

Maya shifted slightly in his arms, so her forehead rested gently against his jaw. Will's lips pressed to her temple and she couldn't stop a quiet moan from escaping her. His hands caressed her waist, smoothing the curves of her sides, sweeping low over her belly, while his lips continued to tease at her hairline. Biting her lip, almost breathless with expectation, she closed her eyes, succumbing to the surfeit of sensation. Will's hands settled on her hips, heavier than before, and he turned her firmly before sneaking his arms back around her and holding her tight.

His caressing lips found her mouth at last. But the touch of his lips on hers brought her up short. Happy as she was, she wasn't delusional. She knew there were still things they had to face, still hurts to overcome, before Will would be ready to commit to this—whatever *this* was. This morning they had shared a kiss just as sweet as this, and it had not stopped him from disappearing into himself a few hours later.

She pushed her hands against his chest and took a step

away from him. Her breathing was heavy, and her arms itched to loop themselves around Will's neck. But she knew that she couldn't let herself. If Will wanted her he had to stop holding back. She hadn't wanted to confront Gwen—not today, not yet. But with help from him she'd done it. And now it was over she felt lighter, freer, and knew that it had been the right thing. She needed the same from Will. She knew there were parts of his story he was still holding back, and if he wasn't prepared to step up, as she had, then they were better off walking away from each other now.

'Maya?' said Will, rubbing at the back of his neck, no doubt confused by her sudden change of mood.

'I'm sorry,' she said as she turned and walked on, down towards the river.

'What is it?' he asked, catching up with her. 'What's wrong?'

She psyched herself up to ask the question she knew they had to face. If they were going to pursue this attraction, this bond that was so tangible between them, she had to know that Will was being open with her, that he wasn't still holding back.

'You mentioned your foster father earlier. I'd like to know about him.'

'Now?' he asked, following closely behind her. His voice was unsteady and he reached for her shoulder. 'That's what you were thinking just now? That you want to know about my *parents*?'

'I want to know *you*.' She reached up and brushed her fingertips across his cheek, meeting his eyes and smiling softly. All the time she wondered if he would see the real question behind her words: *Are you really ready for this?*

CHAPTER TEN

HE HADN'T MEANT to shut her out this afternoon. Hadn't meant to retreat to that quiet, still, cold place in his mind. But he'd been shocked by her reaction when she woke. She hadn't seemed to want him close, so he'd given her space. And then, when he'd started with the cakes, the world had just sort of faded. His hands had got on with the job with little input from him: they'd seemed to remember well enough from long hours in the kitchen with Julia.

But then Gwen had shown up at the door and he'd known he had to help Maya to stand up for herself. He couldn't bear to see her beaten down by her own dizzying expectations of herself. She had been so close he'd only needed to lend her a little support. But that hadn't been enough. It would never be enough. Because once he'd done it he'd had to think about why. And the reason was so clear that he couldn't avoid it.

He cared about her.

And now he had to give more. *Again*. She wanted to know about Neil. The last piece of himself he'd been able to keep from confronting, locked away, secure, where it couldn't hurt him. And he knew that he was out of chances. To push her away after what they had shared last night would be cruel. This was final. If he wanted any sort of future with Maya he had to step up.

He didn't know what he wanted from *her*. Didn't know

how much he could risk. But he knew that if she decided today that she wanted nothing more to do with him he would despair. If talking would stop that happening—give him more space, more time to try and work out what it was that was happening—he would do it.

He dropped down onto a fallen tree trunk by the side of the river and started to speak, his arms resting on his knees.

'After Julia died Neil and I tried to carry on.'

He tried his usual trick, distancing himself from the words as if he was telling someone else's story. But as he spoke he could see the scenes in his mind. See his fifteen-year-old self, lonely and afraid, and his heart broke. He felt the full force of his words now. There was no hiding, no pretending. His words hurt, but he could see past them, see past the pain to what was waiting on the other side: Maya.

'But when I looked at Neil it was as if he wasn't there. I never understood at the time what he was going through. I'd never loved anyone like he loved Julia. I thought that he didn't care.'

Maya leaned against him and he took comfort from her. He knew that however bad his memories were, they were in the past. Maya was *here*. *Now*.

'Oh, Will, I'm sure he loved you,' she said gently. 'It sounds as if he wasn't well.'

'I'm starting to see that.' Yesterday, when Maya had been ill, he'd had the tiniest insight into what Neil might have been feeling, and for the first time he'd started to appreciate the magnitude of his foster father's grief.

He'd been thinking about Neil more and more. It would be so simple and yet so hard to see him again, to speak to him. But part of Will wanted to—to see if he could recapture a part of those happy years of his childhood. But what if Neil didn't want him? What if he was rejected, again?

Will dropped his head into his hands and rubbed at his hair. When he lifted his head one hand stayed at his neck, trying to rub away the tension. He watched the water ripple and the light play on its surface, filtering through the trees.

'So what happened after that?' Maya asked eventually.

A week ago he would have bristled, been angry at anyone prying into his personal life. But he knew that Maya wasn't being nosy, wasn't trying to push. She just wanted to know him.

'Oh, we carried on for a little while,' he explained, his heart heavy as he remembered those horrendous weeks. 'But one day my social worker turned up, asked me a lot of questions and spent a long time locked away with Neil. And then I was off back to the group home.' He tried to sound flippant, but the memory of that day hit him hard in the gut, a physical pain, and his voice broke.

'I'm so sorry.'

Her voice was soft, caring. And it gave him the strength he needed to carry on.

'Losing Julia taught me how much it hurt to lose someone you love.'

He tried to control his voice. Breathed deeply, looking for the calm he'd spent years working on, the new peace he'd found with Maya. It was nowhere to be found, so he just forced the words out as best he could.

'She was pulled from me, and I took some comfort in knowing that she didn't want to go any more than I wanted her to leave. But Neil? At the time it felt like he just didn't care. Didn't love me enough. I knew I couldn't give anyone that power over me again.'

'And that's why—'

'And that's why meeting you terrified me,' he said with a small smile. 'I've never met anyone in my life so impossible to resist.'

'I didn't do it on purpose.'

Her voice was small, worried, and he squeezed her hand, pressed it to his cheek.

'I know, I know.'

He looked up and the sight of her, her red hair and purple dress and bright green eyes, instantly lightened him. When he leaned across and brushed his lips gently across hers more weight fell, and his arm drifted up and around her shoulders.

'I chased you here,' he said, the corners of his mouth turning up. He was amazed that he could smile with his memories so close by. 'I think we have established that beyond any doubt.'

She smiled back at him and then rested her head against his shoulder, looking out over the water.

He had no secrets from Maya now—was completely vulnerable to her. Without doubt, if she wanted to, she could break his heart as soundly as Neil had done. But that knowledge didn't sit heavily on his shoulders. He only felt excited, exhilarated that she could have that effect on him. He should be terrified, but when he saw the light catch the gold in her hair, saw the corners of her mouth turn up at some silent thought, he couldn't regret it.

'There's actually something I need to tell *you*,' Maya said eventually, her words lazy and relaxed.

'Oh?' He sounded worried.

'It's nothing bad. It's just…' She took a deep breath, knowing that she was giving him permission to leave. 'You know that I'll cater your dinner, don't you? It doesn't matter if you don't want to finish the course.'

Her heart fell at the look of unbridled relief and happiness that crossed his face.

'Maya, thank you.' His voice was full of delight, and she cringed at the sound of it. 'You have no idea what that means to me. *Thank you.*'

She bit her lip. She hadn't been prepared for him to be quite so thrilled about the prospect of leaving. Of course she'd thought briefly that maybe he wouldn't stay now that he didn't have to, but his being so pleased by the idea was devastating.

Will must have caught the look on her face, because he trapped it between his palms.

'What's wrong?'

'Nothing,' she lied, trying to hide her heartbreak. 'It's nothing. I guess you were only here because of Sir Cuthbert anyway.'

It had hurt, knowing that was the only reason he had come, but she had thought that what had developed between them was real. That how they'd got here together in the first place wasn't so important. She tried to turn away, cast a glance up at the cottage. She wished they were back up there, so she could escape somewhere, have some privacy.

'You think I'm *going*?'

The incredulous look on Will's face eased the fist gripping her heart.

'Aren't you?'

'No.' He said the word slowly, deliberately. 'I'm staying. I promise.'

She looked up and met the intensity of his gaze head-on. Once her eyes had locked on his she couldn't look away, not until his lips met hers, and she let them drift shut as she drowned in sensation.

He was staying. She still couldn't quite make herself believe it as they started back towards the house. Her heart wanted to soar, but she kept a firm grip on it. He had made no promises for the future, no avowals of love. All she knew—all he had promised her—was the rest of this week.

She shook her head, clearing her thoughts, determined to concentrate on what she did have right now.

'So what culinary delights do I have in store for me tonight?' she asked.

'Ah...'

Maya guessed that Will hadn't thought quite that far ahead in his plan.

'Well, I hadn't thought about the details yet, but I'm sure I can—'

'It doesn't matter. I can cook. Or we can do it together.'

'No. I'm meant to be giving you a break, remember? I'm cooking, and you're going to let me.'

She fought against the urge to argue, to insist, determined to trust him, to give herself a chance to live differently.

'Okay. You know where the fridge is, and there are recipe books on the dresser if you want inspiration.'

He nodded thoughtfully. 'I should keep it simple,' he said. 'I made a cottage pie once. For Julia's birthday—my first time solo in the kitchen. Think I can manage it again?'

Maya smiled, touched that he was making a meal that meant so much to him and by the way he had just dropped Julia's name into conversation. 'I trust you.'

Three hours, seven saucepans, two courses and a visit to the first aid box later, Maya let out a deep, contented breath, leaning back in her seat.

'I'm impressed, Will. Seriously.' She laid down her spoon and fork. Her bowl was scraped clean.

'I know. You've already said that. Twice.' He tried to keep the smugness from his face, but he looked unbelievably thrilled that he had managed to do this for her. For him too.

'But I think back to that first night and—'

He groaned. 'I know I was a pain that night.'

'Not on purpose.'

'No, but I didn't really try to *not* be a pain either.'

'Let's forget about it.' Maya smiled and stood to clear

the bowls, but found herself trapped by a strong arm around her waist. 'Will, I'm just clearing these—'

Words deserted her as he twisted his chair and pulled her towards him so she was trapped between his thighs.

'I know this has been difficult,' he said earnestly. 'That *I* have been difficult.'

'You stayed,' she said simply, trying to think straight through the onslaught on sensation she felt at being in his arms. 'That tells me all I need to know. The fact that you're still here, however difficult it is.'

His legs closed more firmly around hers and his hand found the nape of her neck as he pulled her into his lap. Her eyes closed as she leaned towards him, her tongue moistening her bottom lip. She held her breath, suddenly nervous, unsure, wondering whether this man could truly give her what she needed, whether he was ready for a relationship.

His lips touched against hers, slow, sweet and gentle. She kissed him back instinctively, and heat spread from every point that their bodies met.

After everything Will had told her today she shouldn't be having doubts. He'd trusted her with secrets she was sure he'd never shared with anyone. But she wasn't his therapist. She was his lover. Or she could be. But even with everything they'd talked about there was one subject where she was still in the dark. How did he feel about her? Okay, he'd told her that she was difficult to resist. But he *had* spent the week resisting. Who was to say he wouldn't change his mind?

She deserved nothing less than love and commitment and honesty from the people in her life. No holding back, no playing games. He had shown her that.

Will pulled back and opened his eyes, sensing her hesitation.

'Maya, what is it?' he asked, cupping her face with one hand, brushing her hair back with the other.

She quivered, her every nerve-ending straining for his caress. 'It's nothing,' she said quickly. But then paused, reconsidered. 'No, it's everything. I don't know, Will. I'm just not sure that this is a good idea.'

'Why?' His arms dropped to tighten around her waist.

It was hard to think when he was so close, and her body was urging her on. But she couldn't let herself be persuaded into this if it wasn't right.

'Because I'm not sure how you feel about me,' she said firmly. 'I'm not pushing you to tell me. I'm just not sure that I can do this without knowing.'

He looked floored, and she knew that he hadn't expected her question.

He opened his mouth to speak a couple of times before he finally forced some words out. 'I don't know what I can say to explain.'

She could hear his frustration in every word—not with her, but with himself. 'I've never... I just don't know... You're just so...'

He fell silent, exasperated, and she could see him sorting through words in his head.

He tried again. 'I think that... I'm trying to... I just... *love* you.'

She let out a gasp and sat up straight—and watched as the realisation of what he'd said hit him. His eyes widened and his mouth opened, but he didn't rush to deny the words. Instead as the shock faded it was replaced with a dazed smile.

'I...' She knew she should say something, but she'd no idea what.

Of course she was falling in love with him. But after the shock of his admission just saying his words back to him didn't seem right. It wasn't even the fact that he loved her that had shocked her so much. It was the fact that he had told her. She knew he'd never said those words to anyone.

Understood how much of a risk he was taking by saying them to her.

'Will…' She tried starting again, then realised she didn't have to say anything; she could *show* him how she felt. Show him how much his words meant to her.

Leaning forward, she pressed her lips against his.

As soon as she did so Will's arms tightened around her again.

'I've been wanting to do this all evening,' he confessed breathlessly between kisses.

Maya moaned softly as he shifted her on his lap, his hands moving down from her waist to her hips, gripping her tightly. Her heartbeat thudded in her ears and she gasped, breathless.

'Me too,' she admitted. 'But I didn't think…'

'I know. I'm an idiot,' he said.

She wanted to laugh. Wanted to rejoice that this man, who just a few days ago had seemed so determined to hide himself from her, was here, with his arms around her, laughing, loving her. His fingers skirted the neckline of her sundress and came to rest on the top button; she arched into him, more sure than she'd ever been that she wanted to make love with him. Perhaps this would be one area where he could teach her a thing or two about the sensual.

His lips left the trail they were making up the side of her neck and he whispered urgently in her ear. 'Upstairs?'

She held her breath as she nodded, and then let out a squeal of surprise as Will stood from the chair, taking her with him.

'You're sure?' he asked, pausing as they reached the top step.

'Of course,' she whispered. 'I've barely thought of anything else this week. You've no idea—'

'Oh, you'd be surprised,' Will replied, kicking the door closed behind them.

* * *

Maya stirred beneath the blankets and stretched to ease the delicious ache that had invaded every muscle. As a cool breeze brushed across her cheek she realised something was wrong. She reached across the bed at the same time as she opened her eyes. The other side of the bed was still warm, but unmistakably empty.

She lifted herself up onto her elbows and fear curled instinctively in her belly. Only the dent in the pillow suggested anyone else had been there at all. For a moment she was unsure if she'd imagined the whole thing. But the trail of her clothes from the door to the bed convinced her otherwise. Will had been here—that much was certain. The question was, where was he now?

She felt empty as she acknowledged the question, because gut instinct had told her the answer. She lay still, trying to listen for the whistle of the kettle or the creak of a stair. Eventually she heard footsteps downstairs. Not the quiet padding of bare feet but the purposeful thump of shoes. She knew she had to get up, out of bed, but she hesitated. Once she did that—went down there and faced him—she wouldn't be able to kid herself any longer.

When Will didn't miraculously reappear, she climbed out of bed. And when she reached the bottom of the stairs and saw the suitcase propped by the front door she knew what a mistake she'd made. Her knees weakened and her shoulders slumped as the truth of the situation hit her and nausea rose from her gut. He'd promised her he wasn't leaving, and—stupidly—she'd believed he had a reason to stay.

It was Will who had shown her how she let people use her, take advantage of her to get what they needed. After everything he'd said she hadn't thought Will capable of doing the same thing. But the evidence made it clear how wrong she was.

Will emerged from the kitchen and jumped at the sight of her standing on the bottom step.

'Maya…'

He spoke slowly, warily, and Maya knew her face must be broadcasting her hurt and her anger. When had she ever been able to keep anything like that hidden from Will? His betrayal was absolute—could not have been designed to hurt her more. Her thoughts spun as she stumbled on the stair and leaned against the banister for support.

'I'm sorry,' he said, and she recognised the tone, the blankness in his eyes.

Some time between falling asleep in his arms and waking alone she'd lost him. No, she hadn't lost him—he'd left her. He was walking away, as if this week, last night, had meant nothing. She struggled to swallow, to breathe, to see.

'But you're going?' She forced the words out. The case by the door told her everything that she needed to know.

'I have to.'

She opened her mouth to protest, but couldn't find words as she realised that he was going to break her. It was so much worse than she had imagined it would be. She had let him into her heart and now he would tear his way out. It burnt like acid, radiating from her chest to every atom of her body. She couldn't have spoken even if she'd been able to think; she choked on her grief.

Eventually she managed one word. 'Explain.'

'I don't have time to explain, Maya.' His shoulders were tight, tense, and his eyes moved constantly between her, the door, the clock on the wall. 'The hospital just called. Neil's been rushed in with—chest pains. I have to go. Now.'

The lump cleared from her throat and breath was expelled from her chest in a rush. She sucked in oxygen, relief and sympathy flooding her body. This was not what she'd feared. He was frightened. He was in a hurry. He needed her support—not her anger.

'Oh, Will, I'm so sorry,' she said, turning suddenly and heading up the stairs, her hands trying to comb out her hair as she went. 'Let me just throw something on and I'll come with you.'

'No.'

'I'll be less than a minute, I swear. We'll be out through the door in less than three.' She looked down at the robe she'd thrown on upstairs. 'I just need to grab some jeans or—'

'I said *no*, Maya.'

She stumbled and sat heavily on the stairs as his words stopped her heart and her breath. The cruelty of his words, his actions, tore at her insides and she choked back tears.

'I'm going now,' he continued. 'And I don't want you to come.'

She tried to keep hopeful, to remind herself of what he was going through—the news he had just received—and tried to tell herself that she could understand. He was hurting and lashing out, that was all. He needed her to help him through this.

She gathered herself up, forced herself to a shaky stand, and walked back down the stairs. She reached him and laid a hand gently on his arm.

'I know you're scared.' She forced calm into her voice, tried to hide her fear and hurt. 'But it will be okay. You'll be okay, whatever happens. We'll deal with it together.'

'No!'

He practically spat the word this time, and she recoiled as if he had burnt her.

'Will, I love you. I want to help you. Tell me what I can do?'

He was already at the door, and as he reached for the handle he looked back over his shoulder at her.

'I'm sorry, Maya,' he said, and she knew from the flatness of his voice that he'd already left her. 'But this was a mistake.'

As the door slammed behind him she leaned back against the newel post, letting it take her weight as she slid down to the floor. Grief blurred her vision and she wrapped her arms tight around her body, trying to hold herself together.

Sitting at the bottom of the stairs, Maya tried to understand what had happened, what had led them here. From the minute Will Thomas had walked into that office she'd known exactly where this would lead if she let her guard down. She wanted to scream at the woman she'd been a week ago. Rail at her; tell her never to let him into her heart or her home. Because this was how it had always been going to end: with her heart torn, broken, and him walking away without a backward glance.

Will had told her he loved her—he had promised her he would stay. The scale of his betrayal made it hard to breathe. In the end she had meant nothing to him. She had offered him everything, given him everything, and when she'd told him she loved him he'd brushed the words off as if they were nothing—as if *she* were nothing.

But she'd learnt her lesson now. He could be sure of that. This was it—the last time she would allow anyone to push her around, treat her like a doormat, take advantage. For days Will had been telling her to stand up for herself. She forced the racing of her heart into anger, channelled her desperation into determination. She would never allow this to happen again. It ended now.

CHAPTER ELEVEN

WILL RAISED HIS arms above his head and stretched, wishing it was as easy to soothe the ache in his heart. In the bed, riddled with wires and tubes, Neil slept soundly—as he had since Will had arrived that morning. Watching him, Will felt a mixture of relief and hope; above all, he was grateful that Neil was going to be okay.

A sensation of *déjà vu* had stalked Will since the moment he'd arrived at the hospital. The stale air, the whiff of antiseptic, the scuffed paint along the walls—it felt as if nothing had changed in the fifteen years since Julia had died here. As he'd walked through the corridors he'd clenched his fists, fighting off the surge of adrenaline that had kicked his heart into racing and made his limbs twitchy. He'd had to focus—get to Neil before it was too late.

When he'd heard that Neil was going to be fine the panic and the fear had receded like mist from a warm morning. As adrenaline had drained and his mind had cleared Will had truly understood for the first time what he'd done. He'd lost Maya. No. That would imply some accident, some unfortunate event. He hadn't lost her. He'd pushed her from him.

Bile rose in his throat as he remembered. He'd been cruel and callous. Vicious. He hadn't meant to be. Hadn't planned it. But the end result was the same. She was never going to talk to him again. Guilt churned his stomach as the scene replayed over and over in his mind, and grief tore at his heart at the thought that he might never see her again.

All he had been able to think about in those few minutes before he'd left the house was getting to the hospital as quickly as he could. Holding everything together until he got to Neil. All he had felt was fear. When he'd thought he might lose Neil again he'd remembered all too clearly why he'd made himself those rules that he had. *This* was the reason he didn't let anyone close. *This* was the pain that ruled his nightmares. He'd looked down at Maya and been overwhelmed by the strength of his love— and he'd remembered why he was so scared of this. The enormous price one paid for loving another person. He'd been terrified.

And yet… He was in pain now anyway.

Because the thought of never seeing Maya again—and why would she ever allow him close now?—filled him with despair. All he could see of his future without her was a dark, empty space.

The ironic thing was, if the call had come before he'd met Maya he probably wouldn't even have listened to the nurse, never mind come running. But he'd picked up the phone and when the nurse had mentioned Neil's name he'd risen and snatched up his clothes without thinking. As soon as he'd heard the words 'chest pains' he'd thought 'heart attack', and had known that he would never forgive himself if he didn't try to see Neil again. Make sense of what had happened between them. Make peace with it as well.

He'd been ready to leave in less than fifteen minutes.

The emotions that had coursed through him had been terrifying. And then there was Maya, telling him she loved him. Reminding him that now there was another person to fear losing. In that moment he had panicked. He'd felt his heart racing, his blood pumping, and above it all the cold, metallic taste of fear. And he'd thought that this was better. Better than letting her into his life and having her ripped from him later.

By the time he'd arrived Neil was out of danger and sleeping. The doctor had explained that he had had a severe angina attack but that it was under control now. Will knew that he couldn't leave until he'd spoken to Neil. It had taken a near tragedy to get him to realise it, but this was his family—the only family he had—and he couldn't walk away. And all this was because of Maya—because he'd learnt to love again, learnt how to share his life with another person.

He stood and walked over to the window: he needed something to watch, to occupy his mind. He thought of Maya at her cottage. The way she could sit and look out across the countryside, letting the calm and quiet wash over her. He'd thought that he'd found peace, too, with her. And then in one moment of fear and panic he'd destroyed any chance that he might have had. Because the last ten anguished hours had taught him one thing: he couldn't see a way to be happy again without her. Any thought of a future without Maya in it…he just couldn't face it.

He whipped his head round at the rustle of a sheet and the beeping of an alarm and his heart raced with panic. Neil was struggling in the bed, clawing at one of his tubes. Will hurried to his side without thinking, acting on instinct, out of love. He hit the call button for the nurse and then looked down and met Neil's eyes. His struggling stopped instantly and Will reached for his hand, moving it away from the tubes.

'It's fine,' Will told him, trying to keep his voice steady, even braving a smile. 'You're in hospital, but you're going to be fine.' He breathed out an enormous sigh as he said the words and for the first time truly believed them.

Neil's gaze flickered over Will and realisation, hope, and finally something he could only describe as joy crossed his foster father's face. Neil's smile broadened as he realised that Will was truly there.

'You're here,' Neil said weakly, his eyes still wide.

The nurse arrived then, and pushed Will back from the bed. He fiddled with his phone as he waited, suddenly feeling reticent, a little embarrassed about the way he'd walked in and just expected everything to be the same as it once was.

By the time the nurse left Neil was sitting up, looking if not entirely healthy then a darn sight better than he had half an hour ago. Will recognised the familiar humour in his eyes and the way his mouth naturally settled into a smile. He had not seen him like this since long before Julia had died, Will realised with a shock. It was another reminder of how ill Neil had been back then.

He had worried that conversation would be awkward—how could it not be after all that had passed? But no sooner had Neil started to apologise for everything that had happened than Will stopped him. What Neil had gone through was no more his fault that Julia's cancer had been hers. Will knew that now. And having come so close to losing Neil completely, before they'd been able to make amends, he knew it was the future that was important now—not raking over the past.

Later, Will found himself with his phone in his hand, his eyes automatically checking for a 'new message' symbol, knowing even as he did so that hope was futile. He didn't even remember taking it out of his pocket, but he was so desperate to hear from Maya he couldn't help himself.

'I've told you, Will. I'm fine now. If you need to be at work I know you're very busy...'

'No, it's not work,' he replied soberly, unable to keep the anguish from his voice.

'Ah, I see. Who is she, then?'

Will shifted uncomfortably in his chair. He'd forgotten how Neil could do that—see through whatever front he constructed. Sense every secret he was trying to hide. He rubbed his forehead with the heel of his hand, wondering if he could tell Neil everything that had happened, whether he would judge him for the terrible way he'd treated Maya this morning.

'Come on, Will. Let's have it.'

Suddenly Will felt fifteen again, being quizzed about why he was home an hour after curfew, smelling of perfume.

'You couldn't hide anything from me when you were a teenager, son; I don't know what makes you think you can get away with it now.'

Son. It had been a long time since he'd been called that. A very long time. But even with a hiatus of fifteen years it sounded right, somehow. Through the fog of black, he felt a warm glow of hope.

He had his family back. But it had cost him Maya, and broken her heart too.

He gave a long sigh. 'I've done something terrible.'

Will sat beside Neil's bedside and checked his watch. Eight o'clock. His phone had stayed resolutely still and silent all afternoon and into the evening, but he checked the screen again—just in case.

He didn't even raise his hopes; it was more habit than expectation. But now he knew that Neil was going to be okay all he could think about was how he could start to put things right with Maya. He called her again, even though he didn't expect her to answer. After all, she'd not picked up any of his calls all day. Worry ate at him, and his hands and thoughts were in constant motion.

He had to see her—had to try and make things right. He might have lost Neil today, and he couldn't bear the thought that he might lose her too. He had to apologise— make her see how disgusted he was with himself for the things that he had said.

Will said goodbye to Neil, who pulled him into a hug when he tried to shake his hand, and promised to visit soon. Then he walked down to the car park, fighting himself with every step not to break into a run.

When he reached the end of Maya's lane he stopped and tried to gather his chaotic thoughts, tried to calm the frenzy of emotion in his breast. What would he say if, by some miracle, Maya answered the door and let him speak? He knew that sorry wasn't enough. One word couldn't possibly fix the damage he had done.

All the way up the motorway he'd been trying to think of the magic words that would make her see what she meant to him, make her understand everything that he loved about her, realise how disgusted he was by the way he had behaved. But he hadn't found them. Hadn't been able to think of anything that would make good the fact that he'd promised to stay and been gone before breakfast.

The sound of her feet padding through the hallway heightened his nerves. His palms pricked with sweat and his heart pounded as he waited for her to open the door. The long pause between the silence of her footsteps and the turn of the key told him one thing: she knew he was here and she was preparing for confrontation. He could almost hear the deep breath she must be taking as she lifted the latch. He took one of his own.

She swung the door wide, but stood unmoving in the doorway and didn't say a word. There was pain written across her face, and a puffiness around her eyes that told him she'd been crying. He felt a twist of pain in his guts, knowing that he had done that. He'd do anything, he knew, to make this—her—okay again. He wanted her to be happy more than anything else. Even more than he wanted her back.

Eventually he swallowed down the lump in his throat.

'What do you want?' She held her head high and spoke slowly, evenly.

She sounded strong, he thought, so different from the raging of torrid emotion he was battling through to get his words out. 'Maya, I'm so sorry about earlier.'

'I didn't answer my phone,' she said, with a grit he hadn't seen in her before, 'because I didn't want to speak to you. Not because I wanted you to turn up here. I thought that would be obvious.'

She paused, and he could see indecision in her eyes.

'How's Neil?' she added, and he thanked heaven that she even cared enough to ask, in awe again at the extent of her incredible compassion.

'He's going to be okay. It was angina, not a heart attack. He's going to be fine. I had to see you. I had to explain.'

Her steely calm highlighted the warring of emotions in his chest, the sensation of losing his grip on his life, on everything he'd thought he knew and understood.

'You had plenty of time to explain this morning, Will.' She crossed her arms a little tighter—protecting herself, he saw, pushing him further away. 'Now? Now I'm not interested. I think it would be best if you left.'

'I love you, Maya. I can't take back this morning, but if you let me tr—'

'No.'

Will stopped dead at the power and certainty in her voice. He felt sick. Of course she was right. He wished he could go back, start the day over. He hadn't left because he didn't love her, but he didn't know how he could ever make her believe that. It had been such a long time since he'd had anyone in his life that he'd forgotten how much his actions affected others. How he had the power to hurt people as much as they could hurt him.

'No,' she said again. 'I deserve better than how you treated me this morning. You're the one who showed me that—showed me that I don't have to put up with people taking what they want and giving nothing in return. You can't expect me to forget all that just because you're the one who broke my heart. I can't do it, Will. You have to go now.'

He watched her carefully, taking in the set of her jaw, the clenched fists, the hard eyes. She was right. He'd told her over and over to stand up for what she really wanted. And she'd listened. Part of him was pleased. So proud that she'd finally seen that she was someone who deserved the best from everyone in her life. And another, larger part of him was disgusted, horrified with himself for causing the hurt that was so evident in every part of her body.

He leant against the doorframe, his body drained of energy as he realised he had to go—had to let her go. He didn't want to tempt her or cajole her or try and change her mind. Of all people, *he* knew what it must be costing her to stand her ground. The only thing he could do was leave her now. It wouldn't be right to push his way back into her life.

But a part of him was torn away as he walked back to his car.

Maya sat at the kitchen table, sipping her tea and eyeing the package propped against the fruit bowl suspiciously.

She knew that it was from Will as he'd included a return address on the back. Her pulse had started to race when she'd seen that, and she had felt dizzy as she'd relived that excruciating morning. It looked different to her every time she remembered it. To start with she'd been able to see nothing but his rejection, the way he'd thrown her words of love back at her as if they meant nothing. But as the initial shock had started to wear away she'd seen hurt and nuance and anguish, until she wasn't sure she could be angry for ever.

She'd been staring at the parcel for the best part of half an hour, wondering what more Will could possibly have to say to her. Nothing could undo the hurt he had caused, but the temptation to listen, to try and understand what had gone wrong, was too great. She reached for the envelope taped to the front of the package.

Dear Maya
The book enclosed with this letter is Julia's recipe
collection. I hope that you will accept this gift from
Neil and me. We were looking through some of her
things together, and we both wanted you to have it.

Maya dropped the letter in surprise and reached into the padded envelope. From it she withdrew a hardback notebook, dog-eared and slightly faded with time. She flicked slowly through the pages of neat cursive script, smiling at the evidence of frequent revision: quantities neatly struck through, notes on oven temperatures and timings added in margins. The recipes were diverse, from Christmas cake to meatballs, apple pie to moussaka. They had been added over time, Maya guessed, and captured years of accumulated knowledge and wisdom.

Eventually, after page after page of neat script, she reached one smudged with a sticky handprint and stopped. It couldn't be Julia's hand, Maya knew. The notebook was so neat in every other way. When she glanced at the top of the page she knew instantly who the print belonged to.

Cottage pie. The first meal Will had cooked solo, he had

told her, and here was the evidence. The hand was small, she thought, placing hers over it, comparing the size. Nothing like the large, capable hands of the Will she knew. He'd been a child when he'd first cooked that meal, unaware of the loss and the pain that lay before him. Maybe feeling safe and secure and happy for the first time in his life.

Maya swallowed down the lump in her throat and continued reading the letter.

> *I know that the way I behaved that morning was terrible, and the things I said were unforgivable. You told me you loved me, and instead of telling you that it made my heart swell and ache, that it made me more incredibly lucky than I deserve—which is how I feel now, knowing that you thought it—I lashed out and hurt you.*
>
> *None of this is an excuse. What I did to you that morning, breaking my promise, is inexcusable. But I want you to know how sorry I am. And that if you ever give me another chance I'll never break a promise, walk away from you, hurt you again.*
>
> *There's something else I want you to know, and to remember always.*
>
> *I love you.*
>
> *Wherever you are, whatever you're doing, saying, thinking, I'll love you.*
> *Will*

She refolded the paper and let out a long breath, trying to sort through her thoughts, to make sense of the swirl of her emotions.

He knew her so well—better than she even understood herself. He saw her greatest fears so clearly, and although he couldn't take back what he'd done she knew that she could never be truly alone again, because Will would always love her. She didn't have to try all the time, or even at all. She didn't have to do anything to earn his love. She just had it. Always. He'd never denied that—not even as he was breaking her heart.

But it didn't mean that she could forgive him.

CHAPTER TWELVE

WILL GLANCED AT his phone as he sipped hot, strong coffee. Still nothing. It had been more than a week since he'd sent that letter, since he'd laid himself on the line. And he still hadn't heard a word. He wasn't angry, or even frustrated—he had no right to be; hope had drained away days ago, leaving nothing but a dull, aching pain.

He knew why Maya hadn't answered: he didn't deserve it, didn't deserve *her*. After everything he had said to her, every way he had hurt her, it was impossible that she would forgive him. Even as he'd written the letter he hadn't expected that. But he'd wanted to explain properly. Had to make sure she knew that it was absolutely nothing she had done wrong. That only he was to blame.

Even though he hadn't spoken to her in days he felt Maya's presence all around him, whether he was awake or asleep. She was in every meal and every drink he enjoyed, every caress of soft cotton, even in the warmth of the sun on his face. He felt her presence in everything that brought him pleasure, everything that made him *feel*.

This morning he'd shut his office door, unable to tolerate the looks Rachel was throwing at him every ten minutes: a combination of frustration, pity and 'I told you so'.

At least his work was going well, even if nothing else was. It was the only thing keeping him going, knowing that Julia House was still on track, that he'd not made a mess of everything. But even that was only down to Maya, to the fact that she'd stuck to her word about the fundraiser when she had every reason to change her mind.

Suddenly the shrill bell of his phone shattered the silence of his office, and he knocked over his coffee in his haste to grab it.

Neil.

He pushed down his disappointment as he took the call.

'Hi, Neil. Just give me a minute.' He opened the door and ushered Rachel in to help with his coffee. 'Sorry, I'll have to call you right back.'

He grabbed the napkins Rachel threw at him and blotted the coffee from his keyboard.

'Who was it?' she asked.

'My...my foster dad,' he replied, realising there was no reason he shouldn't say this out loud, no reason to hide his past.

'Oh!' Rachel didn't hide her surprise. 'I didn't... Why don't you call him back from my desk? I'll take care of this.'

'Thanks—he's not been well.'

He sat in Rachel's chair and dialled Neil on his phone, almost unable to believe how simple it was to have Neil back in his life, to reveal this part of himself.

'Neil, sorry about that,' he said with a despondent sigh, leaning forward and resting his forehead in his hand. 'Spilt coffee all over my desk.'

'Let me guess—you thought it was her on the phone.'

He had no idea how this man could still read him like a book after fifteen years, but it brought a small smile to his face, this reminder that the family he'd thought he'd lost wasn't gone for ever. He felt himself relax, just a fraction, felt the darkness lift ever so slightly.

'So she hasn't called?'

'No.'

He leaned back in the chair and watched Rachel mopping up the coffee on his desk, moving the 'Maya Delights' flyer he had propped against his desk-tidy to save it from the flood. He'd told Rachel it was just so he'd have the number handy in case there were any problems about the dinner tonight. She hadn't even bothered to hide her eye-roll.

When he'd returned to his office after a week at Maya's cottage the grey walls had seemed heavy, oppressive. The splash of colour from the flyer made the air seem lighter every time he looked at it.

'And you sent the letter?' Neil said.

'A week ago.'

There was a long silence and Will imagined Neil trying to think of something encouraging to say.

'Well, maybe she wants to do it in person. It's not really the sort of conversation to have on the phone.'

Will shook his head. 'It's not really the sort of conversation to have when we're both working either.' He sighed. Much as he wanted to believe Neil, the weight of Maya's silence was unbearable. 'Maybe she thinks we'll get through the day without talking at all?'

'Are you going to give her that choice?' Neil asked gently.

He took a second to think about it. 'I have to. She knows how I feel. She either wants to try or she doesn't.'

He couldn't keep the defeat from his voice. If she didn't want him he would carry that pain and scar for ever. But he knew that he could never regret meeting her—wouldn't take back having her in his life, not even to spare himself this additional pain.

'You'll definitely be there for the fundraiser?' Will asked.

'Oh, if you're sure? You know these fancy parties aren't

really my thing. But if you think it'll help the charity to have me there—'

'It'll help *me* to have you there,' Will admitted, forcing down the lump in his throat.

'Then I'll be there.'

Will grabbed his cufflinks and patted his jacket pockets again. Wallet, keys, phone—exactly where they'd been the last time he'd checked. He fidgeted while he ran through everything he needed to do before he headed to the ballroom. He'd been working for the last hour from the temporary office Rachel had set up at the venue and all seemed to be going well.

Rachel had emailed earlier, telling him everything was in place. She'd made a point of telling him—twice—that the caterers had arrived as planned. His heart-rate had picked up with every mention of Maya's name until he had no longer been able to sit still. He had paced the office for the rest of the afternoon.

Now, standing at the door of the office, waiting to go down, he felt his heart pounding a tattoo in his chest. But he took a deep breath and opened the door, bracing himself.

And walked straight into Rachel.

'I thought you'd be enjoying the champagne by now,' Will said, trying to keep his nerves and frustration out of his voice.

She held up two glasses—one only half full. 'I am. But I thought you might need a little Dutch courage and a push through the door.'

'Thanks.' He grabbed the glass and took a long slug.

'Now through the door.'

'Fine, fine—I'm going.' He went to take another sip of champagne and then stopped himself. Tempting, he thought, but this night would be hard enough even with a clear head.

He headed downstairs, walking rather than taking the lift, delaying the moment when he'd see Maya, look into her eyes, and know she'd read his letter and it hadn't made any difference. He had to brace himself for rock bottom.

As he reached the door of the ballroom his phone buzzed in his pocket. Neil. He was here, thank goodness. It struck him again how much Maya had given him. He had his family back, and he could never repay her for how incredible *that* was. He answered the phone and told Neil he'd see him at the ballroom door.

He stroked his thumb instinctively over his phone, desperate for distraction. But he stopped himself. If a week with Maya had taught him anything it was that fighting off his feelings only made them worse. So instead he focussed on Maya. With her face fixed in his mind, suddenly his body went still: he was centred. Whatever happened, he would see her again tonight. For now, as that was all he could be sure of, it would have to be enough.

Neil finally approached and gave him a slap on the shoulder.

'You ready for this, son?'

'Which bit?' Will asked through gritted teeth, steadying himself with a hand on the wall. 'The fundraiser or Maya?'

'Either. Both.'

He tried to school his features so they didn't show his despair and desperation. 'No.'

'Well, then, that's the spirit,' Neil said with a stoic smile, propelling Will into the ballroom.

Maya stepped back from the kitchen door and held her breath, wondering if he had seen her. She'd spent the entire day with at least half an eye glued to the window in that door, wondering if and when Will was going to turn up. She didn't even know why she was doing it. If she'd wanted to see him she could have done that before now. But she'd woken up that morning with a spark of anticipation in her chest, and it had grown and grown through the day, pushing against her ribs, forcing out her breath.

Although even if she had wanted to talk to him there'd have been no time. Her wild swings between anger and forgiveness had not helped with her prep, and she was racing the hands of the clock to get everything out on time. And it wasn't over yet. There was still the duck to finish, the plates to dress for the main course, and vegetables to sauté at the last minute.

Difficult enough even *without* the man she loved turning up looking good enough to lick. A rush of love for him hit her like a truck and she felt some of the strength leave her legs, had to lean against the wall. She loved him. She wanted to reach out and touch him. But she couldn't. Because whether she loved him—whether he loved *her*, even—wasn't the question. It was whether she could forgive him, trust him. Whether they had a future together.

She turned it over in her mind time and time again. Would it be risking too much? Asking for her heart to be broken again?

Turning Will away from her house had been only the start of her new life. It was so clear to her now how unbalanced her friendships were—how she'd allowed herself to give everything of herself without ever expecting or even wanting anything in return. And her friendships looked flat, shallow. If she ever wanted them to be anything else the change had to start with her.

So she'd gone to Dylan's birthday party. When Gwen had seen her she had looked a little embarrassed. Stammering out the words, Maya had told her that of course she'd still be happy to watch the children occasionally—as long as Gwen could give her plenty of notice. And perhaps

Gwen could help *her* out by watering her herb garden and taking in deliveries when she was in London.

She'd forced the request out, feeling heat and blood rushing to her face, but Gwen had been quick to agree.

They'd both taken a couple of gulps of their wine after that, but the afternoon that followed had been one of the most enjoyable Maya had ever spent outside of a kitchen. Freed from watching her every word, she'd found herself laughing, joking more than she remembered doing before.

But even that step hadn't helped her to see what to do with Will—what to do with her feelings for him. And then the parcel and the letter had shown up: proof of the changes he was making too, proof that the progress he'd made at her cottage that week hadn't been an illusion. And with that knowledge had come the niggling thought that perhaps they could try again.

The knowledge that he loved her had glowed inside her, growing brighter every day, until eventually it had outshone her anger. Because she'd believed him when he said it. After all, he'd never denied it. Not even at his most heartbreaking. He loved her. But a relationship took more than love: it took courage and commitment.

Maya returned to her starters, carefully placing the scallops and finishing the plates with a scattering of herbs, calling for service as she went.

When the last plate was gone she hurried to the door, allowing herself a quick glance across the room. It was a moment before she realised what she was doing, and then another before she found him. He looked up as her eyes reached him and held her gaze across the hustle of the ballroom. She tried to make herself look away, but in his face she saw every touch and every smile they had shared. She remembered how it felt to be in his arms, how he had looked when he'd told her that he loved her.

One of the kitchen porters shouted from behind her

and her memories were scattered, replaced by the sizzle of duck breasts crisping behind her. She knew she had to get back to work but she couldn't drag herself away, couldn't break this bond between them. It was still palpable, even with distance, a door and a hundred people between them.

But then he moved to stand, and it broke her trance. *He couldn't come in here.* Her hand flew to her throat at the thought that he might try. Whatever happened, whatever was said, she knew it would leave her drained or high or empty. She needed to focus. She needed *him* to focus. If he couldn't secure the funding he needed tonight then all this would have been for nothing; it would be as if the week at her cottage had never happened. As if *they* had never happened.

She returned to the hotplate with a new sense of purpose. When she glanced up at the window again Will was deep in conversation with the older man sitting next to him. *Good.* She just needed to hold this operation together for another hour or two. Then they would talk.

Maya rubbed the back of her hand over her forehead as the last of the desserts went out and then grabbed a cloth, determined to get the kitchen cleared down in record time. Adrenaline was coursing through her as she knew the time when she would see Will, speak to him, drew nearer.

As she wiped the counters near the door she glanced through the window and saw him heading towards the lectern that had appeared at one end of the ballroom. She hesitated and watched him. His expression was a riot of emotion: nerves, pride, guilt, tension. Watching from across the room, she could still feel the connection that had grown between them at her cottage, the energy that pulled them together, held them there, and she wondered if he felt it too.

She knew that this was hard, whatever it was that he

was doing. She could see it clearly in his face and his posture, and she wanted to be here with him. She leaned against the frame and nudged the door open with her foot so she could listen.

Will spoke clearly, thanking everyone there for their support and generosity.

'And now I'd like to say a few words about Julia Wilson and the charity that bears her name,' Will said, with a hint of a waver to his voice.

Her heart ached at the sound of it. Regardless of what he'd done to her, she loved him, and his pain was her pain.

His hands gripped the lectern tightly as he continued. 'I first met Julia when I was twelve years old. Not long after that first meeting she and her husband, Neil, became my foster parents. They welcomed me into their lives with unrivalled generosity. Julia was generous with her time, her home, her family, her kitchen—'

He gave a small smile and his eyes flickered up. Maya was certain that glance was directed at her.

'And with her love. But when I was fifteen cancer took Julia away from us.'

Will's voice wavered again, and Maya ached to wrap her arms around him, to offer him support and comfort— love. But she stayed where she was. Last time she had offered her help he'd pushed her away and broken her heart.

Will took a long pull on the glass of water in from of him and looked out across the tables before starting to speak again.

'Working with a wonderful board of trustees to make this dinner happen has been rewarding, frustrating and at times very painful. For many years after Julia's death I refused to think about my life with her. It was too painful. But my involvement with the charity has helped me to rediscover happy, joyful memories. It has shown me that the loss of a loved one, no matter how painful, is not the end of everything good. Even in the darkest moments there are people who can offer support and hope, help create good memories along with the bad.

'Before its doors have even opened Julia House has already helped its first patient. If it can help even one more person to find moments of peace and happiness even when—*especially* when—the darkness of their situation seems overwhelming, then I'll be immensely proud of what we've done.'

At these last words he glanced towards the kitchen door, and this time Maya knew that he saw her standing, watching. She wanted to look away, but her gaze refused to drop. She didn't want to lose this moment. The words were for her, she knew, and she felt the connection between them pulse again.

There was nothing more to say.

He had apologised; he had explained. It was down to her now, and no one else, to decide if she could trust him again.

As she saw Rachel striding across the room she pulled her gaze down and backed away from the door, suddenly terrified now that it was time.

'Maya, come on,' Rachel urged, holding open the kitchen door. 'Everyone wants to send their compliments to the chef.'

Maya heard Rachel mumble something about an intervention as she grabbed her hand and dragged her towards the door. She wanted to dig her heels in and sit back on her haunches, to beg to be allowed to hide out in here all night. But she knew that this had to be faced. She was a professional, and this was part of her job. And, even terrified, she wanted to see Will. But her whole life could depend on what happened in the next few minutes.

'Wait,' Maya demanded, reaching for the clip in her hair and running the back of her hand over her forehead.

It came away damp with perspiration. 'I'm not going out there like this. I need a couple of minutes.'

Rachel took a step back and folded her arms, a faint smile on her lips. Maya grabbed lipstick, powder and a comb from her bag in the changing room and peered into a mirror.

Applying lipstick under Rachel's scrutiny, Maya blushed as she realised that she knew everything—or had guessed.

'Right, I'm ready.'

The other woman reached across and fluffed her hair a little before leading the way to the door.

The room burst into spontaneous applause as Maya stepped through the door, and it stopped her on the spot. The heat in her cheeks grew even stronger, but her mind was too full of Will to fully take it in. She glanced around the room and stilled momentarily. From the kitchen the room had looked beautiful, but she hadn't truly appreciated the vastness of the space, the opulence of the fabric draped at the floor-to-ceiling windows. Columns towered around the room, and light danced from crystal and silver.

A glamorous older woman on the table next to her reached out to shake her hand.

'Really lovely, dear. I must talk to you about that sauce for the duck.'

Maya seized the opportunity, grateful that it delayed the moment when she would have to decide once and for all what she wanted.

She made her way from table to table, graciously accepting compliments, giving hints about her recipes when people asked, the whole time playing out a weird paradox. She started at the side of the room furthest away from Will, and the knowledge that he was on the other side of the room both drew her to him and slowed her progress. She knew it was inevitable. That she would have to speak to him at some point. But the closer that moment got, the more nervous she felt.

She drew out her conversations, always with her back turned to Will's table, always with him fighting for space in her mind. She tried to force him out, to focus on anything but him—anything but the decision she had to make. But finally there was nowhere else to hide. She took a deep breath, steadied her shaking hands, and turned to face Will.

His eyes were already fixed on her, his expression intense and full of love; she stood motionless as the room and her racing thoughts faded.

'Maya.'

His voice broke the spell and she wanted to turn and run at the naked tenderness and hope she heard. She wasn't sure if she could do this, and nausea crept from her stomach to her throat.

Will stood up as she took a step closer. 'Maya,' he said again, and then cleared his throat. 'You know Sir Cuthbert and Lady Margery, I think? And this is Neil.'

She nodded at Sir Cuthbert and smiled at his wife. She gaped at Neil, and then reached out and shook his hand, looking from him to Will, marvelling at this repaired relationship. At the courage and forgiveness they must have found to get here.

'It's lovely to meet you, Maya,' Neil said. 'I've heard so much about you from Will.'

She blanched at that. Not *too* much, she hoped.

'Pleased to meet you too,' she said. 'I hope you're well?'

'Yes, never better, thanks. Please—have a seat,' Neil said, pulling a chair over from the next table.

She saw her chance to further delay the inevitable, and engaged Neil in conversation.

'Thank you for the recipe book,' she said, angling her body away from Will. 'It was very thoughtful of you. I hope I can do the recipes justice.'

'I'm sure you will,' Neil said, 'if this evening's anything to go by. The chocolate pudding was incredible.'

She managed a genuine smile at last.

'And I'm glad you like the book. But it was Will's idea. I have to thank you, Maya,' Neil continued, his voice dropping low, 'because I understand from Will that we might still not be in contact if it wasn't for you.'

She shook her head slowly, not sure what she could say to that. Neil and Will had managed to rebuild their relationship, and she was happy for them—truly. But that didn't soothe the pain that had ached in her heart since they day of their reunion.

Suddenly talking to Neil, not talking to Will, was more than she could bear. She knew that she had created the situation by delaying talking to him until they found themselves here, but it didn't matter. She couldn't do it. Not like this. Not yet.

She stood abruptly, the sound of her heart beating loud in her head. 'I hope you all enjoyed the food.' She forced the words out. 'But I really ought to get back to the kitchen. Have a good evening.'

She hurried away from the table, knocking her hip against a chair-back, but kept her eyes fixed forward, refusing to allow herself a glance back.

Her brain was impossibly overloaded. The magnitude of her decision made her head spin, and for a second she thought it was another migraine. At the last minute she realised that the lobby would be a safer exit than the still busy kitchen. She slipped through the door into the foyer and then leaned back against the wall, shutting her eyes and trying to catch her breath.

She just needed a minute to gather her thoughts, to work out what the hell she was going to do about what had happened. When she'd arrived there that morning, she hadn't known what would happen between her and Will. She'd hoped—believed—that at some point the right answer would just come to her, fully formed, and she'd accept it.

She hadn't expected her decision, when she made it, to cause such a tumult of emotion. To leave her so desperate to talk to him, but too afraid to do it. She ran her hands through her hair, trying to calm her thoughts, but her heart was thudding and her palms prickling with stress and tension.

She had learnt so much about Will tonight. He wasn't scared of his memories any more. He wasn't blocking out the good for fear of feeling the bad. The progress that he'd made during the week at her cottage wasn't an illusion. It was real. So how—why?—had he hurt her so badly?

Standing in the lobby, she felt it hit her. She knew exactly why. Because he had felt as overwhelmed and as frightened as she did right now, except he'd had a deadline with life-or-death consequences. He had run because he was confused, exactly as she had just done.

Her eyes snapped open at the sound of a door swinging open.

'Will…' She breathed the word, releasing weeks of anger, longing, loneliness.

He opened his mouth but for a long moment stayed silent. She held her breath.

'Hi.'

They stood together in silence for a few more long, awkward seconds as she tried to think what they could say that would heal this rift between them.

'Can I say something?' Will asked eventually.

Maya nodded nervously, her mouth dry, still not convinced that they could really do this—that they could find one another again.

He took a deep breath and raised a hand to rub at the back of his neck. Maya bit her lip at that endearingly familiar gesture.

'If this is going to be the last time I see you,' he said, rubbing a hand over his eyes now, 'I just want you to know how sorry I am about that morning. It's the biggest mistake I've ever made, and I'll always regret it.'

He looked at her and held her gaze steady for a heartbeat. Two. Then he blinked, looked away. She felt colder without his eyes on her, and his words haunted her. *The last time*. It couldn't be. Her chest felt tight and she knew unequivocally that she couldn't allow that. Knew that she could never forgive herself if she didn't forgive him.

A wave of love for him hit her again as she took in the despair on his face, saw that he expected, wanted nothing from her, that he just wanted to apologise. This was all for *her*, not for him.

'I should go,' he said eventually, his voice flat, empty as he turned, his hand already pushing at the door.

'Will—wait.'

She spoke before she'd had the chance even to think the words. But what more was there to think about? She loved him and he loved her. A relationship took courage and trust. If she didn't step up now, with the first of those, then what chance did they have?

'You hurt me,' she said, and saw his features crumple in pain at the memory of it.

'I know,' he said quietly, his voice full of sorrow. 'And I don't know if I can ever show you how sorry I am, how much I regret it. All I can say is that I love you, and the cost of loving someone never felt as sharp or as terrifying as it did that morning.'

'I know,' she said, reaching out to him and taking his hand. And she did. She understood.

'I would never, ever…' He stopped himself.

'Go on.'

'No,' he said. 'I wanted—needed to apologise in person. But I won't pressure you, try and make you take me back.'

She forced out of rush of breath in frustration, wondering when she was going to get *her* say in this.

'I'm a big girl, Will. And we both know I'm past being forced into anything.'

She thought back to the evening when he'd shown up on her doorstep and she'd stood her ground, and knew that Will had helped her find the strength and confidence to do that.

'I can make my own decisions. So make your case, if you want.'

He hesitated, giving her an astute look.

'If you're badgering I'll stop you.' She couldn't quite believe that the calm, steady words had come from her own mouth.

'I've only got one thing left to say: I love you, and I will never hurt you again. The only thing I want is for you to be happy.'

He turned back to the door, his face set, his shoulders stiff, and had one foot through it when Maya cleared her throat. He looked back at her, and for the first time she saw a suggestion of hope in his eyes.

'And do *I* get a say?' she asked, one brow raised, her shoulders relaxing as she planted her hands on her hips. 'Because I'm pretty sure someone spent a lot of time recently telling me how important it is that I get what *I* want. I get to decide what makes *me* happy.'

She took a couple of steps towards him and reached for his hand again.

'I want *you*,' she said, looking him straight in the eye. 'You freaked out and got scared and messed up. And don't worry, because I'm already thinking of a thousand ways you can start making that up to me.' She smiled. 'But I heard the speech you gave in there. I saw you with Neil. And I know how it feels when you know what you need to do and you're absolutely terrified of it at the same time.

I know you're scared too, but you're trying. And I think I can do that too.'

'Maya…'

He still looked pained, but she wanted him to see that he didn't need to be, that they could overcome this, could be happy—both of them.

'No, Will. You want me to make decisions for *me*? Well, this is my decision, and I'm choosing to give us a chance.' She took another step forward, closing the space between them, and then reached up and cupped his cheek with her palm. 'You told me I should start asking for what I want, what I need. I need *you*: are you going to argue with me?'

She stretched up on tiptoes and brought her lips to Will's. He kissed her back, tentatively at first, as if he couldn't quite believe it. And then hungrily, with his arms wrapping tight around her waist, lifting her practically off her feet, pressing her into the wall behind her.

His hand moved from her waist to tangle in her hair, winding tightly, holding her close. Her nerve-endings felt as if they were burning, and every touch of his hands, his lips, his chest, raised another fire. But she sensed desperation in the wild passion of Will's kiss, and it made her sad.

She eased her lips away from his a fraction and looked up, caught his eye.

'Will, maybe…'

'Too much? I just can't quite believe you're giving me another chance. I never want to let go of you again.'

She stroked her fingertips across his cheek, soothing him, and stopped his words with a quick, gentle kiss. 'It was…well, incredible…'

For a second she forgot why she'd stopped him, and was leaning in to him again when she remembered.

'I'm not going anywhere.' She moved her hand back to his cheek and pushed him away from her, made sure he was looking her in the eye. 'It doesn't matter if you grab me tight, or kiss me gently, or if you just throw me a glance from across the room. I'm yours. I love you and I'm going nowhere. Ever.'

Will closed his eyes and leant his forehead against hers, and for the first time that day she sensed a stillness, a peace about him.

'I love you,' he breathed.

She smiled and closed her eyes, absorbing the truth and power of his words.

'So what now?'

What a question, she thought, thinking of the years, the decades of their life ahead of them. And suddenly she knew with startling clarity what she wanted for that life. Simply him. For ever. A smile curled the corner of her lips as the answer formed in her mind, and then nerves fluttered in her belly as she tried to give it voice.

She lifted her head, the smile beaming from her now. 'Marry me.'

Will dropped his hands from her hair, but her smile never faltered. How could it when she trusted his love for her? When she had so much faith in him? She knew she just had to wait, give him a chance to catch up with her.

Then his face broke into a grin. 'Isn't that my line?'

'Nope. It's what I want, so I'm the one who asks for it.'

'You're incredible,' Will said, dipping his head for a kiss.

Maya stopped him with a palm against his chest. 'Are you going to answer?'

'Yes,' Will said with a chuckle. 'Always, always yes.'

Maya curled her hand around his shirt and pulled him to her, meeting his lips with her own.

* * * * *

A CADENCE CREEK CHRISTMAS

DONNA ALWARD

To the Mills & Boon Romance authors – my writing family. You guys are the best

CHAPTER ONE

TAYLOR SHEPARD FROWNED as she assessed the lineup of men before her. All five of them were big, burly and, with the exception of her brother Jack, looked irritated beyond belief.

"Come on, Taylor, can't we take these monkey suits off?"

Her oldest brother, Callum, pleaded with her. Along with his best man and groomsmen, he'd spent the past half hour trying on various tuxedo styles. Callum, being her brother and, of course, the groom, was the spokesman for the lot.

"If you want to show up at your wedding in jeans and boots, be my guest. I don't think your bride would appreciate that too much, though."

A muffled snort came from down the line. Her head snapped toward the sound and she saw one of the groomsmen—Rhys, if she remembered correctly—struggling to keep a straight face.

"Keep it up," she warned severely, "and you'll be the one trying on a cravat."

His face sobered in an instant.

"This was supposed to be a small and simple wedding," Callum reminded her. "Not one of your massive events."

"And it will be. But small and simple doesn't mean it

can't be classy." She pinned him with a stare. "Your soon-to-be wife trusts me. Besides, you need to balance your look with the wedding dress and flower girl dress for Nell." She paused and played her trump card. "They're going to be *beautiful*."

There'd be little argument out of Callum now. All it took was the mention of Avery and his baby daughter and the tough ex-soldier turned into a marshmallow. She thought it was fantastic. He'd needed someone like Avery for a long time. Not to mention how fatherhood had changed him. He had the family he'd always wanted.

She examined each man carefully. "I don't like the red vests," she decreed. She went up to Sam Diamond and tugged on the lapels of his jacket. "And not double-breasted. The green vests, like Tyson's here. The single-breasted jacket like Jack has on, which is much simpler." She smiled up at her brother, easily the most comfortable man in the group. Jack wouldn't give her a moment's trouble, not about this anyway. She got to the last body in the line and looked up.

Dark eyes looked down into hers. A little serious, a little bit of put-upon patience, and a surprising warmth that made her think he had a good sense of humor. She reached up and gave his tie a tug, straightening it. "And not the bolo tie, either. The crossover that Rhys is wearing is classier and still very Western."

Her fingertips grazed the starchy fabric of his shirt as she dropped her hand. It was a negligible touch, barely worth noticing, except the slight contact made something interesting tumble around in her stomach. Her gaze darted up to his again and discovered he was watching her steadily in a way that made her feel both excited and awkward.

Interesting. Because in her line of work she dealt with

all sorts of men every day. Rich men, powerful men, men who liked other men and men who couldn't keep their hands to themselves. She knew how to handle herself. Was never tempted to flirt unless it was a business strategy. She was very good at reading people, figuring out their tastes and wants and knowing what methods she needed to use to deliver them.

So getting a fluttery feeling from barely touching Rhys Bullock was a surprise indeed. And feeling awkward? Well, that was practically unheard of. Of course, it could be that she was just very out of practice. She'd been far too busy building her business to do much dating.

She straightened her shoulders and took a step backward. "Okay, now on to footwear."

Groans went up the line.

She smiled. "Guys, really. This will be the best part. I was thinking black boots which we can get wherever you prefer to buy your boots. No patent dress shoes. Put on the boots you wore here so we can accurately measure your inseam for length. Then we'll finish up your measurements and you're done." She made a dismissive sound. "Honestly, what a bunch of babies."

She was having fun now, teasing the guys. They were good men but not much for dressing up. She got that. Their standard uniform was jeans and boots, plaid shirts and Stetsons. Tuxedo fittings had to be torture.

Still, it didn't matter if this was her brother's wedding or a client's A-list party. Or if she was being paid or doing it as a wedding gift. Avery and Callum's day would be exactly what it should be because she'd oversee every last detail.

And if she were being honest with herself, it was a relief to get out of Vancouver for a while and deal with "real" people. It had been exhausting lately. Most of her clients were rich and used to getting exactly what they wanted exactly when they wanted it. Their sense of entitlement could be a bit much. Not to mention the unorthodox requests. She sometimes wondered what sort of reality these people lived in.

As she looked after the ordering details, one of the alterations staff did measurements. Another half hour and they were all done and standing out in the sunshine again. Taylor pulled out her phone and scanned her to-do list for today. She had to drive back to Cadence Creek and meet with Melissa Stone, the florist at Foothills Floral. The final order was going to be placed today—after all, the wedding was less than two weeks away now. All this should have been done a month ago or even more, but Taylor knew there were ways to get things done in a hurry if needs be. Like with the tuxes and invitations. Both should have been tended to months ago but it had merely taken a few phone calls and it had all been sorted. A little out of Callum's budget, perhaps, but he didn't need to know that. She was good for it. *Exclusive!*—her event planning business—had treated her well the past few years.

Still, there was no time to waste. She closed her calendar and looked up.

The group of them were standing around chatting, something about a lodge north of town and what had happened to the rancher who'd owned it. Jack was listening intently, but Rhys was missing. Had he left already?

The bell on the door chimed behind her, and she turned to see Rhys walking through. He looked far more himself now in black jeans and a black, tan and red plaid shirt beneath a sheepskin jacket. His boots were brown and weathered and as he stepped on to the sidewalk he dipped his head just a little and placed a well-worn hat on top. Taylor half smiled. The hat looked like an old friend; shaped precisely to his head, worn-in and comfortable.

"Feel better?" she asked, smiling.

"I'm not much for dressing up," he replied simply.

"I know. None of you are, really. But it's only for one day. You're all going to look very handsome."

"Is that so?"

Her cheeks heated a little. Rhys's best feature was his eyes. And he was tall and well-built, just the way she liked her men. Perhaps it was growing up the way she had. They'd all been outdoor kids. Heck, Callum had joined the military and Jack had been a pro downhill skier until he'd blown his knee out at Val d'Isère.

But Rhys wasn't classically handsome. Not in the way that Tyson Diamond was, for instance. In this group Rhys would be the one who would probably be overlooked. His cheekbones were high and defined and his jawbone unrelenting, giving him a rough appearance. His lips looked well-shaped but it was hard to tell—the closest she'd seen him come to smiling was the clandestine chuckle while they were inside.

But it was the way he'd answered that piqued her interest. *Is that so?* he'd asked, as if he couldn't care one way or the other if anyone thought him handsome or not.

It was quite refreshing.

"I should get going," she said, lifting her chin. "I've got to be back to town in thirty minutes for another appointment. Thanks for coming out. It'll be easy for you from here on in. Weddings do tend to be mostly women's business." At least with these sorts of men…

"Drive carefully then," he said, tipping his hat. "No sense rushing. The creek isn't going anywhere."

"Thanks, but I'd like to be on time just the same." She gave him a brief nod and turned to the assembled group.

"I've got to go. Thanks everyone." She put her hand on Callum's shoulder and went up on tiptoe to kiss his cheek. "See you soon." She did the same for Jack. "When are you flying out?"

He shrugged. "I'm going to hang around for a few days. I've got to be back in Montana for meetings on Monday, though, and then I'm flying in the Thursday before the wedding."

"Let's have lunch before you go back."

"You got it. Text me."

With a quick wave Taylor hurried across the parking lot, her heeled boots echoing on the pavement. She turned the car heater on high and rubbed her hands together—December in Alberta was colder than on the coast and she felt chilled to the bone all the time.

She was down to twenty-five minutes. As a light snow began to fall, she put her rental car in gear and pulled out, checking her GPS for the quickest route to the highway.

Three weeks. That was how long she had to decompress. She'd take care of Callum's wedding and then enjoy one indulgent week of vacation before heading home and working on the final preparations for New Year's. This year's planning involved taking over an entire warehouse and transforming it into an under the sea kingdom.

It all seemed quite ridiculous. And because it did, she knew that it was time she took a vacation. Even one as short as a week in some small, backwater Alberta town. Thank goodness her assistant, Alicia, was completely capable and could handle things in Taylor's absence.

She turned on the wipers and sighed. Compared to the crazy demands of her normal events, she knew she could do this wedding with her eyes closed.

If that were true, though, why was she having so much fun and dreading going back to Vancouver so very much?

* * *

It was already dark when Taylor whipped out her phone, brought up her to-do list and started punching in brief notes with her thumbs. Her fingers were numb with cold and she'd been out of the flower shop for a whole minute and a half. Where on earth was the frigid air coming from anyway? Shivering and walking toward the town's B&B, she hurriedly typed in one last detail she didn't want to forget. Instead of typing the word "cedar," however, she felt a sharp pain in her shoulder as she bounced off something very big and hard.

"Hey," she growled. "Watch where you're going!"

She looked up to find Rhys Bullock staring down at her, a scowl marking his angular face.

"Oh, it's you," she said, letting out a puff of annoyance.

He knelt down and retrieved her phone, stood up and handed it over. "Hope it didn't break," he said. His tone suggested that he wasn't quite sincere in that sentiment.

"The rubber cover is supposed to protect it. It'll be fine."

"Maybe next time you should watch where you're going. Stop and sit down before you start typing."

"It's too damn cold to stop," she grumbled.

He laughed then, the expulsion of breath forming a white cloud around his head. "Not used to an arctic front? This isn't cold. Wait until it's minus forty."

"Not a chance."

"That's right. You're only here for the wedding."

"If you'll excuse me, I'd like to get out of the cold before my fingertips fall off." She tried to ignore how his face changed when he laughed, softening the severe lines. A smattering of tiny marks added character to his tanned skin. If she had to come up with one word to describe Rhys, it would be *weathered*. It wasn't necessarily a bad thing.

He took a step closer and to her surprise reached into her pocket and took out her gloves. Then he took the phone from her hands, dropped it in the pocket and handed over the gloves. "This will help."

She raised an eyebrow. "That was presumptuous of you."

He shrugged. "Ms. Shepard, I'm pretty much used to keeping things simple and doing what has to be done. If your fingers are cold, put on your gloves."

She shoved her fingers into the fuzzy warmth, her temper simmering. He spoke to her as if she were a child!

"Now," he said calmly, "where are you headed? It's dark. I'll walk you."

Her temper disintegrated under the weight of her disbelief. She laughed. "Are you serious? This is Cadence Creek. I think I'll be safe walking two blocks to my accommodations." Good Lord. She lived in one of the largest cities in Canada. She knew how to look out for herself!

"Maybe I just want to make sure you don't start texting and walk out into traffic," he suggested. "You must be going to Jim's then." He named the bed and breakfast owner.

"That's right."

He turned around so they were facing the same direction. "Let's go," he suggested.

She fell into step because she didn't know what else to do. He seemed rather determined and it would take all of five minutes to walk to the rambling house that provided the town's only accommodation. To her mind the dive motel out on the highway didn't count. She watched as he tipped his hat to an older lady coming out of the drugstore and then gave a nod to a few men standing on the steps of the hardware. He might be gruff and bossy and not all that pretty to look at, but she had to give Rhys one thing—his manners were impeccable.

The light dusting of snow earlier covered the sidewalk and even grouchy Taylor had to admit that it was pretty, especially in the dark with the town's Christmas lights casting colored shadows on its surface. Each old-fashioned lamppost held a pine wreath with a red bow. Storefronts were decorated with garland on their railings and twinkle lights. Christmas trees peeked through front windows and jolly Santas and snowmen grinned from front yards.

Cadence Creek at the holidays was like one of those Christmas card towns that Taylor hadn't believed truly existed. Being here wasn't really so bad. Even if it was a little...boring.

They stopped at a crosswalk. And as they did her stomach gave out a long, loud rumble.

Rhys put his hand at her elbow and they stepped off the curb. But instead of going right on the other side, he guided her to the left.

"Um, the B&B is that way," she said, turning her head and pointing in the opposite direction.

"When did you eat last?" he asked.

She fought the urge to sigh. "None of your business."

Undeterred, he kept walking and kept the pressure at her elbow. "Jim and Kathleen don't provide dinner. You need something to eat."

She stopped dead in her tracks. Rhys carried on for a few steps until he realized she wasn't with him then he stopped and turned around. "What?"

"How old am I?"

His brows wrinkled, forming a crease above his nose. "How could I possibly know that?"

"Do I look like an adult to you?"

Something flared in his eyes as his gaze slid from her face down to her boots and back up again. "Yes'm."

She swallowed. "You can't herd me like you herd your cattle, Mr. Bullock."

"I don't herd cattle," he responded.

"You don't?"

"No ma'am. I work with the horses. Especially the skittish ones."

"Well, then," she floundered and then recovered, ignoring that a snowflake had just fallen and landed on the tip of her nose. "I'm not one of your horses. You can't make me eat just because you say so."

He shrugged. "Can't make the horses do that, either. Trick is to make them *want* to do what I want." He gave her a level stare. "I'm pretty good at that."

"Your ego isn't suffering, I see."

His lips twitched. "No, ma'am. Everyone has a skill. Smart man knows what his is, that's all."

God, she didn't want to be amused. He was a bull-headed, overbearing macho cowboy type who probably called women "little lady" and thought he was all that. But she was amused and to be honest she'd enjoyed sparring with him just a little bit. At least he wasn't a pampered brat like most people she met.

She let out the tension in her shoulders. "Where are you taking me, then?" She'd seriously considered ordering a pizza and having it delivered to the B&B. It wasn't like there was a plethora of dining choices in Cadence Creek.

"Just to the Wagon Wheel. Best food in town."

"I've been. I had lunch there yesterday." And breakfast in the dining room of the bed and breakfast and then dinner was a fast-food burger grabbed on the way back from the stationery supply store in Edmonton.

The lunch had definitely been the best meal—home-made chicken soup, thick with big chunks of chicken, vegetables and the temptation of a warm roll which she'd left behind, not wanting the extra carbs.

Her stomach growled again, probably from the mere thought of the food at the diner.

"Fine. I'll go get some takeout. Will that make you happy?"

He shrugged. "It's not about me. But now that you mention it, I think tonight is pot roast. I could do with some of that myself." He turned and started walking away.

Reluctantly she followed a step behind him. At least he didn't have that darned proprietary hand under her elbow anymore. Half a block away she could smell the food. The aroma of the standard fare—fries and the like—hit first, but then the undertones touched her nostrils: beef, bread and baking.

Her mouth watered as she reminded herself that she had a bridesmaid's dress to fit into as well. Pot roast would be good. But she would absolutely say no to dessert.

It was warm inside the diner. The blast of heat was a glorious welcome and the scents that were hinted at outside filled the air inside. Christmas music played from an ancient jukebox in the corner. The whole place was decorated for the holidays, but in the evening with everything lit up it looked very different than it had yesterday at noon. Mini-lights ran the length of the lunch counter and the tree in a back corner had flashing lights and a star topper that pulsed like a camera flash. The prevalence of vinyl and chrome made her feel like she was in a time warp.

Two-thirds of the tables were filled with people, all talking animatedly over the music. Rhys gave a wave to a group in a corner and then, to her surprise, slipped behind the cash register and went straight into the kitchen.

Through the order window she saw him grin at an older

woman in a huge cobbler's apron who laughed and patted his arm. Both of them turned Taylor's way and she offered a polite smile before turning her attention to the specials menu on a chalkboard. Takeout was definitely the way to go here. This wasn't her town or her people. She stuck out like a sore thumb.

She was just about to order a salad when Rhys returned. "Come on," he said, taking her elbow again. "Let's grab a seat."

"Um, I didn't really think we were going to eat together. I was just going to get something to take back with me."

"You work too hard," he said, holding out a chair for her and then moving around the table without pushing it in—polite without being over the top. "You could use some downtime."

She shifted the chair closer to the table. "Are you kidding? This is slow for me."

He raised his eyebrows. "Then you really do need to stop and refuel."

He shrugged out of his jacket and hooked it over the top of the chair. She did the same, unbuttoning the black-and-red wool coat and shoving her scarf in the sleeve. She wore skinny jeans tucked into her favorite boots—red designer riding boots—and a snug black cashmere sweater from an expensive department store in the city. She looked around. Most of the men wore thirty-dollar jeans and plaid flannel, and the women dressed in a similar fashion—jeans and department store tops.

Just as she thought. Sore thumb.

When she met Rhys's gaze again she found his sharper, harder, as if he could read her thoughts. She dropped her gaze and opened her menu.

"No need for that. Couple orders of pot roast are on their way."

She put down the menu and folded her hands on the top. While the rest of the decorations at the diner bordered on cheesy, she secretly loved the small silk poinsettia pots with Merry Christmas picks. "What amusement are you getting out of this?" she asked. "From what I can gather you don't approve of me but you do enjoy bossing me around."

"Why would you think that?"

"Oh, I don't know. Because so far you've found fault with everything I say or do?"

"Then why did you come with me?"

"You didn't leave me much choice." She pursed her lips.

"You always have a choice," he replied, unrolling his cutlery from his paper napkin.

"Then I guess because I was hungry," she said.

He smiled. "You mean because I was right."

Oh, he was infuriating!

"The trick is to make them want to do what I want." He repeated his earlier sentiment, only she understood he wasn't talking about horses anymore. He'd played her like a violin.

She might have had some choice words only their meals arrived, two plates filled with roast beef, potatoes, carrots, peas and delightfully puffy-looking Yorkshire puddings. Her potatoes swam in a pool of rich gravy and the smell coming from the food was heaven in itself.

She never ate like this anymore. Wondered if she could somehow extract the potatoes from the gravy or maybe just leave the potatoes altogether—that would probably be better.

"Thanks, Mom," she heard Rhys say, and her gaze darted from her plate up to his face and then to the woman standing beside the table—the same woman who had patted his arm in the kitchen. Taylor guessed her to be somewhere around fifty, with dark brown hair like Rhys's, only cut in an efficient bob and sprinkled with a few gray hairs.

"You're welcome," she said, then turned to Taylor with a smile. "You're Callum's sister. I remember you from the christening party."

Right. Taylor had flown in for that and she'd helped arrange a few details like the outdoor tent, but she'd done it all by phone from Vancouver. "Oh, my goodness, I totally didn't put two and two together. Martha Bullock... of course. And you're Rhys's mother." She offered an uncertain smile. Usually she didn't forget details like that. Then again the idea of the gruff cowboy calling anyone "Mom" seemed out of place.

"Sure am. Raised both him and his brother, Tom. Tom's been working up north for years now, but Rhys moved home a few years back."

"Your chicken tartlets at the party were to die for," Taylor complimented. "And I had the soup yesterday. You're a fabulous cook, Mrs. Bullock. Whoever your boys marry have big shoes to fill to keep up with Mom's home cooking."

Martha laughed while, from the corner of her eye, Taylor could see Rhys scowl. Good. About time he felt a bit on the back foot since he'd been throwing her off all day.

"Heh, good luck," Martha joked. "I'm guessing groomsman is as close to the altar as Rhys is gonna get. He's picky."

She could almost see the steam come out of his ears, but she took pity on him because she'd heard much the same argument from her own family. It got wearisome after a while. Particularly from her father, who'd never taken her business seriously and seemed to think her sole purpose in life was to settle down and have babies.

Not that she had anything against marriage or babies. But she'd do it on her own timetable.

"Well," she said, a bit softer, "it seems to me that getting married is kind of a big deal and a person would have to be awfully sure that they wanted to see that person every day for the rest of their lives. Not a thing to rush, really."

Martha smiled and patted Taylor's hand. "Pretty *and* wise. Don't see that very often, at least around here." She sent a pointed look at a nearby table where Taylor spied an animated blonde seated with a young man who seemed besotted with her.

"Well, your supper's getting cold." Martha straightened. "And I've got to get back. See you in a bit."

Taylor watched Rhys's mother move off, stopping at several tables to say hello. Her full laugh was infectious and Taylor found herself smiling.

When she turned back, Rhys had already started cutting into his beef. Taylor mentally shrugged and speared a bright orange carrot with her fork.

"So," she said easily. "How'd a nice woman like your mother end up with a pigheaded son like you?"

CHAPTER TWO

TENDER AS IT WAS, Rhys nearly choked on the beef in his mouth. Lord, but Callum's sister was full of sass. And used to getting her own way, too, from the looks of it. He'd noticed her way back in the fall at the christening, all put together and pretty and, well, bossy. Not that she'd been aggressive. She just had one of those natural take-charge kind of ways about her. When Taylor was on the job, things got done.

He just bet she was Student Council president in school, too. And on any other committee she could find.

He'd been the quiet guy at the back of the class, wishing he could be anywhere else. Preferably outside. On horseback.

Burl Ives was crooning on the jukebox now and Taylor was blinking at him innocently. He wasn't sure if he wanted to be offended or laugh at her.

"She only donated half the genetic material," he replied once he'd swallowed. "Ask her. She'll tell you my father was a stubborn old mule."

Taylor popped a disc of carrot into her mouth. "Was?"

"He died when I was twenty-four. Brain aneurism. No warning at all."

"God, Rhys. I'm sorry."

He shrugged again. "It's okay. We've all moved well beyond the shock and grief part to just missing him." And he did. Even though at times Rhys had been frustrated with his father's decisions, he missed his dad's big laugh and some of the fun things they'd done as kids—like camping and fishing. Those were the only kinds of vacations their family had ever been able to afford.

They ate in silence for a while until it grew uncomfortable. Rhys looked over at her. He wasn't quite sure what had propelled him to bring her here tonight. It had been the gentlemanly thing to do but there was something else about her that intrigued him. He figured it was probably the way she challenged him, how she'd challenged them all today. He'd nearly laughed out loud during the fitting. He could read people pretty well and she had pushed all the right buttons with Callum. And then there was the way she was used to being obeyed. She gave an order and it was followed. It was fun putting her off balance by taking charge.

And then there was the indisputable fact that she was beautiful.

Except he really wasn't interested in her that way. She was so not his type. He was beer and she was champagne. He was roots and she was wings.

Still. A guy might like to fly every once in a while.

"So," he invited. "Tell me more about what you do."

"Oh. Well, I plan private parties and events. Not generally weddings. Right now, in addition to Callum and Avery's details, I'm going back and forth with my assistant about a New Year's party we're putting together. The hardest part is making sure the construction of the giant aquariums is completed and that the environment is right for the fish."

"Fish?"

She laughed, the expression lighting up her face. "Okay,

so get this. They want this under the sea theme so we're building two aquariums and we've arranged to borrow the fish for the night. It's not just the aquariums, it's the marine biologist I have coming to adjust conditions and then monitor the water quality in the tank and ensure the health of the fish. Then there are lights that are supposed to make it look like you're underwater, and sushi and cocktails served by mermaids and mermen in next to no clothing."

"Are you joking?"

She shook her head. "Would I joke about a thing like that? It's been a nightmare to organize." She cut into her slab of beef and swirled it around the pool of gravy. "This is so good. I'm going to have to do sit-ups for hours in my room to work this off."

He rolled his eyes. Right. To his mind, she could gain a few pounds and no one would even notice. If anything, she was a little on the thin side. A few pounds would take those hinted-at curves and make them…

He cleared his throat.

"What about you, Rhys? You said you work with horses?" Distracted by the chatting now, she seemed unaware that she was scooping up the mashed potatoes and gravy she'd been diligently avoiding for most of the meal.

"I work for Ty out at Diamondback."

"What sort of work?"

"Whatever has to be done, but I work with training the horses mostly. Ty employs a couple of disadvantaged people to help around the place so I get to focus on what I do best."

"What sort of disadvantaged people?" She leaned forward and appeared genuinely interested.

Rhys finished the last bite of Yorkshire pudding and nudged his plate away. "Well, Marty has Down's syndrome. Getting steady work has been an issue, but he's very good with the animals and he's a hard worker. Josh is a different story. He's had trouble finding work due to his criminal record. Ty's helping him get on his feet again. Josh helps Sam's end of things from time to time. Those cattle you mentioned herding earlier."

Taylor frowned and pushed her plate away. She'd made a solid dent in the meal and his mother hadn't been stingy with portions.

"So what are your plans, then?"

"What do you mean?"

She wiped her mouth with a paper napkin. "I mean, do you have any plans to start up your own place or business?"

"Not really. I'm happy at Diamondback. Ty's a good boss."

She leaned forward. "You're a take-charge kind of guy. I can't see you taking orders from anyone. Don't you want to be the one calling the shots?"

Calling the shots wasn't all it was cracked up to be. Rhys had seen enough of that his whole life. Along with being the boss came a truckload of responsibility, including the chance of success and the probability of failure. His own venture had cost him financially but it had been far worse on a deeper, personal level. Considering he now had his mom to worry about, he was content to leave the risk to someone else from here on in. "I have a job doing something I like and I get a steady paycheck every two weeks. What more could I want?"

She sat back, apparently disappointed with his answer. Too bad. Living up to her expectations wasn't on his agenda and he sure wasn't about to explain.

Martha returned bearing two plates of apple pie. "How was it?" she asked, looking at Taylor expectantly.

"Delicious," she had the grace to answer with a smile.

"I was trying to be good and avoid the potatoes and I just couldn't. Thank you, Martha."

"Well, you haven't had my pie yet. It's my specialty."

"Oh, I couldn't possibly."

"If it's your waistline worrying you, don't. Life's too short." She flashed a grin. "Besides, you'll wear that off running all over town. I heard you're kicking butt and taking names planning this wedding. Everyone's talking about it."

Apparently Taylor found that highly complimentary and not at all offensive. "Well, maybe just this once."

Martha put down the plates. "Rhys? The faucet in my kitchen sink at home has been dripping. I wondered if you could have a look at it? Consider dinner your payment in advance."

He nodded, knowing that last part was for Taylor's benefit more than his. He never paid for meals at the diner and instead looked after the odd jobs here and at his mother's home.

It was why he'd come back to Cadence Creek, after all. He couldn't leave his mother here to deal with everything on her own. She'd already been doing that for too many years. It had always been hand to mouth until this place. She still worked too hard but Rhys knew she loved every single minute.

"I'll be around tomorrow before work to have a look," he promised. "Then I can pick up what I need from the hardware and fix it tomorrow night."

"That sounds great. Nice to see you again, Taylor. Can't wait to see your handiwork at this wedding."

Rhys watched Taylor smile. She looked tired but the smile was genuine and a pleasant surprise. She had big-city girl written all over her but it didn't mean she was devoid of warmth. Not at all.

When Martha was gone he picked up his fork. "Try the pie. She'll be offended if you don't."

Taylor took a bite and closed her eyes. "Oh, my. That's fantastic."

"She makes her own spice blend and doesn't tell anyone what it is. People have been after her recipes for years," he said, trying hard not to focus on the shape of her lips as her tongue licked a bit of caramelly filling from the corner of her mouth. "There's a reason why the bakery focuses on cakes and breads. There's not a pie in Cadence Creek that can hold a candle to my mom's."

"You seem close," Taylor noted.

She had no idea. Rhys focused on his pie as he considered exactly how much to say. Yes, he'd come back to Cadence Creek to be nearer his mom after his dad's death. She'd needed the help sorting out their affairs and needed a shoulder. He'd been happy to do it.

But it was more than that. They were business partners. Not that many people were aware of it and that was how he wanted it to stay. Memories were long and his father hadn't exactly earned a stellar business reputation around town. Despite his best intentions, Rhys had followed in his footsteps. Being a silent partner in the restaurant suited him just fine.

"We are close," he admitted. "Other than my brother, I'm the only family she's got and the only family here in Cadence Creek. How about you? Are you close with your family?"

She nodded, allowing him to neatly change the subject. "I suppose so. We don't live so close together, like you do, but it's close enough and we get along. I know they were very worried about Callum when he came back from overseas. And they thought he was crazy for buying a dairy farm." She laughed a little. "But they can see he's happy and that's all that matters."

"And Jack?"

She laughed. "Jack is in Montana most of the time, busy overseeing his empire. We don't see each other much. Our jobs keep us very busy. Running our own businesses is pretty time-consuming."

"I can imagine." Rhys had met and liked Jack instantly, but like Taylor, he looked a bit exhausted. Running a big sporting goods chain was likely to have that effect.

Which was why Rhys was very contented to work for Diamondback and spend some of his spare hours playing handyman for the diner and his mother's house. It was straightforward. There was little chance of disappointing people.

Angry words and accusations still bounced around in his brain from time to time. Failing had been bad enough. But he'd let down the person he'd trusted most. And she'd made sure he knew it.

The fluted crust of Taylor's pie was all that remained and she'd put down her fork.

"Well, I suppose we should get going."

"I'm going to have to roll back to the B&B," she said ruefully, putting a hand on her tummy.

"Not likely," he said, standing up, but their gazes met and he was certain her cheeks were a little redder than they'd been before.

He took her coat from the back of the chair, pulled the scarf from the sleeve and held it so she could slide her arms into it. They were quiet now, he unsure of what to say and his show of manners making things slightly awkward. Like this was a date or something. He stood back and grabbed his jacket and shoved his arms in the sleeves. Not a date. It was just sharing a meal with…

With a woman.

Hmm.

"I'm putting my gloves on this time," she stated with a cheeky smile.

"Good. Wouldn't want your fingertips to fall off."

They gave a wave to Martha before stepping outside into the crisp air.

It had warmed a bit, but that only meant that the precipitation that had held off now floated lazily to the earth. Big white flakes drifted on the air, hitting the ground with a soft shush of sound that was so peculiar to falling snow. It draped over hedges and windows, painting the town in fairy-white.

"This is beautiful," Taylor whispered. "Snow in Vancouver is cause for chaos. Here, it's peaceful."

"Just because the wind isn't blowing and causing whiteouts," Rhys offered, but he was enchanted too. Not by the snow, but by her. The clever and efficient Taylor had tilted her head toward the sky and stuck out her tongue, catching a wide flake on its tip.

"I know it's just water, but I swear snow tastes sweet for some reason," she said, closing her eyes. Another flake landed on her eyelashes and she blinked, laughing as she wiped it away. "Oops."

Rhys swallowed as a wave of desire rolled through him. Heavens above, she was pretty. Smart and funny, and while an absolute Sergeant Major on the job, a lot more relaxed when off the clock. He had the urge to reach out and take her hand as they walked through the snow. Odd that he'd have such an innocent, pure thought when the other side of his brain wondered if her mouth would taste like apples and snowflakes.

He kept his hand in his pocket and they resumed strolling.

It only took a few minutes to reach the bed and breakfast. Rhys paused outside the white picket gate. "Well, here we are."

"Yes, here we are. What about you? You walked me back but now do you have to walk home in the snow? Or are you parked nearby?" She lifted her chin and Rhys smiled at the way the snow covered her hair with white tufts. She looked like a young girl, bundled up in her scarf and coat with snow on her head and shoulders. Definitely not like a cutthroat businesswoman who never had to take no for an answer.

"I live a few blocks over, so don't worry about me."

"Do you—" she paused, then innocently widened her eyes "—live with your mother?"

He laughed. "God, no. I'm thirty years old. I have my own place. I most definitely do not live with my mother."

Her cold, pink cheeks flushed even deeper. "Oh. Well, thanks for dinner. I guess I'll see you when we pick up the tuxes, right?"

"I guess so. See you around, Taylor."

"Night."

She went in the gate and disappeared up the walk, her ruby-red boots marking the way on the patio stones.

He had no business thinking about his friend's sister that way. Even less business considering how different they were. Different philosophies, hundreds of kilometers between them... He shouldn't have taken her elbow in his hand and guided her along.

But the truth was the very thing that made her wrong for him was exactly what intrigued him. She wasn't like the other girls he knew. She was complicated and exciting, and that was something that had been missing from his life for quite a while.

As the snowfall picked up, he huddled into the collar

of his jacket and turned away. Taylor Shepard was not for him. And since he wasn't the type to mess around on a whim that meant keeping his hands off—for the next two weeks or so.

He could do that. Right?

Taylor had left the planning for the bridal shower to Clara Diamond, Ty's wife and one of Avery's bridesmaids. Tonight Taylor was attending only as a guest. In addition to the bridal party, Molly Diamond's living room was occupied by Melissa Stone, her employee Amy, and Jean, the owner of the Cadence Creek Bakery and Avery's partner in business.

In deference to Clara's pregnancy and the fact that everyone was driving, the evening's beverages included a simple punch and hot drinks—tea, coffee, or hot cocoa. Never one to turn down chocolate, Taylor helped herself to a steaming mug and took a glorious sip. Clara had added a dollop of real whipped cream to the top, making it extra indulgent. Taylor made a mental note to start running again when she returned home.

"I hope everything's okay for tonight," Clara said beside her. "It's a bit nerve-racking, you know. I can't put on an event like you, Taylor."

Taylor had been feeling rather comfortable but Clara's innocent observation made her feel the outsider again. "Don't be silly. It's lovely and simple which is just as it should be. An event should always suit the guests, and this is perfect."

"Really?"

Indeed. A fire crackled in the fireplace and the high wood beams in the log-style home made it feel more like a winter lodge than a regular home. The last bridal shower she'd attended had been in a private room at a club and they'd had their own bartender mixing custom martinis. She actually enjoyed this setting more. But it wasn't what people expected from her, was it? Did she really come across as…well…stuck up?

Taylor patted her arm. "Your Christmas decorations are lovely, so why would you need a single thing? Don't worry so much. This cocoa is delicious and I plan on eating my weight in appetizers and sweets."

She didn't, but she knew it would put Clara at ease. She liked Clara a lot. In fact she liked all of Callum's friends. They were utterly devoid of artifice.

Clara's sister-in-law Angela was taking puff pastries out of the oven and their mother-in-law Molly was putting out plates of squares and Christmas cookies. Jean had brought chocolate doughnut holes and Melissa was taking the cling wrap off a nacho dip. The one woman who didn't quite fit in was Amy, who Taylor recognized as the young woman from the diner the night she'd had dinner with Rhys. The implication had been made that Amy wasn't pretty *and* smart. But she looked friendly enough, though perhaps a little younger than the rest of the ladies.

She approached her casually and smiled. "Hi, I'm Taylor. You work for Melissa, right? I've seen you behind the counter at the shop."

Amy gave her a grateful smile. "Yes, that's right. And you're Callum's sister." She looked down at Taylor's shoes. "Those are Jimmy Choos, aren't they?"

Taylor laughed at the unconcealed longing in Amy's voice. "Ah, a kindred spirit. They are indeed."

"I'd die for a pair of those. Not that there's anywhere to buy them here. Or that I could afford them."

Her response was a bit guileless perhaps but she hadn't meant any malice, Taylor was sure of that. "I got them for a steal last time I was in Seattle," she replied. She leaned forward. "I'm dying to know. Why is it that everyone else is over there and you're over here staring at the Christmas tree? I mean, it's a nice tree, but…" She let the thought hang.

Amy blushed. "Oh. Well. I'm sure it was a polite thing to include me in the invitation. I'm not particularly close with the Diamond women. I kind of, uh…"

She took a sip of punch, which hid her face a little. "I dated Sam for a while and when he broke it off I wasn't as discreet as I might have been about it. I have a tendency to fly off the handle and think later."

Taylor laughed. "You sound like my brother Jack. Callum was always the thinker in the family. Jack's far more of a free spirit."

"It was a long time ago," Amy admitted. "It's hard to change minds in a town this size, though."

"You haven't thought of moving?"

"All the time!" Amy's blond curls bounced. "But my family is here. I didn't go to college. Oh, I must sound pathetic," she bemoaned, shaking her head.

"Not at all. You sound like someone who simply hasn't found the right thing yet. Someday you will. The perfect thing to make you want to get up in the morning. Or the perfect person." She winked at Amy.

"I'm afraid I've pretty much exhausted the local resources on that score," Amy lamented. "Which doesn't exactly make me popular among the women, either."

"You just need an image makeover," Taylor suggested. "Do you like what you're doing now?"

She shrugged. "Working for Melissa has been the best job I've ever had. But it's not exactly a challenge."

Wow. Amy did sound a lot like Jack.

"We should meet up for coffee before I go back to Vancouver," Taylor suggested. Despite the fact that Amy was included but not quite included, Taylor liked her. She just seemed young and without direction. Heck, Taylor had been there. What Amy needed was something to feel passionate about.

"I'd like that. Just stop into the shop. I'm there most days. It's busy leading up to the holidays."

The last of the guests arrived and things got underway. Taylor was glad the shower stayed on the sweeter rather than raunchier side. There was no paté in the shape of the male anatomy, no gag gifts or handcuffs or anything of the sort. They played a "Celebrity Husband" game where each guest put a name of a celebrity they had a crush on into a bowl and then they had to guess which star belonged to whom. The resulting laughter from names ranging from Kevin Costner who got Molly's vote to Channing Tatum— Amy's pick—broke the ice beautifully.

The laughter really picked up during Bridal Pictionary, which pitted Taylor against Angela as they attempted to draw "wedding night" without getting graphic. After they took a break to stuff themselves with snacks, they all returned to the living room for gifts.

Taylor sat back into the soft sofa cushions and examined the woman who was about to become her sister-in-law. Avery was so lovely—kind and gentle but with a backbone of steel. She was a fantastic mother to her niece, Nell, who was Callum's biological daughter. Taylor couldn't have handpicked a nicer woman to marry her brother. It gave her a warm feeling, but also an ache in her heart, too. That ache unsettled her a bit, until she reminded herself that she was simply very happy that Callum had found someone after all his troubles. A love like that didn't come along every day.

Her thoughts strayed to Rhys for a moment. The man was a contradiction for sure. On one hand he was full of confidence and really quite bossy. And yet he was satisfied with taking orders from someone else and moving back to this small town with very few options. It didn't make sense.

It also didn't make sense that for a brief moment earlier in the week, she'd had the craziest urge to kiss him. The snow had been falling on his dark cap of hair and dusting the shoulders of his jacket. And he'd been watchful of her, too. There'd been something there, a spark, a tension of some sort. Until he'd turned to go and she'd gone up the walk and into the house.

She hadn't seen him since. Not at the diner, not around town.

Avery opened a red box and a collective gasp went up from the group. "Oh, Molly. Oh, gosh." Avery reached into the tissue paper and withdrew a gorgeous white satin-and-lace nightgown. "It's stunning."

"Every woman should have something beautiful for their wedding night," Molly said. "I saw it and couldn't resist."

Taylor watched as Avery stood and held the long gown up to herself. The bodice was cut in a daring "V" and consisted of sheer lace while the satin skirt fell straight to the floor, a deep slit cut to the hip. It blended innocence with sexy brilliantly.

She took another sip of cocoa and let her mind carry her away for a few blissful seconds. What would it be like to wear that nightgown? She would feel the lace cups on her breasts, the slide of the satin on her thighs. She'd wear slippers with it, the kind of ridiculous frippery that consisted of heels and a puff of feathers at the toe. And Rhys's dark eyes would light up as she came into the room, their depths filled with fire and hunger...

"*Helloooo,* earth to Taylor!"

She blinked and focused on the circle of women who were now staring at her. "Oh. Sorry."

"I was just going to say thank you for the bath basket, but you were in another world." Avery was smiling at her.

"You're welcome! Goodness, sorry about that. Occupational hazard. Sometimes it's hard to shut the old brain off." She hoped her flippant words were believable. What would they say if they knew she'd been daydreaming about the only groomsman who wasn't married or a relative?

"Right," Amy said with a wide grin. "I know that look. You were thinking about a dude."

Damn her for being astute. Who had said she wasn't smart, anyway?

Melissa burst out laughing. "Were you? Come on, do tell. Do you have some guy hiding away in Vancouver?"

"No!" The word was out before she realized it would have been the most convenient way out of the situation.

Avery came to her rescue, though. "We're just teasing. Seriously, thank you. It's a lovely gift."

She reached for the last present on the pile and removed the card. "Oh," she said with delight. "It's from Martha. I wonder if she's going to part with her coconut cream pie recipe." Everyone laughed. Martha Bullock never shared her pie recipes with anyone. Even Rhys had mentioned that at dinner the other night.

Avery ripped the paper off the box and withdrew a plain black binder. Opening the cover, she gasped. "It *is* recipes! Look!" She read off the table of contents. "Supper Dishes, Breads and Muffins, Cookies, Cakes, Salads, Preserves." She lifted her head and laughed. "No pies."

Excited, she began flipping through the pages when Amy interrupted again. "That's it!" she called out, causing Avery's fingers to pause and the rest of the group to stare at her in surprise.

"That's where I saw you last," Amy continued, undaunted. "It was at the diner. You had dinner with Rhys!"

Six more sets of eyes swiveled Taylor's way until she felt like a bug under a microscope.

"It wasn't a date. We both ended up needing to eat at the same time. We just met outside on the sidewalk and, uh, sat together."

"It sure didn't look that way," Amy answered, a little too gleeful for Taylor's liking. "Now that is news. Rhys hasn't shown up anywhere with a date since…"

She suddenly blushed and turned her gaze to something over Jean's shoulder. "Well, it doesn't matter how long since."

It was uncomfortably quiet for a few moments until a small giggle broke the silence. Clara was trying not to laugh and failing miserably. Angela and Molly joined in, followed by Jean and Melissa. Even Avery's mouth was twitching. Taylor frowned a little, wondering what the joke could be.

Amy had the grace to look chagrined. "Okay, I know. My track record sucks."

Angela spoke up. "Honey, Rhys Bullock is one tough nut to crack. Someday the right guy's gonna come along."

Amy's eyes glistened. "Just my luck I won't recognize him when I see him."

Everyone laughed again.

Then Avery spoke up. "That's what I thought, too, Amy. Don't give up hope. You just never know." She looked at Taylor. "And I know for a fact that Rhys is smart and stubborn. Sounds like someone else I know. Keep us posted, Taylor."

"Yeah," Clara added, her hand on her rounded stomach. "The old married women need some excitement now and again."

"I swear I bumped into him outside. Literally. Ran smack into him and nearly broke my phone." She brought her hands together in demonstration of the collision. "It was dark, it was dinnertime and we had pot roast. End of story."

But as the subject changed and they cleaned up the paper and ribbons, Taylor's thoughts kept drifting back to that night and how she'd almost reached out to take his hand as he walked her home.

It was such a simple and innocent gesture to think about, especially in these days of casual hookups. Not that hooking up was her style, either. That philosophy combined with her long hours meant she hadn't had time for personal relationships for ages. Not since the early days of her business, when she'd been seeing an investment planner named John. He'd wanted more than a girlfriend who brought work home at the end of a twelve-hour day and considered takeout a sensible dinner. After a few months in, he'd walked. The thing Taylor felt most guilty about was how it had been a relief.

She balled up used napkins and put them in the trash. Time kept ticking. A few days from now was the rehearsal, and then the wedding and then Callum and Avery would be away on their honeymoon and Taylor would move out of the B&B and into their house until Boxing Day, where she planned on watching movies, reading books and basically hibernating from the outside world. It was going to be peace and quiet and then a family Christmas.

Complications in the form of Rhys Bullock would only ruin her plans.

CHAPTER THREE

It was Taylor's experience that if the rehearsal went badly, the wedding was sure to be smooth and problem free. A sentiment which boded well for Callum and Avery, as it turned out, because nothing seemed to be going her way.

First of all, everything was an hour late starting thanks to a winter storm, which dumped enough snow to complicate transportation. The minister had slid off the road and into a snowbank. The car wasn't damaged but by the time the tow truck had pulled him out, the wedding party was waiting and quite worried by his absence. Then Taylor opened the box that was supposed to contain the tulle bows for the ends of the church pews to find that they'd been constructed of a horrible peachy-yellow color—completely unsuited for a Christmas wedding!

The late start and the road conditions also meant canceling the rehearsal dinner that had been organized at an Italian place in the city. Taylor was just about ready to pull her hair out when she felt a wide hand rest on her shoulder.

"Breathe," Rhys commanded. "It's all fine."

She clenched her teeth but exhaled through her nose. "Normally I would just deal with stuff like this without batting an eyelid. I don't know why it's throwing me so much."

"Maybe because it's for your brother," he suggested.

He might be right. She did want everything just right for Callum's wedding. It wasn't some corporate dinner or celebrity party. It was personal. It was once in a lifetime.

God, there was a reason why she didn't do weddings.

"What can I do to help?"

She shrugged. "Do you have a roll of white tulle in your pocket? Perhaps a spare horseshoe I could rub for good luck or something?"

He grimaced. "Afraid not. And you rub a rabbit's foot, not a horseshoe. I'm guessing our plans for dinner have changed."

She looked up at him. He was "dressed up" for the rehearsal—neat jeans, even with a crease down the front, and a pressed button-down shirt tucked into the waistband. His boots made him look taller than ever, especially as she'd decided on her low-heeled boots tonight in deference to the weather. There was a strength and stability in him that made her take a deep breath and regroup. For some reason she didn't want to appear incapable in front of him. "I've had to cancel our reservations."

"I'll call my mom. It won't be as fancy as what you planned, but I'm guessing she can manage a meal for a dozen of us."

"We can't have a rehearsal dinner at a diner."

His lips puckered up like he'd tasted something sour. "Do you have any better suggestions? I guess you could pick up some day-old sandwiches at the gas station and a bag of cookies. You don't exactly have a lot of options."

"It was supposed to be romantic and relaxing and…" She floundered a little. "You know. Elegant."

He frowned at her and she regretted what she'd implied. "What would you do if you were in Vancouver right now?" he asked.

"This kind of weather wouldn't happen in Vancouver."

He made a disgusted sound. "You're supposed to be so good at your job. You're telling me nothing ever goes off the plan?"

"Well, sure it does, but I..."

"But you what?"

"I handle it."

"How is this different?"

"Because it's family."

The moment she said it her throat tightened. This wasn't just another job. This was her big brother's wedding. This was also the chance where she would prove herself to her family. She could talk until she was blue in the face, but the truth of the matter was she still sought their approval. The Shepards were driven and successful. It was just expected. She knew she'd disappointed her dad in particular. He thought what she did was unimportant, and the last thing she wanted to do was fall on her professional face in front of him.

"This isn't Vancouver, or Toronto, or New York or L.A." Rhys spoke firmly. "This isn't a big-city event with a bunch of rich snobs. It's just Cadence Creek. Maybe it's not good enough for you but it's good enough for Callum and Avery and maybe you should consider that instead of only thinking about yourself."

His words hurt. Partly because he was judging her without even knowing her and partly because he was right, at least about things being simpler here. How many times had Avery said they didn't need anything fancy? Taylor had insisted because it was no trouble. Had she messed up and forgotten the singular most important rule: *Give the client what they ask for?*

"Call your mother, then, and see if there's any way she can squeeze us in."

"Give me five minutes."

The words weren't said kindly, and Taylor felt the sting of his reproof. Still, she didn't have time to worry about Rhys Bullock—there was too much left to do. While the minister spoke to Avery and Callum, Taylor fished poinsettia plants out of a waiting box and lined them up on the altar steps in alternating red and creamy white. The congregation had already decorated the tree and the Christmas banners were hung behind the pulpit. The manger from the Sunday School play had been tucked away into the choir loft, which would be unused during the wedding, and instead she set up a table with a snowy-white cloth and a gorgeous spray of red roses, white freesias and greenery. It was there that the bride and groom would sign the register.

The altar looked fine, but the pews and windowsills were naked. In addition to the wrong color tulle, the company had forgotten to ship the candle arrangements for the windows. This would be the last time she ever used them for any of her events!

Her father, Harry, approached, a frown creasing his brow. "What are the plans for after the rehearsal?"

Taylor forced a smile. She would not get into it with her father tonight. "I'm working on that, don't worry."

"You should have insisted on having the wedding in the city, at a nice hotel. Then the weather wouldn't be an issue. Everything at your fingertips."

She'd had the thought a time or two herself; not that she'd admit it to her father. "This will be fine."

He looked around. "It would have been so much easier. Not that the town isn't nice, of course it is. But you're the planner, Taylor." His tone suggested she wasn't doing a very good job of it.

"It wasn't what Callum and Avery wanted," she reminded him. "And it's their day."

He smiled unexpectedly, a warm turning up of his lips

that Taylor recognized as his "sales pitch" smile. "Oh, come now. A smart businessman knows how to convince a client to come around."

Business*man*. Taylor wondered if counting to ten would help. She met her father's gaze. "Callum isn't a client, he's my brother. And he's giving you the daughter-in-law and grandkid you've wanted, so ease up."

Anything else they would have said was cut short as Rhys came back, tucking his cell phone in his pocket as he walked. "Good news. Business is slow because of the weather. Mom's clearing out that back corner and she's got a full tray of lasagna set aside."

It certainly wasn't the Caprese salad, veal Parmesan and tiramisu that Taylor had planned on, but it was convenient. She offered a polite smile. "Thank you, Rhys." At least one thing had been fixed.

"It's no trouble."

With a brief nod, Harry left the two of them alone.

"Everything okay?" Rhys asked.

She pressed a hand to her forehead. "Yeah, it's fine. Dad was just offering an unsolicited opinion, that's all."

He chuckled. "Parents are like that."

"You've no idea," she answered darkly. "I still wish I knew what to do about the pew markers. There's no time to run to Edmonton for materials to make them, even if it weren't storming. And the candles never arrived, either."

"It doesn't have to be perfect. No one will know."

His words echoed from before, the ones that said she was too good for this town. She dismissed them, because she still had a certain standard. "I'll know."

Clara heard the last bit and tapped Taylor on the shoulder. "Why don't you call Melissa and see if she can do something for the pews with satin ribbon?"

"At this late hour?"

Clara nodded. "Worst she can say is no. I have a feeling she'll try something, though. She's a whiz at that stuff. And I might be able to help you out with the windowsills."

Taylor's eyebrows pulled together. "What do you mean?"

Clara laughed. "Just trust me."

"I'm not in the habit of trusting details to other people, Clara. It's nothing personal—it's just how I work."

"Consider it a helping hand from a friend. You're going to be here before anyone else tomorrow anyway. If you don't like what I've done, you can take it out, no hard feelings." She smiled at Taylor. "I'd like to do this. For Avery. She's like family, you know?"

Rhys's hand touched Taylor's back. It was warm and felt good but Taylor got the feeling it was also a little bit of a warning. "I'm sure Taylor's very grateful for your help, Clara."

Dammit. Now he was putting words in her mouth. Perhaps it could be argued that this was "just family" but to Taylor's mind, if she couldn't manage to get the details of one small country wedding right, what did that say about her business?

Then again, in Vancouver she had staff. She could delegate. Which was pretty much what Clara was suggesting. She was just asking her to trust, sight unseen. And then there was the word "friend." She was a stranger here, a fish out of water for the most part and yet everyone seemed to accept her into their group without question. She wasn't used to that.

"Thank you, Clara," she said, but when Clara had gone she turned on Rhys. "Don't ever answer for me again."

"You were being rude."

Now he was judging her manners?

"Look, maybe Callum and Avery are family but I still

hold to a certain standard. This is my job. And it's all carefully planned down to the last detail."

She'd had things go wrong before and it wasn't pretty. She'd been determined never to fail like that again. It was why she dealt with trusted vendors and had a competent staff. She'd pulled off events ten times as complicated as this without a hitch.

Knowing it was like sprinkling salt in the wound.

He put a finger under her chin and lifted it. Considering how abrupt he'd been earlier, the tender touch surprised her. "You don't have to control everything. It'll be fine, I promise. It's okay to accept help once in a while."

"I'm not used to that."

"I know," he said gently. "You're stubborn, strong, bossy and completely competent. But things happen. Call Melissa, trust Clara, pretend to walk down the aisle for the rehearsal and then go stuff yourself with lasagna. I promise you'll feel better."

She didn't like being handled. Even if, at this moment, she suspected she needed it. It was so different being here. More relaxed, laid-back. She was used to grabbing her nonfat latte on her way to the office, not sipping from china cups in a B&B dining room while eating croissants. Maneuvering her SUV with the fold-down seats through city traffic rather than walking the two blocks to wherever. Definitely not used to men looking into her eyes and seeing past all her barriers.

Cadence Creek was a completely different pace with completely different expectations.

"Rhys? Taylor? We're ready for the walk-through," Avery called down the aisle, a happy smile on her face. Despite the wrinkles in the plans, Taylor's soon-to-be sister-in-law was beaming.

Well, if the bride wasn't worried, she wouldn't be, either. She looked up at Rhys. "I'll call Melissa when we're done. But if this goes wrong…"

"I expect I'll hear about it."

The other members of the wedding party joined them at the end of the aisle—first Clara and Ty, then Sam and Angela, Jack and Avery's friend Denise, who'd flown in from Ontario just this morning and thankfully ahead of the storm. Rhys held out his arm. "Shall we?" he asked, waiting for her to take his elbow.

She folded her hand around his arm, her fingers resting just below his elbow as they took slow steps up the aisle. It was just a silly rehearsal, so she shouldn't have a tangle of nerves going on just from a simple touch.

At the front of the church they parted ways and while Taylor slyly glanced in his direction several times, he never looked at her. Not once. He focused unerringly on what the minister was saying, and she found herself studying his strong jawline and the crisp hairline that looked as if his hair had been freshly cut.

The minister spoke to her and she jerked her attention back to the matter at hand, but she couldn't stop thinking about Rhys. It wasn't often that Taylor was intimidated by anyone, but she was by Rhys. She figured it had to be because he found her distinctly lacking in…well, in something.

What she couldn't understand was why on earth his opinion should even matter.

The Wagon Wheel was lit up, the windows glowing through the cold and very white night. Hard flakes of snow still swirled through the air, biting against Rhys's cheeks as he parked his truck in front of a growing drift.

They'd all bundled up and left the church a few minutes ago, the procession of vehicles crawling through town to the diner. There was no way they would have made it to the city for dinner. Even with the roads open, visibility was bad enough that there was a tow ban on. The smart thing was to stay put.

Taylor "Bossy-Pants" Shepard hadn't been too happy about that, though. He'd taken one look at her face and seen the stress that came from dealing with things gone wrong. It was a prime example of why he liked his life simple. If things went wrong out at Diamondback, he might get called to work but the worry belonged to Ty and Sam. Besides, his mother kept him plenty busy with things at the diner when she needed help. There were days he wished she didn't own the place. That she'd stayed on as a cook rather than buying it from the last owner. There was too much at stake, too much to lose.

Frigid air buffeted him as he hopped out of the truck and headed for the door, his head bowed down as far into his collar as possible. This storm had been a good one. Hopefully it would blow itself out by morning and nothing would get in the way of the wedding. For one, he only wanted to get dressed up in that tuxedo once. And for another, Callum and Avery deserved an incident-free day.

It was warm inside, and smelled deliciously like tomatoes and garlic and warm bread. Rhys stamped off his feet and unzipped his jacket, tucking his gloves into the pockets as he walked toward the back corner. His mom had been right. Other than a couple of truckers waiting out the bad roads, the place was empty.

He stopped and looked at the miracle she had produced in a scant hour.

The Christmas tree was lit, sending tiny pinpoints of colored light through the room. The heavy tables were pushed together to make one long banquet style set up for twelve, and they were covered with real linens in holiday red. The napkins were only paper but they were dark green and white, in keeping with Christmas colors. Thick candles sat in rings of greenery and berries—where had she come up with those?—and the candles lent an even more intimate air to the setting. But the final touch was the ice buckets on both ends, and the sparkling wineglasses at each place setting.

"What do you think?" His mother's voice sounded behind his shoulder.

"You're something, Ma," he said, shaking his head.

She frowned a little. "Do you think it'll be okay for Taylor? I know she must have had something fancier planned for the rehearsal dinner."

"You've worked a miracle on short notice. And if Taylor Shepard doesn't like it, she can…" He frowned. "Well, she can…"

"She can what, Rhys?"

Dammit. Her sweet voice interrupted him. He felt heat rush to his cheeks but when he turned around she was looking at Martha and smiling.

"Martha, how did you possibly do all this in such a short time?"

"It was slow in here and I had some help." She grinned. "Jean from the bakery sent over a cake—they were closing early anyway and she was happy to help with dessert. It's chocolate fudge."

"And wine?" Rhys watched as Taylor's eyes shone. Maybe he'd misjudged her. Maybe she'd just been stressed, because the snooty perfectionist he expected to see wasn't in attendance just now.

Or, perhaps she understood she was in a sticky place and was making the best of it. He suspected that faking it was in her repertoire of talents. His jaw tightened. When had he become so cynical? He supposed it was about the time Sherry had promised him to stick by his side—until things got dicey. Then she'd bailed—taking her two kids with her. Kids he'd grown very fond of.

You got to see someone's true colors when they were under pressure. It wasn't always pretty. Sherry hadn't even given him a chance to make things right.

He realized his mom was still speaking. "I'm not licensed, so I'm afraid it's not real wine. But the bed and breakfast sent over a couple of bottles of sparkling cider they had on hand and I put it on ice. I thought at least you could have a toast."

To Rhys's surprise, Taylor enveloped Martha in a quick hug. "I underestimated you," she said warmly. "This is perfect."

Martha shrugged but Rhys could tell she was pleased. "Heck," she replied with a flap of her hand. "That's what neighbors are for."

The rest of the wedding party arrived, complete with laughter and the sound of stomping boots. The next thing Rhys knew, he was seated at the table next to Avery's maid of honor, Denise, and things were well underway. Drinks were poured and he found himself chatting to Harry, who was on his other side. The senior Shepard was a very successful businessman, sharp as a tack and charismatic. Rhys could see a lot of his acumen and energy in Jack, the younger son, and the strength and reliability in Callum, the eldest. Rhys noticed that while Harry spoke proudly about Callum's military career and Jack's business, he didn't say much about Taylor's successes.

What about Taylor, then? She had the dark looks of the Shepard men rather than the more fair coloring of her mother, who sat across the table. But her lips were soft and full, like Mrs. Shepard's, and the dusting of freckles came from there, too. When he met Mrs. Shepard's gaze, he saw a wisdom there that he'd glimpsed in Taylor, too. Wisdom and acceptance. He guessed that it must have been hard to be a girl growing up in a household of such strong males. Had she felt pressure to keep up? Or were the expectations lower because she was female? He'd only known her a short time but he understood that she would hate to be treated as anything less than equal to her brothers. And then there was the tension he'd sensed between them at the rehearsal.

To his surprise, Taylor didn't sit at all but donned an apron and helped Martha serve the meal. When she put his plate before him, he looked up and met her eyes. "Thank you, Taylor."

"You're welcome."

She turned to move away but he reached out and caught her wrist. "What you said to my mother, that was very nice."

Her eyes met his. "I meant it. I apologize for my mood earlier. I was stressed."

"And here I thought it was because you didn't like to be told what to do."

Her eyes flashed at him for a second before mellowing, and then her lips twitched. "I do believe you're baiting me. Now stop so I can finish serving the meal."

He watched as she helped put the plates around, smiling and laughing. He'd thought her too proud for serving but she wasn't. She'd do what it took to pull off an event. There was lots of talking and laughing and toasting around the table, but Rhys frowned. Wasn't she going to sit and eat? While Martha tended to the few customers at the counter, it was Taylor who refilled bread baskets and beverages. Once he spied her in a corner, talking on her cell and gesturing with one hand. When Callum stood and offered a toast Rhys could see her in the kitchen, slicing cake onto plates.

Maybe it was her job, but it was her family, too. She was part of the wedding party, after all. And no one seemed to realize she was missing out.

When the meal was over the party broke up. Callum and Avery departed with a wave, in a hurry to get home to their daughter who was with a sitter. Mr. and Mrs. Shepard left for the bed and breakfast and Jack, being chivalrous, offered to take Denise with him, since they were all staying there anyway.

Angela and Clara offered to help tidy up, but Taylor shooed them away. "You've got Sam and Ty waiting and the kids at home. Go. This won't take but a minute anyway. I'll see you in the morning."

They didn't put up much of an argument, Rhys noticed. Clara put a hand on her swollen tummy and looked relieved.

As they were leaving, another group of truckers came in, looking for hot coffee and a meal before calling it a night. Martha bustled around, attending to them—Rhys knew that on a night like tonight, the tips would be generous.

Meanwhile Taylor grabbed a plastic dishpan and was loading up dirty plates.

She'd missed the entire celebration and was left to clean up the mess. He was pretty sure this wasn't in the job description, and he was annoyed on her behalf. Her family had been utterly thoughtless tonight.

He went around to the opposite side of the table and began stacking plates.

"What are you doing?"

Clank, clank. The flatware clattered on the porcelain as he picked up the dishes. "Helping."

"I got this, Rhys."

He took the stack over to her and put it in the dishpan. "Well, you shouldn't."

"Sorry?"

She looked tired. Tiny bits of hair had come out of her braid and framed her face, and her eyes looked slightly red and weary. "Have you even eaten, Taylor?"

"I'll get something later."

Lord, she was stubborn. "There's no one here now to know that this is your job, because I know that's what you're going to say. And you know what? This isn't your job. For Pete's sake."

"Are you angry at me? Because I'm not leaving all this for Martha. It *is* my job, Rhys. When I plan an event, I sometimes have to chip in and help where it's needed. Even if it's taking out trash or clearing dishes or providing someone with a spare pair of panty hose."

"Not this time. And no, I'm not angry at you."

She lifted her chin. "Then why are you yelling at me? People are staring."

He looked over. Martha was pretending not to watch but he could tell she was paying attention. The truckers weren't so discreet. They were openly staring.

He sighed. "I'm angry at your family. They never even noticed that you didn't sit down. Callum gave the toast without you. And other than Clara and Angela, everyone left without so much as an offer to help clean up. If everyone had pitched in…"

"They had more on their minds." Her posture had relaxed slightly. "It's okay, Rhys. Really."

"Will you go eat, please? Let me look after this."

She sighed. "Tell you what. I'll help clear the tables, and then I'll eat while you put the tables and chairs back to where they normally belong. Deal?"

He could live with that, especially since he figured Taylor wasn't one to generally compromise. "Deal."

With carols playing softly in the background, it only took a few minutes to clear the dirty dishes away. Rhys took them to the kitchen while Taylor stripped away the soiled tablecloths and put the centerpieces in a cardboard box. Together they loaded the kitchen dishwasher and then Rhys put a square of leftover lasagna on a plate, heated it in the microwave and poured Taylor a glass of ice water. When it was hot, he added a bit of salad to the side and grabbed a napkin and utensils.

"That smells delicious."

"Sit. Eat. That's an order."

He knew she was tired when she merely smiled and faked a salute as she sat at an empty table. "Yes, boss."

She'd made a good dent in the lasagna by the time he'd pushed the tables back into place and put the chairs around them. Without a word he went to the kitchen and cut a slice of that chocolate fudge cake she'd missed out on. When he took it to her, she held up her hand. "I couldn't possibly."

"Yes, you can. It's delicious."

"I have a dress to fit into tomorrow."

"Which will look beautiful." He put a bit of cake—complete with fudgy frosting—on the fork and held it out. "Trust me."

"Trust you." She raised one cynical eyebrow so brilliantly he nearly laughed. "As if."

He wiggled the fork. She leaned forward and closed her lips around it, sucking the frosting off the tines.

His body tensed simply from the intimate act of feeding her, feeling the pressure of her lips conducted through metal, the way she closed her eyes at the first rich taste. He enjoyed bantering with her. Matching wits. That didn't happen often around here. But it was more than that. There

was an elemental attraction at work. Something indefin-
able that was more than a physical response to her unusual
beauty. She was the most capable woman he'd ever met.
So why did she seem particularly vulnerable? Especially
around her family?

"That's good," she murmured, licking a bit of chocolate from her upper lip.

"I know." His voice was hoarse and he cleared his
throat. "Have another bite."

"I shouldn't."

In response he put more on the fork and held it out. She
took it, and then he took a bite for himself, feeling adoles-
cently pleased that his lips followed where hers had been.
The room seemed more silent now, and he suddenly realized that the last few customers had gone, the music had
stopped and Martha was turning out lights.

"Oh," Taylor said, alarmed. "We should go."

Martha peered through the kitchen door. "Was everything all right, Taylor?"

"It was lovely, Mrs. Bullock. Thank you so much."

"Don't thank me. You were the workhorse tonight."
When Taylor moved to stand up, Martha flapped a hand.
"Take your time. Rhys will lock up, won't you Rhys?"

"Sure thing, Ma." He never took his eyes off Taylor as
he answered. They were going to be alone—truly alone—
for the first time. Eating cake by the light of the Christmas
tree in the corner. The back door through the kitchen shut,
echoing in the silence.

"I didn't mean to…"

He shook his head. "I have keys to the place. It's okay.
I've locked up plenty of times."

"No, what I mean is…"

She stopped talking, looked into his eyes and bit down
on her lip.

She was feeling it, too. There was something. Something that had been lit the moment that she'd threatened to make him wear a cravat. She meant they shouldn't be alone.

She was probably right.

Instead he gazed into her eyes, unwilling to end the evening just yet. "Do you want some milk to go with your cake?" he asked.

CHAPTER FOUR

SHE SHOULD NEVER have had the cake. Or the milk. Or sat around actually enjoying Rhys's company as the night drew on and on and it was close to midnight and she was still so wired the thought of sleep was ludicrous.

Rhys was bossy and annoying and, at times, growly. He was also the only person to have noticed how she was excluded tonight. When she was working a job she tried to be invisible, behind the scenes. Maybe she'd done her job a little too well, then. Because she'd sure been invisible to her family this evening.

It had stung. In her head she knew she was just doing her job but in her heart it had hurt a little bit, that no one had at least asked her to pause and join the celebration. Not even for the toast.

Except Rhys had noticed.

She was getting used to the sight of his face, rugged and far less refined than most of the men she was accustomed to. Rhys wasn't pretty. But as she looked into his eyes across the table, with the lights of the tree reflected in the irises, she realized a man didn't have to be pretty to be sexy as hell.

"It's getting late. I should get back. Tomorrow's a long day." She balled up her paper napkin and put it on her dirty plate.

"You're probably right," he agreed. "I'll just put these things in the sink."

She followed him to the kitchen. "Rhys. Thank you. I know I blew it off before but it did kind of hurt. That they didn't notice, I mean."

He rinsed the plate and left it in the sink since the dishwasher was already running. "No problem."

She gave a short laugh. "Well, at least being away from the table meant I avoided the 'why aren't you married with a few kids yet' speech."

Rhys gave the kitchen a final check. "Why aren't you, by the way? Or aren't you interested in those things?"

She shrugged. "I like kids. My dad tends to think in lines of traditional roles, like who the breadwinner is and who does the nurturing."

"And you don't?"

She lifted her shoulders. "I don't. I think as long as a couple has a division of labor that works for them, then who am I to criticize? I suppose I'll settle down someday, when I have the time. After I've proved myself."

"And how will you know when you get there?"

She looked up, startled. "What do you mean?"

"I mean, how do you measure that? What do you need to check off on a list to consider yourself a success?"

She floundered. There was no list. "I guess I'll just know."

"Or maybe you'll never know. Let me hit the lights."

She thought about his words as she put on her coat. What was her "yardstick" for success? A dollar amount? Number of employees? Acceptance from her family?

She was so afraid of disappointing any of them, she realized. Callum was a decorated soldier. Jack had been an elite athlete before he'd become a businessman. She loved her brothers but it was hard to compete with their overachievements.

It was a bit of a shock to realize that she'd picked a business where she was behind the scenes, out of the limelight. Where she was protected just a little bit from visibility if she failed.

When had she become so afraid?

Rhys finished up and when they stepped outside she realized just how much snow had fallen—and it was still coming down. Her car was covered and the snowplow had been by, leaving a deep bank right behind her back bumper. She sighed. She didn't even have a shovel, just a brush in the backseat for cleaning off the windshield.

"Come on, I'll take you in the truck," Rhys said, but Taylor shook her head.

"I have to dig it out sometime and I'm due at the golf club by 9:00 a.m. in order to get everything set up for the reception."

"You try driving that little thing out there before the plows make another pass and you're sure to slide off into the ditch." He shook his head. "There aren't even snow tires on it, just all-seasons. I'll take you out there in the morning."

She didn't want to rely on Rhys too much, especially since he seemed very adept at prying into her business. "Jack's rental's a 4x4. I'm sure he'll run me out if the roads are bad."

"Suit yourself." He didn't sound too put out by her refusal, which was a relief. "But for now, you'd best let me take you home."

Home being the B&B. She didn't have a choice. There was no way her car was going to be unstuck tonight and she really didn't feel like walking through the snowdrifts at this hour.

Rhys unlocked the door to his truck and waited while she got in, then jogged around the front and hopped in the driver's side. He started the engine and let everything warm up for a few minutes while Taylor stared at the clouds her breath was making in the air.

The heater kicked in and the air around her feet began to warm. "Gosh, it's cold. I'm so used to the coast. This is full-on winter."

"Complete with whiteouts and a snow removal system that operates at the speed of a slug." Rhys grinned. "Still, with this good dump of snow there'll be lots of sledding happening over the holidays."

"Sledding?"

"Snowmobiles," he confirmed. "Lots of wide-open space here, but a lot of the guys like to go into the mountains and into the backcountry."

"That sounds like something Jack would love."

Rhys grinned. "He might have said something about coming back for a trip later this winter. If he can drag Callum away from his new bride. I get the feeling that Jack's a little more adventurous than Callum."

"Just in a different way," she replied, rubbing her gloved hands together. "Callum got all the adventure he wanted in the army, I think, and he was ready to settle down. Jack's more of a daredevil. Anyway, hopefully this will let up by the morning so nothing interferes with the wedding."

He put the truck in gear. "Right. Well, let's get you home so you can get your beauty sleep."

It took no time at all, even at crawling speed, to reach the B&B. The front porch light was on and white Christmas lights twinkled through the snow that had settled on the porch and railings. Rhys put the truck in Park and left the engine running.

Taylor faced him; saw his face illuminated by the dashboard lights. The snow on his hair had melted, making it darker than usual, almost black. Who was Rhys Bullock anyway? Horse trainer, sure. And clearly devoted to his mother, which was another plus. But what made him tick? What were his thoughts, his views? What went on in that complicated male mind of his? On one hand he claimed he didn't want to be tied down, but there was no doubt in her mind that he'd put down roots in Cadence Creek. What was that about?

Why on earth did she care?

"I, uh, thanks for the drive."

"You're welcome."

"And for making me eat. And…" She wet her lips. "Well, for noticing what no one else did."

There was an awkward pause as if he were deliberating over his next words. "You don't need to prove anything to your family, you know," he finally said quietly. "As long as you're squared away with yourself, that's all that matters."

Her lips dropped open. How could he possibly know that she'd always felt like she came up short? Her dad was always talking about how the boys made him proud. She always felt a few steps behind. There was something in Rhys's voice, too. Something that said that he was familiar with those words. Like maybe he'd said them to himself a time or two. Why?

"Rhys."

She'd unbuckled her seat belt and for several heartbeats the air in the cab held, as if wondering if she were going to stay in or get out. Their gazes met and things got ten times more complicated as neither of them seemed capable of looking away. Somehow they drifted closer. Closer…

She wanted to kiss him. The notion was strange and wonderful and slightly terrifying. Nothing could ever come of this, but he was feeling it, too. He must be, because she saw him swallow as he blindly reached around and undid his seat belt, his dark gaze never leaving hers. Nothing was holding him back now and still the fear and excitement waved over her, amplified in the small space of the truck cab. She didn't do this. She didn't get personal. And still she had the urge to touch, the desire to explore.

"You're going to have to meet me halfway," he murmured, his voice deep and inviting. There was no doubt now, was there? With those words he'd told her that they were on exactly the same page. The air between them sizzled.

"This is probably a mistake," she answered, dropping her gaze, breaking the connection. "I should go inside."

She didn't want to, though. And her pulse leaped wildly as he slid across the seat and reached out with his left hand, curling it around her hip and pulling her across the upholstery. "Hush," he said, and then cupped her cheek in that same hand. "We're both sitting here wondering, so why don't we get this out of the way?"

When his lips came down on hers, it stole her breath. Nothing could have prepared her for the warm insistence of his mouth or the reaction rocketing through her body. One taste and the whole kiss exploded into something wild and demanding. She reached out and gripped the front of his jacket and his arms came around her, pulling her so close she was nearly on his lap. A squeak escaped her lips as he looped one arm beneath her bottom and tugged so she was sprawled across his legs, cushioned by a strong arm as the kiss went on and on, her body ached with trembling need and her head was clouded with sheer desire.

Except somewhere in the fog was the understanding that this couldn't go any farther. She pulled away first, shaking with the intensity of their connection. "Wow," she whispered, their limbs still tangled. Despite the truck being left running, the windows had already fogged up as the sound of their breathing filled the cab.

He let out a soft curse. "I didn't expect that," he said, running his hand over his hair. "God, Taylor."

She had to get some of her bravado back or he'd see exactly how rattled she was. "Too much?" she asked innocently.

"Too much?" He gaped at her for a second, but she wasn't fooled. There was a fire in the dark depths of his eyes that was tremendously exciting.

His voice held a rasp that shivered over her nerve endings. "When I was eighteen I would have been digging for the condom in my wallet by now and heading for the privacy of the gravel pit."

She giggled. He had a condom in his wallet? Or did he mean hypothetically? What was most surprising was how badly she wanted to. Wanted him. That if he'd seriously asked she would have actually considered it even though she totally wasn't into casual anything.

It was too much. Too fast. "That sounds romantic," she replied, the words injected with a healthy dose of sarcasm. She pushed off his lap and back onto the seat of the truck.

"I'm not eighteen anymore," he admitted, letting out a breath. "I'd like to think I've learned some finesse since then. And a quickie in the cab of my truck…" He hesitated, let the thought linger.

Would never be enough. He didn't need to say it for her to hear the words. "I'd better go," she said, sliding all the way over to the door and grabbing her purse. Get out before she changed her mind and crawled into his arms again. "This wasn't such a good idea."

"Because I'm a small-town hick, right?"

She frowned, brought up short. Did he really think she was such a snob? "I didn't say that. It just doesn't make sense to start something when I'm only here until Boxing Day. Then I go back to my world and you stay here in yours. Anything else is just fooling ourselves, Rhys, and you know it."

There was a long, awkward silence. "I'll pick you up tomorrow morning and take you to the club," he offered, but his voice was tight, like she'd somehow offended him.

"Jack will take me."

Rhys let out a frustrated sigh. "Will you call if you need anything?"

She squared her shoulders. "I won't. Thanks for the lift. See you at the church."

She opened the door and hopped down, her boots sinking into eight inches of fresh snow. She wouldn't look back at him. He'd know. Know that if he said the right thing or made the slightest move she'd be in the middle of that bench seat, holding on to his arm as he drove out to the pit or wherever people went parking these days, snowstorm be damned. And she never did things like that. In fact, she hadn't been involved with anyone that way since John. Since he'd said all those hurtful things before slamming the door. She'd put all her energy into the business instead.

Without looking back, she started up the walk to the porch. Rhys gunned the engine the slightest bit—did "Mr. Uptight Pants" have a bit of a rebellious side after all?— and pulled away, driving off into the night.

She tiptoed up the steps and carefully opened the door—a single light glowed from the front window but Taylor expected everyone would be in bed. She'd have to apologize in the morning for coming in so late.

"Aren't you a little old to be parking?" came a voice on her right.

She jumped, pressed a hand to her heart. "Jack. What are you doing up?"

"Big brother was waiting for you. What took you so long?"

She recalled Rhys's criticism of her family and felt her temper flicker. "Someone had to stay and clean up."

"Isn't that the owner's job? What's her name? Martha?"

"Rhys's mother, yes. And considering she was a staff of one tonight and still managed to put on a great dinner for us at a moment's notice, I certainly wasn't going to walk out of there and leave her with a mess. Not that anyone else seemed to mind."

He came forward and frowned down at her. "Touchy," he remarked. "This have anything to do with why you were in Rhys's truck for so long, and with the windows steamed up?"

She didn't want to blush, but the heat crept up her neck and into her cheeks anyway. "That is none of your business."

"Be careful is all I'm saying. He's not your type."

"How would you know what my type is?"

He straightened and it seemed to her that he puffed out his chest. "Oh, I know. You go for the pretty boys who work downtown in two-thousand-dollar suits."

"Men like you, you mean?"

His eyes glittered. "Hardly. You pick guys who aren't a challenge and who don't challenge you. Guys like Rhys Bullock won't let you away with your usual tricks, sis."

She had to keep a lid on her temper before she said something she'd regret. Jack had such a tendency to be cocky and normally she just brushed it off. Tonight it irritated. Could she not do anything right? "Then how convenient for you that he just gave me a lift home after helping me clear away the dishes. Oh, and he reminded me I hadn't had time to eat at the dinner, either, and fixed me a plate. And when we finally went to leave, my rental was completely blocked in by a snowbank so he offered me a drive home. My type or not, Rhys Bullock was very supportive this evening. So you can put that in your pipe and smoke it, Jackson Frederick Shepard."

Unperturbed, Jack merely folded his arms and raised an eyebrow at her.

"I'm going to bed," she announced. "I recommend you do the same. You're taking me to the golf club at eight-thirty so I can be sure it's ready for the reception."

Without waiting for an answer, she swept up the stairs, her pride wrapped around her. It was only when she was settled in her room, dressed in flannel pajamas and curled under the covers that she let down her guard and closed her eyes.

Behind her lids she saw Rhys. And she saw what might have happened—if only they were different people, in a different place and time.

The church was beautiful.

Taylor let out a relieved sigh as she peeked through the nearly closed door leading through the sanctuary. It had taken longer than she'd anticipated, making sure the reception venue was all on schedule and then it had been time to head to Molly Diamond's, where all the bridesmaids were meeting to get ready and have pictures taken. Taylor gave the thumbs-up to the photographer, Jim, who had flown in from Victoria to do the wedding as a personal favor. He was set up at the front of the church, ready for Avery's walk down the aisle.

Taylor's worries about the decorations had been pointless. She wasn't sure how Melissa Stone had managed it, but the end of each pew held a stunning but simple decoration consisting of a red satin bow and a small cedar bough. Not only did it look festive, but the smell was incredible.

And Clara had come through with the sills, too. On each one was a small rectangular plate with three white pillar candles of varying heights. It was incredibly romantic and the warm light radiated through the church. She couldn't have come up with anything more suitable on her own.

With a lump in her throat, she turned to Clara and smiled. "How on earth did you manage that?" she asked. "It's perfect!"

Clara laughed lightly. "I called the owner of the dollar store last night and asked if we could go in early this morning."

The dollar store. Heaven forbid any of her clients ever found out! She gave an unladylike snort and patted Clara's arm. "I swear I need to stop underestimating the women of this town. First Martha with the dinner, then you with the candles and Melissa with the pew markers. I'm starting to feel rather irrelevant."

Avery heard and her face fell with concern. "Oh, don't say that, Taylor! We put this together in such a short time that if it weren't for you we'd be standing in front of the Justice of the Peace and having a potluck. I never dreamed I'd have a wedding day like this. It would never have happened without you."

Taylor's eyes stung. This was so different from anything she'd ever experienced. She hadn't even had to ask for help. Without even knowing her, people had stepped up because it was the right and neighborly thing to do. Maybe Cadence Creek wasn't the hub of excitement Taylor was used to, but never had she ever been made to feel like she belonged so easily. She was starting to understand why Callum was so happy here.

"It was my pleasure, I promise. Now let me check to see what's going on."

Because Avery had no family, they'd decided to forgo

the official ushering in of the parents. Instead Taylor's mom and dad sat at the front, with an adorable Nell, dressed in white ruffles, on their laps. Taylor turned her attention to the side door as it opened and the minister and men came through. At last night's rehearsal it had become glaringly apparent that everyone had an escort up the aisle but the bride. They'd made a quick change of plans, and the women would be walking up the aisle alone with the groomsmen waiting at the front.

Taylor's heart beat a little faster as Rhys appeared, looking so very handsome and exciting in the black tux and tie. The men lined up along their side of the altar, with Rhys positioned right after Jack. The pianist began to play Gounod's "Ave Maria," the signal for the women to begin their walk.

"This is it, girls." Taylor quickly got them in order and then took her place behind Angela. She gave the man at the door a quick nod and it opened, and the procession began.

Clara went first, radiant in dark green, glowing with pregnancy and holding her bouquet in front of her rounded tummy. Then Angela, smiling at her husband at the other end, and then, in the middle of the procession, Taylor.

She stepped on to the white runner, her emerald satin heels sinking slightly into the carpet. She kept slow time with the music, a smile on her face as she winked at her brother who was waiting rather impatiently for his bride. Jack was beside him, grinning like a fool and then…

And then there was Rhys, watching her with an intensity that made her weak at the knees. The smile on her lips flickered until she purposefully pasted it there, but she couldn't deny the jolt that had rushed through her that second their eyes met. Her chest cramped as her breath caught, and then his lips curved the tiniest bit and his gaze warmed with approval. And she was back in the truck last night, feeling his hands on her body and his lips on her lips and she got hot all over.

Then she was in her place, Denise followed and the music changed.

Taylor forgot all about Rhys the moment Avery stepped to the door and on the carpet. Her lace dress was classic and romantic, her solid red rose bouquet perfect. Taylor's throat tightened as she took one quick glance at her brother and found his eyes shining with tears. She couldn't cry. She wouldn't. She never did at these things. But today was different. She knew how Callum had had his heart broken before and how incredible it was that he was even standing here today. Nell stood on her grandfather's lap and everyone chuckled when she bounced and said "Mumm mumm mumm."

Avery reached Callum, and he held out his hand. She took it and they faced the minister together.

The prayers were short and heartfelt, the "I Do's" immediate and clear so that they echoed to the farthest pew. It was when Avery handed her bouquet to Denise and took Callum's fingers in hers that Taylor wished she'd tucked a tissue into the handle of her bouquet.

The vows were simple and traditional, the words solid and true as they filled the candlelit church. "I Callum, take you Avery, to be my wife. To have and to hold from this day forward."

A lump formed in Taylor's throat as she tried to swallow.

"For better or worse, richer or poorer, in sickness and in health."

Taylor took a fortifying breath and told herself to hold it together. But it was so hard, because she could see the look on Callum's face as he gazed into the eyes of his bride. He was so in love. So sure. The promises were the most important he'd make in his life, but they came easily because he loved Avery that much. Taylor had never experienced anything like that. Sometimes she doubted she ever would…if she was actually that…lovable.

Avery's soft, gentle voice echoed them back. "I Avery, take you Callum, to be my husband. To have and to hold, from this day forward."

A single tear splashed over Taylor's lower lashes. She was mortified.

"To love, honor and cherish for as long as I live."

The pair of them blurred as her eyes filled with moisture and she struggled not to blink. The pronunciation was made, there was clapping during the kiss, and then Avery, Callum, Denise and Jack moved to the table to sign the register and wedding certificate. Just when she was sure the tears were going to spill over, a dark figure appeared in front of her and held out a handkerchief.

She didn't need to see the fine details to know it was Rhys. Her heart gave a confused flutter just before she reached out and took the fabric from his hand. The shape of his lips curved slightly before he silently stepped back, and she gave a self-conscious laugh as she turned her head a little and dabbed at her eyes.

She could see again but she didn't dare look at him. A handkerchief—a white one, she could see now, and it smelled like starch and his aftershave. What sort of man these days carried a white handkerchief, for Pete's sake? And why on earth was she charmed by it?

The documents were signed, the minister introduced them as Mr. and Mrs. Callum Shepard and clapping erupted as the bride and groom immediately went to gather their daughter and then swept jubilantly down the aisle.

Taylor swallowed as Rhys offered his elbow. "Shall we?" he asked quietly, smiling down at her.

She tucked her hand in the crook of his elbow. It was strong and warm and she felt stupidly pretty and feminine next to him. "Certainly," she replied as they made their way out of the sanctuary to the much cooler vestibule. They'd form a receiving line there briefly, and then the guests would go on to the golf club for a cocktail hour while the wedding party had pictures taken.

Taylor gave a final sniff and prepared to get herself together. She had the next hour to get through and didn't want smudged makeup or red eyes to mar the photos. The sentimental moments had passed.

What she hadn't prepared herself for was the number of times she'd be forced close to Rhys during the photos; how she'd feel his hand rest lightly at her waist or his jaw close to her hair. By the time the wedding party was dismissed, her senses were so heightened her skin was tingling.

"You want a drive to the club?" Rhys asked, as the groomsmen and bridesmaids gathered by the coatrack.

"Avery said we could all go in the limo that brought us from Diamondback."

"But aren't they doing just some bride and groom photos in the snow first? I guess I figured you'd want to get there and make sure things were running smoothly."

She smiled up at him, making sure to put several inches between them. "You know me too well."

He shrugged. "That part's easy to read. The tears on the other hand? Total surprise." He reached for her coat and held it out so she could slip her arms into the sleeves.

"And yet you were at the ready with a hanky. Impressive." She needed to inject some humor so he wouldn't know how genuinely touched she'd been at the gesture.

He chuckled. "That was Molly's doing. She said that at weddings you never know when a woman might need a hanky. She gave one to all of us."

He brushed his hands over the shoulders of her coat before stepping back. "Didn't think it'd be you, though. You're too practical for that. I guess I figured you'd be thinking two or three steps ahead."

Normally she would have been, and it stung a bit knowing that Rhys only saw what everyone else seemed to see—a woman lacking in sentimentality. But she'd been caught up in the moment just like everyone else. And for the briefest of seconds, she'd felt a strange yearning. Like she was possibly missing out on something important.

"I slipped up," she replied, reaching in the coat pocket for a pair of gloves. "It's just temporary."

She finally looked up into his face. His dark eyes were glowing down at her and whatever other smart reply she'd been about to make fluttered away like ribbons on a breeze. Her gaze inadvertently slid to his lips as she remembered the sound of his aroused breathing in the confined space of his truck. A truck that he was suggesting she get in—again.

This time there would be no funny business. She really should get to the venue and make sure everything was going according to plan. She relaxed her face into a pleasant smile. "I'll accept the drive with thanks. Let me just tell Jack that I'm going on ahead."

"Taylor?" He stopped her from walking away by grabbing her arm, his fingers circling her wrist. "You should slip up more often. It looks good on you."

Maybe he did see more. She wasn't sure if that was a good thing or not. "I'll tell Jack," she repeated.

"I'll warm up the engine," he answered.

She turned around to find her brother and when she turned back again, a cold gust of wind from the just-opened door hit her like an icy wall.

She had to keep her head about her today. Weddings

made people do strange things. It was just as well, then, that she planned on remaining behind the scenes as much as possible.

CHAPTER FIVE

THE RECEPTION WAS going off without a hitch. When Taylor arrived at the club, the guests were already circulating and enjoying the cocktail hour. Platters of crackers, cheese and cold cuts, shrimp rings, crudités and fruit were set out on tables close to the bar, where people were lined up to be served either punch or hot cider.

The place looked lovely. The centerpieces had been lit—boy, Melissa had really outdone herself with those. White candles enclosed in glass sat on real rounds of wood, surrounded by aromatic greenery and winterberries. Each chair was covered in white fabric, a wide red ribbon around the back with more cedar and a single pinecone adding a festive, homey touch. The pew markers had mirrored the design perfectly. She couldn't have planned it any better. Hadn't, actually. Funny how some things worked out.

Rhys showed up at her elbow and handed her a cup. "Have something hot to drink."

"I should check the kitchen."

"You should relax. Maybe enjoy yourself."

"I'll enjoy myself later." But she took the mug anyway. The sweet, spicy scent of the cider was too tempting to resist.

"You look beautiful by the way," he said quietly.

Her pulse fluttered again. "Thank you," she answered

politely, but inside she glowed. She was used to dressing up, but her style usually ran to the classic and conservative. Tailored fits and solid colors that spoke far more to class, confidence and efficiency than femininity and whimsy. But the dress today made her feel very girly indeed. The bodice was strapless and the lace overskirt to the emerald tea-length gown was far more dainty than she normally wore. Not to mention the gorgeous satin shoes on her feet, or the way her hair was gathered in a low chignon with a few pieces left artfully around her face.

"Do you want something to eat? I can bring you something if you like."

What was she doing? Last night she'd lost her senses, but it was the clear light of day now. Sure, weddings brought out the romantic in anyone but she was smarter than that. This wasn't anything. One kiss in a truck at midnight didn't make them a couple today. Or any day for that matter.

"I can get it myself, you know. You don't have to act like we're a couple just because we're paired up in the wedding party," she answered, making a pretense of scanning the room even though everything was moving along seamlessly.

Her breath squeezed in her lungs as she waited for his reaction. When she didn't get one, she turned to say something only to discover that he'd walked away. He'd gone to the buffet table, and she wondered if he'd stay true to form and simply ignore her wishes. But when he'd put a few selections on his plate, he never even glanced her way. He walked over to the other side of the room, greeting a few guests with a smile.

It made no sense that she felt empty and bereft when he'd done exactly as she'd intended.

Fine. She'd go to the kitchens and check on the dinner

prep, and then make sure the sound system was a go for the emcee. That's where she should be anyway. Not trying to impress a stubborn groomsman.

The words had sat on Rhys's tongue but he'd kept them to himself. At a wedding reception was no place to tell her exactly what he thought of her rude response. But he was plenty put out. He'd only been trying to be a gentleman. Sure, he enjoyed pushing her buttons. But after last night...

Never mind that. Even if that kiss had never happened, he would have been courteous to any woman he'd been paired with for the day. That was just plain manners where he came from. But she was too damned independent. Wanted to do everything by herself. Was it to prove she could? She didn't have to prove anything to him. Anyone with eyes in their head could see she was good at her job. She'd pulled this whole event together in a few weeks. That took organizational skills and long hours and, he suspected, a good amount of money. He felt like saying, "I get it. You're successful and you earned it all by yourself."

The contrast between them was laughable. So why did he bother? He got the feeling she'd never understand his point of view anyway.

He mingled a bit, visiting with neighbors and acquaintances. The Diamonds arrived, and then fifteen minutes after that Avery and Callum followed, along with Denise and Jack and of course, the adorable Nell. His gaze lit on the little girl for a moment, all in ruffles with a tiny green bow in her dark curls. Humph. Taylor probably didn't even want kids. It would take too much time away from her business and important tasks. How much more reminding did he need that she was not for him? Her work was her top priority.

Rhys's heart constricted as he thought of the two little

boys he'd grown so attached to. For a while he'd been so focused on saving the business that he'd neglected the people closest to him. Funny how your perspective changed when you lost what you didn't appreciate in the first place.

So why did he kiss her last night? Why had he made an effort today? And why in hell couldn't he stop thinking about her eyes swimming with tears as he handed her a stupid square of cotton during the ceremony?

Sam took the mic and introduced the happy couple and asked everyone to take their seats. "You, too, Taylor," he added, glimpsing her talking to one of the wait staff by the door. She smiled and gave a little shrug, making people chuckle as she came his way.

Rhys waited. And when she got to his side, he held out his arm.

He could tell her teeth were clenched as she smiled and put her hand on his arm. "You did that on purpose," she accused, smiling brightly.

He smiled back. "Yes, I did. Just to annoy you."

Her eyes sparked. "Why would you do that?"

"Because pushing your buttons amuses me," he replied. "I know I shouldn't." He pulled out her chair with a flourish and noticed her cheeks were flushed. "It's pretty clear where we stand. But I can't resist."

She took up her napkin and gave it a sharp flap before settling it on her lap. "Hmm. I took you for a rule follower. Straight and narrow. Didn't take you as a bit of a scamp."

Once upon a time he'd been far more carefree and less careful. A risk taker. Circumstances had made him grow up in a hurry. "Funny," he answered, taking his seat and retrieving his own napkin. "I never pictured you as the sappy type either, but…"

"Maybe we bring out the worst in each other," she said in an undertone, reaching for her water glass.

"See? We're getting to know each other better. Now I know that you see both fun and sentimentality as flaws."

"You're deliberately twisting my words."

"Be quiet. The minister is going to say the blessing."

He was gratified when she clamped her lips shut—score one for him. After the blessing, Sam took to the mic again, explaining the order of the evening while the salads were served. Even the salads matched the Christmas decor—greens with candied pecans, red cranberries and creamy feta. Her attention to the smallest detail was starting to get annoying.

Staff were on hand at each table to pour the wine, and he noticed that when Taylor's glass had been filled with red, she reached for it immediately and took a long sip.

Maybe he shouldn't bug her so much. She had a lot on her mind today. He didn't need to add to the stress.

Then again, there was something to be said for distraction. And he did enjoy pushing her buttons. It was a nice break from his self-imposed "dry spell."

"Good wine?" he asked, reaching for his glass.

"One of my favorites, from Mission Hill. Do you like it?"

He did, though he wasn't much of a wine drinker. "It's okay."

"What's wrong with it?"

"Nothing. I said it was okay."

A look of understanding lit in her eyes. "You don't drink much wine, do you?"

He shrugged. "Not as a rule." When would he drink wine? It wasn't like he went on dinner dates or was the kind to chill out at the end of the day with a nice chardonnay. At her distressed look, he took pity on her. "Look, I'm a guy. Most of us around here are beer men, that's all. Which would be totally out of place at this dinner."

"Oh, is it too fancy? I tried to keep it fairly traditional. Nothing that people can't pronounce, that sort of thing, you know?"

Gone was the sharp tongue and sassy banter. She was actually concerned. A few days ago he might have taken her comment differently, like maybe she meant the people of Cadence Creek weren't as sophisticated as she was. But that wasn't it. Her brow was wrinkled in the middle. He knew without asking that she'd tried very hard to come up with a menu that people would like.

"What's the main course?" he asked.

"Beef Wellington, Duchess potatoes, green beans and roasted red pepper."

"Sounds delicious."

"Well, Avery approved it, but then she approved just about everything I suggested." Her eyes widened. "Oh, Rhys, did I railroad her into stuff? Did she feel she couldn't say no?"

"Hey," he said, beginning to take pity on her. "Where is all this doubt coming from? You've said from the beginning that this is your thing."

"It is, but…"

He nudged her elbow. "Why did you pick this as the menu?"

She picked at her salad without eating. "Well, I tried to come up with something that was fancy enough for a wedding, something special, while keeping in mind the guest list. This is a meal for ranchers and, well, regular people. Not crazy movie stars or visiting dignitaries who only eat fish and sprouted grains or that kind of thing, you know?"

"So you tailored the food to the guest list?"

"Of course. I always do."

"Then why are you so worried? Know what I think? I think that for most people this is going to taste like a fancy meal out that's not intimidating, you know? Nothing they can't recognize or need to pronounce in a foreign language."

Their salads were removed and the main course put in front of them. Rhys's stomach growled. He'd only managed a few bites of the salad and the beef smelled delicious.

"I swear I'm not usually like this. Not so insecure."

"Is it because it's Callum?"

"Maybe. Then again, I don't usually do weddings. That's the one day everyone wants utterly perfect. There's more freedom with parties. But wedding days?" She took another sip of wine. Was quiet for a moment. "I screwed one up once."

"You did?" Was Taylor actually going to admit she'd made a mistake? It didn't strike him as her style.

She nodded. "The bride was allergic to strawberries. I'd forgotten. You don't mess with a bride on her wedding day, you know? She had a breakfast for her bridal party. I never thought twice about giving the chef dominion over the menu. I trusted him completely." She winced at the memory. "The wedding colors were pink and cream. The chef added strawberry coulis to the pancake batter. She got hives and her face swelled up like a balloon. Four hours before her walk down the aisle."

Rhys was intrigued. "What did you do?"

"We tried cold cloths, creams…it wasn't until the antihistamine shot that she really started to improve. But the 'getting ready' photos never happened, and she still looked rather pink and puffy in the pictures. Not to mention the fact that she nodded off in the limousine on the way to the hotel and reception because the drug made her drowsy. Not my finest moment as an event planner."

She speared her golden-browned potatoes with a somewhat savage poke. "I'm telling you, Rhys, you do not mess with a bride on her wedding day."

She looked so fierce he nearly smiled. But there was something else in her expression, too. She didn't like failure, or anything that would reveal a chink in her perfect armor. He wondered why.

"Have you always been a perfectionist?"

She didn't even take it as a slight criticism. "Yes."

"And doesn't that stress you out?"

She shrugged. "Occasionally. As long as I stay organized I'm fine. And I do work best under pressure. It's just now and again something will crop up and I'll chew antacids for a few days."

He wanted to ask her how that could possibly be fun, but they were interrupted as the speeches began. Mr. Shepard welcomed Avery to the family, and then Avery and Callum stood to speak together, thanking their family and friends. They took a moment to thank Taylor for pulling it all together, and Rhys saw her relax a little in her chair. The day was nearly done. The ceremony had gone without a hitch; the reception was lovely and the food delicious. Perhaps she could actually enjoy herself a little during the dancing.

Dessert was served—pastry baskets filled with chocolate mousse and topped with berries and whipped cream. They were almost too pretty to eat, and Rhys noticed that Taylor had slowed down on the wine and accepted a cup of coffee instead.

He frowned. He shouldn't care. Shouldn't bother him that she was wound tighter than a spring or that she was so deliberate in each choice and move. Except he knew now. He knew that there was a vulnerable side. He'd seen it last night when he'd mentioned how her family had ignored her. Whether she acknowledged it or not, she was desperate for her family's approval.

And he knew there was an unpredictable side to her, too, that rarely had a chance to get out to play. Because he was pretty sure that the heavy kissing they'd been doing in the cab of his truck last night had not been planned out and put on a list of pros and cons. It had been spontaneous. And combustible.

When the meal ended, the wedding cake was rolled in. "Oh, it's stunning," Taylor gasped, leaning forward to see better.

"You didn't know? A detail escaped your notice?"

She laughed. "No one was allowed to see it. Avery's friend Denise did it as a wedding gift. Avery insisted I trust her on this and so I did."

"It bothered you, though, right?"

She tore her gaze away from the cake and slid it up to meet his. "A little," she admitted. "This whole experience has been weird. I've had to give up way more control than I normally do. Usually no detail ever escapes my approval."

"Sometimes it's good to let someone else take the reins."

She chuckled. "Not my style, Bullock."

The cake really was pretty, even Rhys could see that. It looked like three presents stacked on top of each other, each layer turned on a slight angle and alternating red and white. The topper looked like a giant red bow. "What's the bow made out of?" he asked Taylor.

"Fondant," she said, smiling. "Okay, so the only thing to worry about now is the music, and the DJ should be fine, so maybe you're right. Maybe I can relax." She sighed. "And finally get some sleep."

He wondered if her lack of sleep was to do with the wedding or if she'd been like him last night, staring at the ceiling wondering what it would have been like to finish what they'd started.

It had been a long time since he'd come that close. He

certainly hadn't wanted to sow any wild oats here in Cadence Creek. The town was too small. Things got around. And before he knew it he'd be tied down, worrying about what he had to offer a wife, wondering how long it would be before he disappointed her.

No danger of that with Taylor, was there? She wasn't staying long enough for that.

Cheers went up as Avery and Callum sliced into the cake. Nell, clearly exhausted, was curled up in Mrs. Shepard's arms, sound asleep. The wait staff cleaned away the remaining dishes and business at the bar picked up. The show was over. Now it was time for fun.

He looked over at Taylor, who was more relaxed but looking increasingly exhausted. He was starting to wonder if she knew what fun was—or if it was all work and no play with her.

She wasn't sure how much more she could take.

Rhys was beside her every moment. He smelled so good. Like those peel-away cologne ads in magazines only better, because the scent came alive from the contact with his warm skin. He knew how to push her buttons and she'd started to realize he did it intentionally, trying to get a rise out of her. It was sexy as all get-out, like a strange mating dance that sent her heart racing and blood to her cheeks.

Which was all well and good except she kept feeling her control slipping and the balance of power was not in her favor. She found herself admitting things that she'd normally never dare breathe. Like that wedding story. She never shared that. It was too humiliating! At least she'd stopped before she'd said anything about how that day had ended—with John walking out. Professional and personal failure in one twelve-hour period. Talk about overachieving…

She didn't quite know where she stood with Rhys. It was partly exhilarating and mostly maddening and now, at the end of a very long day, she was feeling a bit off her game.

She decided to take a few minutes to chill out. She'd done her job. Everyone was doing theirs. It would be okay to relax for a bit. Especially when she could watch her brother and brand-new sister-in-law take to the dance floor for their first waltz.

Rhys disappeared momentarily to the bar and she let out a breath. Avery and Callum swept across the parquet as everyone watched, but her gaze slipped away from the floor and to Rhys, who stood chatting to the bartender while he waited for his drink. She swallowed. His tux fit him to perfection, the trousers showcasing long, lean legs that led to a gorgeously tight bottom. He'd taken off the jacket, and the tailored vest over the white starched shirt accentuated the breadth of his shoulders. He wasn't classically handsome, but his physique was as close to perfect as she could imagine.

When he turned back from the bar he caught her staring. She gasped a little as heat snapped between them, even from across the room. Maybe his face would never be in a magazine, but there was an intensity to it, a magnetism, that she couldn't deny.

He was holding two glasses in his hands.

When he got back to the table, he held one out to her. "Here," he said, taking his seat. "You look like you could use this."

"Champagne?"

He grinned, and it lit her up from the inside. "They managed to have a couple of bottles back there."

"You're more of a beer guy."

"It depends on the occasion. And you—" his gaze traveled over her for about the tenth time today "—look like a girl who needs champagne in her hand."

She took the glass.

"To a job well done."

She raised her glass to touch his but he wasn't done.

"And some well-deserved R&R."

That's right. After tonight she was on vacation for a whole week. She wasn't sure if it was a blessing or if it was going to drive her stir-crazy. She wasn't used to being idle.

She sipped at the champagne, the bubbles exploding on her tongue. A waitress stopped at the table, offering small pieces of cake. What the heck. Taylor took one, and so did Rhys. She took a bite. Not straight up chocolate... She closed her eyes. It was lavender. "Holy cannoli," she whispered, taking another sip of champagne, which only intensified the flavors on her tongue. "That is some serious cake."

"You," he said in a low voice, "are killing me here."

She held his gaze. Put a bit of cake on her fork and held it out while the events of the previous night leaped to the front of her mind. "What's good for the goose," she said lightly, offering the cake. "I promise you, this cake is a life-altering experience."

He took it from the fork. "I don't think it's the cake," he answered, reaching out and circling her wrist with his fingers. "Taylor, what are we doing?"

Clapping erupted as Avery and Callum finished their dance. "Now could we have the wedding party on the floor, please?" the DJ called.

Their gazes clung for a brief second as the words sunk in. For all her "you don't have to act like we're a couple" bit, the truth was they *had* been seated together for the reception and they *were* expected to dance together. The other bridesmaids and groomsmen seated along the head table were getting up from their chairs. Rhys held out his hand. "That's our cue."

She put down her fork. For heaven's sake, it was one dance at a wedding. Nothing to get in such a lather over. She'd put her hand in his, the other on his shoulder, and stare at the buttons on his shirt. It would be fine.

Except the moment they hit the parquet, he pulled her close in his arms and the scent that had teased her earlier enveloped her in a cloud of masculinity. Even in her heels—and she wasn't a short girl—he had a few inches on her. His palm was wide and warm and her plan to simply put her other hand on his lapel was a total fail because she remembered he'd removed his jacket and the flat of her hand was pressed simply to his white shirt. And the hard, warm wall of muscle beneath it.

"For goodness' sake, smile," he commanded as their feet started moving to the music.

She looked up into his eyes. He was smiling down at her but rather than feeling reassured she got the feeling that she was looking into the face of the Big Bad Wolf.

CHAPTER SIX

WHOEVER DECIDED THAT slow, angsty songs were appropriate for weddings needed to be shot.

Taylor made her feet move, determined to keep her distance from Rhys as best she could, which was a rather daunting task considering they were slow dancing. It might have been easier if the song choice had been a wedding standard, something she was used to hearing time and again over the years and could dismiss as cliché and trite. But this was something new and romantic, and an acoustic version to boot that only added to the intimacy. Rhys's hand rode the small of her back, fitting perfectly in the hollow just below the end of her zip. The warmth of his touch seeped through the lace and satin to her skin.

During the planning, a wedding party dance had sounded nice. Since Avery didn't have any family, the traditional Groom/Mom of the Bride, Bride/Father of the Groom dances couldn't happen for the second dance of the night. This was Avery's idea of including everyone. Little had Taylor known that something so innocuous sounding would create such havoc.

"This isn't so bad, is it?"

His breath tickled the hair just above her ear and goose bumps popped up over her skin. How could she say how she really felt about it? That it was pure torture being in his arms this way, determined not to touch, wanting to desperately, knowing she couldn't with such an audience watching their every move?

"Not so bad I guess," she answered.

More shuffling steps. Was she imagining it or did his hand tighten against her back, pulling her closer? She swallowed heavily, the nerves in her stomach swirling with both anxiety and anticipation. Oh, God, now his jaw was resting lightly against her temple and his steps were getting smaller.

Her fingers slid over his shoulders as she imagined the smooth, muscled skin beneath the pure white fabric. Each breath caught for just a moment in her chest, making it hard to breathe as the song went on interminably. His fingers kneaded gently at the precise spot of the dimple at the top of her...

They had to stop this. And yet she lacked any will to back away, to put space between them. What she really wanted was to tilt her head so that his jaw wasn't riding her temple but closer to her mouth.

Holy Hannah.

"What are you doing to me, Taylor?"

If he kept talking in that husky voice she was going to have a meltdown right here on the dance floor.

"Nothing," she replied. "I'm not doing anything."

But she was and she knew it. And he wasn't exactly backing off, either.

"You..." Fear crowded her breath. She was getting in way too deep. "You don't even like me. You criticize everything."

"You're not the only one who enjoys a challenge," he replied, his thumb making circles against her tailbone. "You know as well as I do all that baiting was just foreplay."

Melt. Down.

"You're forgetting," he said softly, "who was with you in that truck last night."

She finally braved a look at him. His dark eyes glittered at her and she knew in a heartbeat where this would lead if she let it. The big question was did she want to?

Her body said yes. Her brain was another matter entirely. And while it was a close-fought battle, her brain was still in charge. By a very narrow margin.

"Not going to happen," she said, sounding far more certain than she felt.

"You sure? No gravel pit required. I have my own house, with a nice big bed in it."

Oh. *Oh.*

While that was a temptingly delicious thought, Taylor knew one of them had to be sensible. "I haven't had that much champagne, Rhys. If you're looking to hook up with someone, maybe you can find someone local. I'm sure there are some pretty girls in town who'd be interested."

He lifted his chin and his hot gaze slid away. "I don't date town girls."

"Ever?"

"Ever," he confirmed tightly.

Well. There was a story there, she was sure. But she wasn't about to ask. The farther away from Rhys she could manage the better. She did not want to get involved. A couple of stolen kisses were one thing. Start to probe into his personal life and it was going to get intimate.

"So I'm what? Not hanging around after Christmas, which makes me convenient?"

He let out a short laugh, dropped his gaze to her lips and pulled her close. Her breath came out in a rush as she found herself pressed against his hard length. "Trust me. You are anything but convenient."

The contact rippled through them both until suddenly

he released his hold and stepped back. The song ended and a new one began. Other guests crowded the floor as a popular, upbeat song thumped through the speakers.

Taylor stepped back. "Thank you for the dance."

Before he could say anything else, she turned her back on him and went to their table, ready to pick up her purse and go. Except she hadn't brought a vehicle, had she? She'd gone to the church in the limo and to here with Rhys and now she'd have to beg a ride back to the B&B. Which she'd planned to do with Jack, but she caught sight of him dancing with Amy Wilson, having a good time.

She grabbed her champagne glass and drained what was in it.

Callum and Avery stopped for a moment, happy and glowing. "Taylor, we can't thank you enough," Avery said. "Today was just perfect."

She was relieved to have something to think about other than Rhys. "It was my pleasure. And I did have some help you know. Your florist is a gem and your cake was out of this world. Not to mention Clara saving the day with the church candles." She looked up at Callum. "You've landed in a very nice place, brother."

He winked at her. "I know it. Sure you don't want to hang around a little longer?"

She shook her head. "A nice diversion but not my style. The week of relaxation that I'll get housesitting for you is enough small-town for me, thanks."

"You sure? Seems to me you've made a friend." He raised his eyebrows.

"I'm a big girl. And that's going nowhere, so don't you worry your head about it."

"That's not what Jack says. He said you were necking with Rhys in his truck last night."

This was what she didn't miss about having brothers

underfoot. They always thought it was okay to stick their noses in her business under the guise of "looking out for their sister." All of it was a pain in the butt.

"Callum," Avery chided softly, elbowing her husband in the ribs.

"Well, they weren't exactly discreet on the dance floor, either."

Taylor's cheeks burned. "Rhys Bullock is a bossy so-and-so who likes to push my buttons. I'm no more interested in him than…than…"

A hand appeared beside her, reaching for the other champagne glass. She turned on him. "Could you please stop showing up everywhere I am?"

He lifted his glass in a mock toast, totally unperturbed. "I'll disappear somewhere more convenient," he said.

He did, too. Right back to the dance floor. The DJ had put on a faster number and Rhys snagged Amy from Jack and swung her into a two-step. He turned her under his arm and she came back laughing.

"You're jealous," Callum noted.

"I most certainly am not."

"You're no better at lying now than you were when we were kids. Dad always said the poker face gene passed you by." Callum grinned, but he couldn't possibly know how much the words stung. Another criticism. She never measured up. She was always one step behind her brothers as far as her dad was concerned. One of these days she was going to show her father her accounts and watch his eyebrows go up. Those "frivolous" parties she planned brought in a boatload of cash.

Funny how the idea of that future moment had always seemed so sweet in her mind, but lately it had lost a little of its lustre. It was only a bank statement after all. There had to be more, right? Something more satisfying than the account balance?

"Don't you have cows to milk or something?"

He laughed. "I hired someone to do that today." His eyes twinkled at her. "And you won't have to worry about any farm work, either, while you're at the house. It's all taken care of."

"Good. Because you used to enjoy mucking around in the barns but I'd rather keep my boots nice and clean."

He laughed, then leaned forward and kissed her cheek. "We'll be gone tomorrow before you get to the house. I'll leave the key under the Santa by the door. Make yourself at home and we'll see you on the twenty-third."

She relaxed and kissed him back. "Love you, Callum."

"I love you, too, brat."

They moved off to visit with other guests. Taylor took a turn on the floor with Ty, and Sam, and even once with her father. True to form, he complimented the wedding but in such a way that it made her feel inconsequential.

"You planned a nice little party," he said, smiling at her.

Her throat tightened. Eighty guests, wedding party, church, venue, catering, flowers and all the other tiny details it took to put a wedding together in a ridiculously short amount of time. And it was "little"?

"Thanks," she said, deflated but unwilling to rise to any bait tonight. Not on Callum's day.

"When are you going to stop playing and start putting that business degree to good use?" he asked.

"I am putting my degree to use," she returned, moving automatically to the music. "Just ask my accountant."

"Planning parties?"

"I know you've never understood that. You wanted me to be a fund manager. I'd be bored to death, Dad."

She made herself look into his face as she said it. For

a moment he'd almost looked hurt. How was that even possible?

Conversation dropped for a minute or so before Harry recovered and changed the subject, talking nonstop about Nell and how it was wonderful to have a grandchild to spoil. The dance ended just in time—she was starting to worry he was going to ask her when she was going to do her duty and provide some more grandchildren. Her father's opinions were clear enough and pretty much paralleled with what John's had been. Personal and professional failure. And if not failure, at the least disappointment.

When the dance was over Rhys gave her a wide berth and she attempted to perk up her mood by spending a half hour with the pregnant Clara, chatting about Angela's charity foundation Butterfly House, and the other initiatives the Diamonds were involved in. It was all quite fascinating and before she knew it, the call went up for the single women to gather on the floor for the throwing of the bouquet.

She was not going to do that. Not in a million years.

Except Avery put up the call and every eye was on her. "Come on, Taylor, you, too!" Taylor spied Rhys standing against a pillar, his arms folded smugly as his eyes teased her, daring her to take part in the silly custom. She lifted her chin and ran her hands down her skirt before joining the half-dozen or so women ready to do battle for the mythical status of the next to be married. She wouldn't give him the satisfaction of backing out. Not that she'd actively try to catch it…

When Avery let the bouquet fly, Taylor had a heart-stopping moment when she realized it was heading right for her. Without thinking she simply reacted, raising her hands. But just before the ribbon-wrapped stems reached her, another hand neatly plucked it from the air.

Cheers went up when Amy Wilson held up the bouquet in a sign of victory.

Taylor was really ready to leave now. As she backed off the dance floor, she looked over at her mother, smiling from the sidelines, still cradling a sleeping Nell in her arms. Taylor wondered if her mom knew how much Taylor admired her. It was always her dad in the spotlight, but Taylor knew how hard her mom worked to keep the ship on course. Once, when she'd been about ten years old, she'd discovered her mother in the kitchen, making lists for an upcoming party they were hosting. That was when Taylor understood how, when everything seemed smooth and effortless on the surface, it was because of a well-oiled, well-organized machine running things behind the scenes. The machine, in that case, had been her mother, who handled everything from start to finish and still found time to run the kids to sports and especially Jack to his ski meets.

Maybe her dad was the one with his picture in the business magazines, but it was her mother Taylor truly admired. Her mother was the reason she'd chosen event planning as her career. Taylor hated how her father minimized the hard work she did, so why did her mother not resent his attitude? Why had it never been an issue for them?

There was another loud shout and Taylor lifted her head to see a stunned Rhys holding the bridal garter. According to tradition, Amy then took the chair in the middle of the dance floor while Rhys slid the garter on her leg. Taylor stifled a laugh. He didn't look too happy about it, especially when the DJ announced that the next dance was for the "lucky couple." Served him right.

As the music started, she headed toward her parents. "I don't suppose you're heading back to the B&B anytime soon, are you?" she asked, kneeling by her mom's chair.

"As a matter of fact, I was just suggesting to your dad

that we should take Nell and go. She's staying with us to-night so Callum and Avery can have the place to them-selves before they all fly out tomorrow. Poor little mite's had enough excitement for today."

"So has this big mite. I'm beat. Mind if I catch a lift?"

"Of course not, but don't you want to stay at the party?"

Taylor saw Rhys and Amy out of the corner of her eye. For all he said he didn't date local girls, Amy sure was snuggled close to him, her arms wrapped around his ribs and her head nestled into his shoulder. "I'm sure. I've had a long few days and this will pretty much run itself now."

"Get your things then. You did a beautiful job, sweet-heart. Proud of you."

The words warmed Taylor's heart. "Thanks, Mom. I had a good teacher."

"Oh, go on."

But Taylor took a moment to press her mother's hand in hers. "I mean it. I don't know that you were appreciated enough for all you did to keep things running smoothly. I should have said this before, but when I started my busi-ness you were the inspiration behind it."

"I didn't know that."

"Well, it's true."

Taylor went to pull away but her mom held tight to her hand. "Mind if I give you a little extra food for thought?"

Surprised, Taylor paused. "Sure."

Susan looked into Taylor's eyes and smiled. "None of it would have meant a thing without your dad and you kids. I know sometimes it looked like I played the dutiful wife…"

"You worked hard."

"Yes, I did, and I enjoyed it. Still, I would have missed out on so much if I hadn't had you kids. I could have gone on and done anything I wanted, you know? And I don't regret my decision for a second. Work is work, but family is forever."

"Didn't it ever bother you that Dad, well, took you for granted?"

Susan laughed. "Is that what you think? Oh, heavens. He wanted you kids, too. Honey, you get so wound up and defensive about this division of labor expectation, but it goes both ways. We did what worked for us. Being home with you three was my choice to make."

"Is this leading to a speech about settling down?"

Susan smiled and patted her hand. "I know better than that."

Taylor let out a breath. "Phew." But after a moment she looked at her mother again. "Mom, maybe I will settle down. When I find the right guy."

"That's a good answer," her mother replied. "Now, let's get going. I want to spend a little more time with my new granddaughter tonight."

Taylor got her coat from the coat check, snagged her purse and checked in with the staff one last time. Her mother was making sure they had all of Nell's stuff—including her car seat—while her dad went to warm up the car. She was just pulling on her gloves when Rhys came up behind her.

"You were just going to leave without saying goodbye?"

She held on to her purse strap. "It's been a long day and I'm catching a ride with my folks."

"That didn't answer my question."

She frowned. "What do you care? You've amused yourself with me a bit for the last few days but the wedding's over, we're not paired up anymore and we can both go about our business."

Rhys stared at her quizzically. "Really?"

"Is there some reason why we shouldn't?"

He looked like he wanted to say something, but held back. She wondered why. And then got a bit annoyed that she kept wondering about Rhys's state of mind at all. She blew air out her nose in an exasperated huff. "What do you care anyway? You seemed to enjoy having Amy Wilson plastered all over you."

"Jealous?"

She snorted. "Hardly."

He stepped forward until there was barely an inch between them. "Amy Wilson is the last woman on earth I want to be with!"

Silence rang around them, and then, almost as one, they realized someone had heard the entire outburst. Amy stood not ten feet away, her creamy skin stained crimson in embarrassment as humiliated tears shone in her eyes.

"Amy…" Taylor tried, taking a hesitant step toward the woman.

But Amy lifted a hand to halt Taylor's progress, and without saying a word she spun on her heel and disappeared into the women's powder room.

Rhys sighed heavily, let out a breathy expletive.

"Good night, Rhys."

"Taylor, I'm…"

But she didn't listen to the end. She turned and walked, quickly, toward the exit. She could see the headlights of her dad's rental car as it waited by the front door, saw him helping her mom in the passenger side. She went outside and was met by a frigid wall of arctic air. As she climbed into the backseat, she made a promise to herself.

Tomorrow she was going to stock up on groceries, wine and DVDs. Then she was going to go to Callum's house and as God as her witness, she wasn't going to venture out into the icy cold for the entire week. She was going to be a hermit. No work. No worrying about freezing her tail off.

And especially no men!

CHAPTER SEVEN

TAYLOR ROLLED OVER and squinted at the sunshine coming through the bedroom window. Why hadn't she thought to close the blinds last night? Her first full day of vacation and she'd looked forward to sleeping in. She checked her watch. It was only eight-fifteen!

She burrowed into the warm blankets and closed her eyes. Maybe if she breathed deeply and relaxed, she could fall back asleep. But after just a few minutes she knew she might as well get up. She was awake for good now. Besides, just because she was up didn't mean she had to actually "do" anything. She could lounge around in her fuzzy pajamas, drink coffee, read one of the paperbacks she'd brought along.

Come to think of it, that sounded pretty darn good. Especially the coffee part. It was going to be awesome having some peace and quiet. No ringing phones, no buzzing email, no wedding plans and especially no Rhys Bullock to get in her way now that the wedding was over.

She was terribly afraid she was going to be bored to tears within forty-eight hours.

She rolled out of bed and shoved her feet into her favorite sheepskin slippers. On the way to the kitchen she pulled her hair back into a messy ponytail, anchoring it with a hair elastic that had been left on her wrist. While the coffee was brewing she turned up the thermostat and chafed her arms. Even the soft fleece of her winter PJs was no protection against the December cold.

She poured her first cup of coffee and, in keeping with the celebratory nature of the week, substituted her usual cream with the festive eggnog she found in the refrigerator.

She was halfway through the cup when she chanced a look out the front window. The mug paused inches away from her lips as she stared at a familiar brown truck. What on earth was Rhys doing here?

As she stared, the man in question came out of the barn. Even with the hat pulled low over his head, she'd recognize that long-legged stride in a heartbeat.

Irritation marred her idyllic morning and before she could think twice she flung open the door and stepped to the threshold. "What on earth are you doing here?"

His head snapped up and even though he was too far away for her to see his eyes, she felt the connection straight to her toes. Stupid girl. She should have stayed inside. Pretended she wasn't home. Not risen to the bait, except Rhys seemed to get on her last nerve without trying. She swallowed thickly, feeling quite foolish but standing her ground as a matter of pride. He hadn't actually baited her at all. He hadn't done *anything*.

Except show up.

"Well?" she persisted.

"I'm doing the chores." His tone said, *What does it look like I'm doing?*

She frowned. Callum had said at the reception that someone had looked after the chores and would continue to do so during his absence. He couldn't have meant Rhys. Rhys had been occupied with the wedding all day on Saturday. She would have noticed if he'd slipped away.

"Why?"

He came closer, walking across the yard as if he owned the damned place. "Well, I would suppose that would be because Callum hired me to."

"He did not. He hired someone else."

Rhys was only twenty feet away now. "He told you that?"

The wrinkle between her eyebrows deepened. Was that exactly what Callum had said? "He said he hired someone to do the chores during the wedding and during his absence, too."

Rhys stopped at the bottom of the steps to the veranda. "He hired Keith O'Brien on the day of the wedding, because I was in the wedding party."

Oh, hell.

"Why didn't he just hire him for the whole time, then?" She gave a huff that went up in a cloud of frosty air.

"Because Keith left yesterday to go to Fort McMurray to spend the holidays with his family."

"So you're…"

He shifted his weight to one hip, a move that made him look unbearably cocky. "Here for the week," he finished for her, his whole stance screaming *deal with it*.

And then he smiled, that slow grin climbing up his cheek that was at once maddening and somehow, at the same time, made her whole body go warm. His gaze slid over her pajamas. "Penguins? Seriously?" he asked.

Her mouth dropped open as she realized she was standing in the doorway still in her nightwear. Jolly skiing penguins danced down the light blue pant legs. The navy fleece top was plain except for one more penguin on the left breast.

She stepped back inside and slammed the door.

It was eerily quiet for the space of five seconds, and

then her heart beat with the sound of his boots, heavy on the steps, then two more as he crossed the narrow porch.

He was just on the other side of the door. Less than two feet away. He didn't even have the manners to knock. It was like he knew she was standing there waiting for him because he said, in a low voice, "Aren't you going to ask me in for coffee?"

"Humph!" she huffed, taking a step backward and fuming, her hands on her hips. As if. Presumptuous jerk!

"Come on, Taylor. It's cold out here. A man could use a hot cup of joe. I can smell it, for Pete's sake."

"I hear the coffee is good at the Wagon Wheel. Price is right, too."

Was that a chuckle she heard or had she just imagined it?

Softer now, he answered, "But the company isn't nearly as good."

She shouldn't be persuaded or softening toward him at all. He was used to getting his own way and she wouldn't oblige.

Then he said the words she never thought he'd ever utter. "I'm sorry about the other night."

Damn him.

She opened the door. "Come in then, before you let all the heat out. It's like an igloo in here."

He stepped inside, all six-feet-plus of him, even taller with his Stetson on. She wasn't used to seeing him this way—he looked like the real deal with his boots and hat and heavy jacket.

"You smell like the barn."

"My grandfather would say that's the smell of money."

"Money?"

He grinned. "Yeah. Anyway, sorry. Occupational hazard. Me smelling like the animals, that is. Though usually I smell like horses. They smell better than cows."

She didn't actually mind. While she wasn't interested in getting her own boots dirty, she did remember days on her uncle's farm. The smell was familiar and not too unpleasant.

"Just take off your boots if you're coming in for coffee."

While he toed off his boots she went into the kitchen to get a fresh cup. "What do you take in it?" she called out.

"Just cream, if you've got it," he answered, stepping inside the sunny kitchen.

She handed him the cup and then took a plastic container from a cupboard. "Are you hungry? Avery left a mountain of food, way more than I can eat in a week. This one is chocolate banana bread."

"I couldn't turn that down."

She cut several slices and put them on a plate. "Come on and sit down then."

Before Rhys sat down, he removed his hat and put it carefully on a nearby stool. She stared at him as he sat, pulled his chair in and reached for his coffee cup.

"What?" he asked, pausing with the cup halfway to his lips.

She shrugged. "You can be very annoying. But you have very good manners."

He laughed. "Blame my mom, I guess. So, enjoying your vacation?"

"Well, I've only officially been on holiday for a few hours. Yesterday I slept in, then spent last night hanging with my family. My mom and dad booked a place in Radium for the week and are coming back on the twenty-third for Christmas with Callum and the family. And Jack flew back to Montana this morning for a meeting of some sort. Lord only knows what deal he's cooking up this time.

Anyway, I'll probably enjoy my vacation for a few days. And then I'll start going stir-crazy."

Rhys reached for a slice of cake. "You strike me as one of those ambitious, type A personality people."

"You mean I'm driven? Yeah, I guess." She sighed. "I might as well 'fess up. I like being my own boss. Sometimes it's stressful because it's all on me, you know? But I don't like being told what to do."

He began coughing, crumbs catching in his throat. When he looked up at her again his eyes had watered and he was laughing. "Sorry. Stating the obvious shouldn't have been that funny."

"Hey, I know how you feel about it. You think I'm crazy. Most guys are intimidated by it."

"Most guys have a hard time with a woman who is smarter than they are."

She nibbled on her cake. "Careful, Rhys. That almost sounded like a compliment."

He laughed.

"So why aren't you?"

"What?" He tilted his head curiously. "What do you mean?"

"Why aren't you intimidated?"

He smiled again and the dark depths of his eyes warmed. "Oh. That's easy. I said that most guys have a problem with women who are smarter than they are..."

"And you're not most guys?"

"I never said you were smarter than me."

Without thinking, she kicked him under the table. Her toe hurt but he barely even flinched. "You are an infernal tease!"

"And you love it. Because you like a challenge."

How did he possibly know her so well? It was vastly unsettling.

She picked at her cake another moment or two before putting it down and facing him squarely. "What do you get out of this, Rhys? You and me. We're doing this dance and I'm not sure I see the point of it."

"You mean because we're so different and all?"

She lifted one shoulder. "That's only part of it. We both know that on Boxing Day I'm headed back to my life, so why bother?"

Taylor lifted her gaze to meet his. Something curled through her insides, hot and exciting. This simmering attraction they had going on made no sense. They were as different as water and air. But it was there just the same. This chemistry. Rhys Bullock was exciting. A small-town farmworker who hadn't the least bit of initiative and she couldn't stop thinking about him.

And yet, maybe the attraction stemmed from his confidence, a self-assurance that he knew who he was and was exactly where he wanted to be. While she didn't quite understand his choices, she had to admit she was the tiniest bit jealous that he'd gained that understanding while she was still trying to figure it all out. He didn't need accolades. Rhys Bullock had the confidence to know exactly who he was. He was comfortable in his own skin the way she'd never been.

"Why you?" He leaned forward a little. "Beyond the obvious fact that you're crazy hot and my temperature goes up a few degrees when you enter the room?"

She suppressed the urge to fan herself. "Rhys," she cautioned.

"You asked. And for what it's worth, I'm not looking for ties and commitments."

"Funny, because you're a pretty grounded guy. I'd kind of expect someone like you to be settled down with two-point-five kids and a dog, you know?"

Something flickered across his face. Pain? Anger? It disappeared as fast as it had arrived. "Start dating in a town this size and suddenly the town gets very, very small. Especially when things go wrong."

"Ah, like that old saying about…doing something where you eat."

He chuckled. "Yeah. Exactly like that. Look, you're a novelty, Taylor. An adventure. A safe one, because in a week's time you're going to be gone."

"So I'm a fling?"

His gaze sharpened. "A couple of kisses hardly constitutes a fling." He took a calm sip of his coffee. "You're an anomaly. You intrigue me. You know how to keep me on my toes."

"I'm glad I'm so amusing."

"Don't act like your feelings are hurt. We both know that the last thing you want is to be ordinary."

"Yeah, well, not everyone appreciates the alternative."

"That's because you highlight every single one of their flaws. You're not always right, but you're committed." He put his hand over hers. "That kind of commitment can take a toll. I can see you need the break."

"Don't be silly. I'm perfectly fine." She looked away, unexpectedly touched by his insight. How could he see what everyone else did not? The whole wedding she'd felt like she was losing her edge. Normally she'd be fired up and excited about the New Year's job, but instead she was dreading it. What on earth was wrong with her?

He squeezed her fingers. "Oh, Taylor, do you think I don't recognize burnout when I see it?"

She pulled her hand out of his grasp and sat back. "I'm not even thirty years old. I'm too young for burnout. Besides, what would you know about the pressures of running a business, with your 'put in your shift and go home' attitude?"

Silence rang in the kitchen for a few seconds. "Okay then." He pushed out the chair, stood and reached for his hat. "I should get going. I have some work out at Diamondback before coming back tonight to do the evening chores. Thanks for the coffee and cake."

She felt silly for going off on him like that—especially when he was right. At the same time, she didn't need to have it pointed out so bluntly. And the way he'd spoken so softly and squeezed her fingers? Argh! The sympathy had made her both angry and inexplicably tearful.

"Rhys, I…"

"Don't worry about it," he said evenly, going to the door and pulling on his boots. "I'll see you later."

He was gone before she had a chance to do anything. To take back the snippy words. She'd judged him, when she knew how it felt to be on the receiving end of such judgment.

She turned her back to the door and leaned against it, staring at the Christmas tree, fully decorated, standing in the corner. She couldn't even muster up a good dose of Christmas cheer.

Maybe Rhys was right. Maybe she was a little burned out. But she couldn't just take off and leave things. She had clients and commitments. She had employees who were counting on her for their livelihoods.

One week. Somehow she needed to recharge during this one week. With a heavy sigh, she went to the kitchen, retrieved her coffee and headed back to the bedroom. Coffee and a book in bed was as good a start as she could come up with right now.

Rhys was glad of the physical labor to keep him going. He'd been up early to head to Callum's for chores, then to

Diamondback, and now back at Callum's for the evening milking. Plus he hadn't been sleeping well. He'd had Taylor on his mind. Something had happened between them as they'd danced at the wedding. Then there was this morning in the kitchen. Lord, how he loved bantering with her. She was quick and sharp and it was like a mating dance, teasing then pulling away. Except that when it got a little too honest she ran scared and the game was over.

It was fully dark outside as he finished tidying the milking parlor and went to the stainless sink to wash his hands. What was she doing now? Having dinner? A bubble bath? His fingers paused for a moment as that idea saturated his consciousness, crowding out any other thoughts. He imagined her long, pale limbs slick with water and soap, tendrils of hair curling around her face from the steam rising from the bath.

Not dating came with a price. It was like anything else, he supposed. Deny yourself long enough, and temptation was nearly too much to bear. And Taylor Shepard was tempting indeed.

But he knew what she really thought of him. That fact alone would keep him from knocking on her door again.

He shut off the tap. He knew a damn sight more about running a business than she thought. His livelihood and his mother's future were tied up in the diner. And he knew the pain of failure, too. It wasn't even a matter of his savings. It was a matter of trying to make things right for employees. Creditors. Putting himself last, and scraping the bottom of the barrel to keep from declaring bankruptcy. The unfortunate part was that he hadn't just messed things up for himself. It had messed up Sherry's life. And by extension, that of her kids.

He rubbed a hand over his face.

Never again. Punching a clock made for a lot less stress in the end. Taylor had no right to judge him for it.

He shoved his gloves on his hands and stepped outside into the cold. His feet crunched on the snow and he was nearly to his truck when the front door to the house opened.

"Rhys?"

He turned. His breath formed a frosty cloud as he saw her standing in the circle of porch light, her arms crossed around her middle to keep warm. Her long braid fell over her shoulder again, neat and tidy. Just once he'd like to take that braid apart with his fingers and sink his hands into the thick softness of her hair.

"You need something?" he called out.

There was a slight hesitation. "I… Do you want to come in for a few minutes?"

Hell, yes. Which was exactly why he shouldn't.

"It's been a long day, Taylor." He put his hand on the door handle.

"Oh."

That was all she said. Oh. But he was just stupid enough to hear disappointment in her voice as well as a recognition that it wasn't about the long day at all.

He closed his eyes briefly. This was very likely going to be a big mistake. Huge.

"Maybe just for a minute."

She waited for him, though she had to be nearly freezing by now. She stepped aside as he climbed the steps and went inside to where it was warm. He heard the door shut behind him and fought the urge to turn and kiss her. The desire to take her in his arms was so strong it was nearly overwhelming. Whatever differences they had, the connection between them was undeniable. It made things very complicated.

"Did you need something?" he asked. "I'm pretty handy if something needs fixing."

Taylor slid past him into the living room. He noticed now that the tree was lit up, a beautiful specimen glowing with white lights and red and silver decorations. A few presents were beneath it, wrapped in expensive foil paper with precise red and green bows. "Tree looks good."

"Avery did it before she left."

"I didn't notice it this morning."

She met his gaze and he'd swear she was shy. "It looks different when it's lit up."

"So do you."

He shouldn't have said it. Keeping his mouth shut had never been much of a problem for him before. But there was nothing usual about Taylor, was there? She provoked all kinds of unexpected responses.

"About this morning," she said quietly. "I asked you in tonight because I owe you an apology."

He didn't know what to say. Taylor didn't strike him as the type who apologized. Or at least—came right out and said it. He recalled the night of the rehearsal dinner, and how Taylor had told Martha that she'd underestimated her. She'd expressed the sentiment in a roundabout way when talking to Rhys. But not a full-on apology.

She came forward and looked up into his eyes. "I was overly sensitive this morning, and I said something I shouldn't have. It's not up to me to judge your life choices. Everyone makes their own decisions for their own reasons and their own happiness. I don't like it when people do it to me, and I shouldn't have done it to you."

He'd respected her intelligence before, admired how capable she was. But this was different. Taylor had a lot of pride. Making a point of saying she was sorry took humility.

"It's a bit of a hot-button with me," he admitted. "I tend to be a bit sensitive about it."

"Why?" She cocked her head a little, and the motion made him smile.

"It's a long and boring story," he said lightly.

"I bet it's not. Which is why you're not talking."

He couldn't help it, he smiled back. It might be easier to stay away if he didn't actually *like* her—but he did. She was straightforward and honest and made him laugh.

"Listen," she said, her voice soft. "I made cannelloni for dinner and there's enough to share. Have you eaten yet?"

Her lips had some sort of gloss on them that didn't add much color but made them look shiny and plump. He swallowed and dragged his gaze from her mouth back to her eyes. "Um, no."

"Take your boots off, then, and come inside. I promise that I won't poison you."

She said it with one eyebrow raised and her lips curved up in good humor.

He questioned the wisdom of hanging around, and then his stomach rumbled. As Taylor laughed, he took off his boots and left them by the door.

"Bathroom's through there, if you want to wash your hands. I'll dish stuff up."

When he arrived back in the kitchen, the scent of tomato and garlic seduced his nostrils. "That smells so good," he commented, pausing in the doorway.

She'd only left on the under-counter lighting, which cast a warm and intimate glow through the room. A cheery red and green plaid tablecloth covered the table, and she'd lit a couple of stubby candles in the middle.

Suddenly he wondered if he'd fallen very neatly into a trap. And if he actually minded so very much.

"Do you eat like this every night?" he asked casually, stepping into the room.

Taylor blushed. "Confession time, I guess. I planned dinner a little late because I was hoping you'd say yes." She placed a glass casserole dish on a hot mat on the table, then added a bowl of salad and a bottle of white wine. "I thought I'd have some wine, but if you'd prefer something else?"

"Wine is fine. Just a single glass, though." He was trying to decide what he felt about her admission that she'd planned dinner with him in mind. "You wanted me to come to dinner, and yet this morning you were pretty mad about seeing me here."

She hesitated, wine bottle in hand. "You complicate things for me. But I was here today at loose ends, no work to do, no one to talk to. It seemed lonely to eat here alone and I didn't want to go into town again."

"So I'm a chair filler."

"I decided to stop being annoyed with you and enjoy your company instead." She finished pouring the wine.

When she was seated he sat, and reached for the cloth napkin. "What do you do in Vancouver, then? I mean, at meal times?"

It occurred to him that maybe she didn't eat dinner alone. A beautiful woman like her. It was stupid to think she wasn't taken, wasn't it?

She took his plate and served him a helping of the stuffed pasta. "I usually pick up something on my way home. Or I get home so late I just grab something quick in front of the TV before hitting the bed."

"This pace must be a real change for you."

"A bit. Different, but not entirely unwelcome, actually."

She added salad to his plate and handed it back. "I'm very good at what I do, Rhys. I've built the business from the ground up and I'm proud of it. But sometimes I do wonder if I'm missing out on something."

He nearly bobbled his plate. "You're joking, right?"

"Not really." She sighed. "Of course, it's entirely possible I just need a vacation. I haven't taken any time off in a while."

"Since when?"

She served herself and picked up her fork. "Nearly three years. I took a very brief four-day trip to Hawaii. A few days of sun, sand and fruity drinks with umbrellas."

"Four days isn't much time."

"It was what I could manage. It's not like punching a clock and putting in for two weeks of holiday time."

"I know that." He tasted his first bite of cannelloni. Flavor exploded on his tongue—rich, creamy cheese, fresh basil, ripe tomatoes. "This is really good, Taylor. I never knew you could cook."

"My mom taught me."

"Your mom? Really? She strikes me as a society wife. Don't take that the wrong way," he warned. "Your mom seems very nice. But I kind of see her as someone who, I don't know, has things catered. Who outsources."

Taylor nodded. "Sometimes. But growing up—we weren't hurting for money, but we didn't have household staff, either. Mom kept us kids in line, helped with homework, decorated like Martha Stewart and cooked for her own dinner parties. At least until we were much older, and Dad's firm was on really solid ground." She speared a leaf of lettuce. "I learned a lot about my event planning biz from my Mom. She's an organizational whiz."

"Hmm," he mused. "Seems we have something in common after all. While my old man was out taking care of business, my mom held down the fort for me and my brother. I've never met another woman who could make something out of nothing. She worked at the diner during the day, but she was always helping my dad with his ventures."

"What did he do?"

Rhys shrugged. "What didn't he do? He sold insurance for a while, a two-man operation here in Cadence Creek. When that didn't fly, he was a sales rep for some office supply company, traveling all around Alberta. He sold used cars after that if I remember right."

And a bunch of other jobs and schemes that had taken him away more than he was home, and never panned out as he'd hoped. Time and again he'd moved on to something newer and shinier, and financially they'd gone further and further in the hole.

"Sounds industrious," Taylor commented easily, reaching for the wine and topping up her glass.

"Yeah, he was a real go-getter," Rhys agreed, trying very hard to keep the bitterness out of his voice and not doing such a great job. He'd loved his dad but the legacy he'd left behind wasn't the greatest.

She put the bottle down carefully and frowned. "You aren't happy about that, are you?"

He focused on his pasta. "Dad was full of bright ideas and a little fuzzier on the execution. It was my mom who kept her feet on the ground and really provided for us kids. Problem was, every time Dad moved on to something better, he usually left some damage in his wake. Debts he couldn't pay and employees out of a job. It didn't get him the greatest goodwill here, you know? We were lucky that everyone loved my mom. Otherwise maybe we would've been run out of Cadence Creek."

"Surely it wasn't that bad," Taylor said, smiling.

"I know I wasn't supposed to hear, but one day I was passing by the hardware store and I heard these guys outside talking. They called him 'Big Man Bullock' and not in a nice way."

He couldn't look at her. For some reason that single memory had shaped him so much more than any other from his childhood, good and bad. In that moment he'd decided he would never be like his father. Never. Only for a while he had been. He'd let so many people down. It was his biggest regret.

"So that's why you don't want to own your own business? You don't want to fail like your dad did?"

Rhys nodded and stabbed some salad with his fork. "That's exactly why. You said it yourself—you're responsible and can't just take off on a whim. You have other people relying on you." His throat tightened and he cleared the lump away. "You mess up and it's other lives you're affecting, not just your own. I would never want anyone to speak about me the way they were speaking about him that day. My brother and I both left home after high school. It was two less mouths for my mom to try to feed, to be honest."

Silence hummed through the kitchen. It hadn't turned out to be a very pleasant conversation after all. All it had done was stir up things he'd rather forget.

"Well," she said softly. "You're back in Cadence Creek now, and the diner is the heart of this town, and your mom is fabulous. You're steady and reliable, Rhys. There are worse things." She patted his hand. "You don't have to live down your father's reputation. That was his, not yours. You came back to help your mom. Not everyone would do that."

She seemed so sure that she said the right thing as she smiled again and turned back to her meal.

Rhys's appetite, though, shriveled away to nothing as he picked at his food. She had no idea, none at all. Yes, he'd come back when his father died because Martha had needed him. And he'd gone against his instincts and done what she'd asked of him because she was his mother and he couldn't stand the thought of disappointing one more person. He wondered what Taylor would say if she knew he'd gone from one bad venture into immediately investing in another?

He'd come back to Cadence Creek with his tail between his legs. He was more like his old man than anyone knew.

And he hated it.

CHAPTER EIGHT

THEY RETIRED TO the living room after dinner. Taylor made coffee and insisted they leave the dishes. She'd need something to keep her busy tomorrow anyway. Besides, Rhys had turned surprisingly quiet. She wondered what that was about.

"You okay?" she asked, offering him a shortbread cookie.

"Sure, why wouldn't I be?" he responded, taking one from the plate.

"I don't know. You got quiet all of a sudden. After we talked about your dad."

She looked over at him. Despite his relaxed pose, his jaw was tight. "Rhys," she said gently, "did you feel like it was your job to look after everyone after he died?"

"Why are we talking about this?" He shoved the cookie in his mouth, the buttery crumbs preventing him from saying more. But Taylor waited. Waited for him to chew and swallow and wash it down with a sip of coffee.

"Because," she finally answered, "it seems to me you could use a friend. And that maybe, since I'm not from Cadence Creek, I might be a logical choice."

Confusion cluttered his eyes as they met hers. "Do I strike you as the confiding type?"

She smiled. "Maybe you could make an exception. This once."

He seemed to debate for a while. Taylor pulled her knees up toward her chin and sank deeper into the cushions of the sofa, cradling her cup in her hands. How long had it been since she'd spent an evening like this, with a warm cuppa in front of a glowing tree? No files open, no cell phone ringing. Just a rugged cowboy and coffee and cookies.

Simple. And maybe it would bore her in a couple of days, but for right now it was quite heavenly.

"I had my own business once," he confided, staring into his cup. "I had an office based in Rocky Mountain House. I'd wanted to start something away from Cadence Creek, away from my dad's reputation. I was determined to make a go of it, the way he'd never been able to."

She got a sinking feeling about where this was headed. "What kind of business?"

"Feed supplements," he said simply. "I had an office, a couple of office staff and a few reps other than myself who traveled the area to the various ranches. For a while it was okay. Then I started losing money. It got to a point where I wasn't even drawing a salary, just so I could pay my staff. I fell behind on the office rent and we shifted it to run from my house."

His face took on a distant look for a few seconds, but then he gave his head a little shake and it cleared. "It wasn't long before I knew I had to shut it down or declare bankruptcy. Since I didn't want the mark on my credit rating, I closed my doors. My final accounts owing paid my back rent and wages and I got a job as a ranch hand. I got to bring home a paycheck while my employees had to file for Employment Insurance since I laid them off. They had families. Little kids. Mortgages."

"But surely they didn't blame you!"

He shrugged, but the distant look was back. "A million times I went over what I might have done differently, to manage it better. The jobs I took—working the ranches I used to serve—kept a roof over my head. When my dad died, I quit. Sold the house and moved back here to help my mom."

He opened his mouth and then suddenly shut it again.

Intrigued, she unfolded her legs and sat forward. "What were you going to say?"

"Nothing," he answered, reaching for another cookie from the plate on the coffee table.

"You were going to say something and stopped." She frowned. There was more to this story, wasn't there? Something he didn't want to talk about. Something about coming home.

"You're nosy, you know that?"

She grinned. "I'm a woman. We don't let anything drop."

"You're telling me." He sighed. "Look, let's just say I wasn't a big fan of my mother buying the diner. Running a small business is tough and she's worked hard her whole life. She's over fifty now and working harder than ever."

"You wished she had stuck with working her shift and going home at the end of the day. Leaving the stress behind."

"Yes."

She understood. He'd felt terrible when his own business had failed. He'd seen the bad reaction from people when his dad had failed. He wanted to spare his mother any or all of that. She got it. She even admired him for his protective streak.

"Some people aren't satisfied with that, Rhys. I wasn't. I wanted to build something. I wanted to know I'd done it and done it on my own. But I understand where you're coming from. I'm responsible for my employees, too. It's a big responsibility, not just financially but morally. At least for most people, I think, and if not it should be. People need to look at their employees like people and not numbers. Even if I wanted to make a change, I know I'm not the only one to consider."

"You thinking of changing?"

The question stirred something uncomfortable inside her. "Nah, not really. Like I said—I'm just overdue for a break, that's all."

She liked it better when they were talking about him. She put her hand on his knee. "You help her a lot, don't you? Around the diner. Fixing things and whatever needs to be done."

He looked away. "Of course I do."

"And you don't get paid."

He hesitated. "I'm not on the payroll, no," he said.

"You're a good man, Rhys."

She meant it. The things he said made perfect sense and only served to complicate her thoughts even more. She was enjoying the downtime too much. She hadn't truly loved the work for a while now, and she was finally admitting it to herself. Sometimes it felt pointless and frivolous, but every time she considered saying it out loud, she heard her father's voice proclaiming that very thing. She was just stubborn enough to not let him be right. Damn the Shepard pride.

Every time she thought about making a change, she was plagued by the realization that it wasn't just her who would be affected. Her employees needed wages. Her landlord was counting on her rent. Suppliers, caterers… All of that would trickle down, wouldn't it? Walking away would be just about the most selfish thing she could do.

They were quiet for a few minutes, until Rhys finally spoke up. "This business of yours, you've had to fight hard for respect, haven't you?"

"I'm sorry?"

"With your family. Your father's hugely successful, Jack's running what can only be considered an empire and Callum, while way more low-key, has fulfilled the family requirement for a spouse and grandchild. Must be hard standing next to that yardstick."

"I'm doing just fine, thank you." Indignation burned its way to her stomach, making it clench. She wanted to be able to tell him he was dead wrong. Problem was she couldn't.

"Hey, you don't have to tell me that. You're one of the most capable women I've ever met. But seeing your family at the rehearsal dinner, I got the feeling that you had to work just a little bit harder for the same recognition."

"You're a guy. You're not supposed to notice stuff like that."

She put her cup down on the table and folded her hands in her lap.

His voice was low and intimate as he replied, "I only noticed because I can't seem to take my eyes off you whenever you're around."

And there it was. The acknowledgment of whatever this was. Attraction. Curiosity. Carnality.

"I thought we weren't going to do this," she said softly. She kept her hands folded tightly in her lap to keep them from going where they wanted to go—on him. "I'm only here for a few days."

"Then there's no danger. We both know what's what. We're going in with our eyes wide open."

She looked up at him and was caught in his hot, magnetic gaze.

"Since that night in my truck, I can't stop thinking about you," he murmured, reaching out and tucking a piece of hair behind her ear. "I've tried. God knows I've tried." His fingers grazed her cheek and before she could reconsider, she leaned into the touch, the feel of his rough, strong hand against the sensitive skin of her face.

"Are you seducing me, Rhys?" His thumb toyed with her lower lip and her eyes drifted closed.

"With any luck." He moved closer, leaning forward slightly so she began to recline against the cushions. "We're adults," he stated. "We're both wondering. It doesn't have to go any deeper than that."

Tentatively she lifted her hand and touched his face. "Usually I'm the confident one who goes after what she wants."

He smiled a little, his gaze dropping to her lips. "You don't want this? I could have sworn you did."

"I didn't say that," she whispered, sliding deeper into the cushions.

"That's what I thought." His voice was husky now, shivering along her nerve endings. He leaned closer until he was less than a breath away.

The first kiss was gentle, soft, a question. When she answered it his muscles relaxed beneath her hand and he pressed his mouth more firmly against hers. Her pulse quickened, her blood racing as he opened his mouth and invited something darker, more persuasive. His hand cupped her breast. Her fingers toyed with the buttons of his shirt. He sat up and stripped it off, leaving him in just a T-shirt. She expected him to reach for the hem of her sweater but instead he took it slow, braced himself over top of her and kissed her again. His lips slid along her jaw to her ear, making goose bumps pop out over her skin and a gasp escape her throat.

"I'm in no rush," he whispered just before he took her lips again, and they kissed, and kissed, and kissed until nothing else in the world existed.

Taylor's entire body hummed like a plucked string. Rhys felt so good, tasted so good, and it had been too long since she'd felt this close to anyone. Yearning and desire were overwhelming, and his leisurely approach had primed her nearly to the breaking point. The words asking him to stay were sitting on her lips when he softened his kiss, gently kissed the tip of her nose, and got up off the sofa.

She felt strangely cold and empty without his weight pressing upon her. Maybe he was going to hold out his hand and lead her down the hall, which would suit her just fine. If he could kiss like that, she would only imagine his lovemaking would be spectacular and…thorough. She swallowed roughly at the thought and got up, ready to take it to the next step.

Except he was reaching for his coat.

Her stomach dropped to her feet while heat rushed to her face. "What…? I mean where…?" She cleared her throat, crossed her arms around her middle, feeling suddenly awkward. "Did I do something wrong?"

He shoved his arms into the sleeves but wouldn't meet her gaze. "Not at all. It's just getting late. I should go."

She wasn't at all sure of herself but she lifted her chin and said the words on her mind anyway. "For a minute there it kind of looked like you weren't going to be leaving."

For a second his hand paused on the tab of the zipper and the air in the room was electric. But then he zipped his coat the rest of the way up. "I don't want to take things too fast, that's all."

Too fast? Good Lord, she was leaving in a matter of days and he was the one who'd said he couldn't stop thinking about her. She wasn't innocent. She knew where this sort of make-out session was headed. And he was putting on the brakes without so much as a warning? Just when she thought she understood him, he did something else that made her wonder who the heck he was.

"What happened to 'we're both grown-ups'?"

Now he had his boots on. One moment they were sprawled on the couch and the next he couldn't get out of there fast enough. What in heaven's name had she done wrong?

"Let me take a rain check, okay?"

This night was getting stranger by the minute. "Rhys?"

He took a step forward and pressed a kiss to her forehead. "It's fine, I promise. I'll see you tomorrow."

Right. Because he'd be here twice. Great.

Still dumbfounded, she heard him say, "Thanks for dinner." Before she could wrap her head around what was going on he was out the door and headed for his truck. He didn't even let it warm up, just got in, started it up and headed out the driveway to the road.

What had just happened?

In a daze she gathered up the cups and the plate of cookies and took them to the kitchen. She expended her pent-up energy by washing the dishes and tidying the supper mess, and then went back to the living room to turn off the Christmas lights, still reeling from his abrupt change of mood.

His cotton shirt was still lying on the floor in a crumpled heap. He'd been in such a hurry to leave he'd forgotten to pick it up. She lifted it from the floor and pressed it to her nose. It smelled of soap and man and aftershave, a spicy, masculine scent that, thanks to the evening's activities, now elicited a physical response in her. Want. Need. Desire.

She stared at it while she brushed her teeth and washed her face. And when she went to bed, she left the penguin pajamas on the chair and instead slid into Rhys's soft shirt.

Having the material whisper against her body was the closest she was going to get to Rhys. At least tonight!

But the week wasn't over yet. And she was pretty sure he owed her an explanation.

Rather than drive into Edmonton to shop, Taylor decided to explore the Cadence Creek stores for Christmas gifts. After her conversation with Rhys about running a small business, she felt the right thing to do was to buy local and support the townspeople who made their livelihood here. For Avery and Callum, she bought a beautiful evergreen centerpiece for their table from Foothills Floral. The craft store sold not just yarn but items on consignment, and she bought Nell a gorgeous quilt in pink and blue with patchwork bunnies in each square. The men were a little harder to buy for, but she ended up being delighted at the silversmith, where she purchased both her father and Jack new tie clips and cuff links, the intricate design a testament to the artist's talents.

While she was browsing the handcrafted jewelry, a particular display caught her eye. Beautiful hammered and sculpted silver pendants on sterling chains shone in the morning sunlight. She picked one up, let the weight of it sit on her fingers, a delicate horseshoe with tiny, precise holes where nails would go. She smiled to herself, remembering asking for a lucky horseshoe at the wedding and how Rhys had informed her that a rabbit's foot got rubbed for luck.

He'd amused her, even then when she'd been her most stressed.

She let the pendant go and moved on. She still had her mother's gift to buy and then the groceries for Christmas dinner.

At the drugstore she picked up a gift set of her mother's favorite scent, and hit the grocery store for the turkey and vegetables needed for dinner, loading everything in the trunk of her car. She must have done okay, because the bags nearly filled it to capacity.

The last stop was the bakery, where she figured she could grab something sweet and Christmassy for the holiday dinner and maybe sit and have a coffee and a piece of cake or something.

Anything to avoid going to the Wagon Wheel. She was too afraid of running into Rhys, and she had no idea what to say to him. Sleep had been a long time coming last night. This morning he'd been by early to do the chores, and was already gone when she'd finally crawled out of bed.

The first thing she noticed as she went inside was the welcoming heat. Then it was the smells—rising bread and spices and chocolate and vanilla all mingled together. Browsing the display, she immediately decided on a rich stollen, her mouth watering at the sight of the sugar-dusted marzipan bread. She also ordered a traditional Christmas pudding which came with a container of sauce and instructions for adding brandy.

They were going to have a traditional Christmas dinner, with all of them together for the first time in as long as Taylor could remember.

She was just sitting down to a cup of salted caramel hot chocolate and a piece of cherry strudel when Angela Diamond came in, her cheeks flushed from the cold. She spotted Taylor right away and came over, chafing her hands together and smiling. "Well, hello! I didn't expect to meet you in here this morning."

"I thought I'd do a little shopping before the honeymooners get back. It's hungry work."

"Amen. I like to cook but my talents can't compare to the goodies in here. Do you mind?" She gestured to the chair across from Taylor.

"Of course not! I'd love the company."

Angela sat and took off her gloves. "God, it's cold. I wish a Chinook would blow through and warm things up a bit. What are you having? It looks good."

Taylor laughed. Angela was quite chipper this morning. "Hot chocolate and strudel."

"I'll be right back. I need something decadent."

Angela returned shortly with a cup of chocolate and a plate holding an enormous piece of carrot cake. "I'll tell you a secret," she confided, leaning forward. "Since Avery joined forces with Jean, the quality has gone way up. The specialty in here used to be bread and that's it. Now it's everything."

"I bought a Christmas pudding," Taylor admitted. "It's the first time we've all been together in a long time. I'm thinking turkey and stuffing and the whole works this Christmas." She took a sip of her hot chocolate.

"When are Callum and Avery back?"

"The afternoon of the twenty-third."

"And when do you head back to Vancouver?"

Taylor sighed. "Boxing Day."

Angela put a piece of cake on her fork. "Sounds to me like you're not too excited about it." She popped the cake in her mouth.

"I should be. I've got a ton of work to do and not much time to do it in. Big New Year's party happening. I've left most of the work to my assistant. She's very capable, thank goodness."

"You're not enjoying the project?"

Taylor brushed a flake of strudel pastry off her sweater. "I've been doing this for a while now. When I started, some of the unorthodox requests I got were exciting. And I really liked being creative and working under the gun. But lately—"

She broke off. She really *was* having doubts, wasn't she? And then there was the conversation with Rhys last night. How could she even flirt with the idea of walking away when so many people depended on her?

"Lately what?" Angela asked.

"I think I'm getting jaded or something. Most of the events seem so extravagant and pointless."

"You're looking to create something meaningful."

Taylor put down her mug. She'd never quite thought of it that way. "I suppose I am. This party on New Year's Eve? It's just some rock star throwing cash around and showing off, you know? And it'll be fun and probably make some entertainment news and then it'll be gone twenty-four hours later and no one will remember. Weeks of planning and thousands of dollars for what?" She sighed. "It lasts for a few hours and then it's gone like that." She snapped her fingers.

For a minute the women nibbled at their treats. Then Angela spoke up. "You don't have to give up the business to make a change. Maybe you just need to switch the focus."

"What do you mean?"

Angela shrugged easily, but Taylor knew a sharp mind at work when she saw one. Angela had single-handedly started her own foundation for helping battered women. She was no lightweight in the brains or in the work department, and Taylor knew it would be smart to pay attention to what Angela said.

"Say, for instance, there's a non-profit looking to hold a fund-raiser. The board of this foundation is pretty on the ball, but organizing social events is not where their strongest talent lies."

"You're talking about the Butterfly Foundation."

Angela smiled. "Well, yes, in a way. But we're small.

We wouldn't have enough work to keep you going. But there's the housing organization that helped build Stu Dickinson's home after they lost their things in a fire. And many others in any part of the country you choose. I think you'd be very good at it, Taylor."

The idea was interesting, and to Taylor's surprise she didn't dismiss it right away. That told her something.

Angela put down her fork. "Look, I was a social worker before I started Butterfly House and the foundation. I was good at my job but I was frustrated, too, especially as time went on. I'm still using much the same skill set, but I finally started doing something I'm really passionate about—helping abused women get back on their feet. Anyway, think about it. We're going to be planning something for later this spring. I'll give you first crack at the job if you want it. Get your feet wet."

"Thanks," Taylor replied, her mind spinning. "But I can't just up and walk away from what I've built, you know?" It certainly wasn't as easy as putting in two weeks' notice and going on her way.

"Of course." Angela checked her watch. "And I've got to go. I'm picking my son up from a play date in twenty minutes. But I'm really glad we ran into each other."

"Me, too."

Angela got up and slid her gloves back over her fingers. "And merry Christmas, Taylor. To you and your family, if I don't see you again."

"You, too. Say hi to Molly and Clara for me."

After Angela was gone, Taylor sat at the table, her hot chocolate forgotten. Angela had been so right. What was missing from Taylor's job was meaning. It was why she'd been so flustered about things not being perfect at the wedding—it had been important to her on a personal level.

Right now she did a job because she was paid good

money to do so. And she had enjoyed the challenges that went along with the position of being sought after. But at the end of the day, all she had left was the satisfaction of a challenge met. She hadn't given anything back. What Angela suggested, an event like that had the power to make ripples throughout communities, a difference in peoples' lives. It would matter; last longer than a single night. Wouldn't that be amazing?

And then Taylor thought of her staff, and her leases, and the fact that they, too, had lives, and bills to pay.

Maybe Rhys was on to something after all. Maybe working nine-to-five was way easier. He'd just learned his lesson faster than Taylor, that was all.

But then, he'd been forced to shut down his company. As Taylor stood and put on her coat again, she let out a long breath. She didn't have that worry. Her company was well into the black. And as long as they stayed there, she was sure she could find an answer.

CHAPTER NINE

RHYS HOVERED AT the door to the barn, wanting to go to the house, but hesitating just the same. He'd been an idiot last night. It had all been going great. He hadn't even minded talking about the past so much. Maybe Taylor was right. She was an outsider and completely impartial, and it made a difference. She certainly hadn't judged.

But it hadn't just been about talking. Oh, no. Every time he was around her the sensible, cautious part of his brain shut off. The physical attraction was so strong and sitting alone, in front of the tree, with the cozy lighting and the way her eyes shone and her hair smelled...

Yep. He was an idiot. There'd been no room for logic. Just justification for doing what he wanted rather than what was smart.

He'd been ready to take it to the next level when warning bells had gone off in his head. At first it was knowing that he was on the verge of losing control and pushing his advantage, which he made a practice of never doing. Taylor wasn't as ready as she thought she was. It was in the sweetness of her kiss, the tentative way she touched him, the vulnerable look in her eyes. And just like the horses he worked with, he knew she had to be sure. She needed to come to him.

Except she hadn't, not this morning. He'd hung around

for a while, hoping to see her at the window or door, but nothing, and he'd been due for work at Diamondback and couldn't stay forever. Now he'd finished the evening chores and the lights were glowing at the house and still there was no sign of her. His hasty exit had probably hurt her feelings, he realized.

But there'd been a second issue, too, and one equally if not more important. He'd known exactly where things were headed and abruptly realized he had absolutely no protection. He was a guy who was generally ready for any eventuality, and he should have had a clue after the way the passion had exploded between them while parked in his truck. But he hadn't. And if he'd let things go any further, he might have been very irresponsible. Might have lost his head and let his body override his brain. He wanted to think he wouldn't, but he wasn't exactly objective when it came to Taylor, for some reason.

So he'd pulled the pin and gotten out. And not exactly gracefully.

It wouldn't happen again. A condom packet was nestled in his back pocket. He'd driven out to the gas station on the highway to buy it, because this town was so damn small that it would be just his luck that he'd be spotted at the drugstore and the rumors would start.

He told himself that the condom was just a contingency plan. He could get in his truck and go back home, or…

Resolutely he left the barn and latched the door behind him, and with his heart beating madly, took long strides to the house. He made no secret of his approach, his boots thumping on the steps and he knocked firmly on the door. Whether this went further or ended, some decisions were going to be made right now. He had to stop thinking of her like some nervous, inexperienced filly, afraid of her own shadow. Taylor Shepard was the most self-assured, confident woman he'd ever met. She knew her own mind.

The door opened and anything he'd considered saying died on his lips.

She looked stunning. She'd left her hair down, the dark mass of it falling in waves past her shoulders. Her jeans hugged her hips and legs like a second skin and the red V-neck shirt was molded to her breasts, clinging to her ribs and giving her the most delicious curves he'd ever seen.

"It's about time you got here," she said softly, holding open the door.

He didn't need any other invitation. He stepped inside and, with his gaze locked with hers, kicked the door shut with his foot. She opened her lips to say something but he caught her around the waist and kissed her, erasing any words she might have uttered. When he needed to come up for air, he released her long enough to shed his jacket and boots.

"Hello to you, too," she said, her voice rich and seductive. "Not wasting any time, I see."

"I'm done wasting time. Aren't you?"

The moment paused as her gaze held his. "I think I am, yes."

It was all the encouragement he needed. As a saucy grin climbed her cheek, he chuckled. And then he reached out, threw her over his shoulder in a fireman carry and headed for the hallway as her laughter echoed off the walls.

It was still dark in the bedroom but Taylor's eyes had adjusted to it and she could see shadows cast by the moonlight streaming through the cracks in the blinds. The dark figure of the dresser, a small chair, a laundry basket.

Rhys, snuggled under the covers beside her, his hair flattened on one side where he'd rested against the pillow.

Her heart slammed against her ribs just looking at him. Not in her wildest dreams had she been prepared for last night. Any impression she'd had of him as…well, she supposed ordinary was as good a word as any…was completely false. He'd been an exciting lover, from the way he'd taken control and carried her to the bedroom, to how he'd managed to scatter their clothes in seconds, to how he'd expertly made love to her.

She swallowed thickly. It had been more than exciting. It had been much, much more. He'd been physical yet gentle, fun yet serious, and he'd made her feel things she'd never felt before in her life. She'd felt beautiful. Unstoppable. Completely satisfied. And in the end, rather than skedaddling home as she expected, he'd pulled up the covers and tucked her securely against him.

She'd felt cherished. More than she'd ever imagined, Rhys Bullock was turning out to be someone very, very amazing. Someone who might actually have the power to chase away some of the ghosts of the past.

His lashes flickered and his lips curved the tiniest bit. "You're staring at me, aren't you?"

Heat climbed her cheeks but she braced up on her elbow and rested her jaw on her hand. "Maybe."

"I can't blame you. I'm really quite handsome."

Her smile grew. Had she really ever thought him plain and unremarkable? There was a humor in the way he set his mouth, the way his eyes glowed that set him apart, wasn't there? And then there was his body. She'd had a good look at it now—all of it. There was nothing plain about Rhys.

"Your ego knows no bounds."

"I'm feeling really relaxed this morning." He opened his eyes. "Why do you suppose that is?"

She dropped her gaze for a moment. "Rhys…" she said shyly.

"Is it okay I stayed all night?"

Her gaze lifted. "Of course it is." She preferred it. Things had happened so quickly. They'd touched and combusted. At least by him staying she didn't get the feeling it was only about the sex.

Which was troubling because there really couldn't be anything more to it, could there?

His hand grazed her hip, sliding beneath the soft sheets. "It was good."

She smiled, bashful again because they were still naked beneath the covers. "Yeah, it was."

For a few minutes his hand lightly stroked and silence filled the room. Taylor wished she could abandon all her common sense and simply slide into his embrace again, but being impulsive wasn't really her way. Last night she'd waited for him. She'd wanted this. But now? It was how to go on from this moment that stopped her up.

"Listen, Rhys…"

"I know what you're going to say." His voice was husky-soft in the dark. "You're going to say there's only the weekend left and Callum and Avery will be back and you'll be going to Vancouver."

Nervousness crawled through her belly. "Yeah, I was going to say that."

"Since we're both aware of that, the way I see it we have one of two choices."

She couldn't help but smile the tiniest bit. Rhys was used to being in charge. Even now, he was taking control of the situation. When they'd first met it had grated on her last nerve. But now not so much. It was kind of endearing.

"Which are?" she asked.

"Well, I could get out of bed and get dressed and do the

chores and we could say that this is it. No sense going on with something that's going to end in a few days anyway."

"That sounds like a very sensible approach."

"Thank you."

She might have believed him, except his fingers started kneading the soft part of her hip. She swallowed, trying to keep from rolling into the caress. "And the second?"

"I'm glad you asked. The second option, of course, is that we enjoy this for however long it lasts and go our inevitable separate ways with the memory of the best Christmas ever."

"Not as sensible, but it sounds like a lot more fun."

"Great minds think alike."

The smile slid from her face as she turned serious, just for a moment. "Do you think it's possible to do that?" she whispered.

Dark eyes delved into hers. "I'm not ready to say goodbye yet. I don't see as we have much choice."

She slid closer to him until they were snuggled close together, skin to skin. She hadn't counted on someone like Rhys. She'd thought she'd come here, watch her brother get married, recharge, go back to her life. Instead she was…

She blinked, hoping he didn't notice the sudden moisture in her eyes. She would never say it out loud. Couldn't. But the truth was, she suspected she was falling in love. She recognized the rush. The fear. The exhilaration. Something like that only happened once in a while, and it had been a long, long time for Taylor. It wasn't just sex. She had real feelings for Rhys. Saying goodbye wasn't going to be easy.

"Can I ask you something?"

"Sure." He, too, braced up on an elbow, more awake now.

"Why did you leave so fast the other night?"

"Oh, that." He smiled, but it had a self-deprecating tilt to it that she thought was adorable. "Truth is, things were happening really fast. And you caught me unprepared."

That was it? Birth control? She suppressed a giggle, but a squeak came out anyway. "You could have just said that," she chided. "Instead of rushing out like you couldn't stand being near me another moment."

"Is that what you thought?" His head came off his hand.

"Maybe."

He leaned forward and kissed her lightly. "Nothing could be further from the truth. If I was in a hurry, it was because I was in danger of not caring if I had a condom or not."

Her heart turned over. She wondered if he realized how much he truly tried to protect those around him.

"Now, as much as I'd like to repeat last night's performance, I've got cows that need to be milked," Rhys said quietly.

"And then what?" She lifted her chin and looked into his eyes. The dark light was turning grayer as the night melted into day, highlighting his features more clearly.

"It's Saturday. I'm not due at Diamondback. I'm not expected anywhere, as a matter of fact."

"Then come back in for breakfast," she invited. "I'll make something good."

"You got it." He slid out of bed and she watched as he pulled on jeans and a T-shirt. He turned and gave her a quick kiss. "Look, I'll be a while. Go back to sleep."

"Okay."

He was at the doorway when he turned and looked back at her. "You look good like that," he said softly, and disappeared around the corner while her heart gave a little flutter of pleasure.

They had the weekend. She rather suspected a weekend wouldn't be nearly enough.

After breakfast Rhys went back home to shower and grab fresh clothing. In his absence Taylor also showered and did her hair and put on fresh makeup. She vacuumed the rugs and tidied the kitchen and wondered if he'd bring his things to stay the night. When he arrived again midmorning, he carried a bag with him containing extra clothes and toiletries.

Seeing the black case brought things into rather clear perspective. Their intentions were obvious. There was no need for either of them to leave the house now.

After a rather pleasurable "welcome back" interlude, they spent the rest of the day together. Rhys helped Taylor wrap the presents she'd bought the day before, cutting tape, tying ribbon and sticking a red and gold bow on top of her head while making a lewd suggestion. She made soup and grilled cheese and the long awaited Chinook blew in, raising the temperature and softening the snow. They went outside and built a snowman, complete with stick arms, a carrot for a nose, and rocks for the eyes and mouth. That event turned into a snowball fight, which turned into a wrestling match, which ended with the two of them in a long, hot shower to ward off any damp chill.

He did chores. She made dinner. They curled up in front of the television to watch a broadcast of White Christmas while Rhys complained of actors feeling the need to sing everything and Taylor did a fair impression of the "Sisters" song. And when it was time, they went together to Taylor's room.

By Monday morning Taylor's nerves were shredded. The weekend had been nothing short of blissful but in a few hours Callum would be home and her time with Rhys would be over. There was no question in her mind—her feelings for Rhys were real.

But what hope did they have? He would never be happy living in a city like Vancouver, and she could tell by the way he spoke and how he'd acted since they'd met that he wanted to stay close to his mother to look after her. She realized now that his desire to hold a steady job rather than being the boss was all about taking care of his family. What she'd initially seen as complacency was actually selfless and noble. From what she could gather, his need to care for Martha was, in part, a way to make up for the instability in her past. He'd hold things together the way his father never had—no matter how well-intentioned.

Despite Angela's ideas, Taylor couldn't see any way to avoid going home either. She had commitments and responsibilities at *Exclusive!* This was nothing new. She just hadn't expected that even the thought of leaving him would cause the ache she was feeling in her chest right now.

"Hey," he said softly, coming up behind her. She was standing at the kitchen window, looking out over the fields. "You look like you're thinking hard."

"Just sad the weekend's over, that's all."

"Me, too."

She turned to embrace him and noticed his bag by the kitchen door. "You're leaving already?"

"It's Monday. I'm due back at Diamondback, remember? I should have been there an hour ago."

Right. His job. Time hadn't stood still, had it? "You're working today?"

"And tomorrow."

Emptiness opened up inside her. This was really it then. She might not even see him again before her flight out on the twenty-sixth.

"Rhys…"

"Don't," he said firmly. "We both knew what this was from the start."

Dread of losing him sparked a touch of anger. Was she so easy to forget? So easy to leave—again? "And you're okay with that? Just a couple of days of hokey pokey and see you later, it's been fun?"

He gripped her upper arms with strong fingers. "We weren't going to do this, remember?"

"Do what?"

"Get involved."

"I am involved. Up to my neck, as it happens."

"Taylor."

He let go and stepped back, his dark eyes clouded with confusion. He ran a hand through his hair. "I should never have come back. I should have left well enough alone."

"You didn't. We didn't. I don't know how to say goodbye gracefully, Rhys."

To her chagrin she realized tears were running down her face. She swiped them away quickly. "Dammit," she muttered.

He came closer, looked down at her with a tenderness in his eyes that nearly tore her apart. "Hey, we both knew it would come to this. My life's here. Yours is there. You have *Exclusive!* to run."

Yes, yes, the damn business. When had she started resenting it so much? Even a quick check of her email on her phone this morning had made her blood pressure spike. She couldn't ignore reality forever. Didn't mean it didn't stink, though.

"Thanks for the reminder." She stepped back, wished she had something to occupy her hands right now.

Rhys frowned. "Look, Taylor, we both know you're competitive and a bit of a perfectionist. I like those things about you. I really do. But I also know that the drive and determination that made you so successful is going to keep you in Vancouver until you set out to do what you've wanted to achieve."

"Even if what I'm doing isn't making me happy?"

It was the first time she'd come right out and said it.

His frown deepened. "The only person who can decide that is you. But I'll caution you right now. Letting go of that goal isn't easy. There are a lot of things to accept. And I'm not sure you'd be happy walking away."

"And if I did walk away, would you be here waiting?"

Alarm crossed his features. She had her answer before he ever opened his mouth, didn't she? Oh, she should have listened to what he'd said ages ago when they'd first kissed. She was different from local girls, and she was low risk because she wasn't staying. The idea of her not going was scaring him to death.

"Look, Taylor…"

"No, it's okay," she assured him. "You're right. This was what we agreed and I don't have any regrets." That, at least, was the truth. She didn't regret the last few days even if there were mixed feelings and a fair bit of hurt. They'd been magical when all was said and done. And Rhys Bullock would be a nice memory, just like he said.

He came forward and tilted up her chin with his finger. "I know I'm where I belong. I learned my lessons, had my failures and successes. You're not there yet, that's all."

She pulled away, resenting his attitude. What did he know? She had her own failures, but she was glad now that she'd kept the baring of her soul to one messed up wedding and not the disaster that was her last relationship. "You're leaving anyway, Rhys. I'd appreciate it if you weren't patronizing."

The air in the room changed. There was a finality to

it that had been absent only moments before. Rhys went to the doorway and picked up his bag. Silently he went to the door and pulled on his boots and jacket. When he was ready he looked up and met her eyes. "I don't want to leave it this way," he said bleakly. "With us angry at each other."

"I'm not angry," she said quietly. "I'm hurting, and the longer you stay, the worse it is."

He stepped forward and pulled her into his arms for one last hug. "Hurting you is the last thing I wanted to do," he murmured in her ear. "So I'll go." He kissed the tip of her ear. "Take care, Taylor."

She swallowed against the lump of tears and willed herself to stay dry-eyed. "You, too, Rhys. And Merry Christmas."

He nodded and slipped out the door. The milder temperatures of the Chinook had dipped slightly and she could see his breath in the air as he jogged down the steps and to his truck.

She shut the door, resisting the opportunity to give him one last wave.

They'd set the ground rules. Leaving was supposed to be easy. It definitely was not supposed to hurt this much.

CHAPTER TEN

CALLUM AND AVERY arrived back home, happy and tired from their trip and with tons of pictures from Hawaii. Taylor found herself bathing Nell after dinner while Callum checked on the stock and Avery started to make a dent in the mountain of laundry from their luggage. When Taylor suggested she go back to the B&B for the next few nights, Avery insisted she stay. "The couch pulls out. Please, stay. I've missed having a sister around."

Taylor had no good argument against that so at bedtime the cushions came off the sofa and the mattress pulled out. Avery brought sheets from the linen closet. "Sorry it's not as comfortable as our bed," she apologized.

A lump formed in Taylor's throat. Memories she wished she could forget crowded her mind, images of the last few nights spent in the master bedroom. This morning she'd stripped the bed and put the sheets in the washer. Rhys's scent had risen from the hot water and she'd had to go for a tissue.

"Taylor, are you okay?"

"Fine," she replied. "Hand me that comforter, will you?"

Avery handed it over while putting a pillowcase on a fat pillow. "Callum said Rhys did fine with the stock. Did you see him much while he was here?"

Taylor met Avery's innocently curious gaze, watched

as her expression changed in reaction to Taylor's. "What's wrong? Did something happen with Rhys?"

Taylor focused on tucking the bedding around the mattress. "Of course not."

"Taylor." Avery said it with such meaning that Taylor stopped and sat down on the bed.

Avery came over and sat beside her. "I saw you dancing at the reception. And Callum said Jack said something to him about you and Rhys kissing in his truck the night of the rehearsal. There's something going on between you, isn't there?"

"Not anymore," she replied firmly. She wondered if she sounded convincing.

Callum came through to the kitchen carrying an empty baby bottle. "Hey, what's going on?"

Avery looked up at him. "Girl talk. No boys allowed."

Taylor saw her brother's expression as he looked down at his wife. He was utterly smitten. Having someone look at her that way hadn't been so important even a month ago. Now it made her feel like she was missing out on something.

"Who am I to get in the way of my two favorite girls?" he asked, then looked down at the bottle with a stupidly soft expression. "Well, two of my three favorites anyway."

Callum knew where he belonged. He was contented, just like Rhys. So why was it so hard for her to figure out?

"I'll leave you ladies alone, then. Gotta be up early anyway."

When he disappeared back around the corner, Avery patted Taylor's arm. "Wait here," she commanded, and she skipped off to the kitchen. She returned moments later carrying two glasses of wine. "Here," she said, handing one to Taylor. "Sit up here, get under the blanket and then tell me how you managed to fall in love with Rhys Bullock within a week."

"How did you know?" Taylor asked miserably.

Avery laughed. "Honey, it's written all over your face. And as an old married woman, I demand to know all the details." She patted the mattress. "Now spill."

Christmas Eve arrived, along with Callum and Taylor's parents and Jack, back from Montana bearing presents and a strained expression. His trip hadn't gone all that well, as the manager for his corporate retreat business had been in an accident, leaving no one to run things at his Montana property. He was going to have to go back down there right after Christmas instead of taking the break he'd planned.

But nothing kept Jack down for long, and as they all gathered in Callum's small house laughter rang out in the rooms.

"I wish we had room for everyone here," Avery mourned.

"The bed and breakfast is lovely, don't you worry," Susan assured her. "And Harry and I have a surprise for you. We're taking you all out for Christmas Eve dinner."

A strange sort of uneasiness settled in Taylor's stomach. Please let her say it was out of town and not at the diner...

Susan went on happily. "You two just got back from your honeymoon and you're hosting us all tomorrow for Christmas. Tonight someone else is going to worry about the cooking. It's all arranged. Martha Bullock is doing up a prime rib for us and then we'll go to the Christmas Eve service."

Oh, God. The Wagon Wheel? Really?

Taylor pasted a smile on her face. "Surely the diner closes early on Christmas Eve?"

Harry shrugged. "Mrs. Bullock said it would be no trouble, especially for just the six of us."

Avery caught sight of Taylor's face and jumped in. "What a lovely thought. But really, we can have something here. There's no need…"

"Are you kidding?" Jack interrupted. "Prime rib? I've been living on sandwiches for a week. I'm so there."

Avery looked over at Taylor. What could she say? Besides, there was no guarantee that Rhys would be there. It was Christmas Eve after all.

She gave a short nod. "Sounds good to me," she answered, trying to inject some enthusiasm into her voice. This great Shepard family Christmas wasn't going to be brought down by her bad mood.

During the afternoon everyone brought out their presents and put them under the tree, which was a major source of frustration to Nell, who got sick of the word *no* as she crawled through the living room and pulled herself up on the chair next to the decorated spruce. She went down for an afternoon nap and everyone relaxed with a fresh batch of one of Avery's latest creations—eggnog cupcakes—and hot spiced cider. It was supposed to be perfect. Magical. And instead Taylor could only think about two things—the work waiting for her back in Vancouver, and how much she missed Rhys.

Jack pulled up a footstool and sat beside her, bringing his mug with him. "You're awfully quiet today. What's going on?"

She shrugged. "Too long away from the city, I guess."

He nodded. "Can I ask you something?"

"Sure." Jack and Taylor were the most alike in her opinion. He tended to see the big picture in much the same way that she did. And they were the ones still single now, too.

"Are you happy, sis?"

The question surprised her. "What do you mean?"

He raised an eyebrow. "I recognize the look on your face."

Oh, Lord. If he guessed about Rhys she was going to wish for the floor to open up and swallow her.

"I saw it when I first got here, when you were planning the wedding," he continued. "How's business?"

"Booming," she replied.

"And how do you feel about that?"

She met his gaze. "What do you mean?"

Jack hesitated for a minute. "A few years ago, remember when the company expanded? New franchises opened up, and Shepard Sports launched south of the border. It was all very exciting, right?"

"Dad was ready to burst his buttons with pride."

"I wasn't. It was everything I'd worked for and yet…do you know what ended up making me happiest?"

Curious now, she leaned forward. "What?"

"The property I bought in Montana. The corporate retreat and team-building business. The sporting goods, well they're like numbers on a page. Units in and out. Sure, we do some special work with schools and organizations and that sort of thing. But it's just selling. The team building stuff, though, it's about people. I like that. I like meeting different people and finding out more about them. I like seeing groups come in and leave with a totally different dynamic. They come in and push themselves in ways they don't expect, which was the very best thing I liked about competing."

"That's really cool, Jack."

"I know. And because of it, I can look at you and see that what you're doing isn't giving you that same buzz. Something's missing."

"I've been doing some thinking," she admitted. "But you know what it's like. The bigger you get the bigger the responsibility. You can't just pull up and abandon what's already there."

Jack nodded. "There's always a way. And anyway, you've got good people working for you. You've been gone quite a while and everything's run in your absence, hasn't it?"

It had. Sometimes a little too well. Even when trouble popped up, a quick email giving her assistant the green light to solve the problem was all it took.

"Just think about it," Jack said. "Responsibility or not, there's no sense doing something if you're not happy at it."

"Thanks," she answered, taking a drink of cider. She was glad he hadn't assumed her reticence was caused by a man. That would have been a whole other conversation. Then Avery called her to the kitchen to taste Susan's recipe for cranberry sauce and the afternoon passed quickly.

They arrived en masse at the Wagon Wheel at six on the dot. A sign on the door stated that Christmas hours went to 5:00 p.m. on the twenty-fourth and closed on Christmas Day and Boxing Day. Just as she thought, Martha had stayed open for their family and Taylor was a bit upset at her parents for requesting it. Martha had family of her own, probably had plans too.

Inside was toasty-warm and two tables were pushed together to make plenty of room for the six of them plus the high chair for Nell. Nell was dressed in soft red pants and a matching red velour top with tiny white snowflakes on it. After her nap she was energized, tapping a toy on the tray of the high chair and babbling at the blinking tree lights. Taylor was laughing at her antics when a movement in the kitchen caught her eye. It was Rhys, dressed in one of Martha's aprons, taking the roast out of the oven to rest.

He was here. Her stomach tangled into knots and her mouth felt dry. They hadn't seen each other or spoken since the morning they'd said goodbye. From the strained expression on his face, he wasn't too happy about tonight, either. As if he could sense her staring, he looked up and met her eyes across the restaurant. She looked away quickly, turning to answer a question of her mother's about the upcoming event her company was planning.

Martha brought them all glasses of iced water and placed a basket of hot rolls in the center of the table. That was followed by a fresh romaine salad with red onion, peppers and mandarins in a poppy seed dressing that was delicious. Rhys stayed in the kitchen, out of everyone's way. The fact that he seemed to be avoiding her stretched her nerves taut, and by the time the main course was served she was a wreck.

Martha had outdone herself. Glazed carrots, green beans with bacon, creamy mashed potatoes and puffy Yorkshire pudding and gravy complemented the roast, followed by a cranberry bread pudding and custard sauce. By the time the plates were cleared away, Taylor was stuffed to the top. Her father checked his watch. "Seven-fifteen. We'd better get going," he announced. "The church service starts in fifteen minutes."

Everyone got up to leave, reaching for coats and purses and gloves. Everyone but Taylor. They really didn't see, did they? She'd bet ten bucks that Martha and Rhys probably wanted to go to church, too. According to Callum, most of the community showed up at the local Christmas Eve services. And the Bullocks were going to be stuck here cleaning up the mess instead of enjoying their holiday.

"Taylor, aren't you coming?"

"I'll be along," she said lightly. "You go on without me."

Avery gave her a long look, then a secret thumbs-up. Taylor returned a small smile, but it was quickly gone once the Shepard crew hit the door.

She went back to the table and started clearing dessert plates and coffee cups.

Martha hustled out from the kitchen. "Oh, heavens, girl, don't you worry about that! You head on to church with your family."

"What about you? Aren't you planning to go to church?"

Martha looked so dumbfounded that Taylor knew she had guessed right. "If I help it'll get done faster and we can all make it."

"Bless your heart."

"Where's Rhys?" Taylor looked over Martha's shoulder into the kitchen.

"He just took a bag of trash to the Dumpster out back. I swear I don't know what I'd do without that boy. He always says we're in this together, but he's got his own job." She handed Taylor the bin of dirty dishes and briskly wiped off the tables. "It was more than enough that he invested in this place for me. He's supposed to be a silent partner, but not Rhys. He thinks he needs to take care of me."

Taylor nearly dropped the pan of dishes. Silent partner? But Rhys was so determined to stay away from owning a business. How many times had he gotten on her case about it? And this whole time he was part owner in the diner and just neglected to mention it?

For the briefest of moments, she was very, very angry at him. How dare he judge her? And maybe he hadn't exactly lied, but he hadn't been truthful, either.

She remembered pressing him for something he'd been going to say. Now she got the feeling he'd almost let his stake in the diner slip while they'd been talking, and caught himself just in time.

"Rhys is part owner of the diner?"

Martha looked confused. "He didn't tell you? I mean, he

doesn't say much about it, but I thought the two of you…" Her cheeks flushed. "Oh. I've put my foot in it."

Taylor shook her head. "Not at all. We're not…"

But she didn't know how to finish that sentence. They weren't together but they weren't *not* together, either.

"I'm sorry to hear that," Martha said quietly, putting her hand on Taylor's arm. "You've been real good for him these last few weeks. And I think he's been good for you, too. You smile more. Your cheeks have more color. If I'm wrong tell me to mind my own business."

"You're not exactly wrong."

"He's needed someone like you, Taylor. Not that he's said a word to me about it." Her lips twitched. "He's not exactly the confiding type. Bit like his father that way."

Taylor knew that Rhys probably wouldn't like that comparison.

"My husband had his faults, but he always meant well. And he loved his family. I wish you were staying around longer, Taylor. You're a good girl. Not afraid to work hard. And I can tell your family is important to you."

She was perilously close to getting overemotional now. "Thanks, Martha. That means a lot to me. And Rhys is a good man. I know that. I'm sorry things can't work out differently."

"Are you?"

She swallowed. "Yes. Yes, I am."

Martha smiled. "Well, never say never."

The back door to the kitchen slammed and he came back in. A light snowfall had begun and he shook a few flakes off his hair. Their gazes met again and she fought to school her features. She should be angrier that he hadn't been totally honest, but instead all she could think of was how he had said he didn't want his mom to own the place. He'd gone against his own instincts and wishes to make her happy, hadn't he? Did Martha realize what a personal sacrifice he'd had to make?

They couldn't get into this now, if for no other reason than Martha was there and she should talk to him about it in private.

She marched the dishes into the kitchen. "Should I put these in the dishwasher?"

"What are you still doing here?"

"Helping. I thought you and your mom might like to go to the service."

"Then maybe you shouldn't have requested a private dinner after we closed."

Guilt heated her cheeks at his condemning tone. "I didn't know about that until it was a done deal. Avery even suggested they do something at home but my parents insisted."

"Really? It kind of struck me as exactly the kind of thing you'd be comfortable asking for. You know, like when you're planning an event and you just 'make things happen.' Right?"

"Are you really that mad at me, Rhys?" She tried to muster up some annoyance, some justifiable anger, but all she felt was a weary sadness.

He shoved a cover on the roaster and placed it—none too gently—in the commercial fridge. "I don't know what I am. I know my mom is tired and was looking forward to a quiet Christmas Eve. Instead she ended up here after hours."

"None of the staff would stay?"

"She insisted they go home to their families. It's their holiday, too." His voice held a condemning edge that made her feel even worse.

He really was put out and honestly she didn't blame him.

She hurried to put the dishes in the dishwasher while Martha put the dining room back to rights. "So you helped."

"Of course I did."

Yes, of course he did, because this wasn't just Martha's diner but his, too. "I'm sorry, Rhys. My parents didn't think. What can I do now? Can we still make it to the church?"

"Run the dishwasher while I finish up these pots and pans. We'll be a little late, and not very well dressed, but we'll get there."

Martha bustled back into the kitchen, either too busy or simply oblivious to the tension between Rhys and Taylor. "My goodness, you're nearly done in here. Rhys, let's just leave the sweeping up and stuff until Boxing Day. It's always slower then anyway."

"If that's what you want."

Martha grinned. "Well, what I want is to get a good dose of Christmas carols and candlelight, followed by a double dose of rum in my eggnog."

Taylor laughed. "Get your coat while I start this up."

Martha disappeared into the office. Rhys frowned at Taylor. "Why did you stay? You could have gone on with your family and been there with time to spare."

She shrugged. "Because tonight isn't about just my family. There are other people to consider, too." She tilted her head to look at him. "Why didn't Martha just say no when my father asked?"

What little softening she'd glimpsed in his expression disappeared as his features hardened. "Your father offered a Christmas tip she couldn't refuse."

Taylor winced. Her dad, Jack, her—they were all used to getting what they wanted. It simply hadn't occurred to her father that Martha would say no. And it wasn't that he was mean or unfeeling. Of course he would consider it fair to properly compensate Martha for the inconvenience.

But she rather wished he hadn't inconvenienced the Bullocks at all. It would have been more thoughtful.

"I'm sorry, Rhys. Can we leave it at that and get your mom to the church?"

His gaze caught hers for a prolonged moment. In that small space of time she remembered what it was to hear him laugh, taste his kiss, feel his body against hers. It had happened so fast, and now here they were, as far apart as ever. Trying to keep from being hurt any more than they already were.

"You'd better get your coat. You can drive over with us."

She rushed to grab her coat and purse and by the time she was ready Rhys was warming up Martha's car and Martha was shutting off the lights to the diner and locking the door. The parking lot at the church was packed and inside wasn't any better; the only seats were on the two pews pushed against the back wall. Taylor spied her family, several rows up, but the pew was full from end to end. She squeezed in with the Bullocks, sitting on one side of Rhys while his mother sat on the other. As the congregation sang "The First Noel" she realized that while everyone here was dressed up in their best clothes, Rhys wore jeans and Martha wore her standard cotton pants and comfortable shoes from work.

It didn't seem fair.

They turned the pages of their hymnbook to "Once in Royal David's City." It was less familiar to Taylor, and Rhys held out the book so she could see the words better. Their fingers never touched, but there was something about holding the book together that healed the angry words of before. When they finally sat down, Taylor took advantage of the hushed scuffle. "I'm sorry," she said, leaning toward his ear. "I really am."

The minister began to speak and she heard the words "Let us pray," but she couldn't. Rhys was staring down into her eyes and she couldn't look away. Not now. She wanted to tell him how much she hated the way they'd left things. Wanted to ask him why he'd never told her the truth about the diner. Wanted to kiss him and know that she hadn't just imagined their connection. Instead she sat in a candlelit church that smelled of pine boughs and perfume, the fluid voice of the minister offering a prayer of thanks for the gift of Christmas, and wondered at the miracle that she'd managed to fall utterly and completely in love for the first time in her life.

Her lower lip quivered the tiniest bit and she looked away. What was done was done.

And then Rhys moved his hand, sliding it over to take hers, his fingers tangling with her fingers. Nothing had really changed, and there was a bittersweet pain in her heart as she acknowledged the truth of that. At least he wasn't angry at her anymore.

During the sermon Taylor looked around at the people gathered to celebrate the holiday. Her big brother cuddling a sleeping Nell in the crook of his arm. Her parents sat in between with Jack on the other side and Amy Wilson beside him—an odd surprise. There was the whole Diamond clan—Molly, Sam, Angela, Clara, Ty, the kids. Melissa Stone and her fiancé, Cooper Ford, sitting with two older couples she assumed were their parents. Many others she recognized as guests from the wedding. Business people, professionals, ranchers. Ordinary folks. This was real. This was life. Not the glammed-up high-paced craziness she was used to living in. Somehow, between Clara's sunny generosity, Angela's steady advice and Martha's ready acceptance she'd managed to become a part of this town instead of remaining on the fringes, where she usually made it a policy to stay.

She'd changed. And she couldn't find it within herself to be the least bit sorry.

As if she could sense her thoughts, Angela Diamond turned in her seat and caught Taylor's eye. She smiled and turned back around.

For the first time ever that she could remember, Taylor had no idea what to do next.

An usher brought around a box with tiny white candles in plastic holders. As the service ended, the choir started with the first verse of "Silent Night" as the minister went along and lit the first candle on the end of each pew. The congregation's voices joined in for the second verse as Rhys leaned over a little and let the flame from his candle ignite hers. Soon they were all standing with their candles, singing the last verse as the piano stopped playing and there was no sound but two hundred voices singing the age-old carol a cappella.

It was the most beautiful Christmas tradition Taylor had ever seen.

And when the song ended, everyone blew out their candles, the minister gave the benediction and a celebratory air took over the sanctuary.

In the midst of the confusion, Rhys leaned over. "Are you staying at the house or the B&B?"

"At the house." She waved at someone she only half recognized and smiled. "Callum and Avery insisted. I got the sofa bed."

Rhys's dark complexion took on a pinkish hue. She shouldn't have mentioned sleeping arrangements.

"Can I drive you home?"

"What about your mom?"

"I'll take her now and come back for you."

She wasn't at all sure what she wanted. She had no idea where things stood or even where she wanted them to stand. And yet they both seemed determined to play this out for as long as possible.

"I'll wait."

He gave her a quick nod and turned to Martha. The older woman had clearly decompressed during the service, and now she looked tired. It didn't look like Rhys was going to have much fight on his hands, getting her to leave.

There was a lot of socializing happening in the vestibule. Avery and Callum were working on getting Nell into her snowsuit without waking her up and the other three Shepards were putting on their coats and wishing a Merry Christmas to anyone who stopped by and offered a greeting. Susan saw Taylor and frowned. "You don't have your coat on! We're nearly ready to leave."

"I'll be along a little later."

"But you didn't bring your car."

Callum joined the group, a blurry-eyed, half-awake Nell fully dressed and snuggled into his shoulder. "We ready to go? Santa will be along soon."

"I was just telling Taylor to get her coat."

Taylor let out a breath and smiled brightly. "I've got a lift home, actually. No worries. You go on ahead."

"A lift home?"

"Rhys is going to drive me."

"I just saw him leave with his mother."

Taylor resisted the need to grit her teeth. "He's coming back."

Harry stepped in. "Rhys. He was one of Callum's groomsmen, right? Is there something going on there?"

Avery looked panicked on Taylor's behalf and Callum's brows were raised in brotherly interest but it was Jack, bless him, who stepped in, Amy Wilson hanging back just a bit, as if she was uncertain whether to join the group or not. "Hey, Dad, I've been meaning to ask you something about a new property I'm interested in buying."

The topic of a property investment was enough to lure her father away and Taylor relaxed. "Don't worry," she said to her mother. "We'll be right behind you."

"You've got your phone?"

Taylor laughed. "Of course."

"We'll see you in a bit, then." She hurried off in the direction of Jack and Harry. Avery came over and gave her a hug. "We're off, too. Good luck."

"Thanks."

As Avery and Callum walked away, Taylor heard Callum say, "Good luck? What do you know about this, wife?"

The vestibule thinned out until there were just a handful of people left. Jack got their parents on their way and came back for Amy, offering her a lift home. They'd just turned out of the lot when Taylor saw Rhys pull back into the yard in his truck.

Her boots squeaked in the snow as she crossed the parking lot, opened the door and hopped up inside the cab. She wasn't sure what to say now, so silence spun around them as he put the truck in Drive and headed out of the parking lot.

"I'm sorry I was so hard on your family." He finally spoke when they hit the outskirts of town.

"Don't be. You were right. About a lot of things."

"Such as?"

"Such as this is exactly something I probably would have done. Like you said, I make things happen. That's my job."

"I shouldn't have said that, either."

She chuckled then. "Boy, we can even turn an apology into an argument. We're good."

He laughed, too, but it didn't do much to lighten the atmosphere in the truck.

"So you're really going day after tomorrow."

"Yeah."

More silence.

It was only a short drive to the farm. Taylor longed to ask him about the diner but didn't want to get in another argument and she sensed it would be a sensitive subject. Besides, what did it truly matter now? It really didn't change anything.

The damnedest thing was that she did want something to change. And she couldn't figure out what or how. She just knew it felt wrong. Wrong to leave here. Wrong to say goodbye.

"You've got a couple days off from Diamondback?"

"Yeah," he answered. "Actually Sam suggested we all take Friday off, too, so I don't actually have to be back to work until Monday. I thought I'd sneak Mom to Edmonton one of those days, let her take in some of the Boxing Week sales."

"You're good to your mom, Rhys. She appreciates you, you know."

"Someone has to look out for her. She's my mom. She doesn't have anyone else."

It made even more sense now, knowing he had a stake in the Wagon Wheel. "You're very protective of the people you care about."

"Is that a bad thing?" He slid his gaze from the road for a moment.

"On the contrary. It's one of the things I l…like most about you."

Yeah, she'd almost said "love." She took a deep breath.

This would be a stupid time to get overly emotional, wouldn't it?

They turned onto Callum's road. "The thing is, Taylor…"

"What?"

He frowned. "You're competent. Everyone can see that. You're confident and successful and clearly you know how to run a business. I don't know why you feel you have to prove yourself. Why you have this chip on your shoulder."

"Sometimes I ask myself the same thing, Rhys." She turned in her seat. "Remember the time you said that most guys were intimidated by smart women? You had something there. There's a lot I don't know and more I'm not good at, but I'm not stupid. I've never understood why I should hide that fact just because I'm a woman."

"So you push yourself."

"Yeah. I guess if this trip has shown me anything, though, it's that I don't need to try so much. That…" She swallowed, hard. "That there are things more important that I've maybe been missing out on. In the past I haven't paid enough attention to personal relationships." She sighed. "I've made my share of screw-ups."

"Figuring that out is a good thing, right?"

"To be honest, it's been a little bit painful."

They pulled into Callum's driveway. Rhys parked at the far side, giving them a little space away from the house, and killed the lights.

"Sometimes the best lessons we learn are the ones that hurt the most."

She laughed a little. "Helpful."

But he reached over and took her gloved hand in his. "I mean it, Taylor. My mother told me once that we rarely learn anything from our successes, and the best teachers are our failures. It hurts, but I have to believe it always comes out better on the other side." He squeezed her fingers. "I wish you didn't have to go."

She wanted to say "me, too," but it would only make things worse, wouldn't it? Why wish for something that wasn't going to happen?

"Right. Well. Before you go in…I uh…" He cleared his throat. "I saw this earlier in the week and…"

He reached into his pocket and held out a small rectangular box. "Merry Christmas."

"You got me a present?"

"It's not much."

"Rhys, I…"

"Don't open it now, okay? Let's just say good-night and Merry Christmas."

She tucked the package into her purse. "Merry Christmas," she whispered, unbuckling her seat belt.

She looked up into his face. How had she ever thought it wasn't handsome? It was strong and fair and full of integrity and sometimes a healthy sense of humor. Before she could change her mind she pushed against the seat with one hand, just enough to raise her a few inches so she could touch her lips to his. The kiss was soft, lingering, beautiful and sad. It was the goodbye they should have had yesterday morning. It filled her heart and broke it in two all at the same time.

"Goodbye, Rhys."

She slid out of the truck before she could change her mind. Took one step to the house and then another. Heard the truck engine rev behind her, the creak and groan of the snow beneath the tires as Rhys turned around and drove away for the last time.

She took a few seconds on the porch to collect herself. She didn't want her family to see her cry or ask prying questions. She had to keep it together. Celebrate the holiday the way she'd intended—with them all together and happy. And if she had to fake it a little bit, she would. Because she was starting to realize that she'd been faking happiness for quite a while now.

She was just in time to kiss Nell good-night; to sit with her family and share stories of holidays gone by. Jack arrived and added to the merriment. After her brother and parents left for the B&B, she stayed up a little longer and chatted with Callum and Avery before the two of them went down the hall hand in hand. No one had asked about Rhys, almost as if they'd made a pact to spare her the interrogation. But as she finally burrowed beneath the covers on the sofa bed, she let the emptiness in. Because in the end she was alone. At Christmas. And her heart was across town, with Rhys.

CHAPTER ELEVEN

CHRISTMAS MORNING DAWNED cool and sunny. Taylor heard Callum sneak out just after five to do the milking; she fell back to sleep until Avery got up and put on coffee around seven. With Nell being too young to understand it all, there was no scramble for presents under the tree. Nell slept late after the busy night before, and Avery brought Taylor a coffee then slipped beneath the covers with her own mug.

Taylor looked over at her sister in law. "I think I would have liked having a sister if this is what it's like. Jack and Callum's idea of this would be to count to three and jump on the bed and see if they could make me yell. Extra points if they left bruises."

Avery smiled. "It was like this for me and my sister. I'm really glad you're here, Taylor. It's been so very nice."

"I'm glad I came, too."

"Even though it's bothering you to leave Rhys?"

Taylor nodded.

They sipped for a moment more before Avery took the plunge. "Did you fall in love with him? Or was it just a fling?"

Taylor curled her hands around the mug. "It would be easier to say it was a fling."

"But it wasn't?"

She shook her head.

Avery laughed. "I don't know whether to offer my congratulations or my sympathy."

"What do you mean?" Taylor looked over at her. "Do I look happy about it?"

"Yes. And no. You light up when you talk about him, you know."

No, she hadn't known. Damn.

"Falling in love is a bit of a miracle, don't you think? So that's the congrats part. And the sympathy comes in because I can tell you're confused and that's not easy."

"I live in Vancouver."

Avery nodded. "When I met Callum, I lived in Ontario. My life and job were there."

"But you could quit your job. It's different when you own your own venture. It would be harder for you now, with your bakery business, wouldn't it?"

"Difficult, but not impossible."

Taylor let out a frustrated sigh. "Avery, I get what you're saying. I do. But I've spent years building this business and my reputation. I've known Rhys less than a month."

Avery smiled softly. "I know. If you didn't have the business in the way, what would you do?"

See where it leads.

The answer popped into her mind with absolute ease. But it wasn't just up to her. "Rhys never once asked me to stay or hinted at anything past our…"

"Affair?"

Taylor blushed.

Avery finished her coffee. "It's that serious, then."

"Look," she said, frustration in her voice. "Last night he said he wished I didn't have to go but that's not the same thing as asking me to stay or when I'm coming back."

"Why would he ask when he's sure of the answer? Have

you given him any reason to think you would stay? Told him how you feel?"

She hadn't.

"Only because I'm positive nothing could come of it except our being hurt even more. Besides, there's a good chance he doesn't feel the same way. He told me straight out that he liked me because I was a challenge. That I was low risk because I was leaving anyway."

Avery snorted. "Oh, my God, that's romantic."

Taylor couldn't help it. She started laughing, too. "I'll be fine, Avery, promise. I just need to get back to a normal schedule. And first we have a Christmas breakfast to cook. You're the whiz, but I'm happy to be your sous-chef today."

"Deal," Avery said.

Babbling sounded from the second bedroom and Avery grinned. "Let me get the princess changed and fed first."

While she was gone and the house was quiet, Taylor snuck out of bed and got the box from her coat pocket. She didn't want to open it when anyone else was around. Sitting on the bed in her pajamas, she carefully untied the ribbon and unwrapped the red foil paper.

Inside the box was a necklace—the very same horse-shoe necklace she'd been admiring at the silversmith's the other day. She lifted it gently and watched the U-shaped pendant sway as it dangled from the chain. How had he known it was just what she liked? It was simple but beautiful. When she went to put it back in the box, she heard a strange ruffle when her fingers touched the cotton padding. Curious, she moved it out of the box and saw the folded note hidden beneath.

For all the times you need a horseshoe to rub for good luck. Merry Christmas, Rhys.

He remembered, but he'd hidden the note, as if he didn't want her to find it right away. As if—perhaps—he'd meant her to discover it after she was home again and it would remind her of the time they'd spent together.

She didn't know whether to laugh or cry.

She tucked the necklace back in the box. She wouldn't wear it today, not when everyone was around. She didn't want any more questions about her relationship with Rhys. She just wanted to keep this one thing private, like a secret they shared. Cherished.

But she thought about it as the rest of the family arrived, breakfast was served, presents were opened. And when there was a lull, she took the necklace out of her bag and tucked it into her pocket, where it rested warmly within the cotton.

An hour or so before dinner, it all got to be too much so she excused herself and bundled up for a short walk and some fresh air to clear her head. She was partway down the lane when a dull thud echoed on the breeze. She turned around to see her dad coming down the steps, dressed in Callum's barn coat and a warm toque and gloves. "Hey, wait up," he called.

She had no choice but to wait.

When he reached her they continued walking, the sun on the snow glittering so brightly that Taylor wished she'd put on her sunglasses. "It's been a good day," Harry said easily, falling into step.

"We haven't all been together like this in a long time." Taylor let out a big breath. "It's been good."

"Yes, it has."

Silence fell, slightly awkward.

"Taylor, I've gotten the impression you're not completely happy. Are you okay?"

Her heart clubbed. "What gave you that idea?"

"Your mother pointed out a few things. And then

there's this Rhys guy. You seem half miserable, half thrilled about it."

She huffed out a laugh. "That about sums it up."

"Is it just this guy? Or is it work, too?"

She frowned. "You don't have to sound so hopeful about it. I know you don't like what I do and you'd love to see me settled with kids like Callum."

There. She'd come right out and said it.

Harry let out a long sigh. "I haven't been very fair. Or put things the right way."

Her feet stopped moving, as if they had a mind of their own. "What?"

She looked up at him, suddenly realizing why his eyes seemed so familiar. They looked like hers.

"I don't hate what you do. I resent it a bit, that's all."

"I don't get it."

Harry started walking again. "Callum joined the military instead of going to college. It wasn't my first choice, but when your son says he wants to serve his country, it's a hard thing to find fault with. Then with Jack…we both knew he couldn't ski forever. But after his accident and after the scandal…" There was a telling pause. "When he came to me asking to help him start Shepard Sports, I couldn't say no. It was good to see the light in his eye again. He could have died on that hill."

"What does this have to do with me, Dad?"

"I built my company from the ground up, Taylor. Neither of my boys were interested in finance. But you… you weren't just my last chance to pass it on to one of my kids. I could see the talent in you. You're good at making money, maybe even better than Jack. And you weren't interested in the least in the market or fund management or anything I do."

"You wanted me to work for you?"

"With me. Eventually."

"I thought you thought what I do is stupid."

He stopped walking again. "I was jealous of it."

"You never said anything."

"I kept hoping you'd come to me. I didn't want to pressure you."

"Instead you just made me feel like a disappointment." She wasn't holding anything back today. Maybe Rhys's way of plain speaking was rubbing off.

"I know. And I'm sorry. The truth is that you should do what makes you happy. I can't put my wishes on you kids. I'm proud of all of you for being strong and smart enough to make your own way."

"Even if it's planning frivolous parties?"

He chuckled. "I've seen your mother work her magic enough times at our small functions to know that a big event takes massive planning. You've got a talent, Taylor. And again, I'm sorry that my selfish pride took away from that."

They turned around and headed back, the house waiting for them at the end of the lane, snowbanks curling along the driveway and the remnants of her snowman listing lazily to one side. Her father's approval meant a lot. But she was also realizing that his validation wasn't everything. Her restlessness and drive wasn't about proving herself. It was about looking for something that was missing. It was about meaning, not accomplishment.

"I wish I could tell you that I could join the firm, but I need something that makes me excited to get up in the morning, Dad. I know fund management isn't it. I'm sorry, too. I wish you'd told me sooner."

"All I've ever really wanted for my kids is for them to be happy. If you're not, I want to know if there's anything we can do to help."

"Oh, Daddy." She stopped and gave him a hug, warmth spreading through her as he put his strong arms around her and hugged her back. "Thank you for that. I've got to figure it out on my own, that's all."

"Well, anything worth having is going to take a lot of work. If it was easy it wouldn't mean half so much. And none of my kids are quitters."

"No, we're not."

"You'll figure it out," he assured her. "Now, let's get back. I'm getting cold and I swear I can smell the turkey clear out here."

Taylor walked beside her father, feeling like a weight had been lifted. And yet a heaviness remained, too. Because their conversation hadn't offered any insight into what she should do about her current situation. So much for her creative, problem-solving mind. All she could see right now was a massive New Year's party that needed finalizing and about a dozen employees who were counting on her to keep their lives afloat. Where could she and Rhys possibly fit into that?

No stormy weather or mechanical failures had the grace to delay her flight, so bright and early on Boxing Day Taylor took the rental car back to the depot and walked into the departures area of the airport. Her feet were heavy and her stomach felt lined with lead as she tugged her suitcases behind her. She should be glad to be going home to her apartment, her regular routine, familiar things. Her muffin and coffee from the café around the corner each morning. Walks in Stanley Park. Warmer temperatures. Shopping. Work.

It would be good. It would be fine.

After she checked her bags she went through security and to the gate, even though she had nearly an hour to spare. She checked her phone, going through the email that was waiting for her attention. There was a rather frantic one from her New Year's client, and Taylor's blood pressure took a sudden spike. It was only five days to the party and the construction of the aquariums was delayed. He'd emailed her on Christmas Day, for heaven's sake. Like she could—or would—have done anything during that twenty-four hour period. People did celebrate holidays, she thought grumpily. Even workaholics.

Her fingers paused over the keypad. Was that what she was? A workaholic?

She scanned through the rest, knowing she should cool off before responding, and saw an urgent reply from her assistant, Alicia. Everything was under control. The aquariums were set to be delivered on the morning of the thirtieth, the fish would come a day later when the tank conditions were at the proper levels, and everything else was on schedule.

Taylor let out a breath. Why had she even worried? Alicia could handle anything their clients dished out. She never panicked and she was incredibly resourceful. Heck, Taylor wasn't even really needed.

She put the phone down on her lap as the thought sunk in.

She wasn't really needed.

The truth should have been obvious before. She was great at her job. She knew how to make the impossible happen. It stood to follow that she'd train her staff the same way. Alicia had been her right-hand girl for three years. She'd managed smaller events on her own. This party was probably the biggest challenge they'd had in a while and all Taylor had done was been available by email simply to confirm or approve changes in plan. Alicia had done the grunt work. She and her team had put it together.

And yet Taylor couldn't just walk away. She owned the business after all.

Suddenly her conversations with family came back with disturbing clarity. *What you're doing isn't giving you that same buzz,* Jack had said. *Something's missing.* And he'd gone on to say that what had given him the most fulfillment was his corporate retreat business. That it was more than just buying and selling. That it was about people.

An even bigger surprise was how her father had taken her aside yesterday afternoon. Just before they'd gone inside, he'd added one little addendum to their conversation. "I want you to know that I couldn't have done what I have all these years without your mother. Without all of you. Don't let life pass you by, sweetheart. Build your business with people you trust, but build your life with people you love."

People you trust. People you love.

The solution was so clear she couldn't believe it had taken her so long to put it together.

Even though it was still a statutory holiday, she scanned through her directory and found the number she was looking for. A quick call later and she was heading to the gate desk where two service agents had just arrived.

"I need you to pull my bags, please," she said, holding out her boarding pass.

The first agent came to the desk. "I'm sorry? This is the flight to Vancouver, leaving in forty minutes."

"Yes, and I checked in and this is my seat, 12F. But I'm not going to be leaving on it, so I need you to pull my bags."

"Miss." She checked the boarding pass. "Miss Shepard. We're going to be boarding in about fifteen minutes."

"I'm not going to be on it." She tried to stay calm and

smiling. "And if I'm not on it, you're going to have to pull the bags anyway, right?"

"Yes, but…"

"I don't even care if I take them with me now. I can come back to get them. I don't care if my ticket can't be refunded." Her smile widened even as the agent's expression grew more confused. She leaned forward. "Would it help if I told you I fell in love and decided I can't leave after all?"

The confused look morphed into sentimental amusement. "You're absolutely sure you're not boarding this flight?"

"I've never been more sure of anything in my life."

"It might take a while. You'll have to pick them up at baggage services." She sent Taylor a wink. "I'll call down."

"Thank you! I'm sorry for the trouble. And Merry Christmas!"

"Merry Christmas," the agent returned, picking up the phone. "And good luck."

CHAPTER TWELVE

RHYS PUT THE BROOM back in the storage closet and began running hot water for the mop bucket. He'd left Martha in bed with a cold; she'd insisted on getting up and coming with him to give the diner a good cleaning but he'd convinced her to stay in bed since she'd be needed when they opened tomorrow. Knowing she'd likely change her mind, he'd made sure to give her a good dose of cold medicine. She'd be asleep for a good few hours, getting some much deserved rest. He could mop the floors and do up the bank deposit without any trouble.

If only he could stop thinking about Taylor as easily. That last kiss she'd given him had been so sweet—a bit shy and a bit sad. He knew he had no choice but to let her go, but it was killing him. She'd awakened something in him that was unexpected and he didn't know how to make it go back to sleep. At least a dozen times in the past thirty-six hours he'd grabbed his car keys, ready to drive over to Callum's and tell her he wasn't ready to let what they had end. But he'd put the keys back on the hook every time. It already hurt to let her go. To prolong it would only make it worse.

Something made him shut off the water, a persistent thump that came from out in the main part of the restaurant. Frowning, he stuck his head out of the kitchen and called out, "We're closed!"

He'd nearly pulled his head back in when he saw the red boots.

His heart gave an almighty *whomp*.

She was supposed to be gone. Her flight was supposed to have left almost an hour ago. Maybe he'd been mistaken about the boots?

He slowly stepped through the kitchen door and into the front of the diner. There was no question, they were red boots. The only red boots like them he'd ever seen in Cadence Creek. Most of her body was hidden by the gigantic pine wreath hanging on the door, but he saw her long legs and the tails of her soft black and red coat.

He smiled as she knocked again, harder.

"Rhys, I know you're in there. Your truck is parked right outside."

His smile widened. God, he loved it when she got all impatient and bossy.

"I said we're closed."

There was a moment of silence. Then her voice came again, mocking. "Don't be an ass. Open the door."

He rather thought he could play this game all day. Except he did really want to see her. And find out why she was still here.

"Rhys!" she commanded. "It's freezing out here!"

He couldn't help it, he burst out laughing, half in surprise and half in relief that he actually got to see her again. He went forward and turned the lock back. Gave the door a shove and then there she was, standing in the snow, her dark hair in the customary braid and her eyes snapping at him from beneath a black hat, one of those stylish things women wore in the winter that wouldn't ruin their hair.

"Hello, Taylor."

She stepped inside, reached up and swiped the hat from her head and shoved it in her pocket. "Hi."

"I thought you were leaving today."

"I was."

He locked the door again and faced her, his pulse leaping as he registered the fact that she'd used past tense. "Wait. Was?"

She nodded.

"Your flight get canceled or something?"

"Nope."

"I don't understand."

For several seconds Taylor remained silent. "Do you have any coffee on or anything?" she asked. "I'm freezing."

She was stalling, and the only reason she'd do that was that she was nervous. "I put a pot on when I got here. Have a seat."

She went to one of the lunch counter stools and perched on it. He added the right amounts of cream and sugar to her cup and handed it over. "It's probably not as good as mom's."

"Where is she, by the way?"

"Home in bed with a cold."

"Oh, I'm sorry to hear that." Her face seemed to relax a bit, though—was she glad they were alone? He was still confused as hell. She was insistent on coming in but now that she was here, trying to get anything out of her was about like working with a pigheaded colt who refused to be bridled. Trying on the patience. Once he got the bit in her mouth she'd be just fine, he realized. It was just figuring out what to use to lure her in, make her explain.

"You're probably wondering why I'm here," she said softly, looking up at him with wide eyes.

Feelings rushed through him as he held her gaze. Pain, because prolonging the inevitable was torture of a special kind and they'd done it twice now. Hope, because for some reason she was here and not crossing thirty thousand feet over the Rockies. And tenderness, because he knew now that beneath the dynamo that was Taylor Shepard was one of the most caring, generous people he'd ever met. At the very least he could admit to himself that he'd fallen for her. Hard.

"The thought crossed my mind," he replied.

"I forgot to give you your Christmas present," she said, reaching into her handbag. "I apologize for the poor wrapping job."

She held out a thin plastic bag that bore the logo of one of the airport gift shops.

Amused, he reached inside and pulled out a key chain with a fuzzy fake rabbit's foot on the end.

"Someone told me that you rub a rabbit's foot for good luck." Her voice was barely above a whisper.

It was then he noticed the horseshoe hanging around her neck, just visible in the "V" of her coat and sweater. She was wearing his Christmas present. That pleased him more than it probably should.

"Do you think I'm in need of some good luck?"

She put down her coffee cup but not before he noticed her hand was trembling the slightest bit. She was nervous. So was he. He had no idea what this all meant but he got the feeling they were standing on the edge of something momentous. Somewhere he'd never wanted to be again. Until now.

"Why don't you try rubbing it and find out?" she suggested.

He felt like a fool, but she was here, wasn't she? He'd indulge her. He rubbed the tiny faux-fur foot.

"Ok, Luck," he said when he was done, spreading his arms wide. "Here I am."

She got up from the stool, went around the counter, and grabbed onto his shirt, just above where he'd fastened the last button. "And here I am," she whispered as she tilted up her head and kissed him.

His arms came around her by sheer instinct, pulling her against his body into the places where she fit so well. There was relief in holding her in his arms again, passion that ignited between them every time they touched. She tasted good and he kissed her back, loving the feel of her soft lips against his, the sleek texture of her mouth, the way she made the tiniest sound of pleasure when he nibbled on her lower lip.

"You're right," he murmured. "It *is* lucky."

She smiled against his lips, but then pulled away a little and simply rested in his arms, her head nestled in the space between his shoulder and neck. A lump formed in his throat. Whatever he'd said over the last few weeks, he'd been a liar. There was nothing easy or casual or temporary about his feelings for her. They were very, very real. It wasn't all physical. The way they were embracing now was much, much more than that. What a mess.

"Why didn't you tell me about the diner?" Her voice was slightly muffled against his shirt but he heard her just the same. It was not what he expected her to say.

"What?"

She pushed back out of his arms and met his gaze. "This place. Why didn't you tell me you were part owner?"

Nothing she could have said would have surprised him more. "Who told you that?"

"Your mother. Though I don't think she meant to. It slipped out the other night."

"It's not a big deal."

"It's a very big deal." She frowned, a cute little wrinkle forming between her eyebrows. "For all your talk about not wanting to own your own business, not wanting to be the boss. Heck, you even said you hadn't wanted your mother to buy this place."

"I really didn't want her to buy it. But she was determined. Once my mother gets something in her head…"

"Sounds like someone else I know. And you invested because?"

He frowned. "If I hadn't invested all the money I'd gotten for my house in Rocky, she would have mortgaged herself to the eyeballs to have it. As it is, this place is free and clear in another four years."

"You did it to protect her."

"Of course I did. I couldn't stop her from taking the risk, but at least I could help cushion the fall."

"You did it thinking that you'd never see your money back."

He remembered the heated discussions he'd had with his mother about taking such a big step. In the end he'd had no choice. Money was just money. This was his mother and Rhys knew he had to look out for her. "I did it knowing that was a very real possibility, yes. And not because I didn't think she could do it. I just know from painful experience how many small businesses fail. She'd already lost enough over her lifetime. Her whole nest egg went into buying it, plus Dad's life insurance money. If the diner went under, she'd lose everything."

Taylor must think him an idiot. He'd made a business decision for reasons that had very little to do with business.

"You did it for your mother."

"I know it was foolish. But she's my mom."

"And the job at Diamondback?"

"Security. The best way to take care of her, to protect her, was to minimize financial risk. At least I bring in a regular paycheck that I, or rather we, can rely on."

Taylor reached out and pressed her hand to the wall of his chest. "You are a dying breed, Rhys Bullock. You protect the people you love no matter what. There's nothing foolish about that. What about your brother?"

"He's been gone too long, I think. He's off doing his own thing. He just said, 'Whatever she wants.'"

It had been Rhys who'd come home and helped his mom through those first days of grieving. Who'd met with lawyers and bankers. There had been no way he was going to let her go through that alone.

Taylor squeezed his hands. "Let me guess, Martha insists on you taking your share of the profits."

"Of course. I draw out the same percentage of profit as I initially invested."

He didn't quite like the keen way she was looking up at him. Like she could see right through him. He wasn't exactly lying...

She lifted one eyebrow. "You use the profits to pay down the loan, don't you?"

Busted. "Perhaps."

"And your house?"

He met her gaze. If she was after the whole picture, she might as well have it. She could probably still catch another flight today.

"Rented." Because by using all his equity he'd had nothing left for a down payment.

"And Martha doesn't know. She thinks you own it?"

He nodded. "That's right. You're looking at a full-time ranch hand with a rented house, truck payment and not a scrap in savings."

"So that's why you didn't tell me? Pride?"

She was here. Things were bigger between them than he'd ever planned. "No, not just pride. There's more. You know I never wanted to be like my dad. I was so determined that I'd do better. That no one would suffer because of my mismanagement."

"But someone did?"

He nodded. "Her name was Sherry. She had a couple of kids. She was my office manager—and my girlfriend."

"Oh, Rhys."

"I let them down so completely," he explained. "She blamed me, too. For losing the business. For putting her out of a job when she had the children to support. For..." He cleared his throat. "For breaking her heart."

"So you carried that around, on top of losing the business?"

"She depended on me. I can't blame her for being angry." He ran a hand over his hair and looked in her eyes, feeling miserable. "So you see I don't have a lot to offer in the way of brilliant prospects."

She took his hand. "That's not true! You work hard and you put the ones you love first. You made your mom's dream come true. You're strong and honest and loyal. You've got two strong hands and the biggest heart of anyone I've ever met." Her smile widened. "Know what else you've got?"

"What?"

"Your ace in the hole. Me."

Taylor gazed up at him, filled with admiration for the man he'd become. He really had no clue, did he? Rhys was self-assured, knew his place in the world. But he didn't understand how extraordinary he was.

"You? Come on, Taylor," he said, pulling away a little. "Look at you. You're successful. Your business is profitable enough to keep you in designer boots and who knows what else. We're as different as night from day."

"Not as different as you think. Just so happens that

we're peas in a pod, you and me. I was in a relationship a while ago, too. At the same time as that wedding story I told you about—remember the bride with the allergy? I was so upset about that. I mean disproportionately freaked out. John accused me of being cold. Of caring more about the business than I did about our relationship. The thing is he was right. And so your little digs about proving myself really hit a nerve. I was at a crisis point and he bailed. You weren't the only one who thought you were incapable of making a personal relationship work, and I really wasn't interested in risking myself like that again, you know?"

"He was an idiot."

She smiled at Rhys's blind loyalty. "No, he was honest. And the truth is, I didn't invest enough in our relationship. Probably because I didn't love him. I loved the idea of him. But not him. The idea of losing him didn't make me lose sleep. It didn't break my heart or make this heavy pit of despair settle right here." She pressed her fist to her stomach. Her voice lowered to a whisper. "Not like it felt about an hour and a half ago while I sat in Edmonton airport wondering how I could ever be happy if I left you without telling you how I feel."

His lips dropped open. He hadn't been expecting that. Neither had she. Neither of them had expected any of this.

"Do you really think I care about your bank statement? Truly? When have I ever given the impression that my goals are about making money?"

He shook his head. "You haven't," he admitted. "It's always been about proving yourself, meeting challenges."

"That's right." She tugged on his hand. "Come sit down. I want to run something by you."

"Me? Why?"

"When we first met, you told me that a smart person knows their strengths, do you remember? My dad taught me that a smart person also sees the strengths in others. I want your honest to goodness opinion about something. Will you help?"

"Of course."

They sat side by side on the stools, swiveled so they were facing each other and their knees were nearly touching. Rhys wasn't just some ranch hand. He had a lifetime of experiences to draw upon and she trusted his judgment. "Do you think I could keep the event planning business in Vancouver going and branch out into something else that excites me personally? Can I do both?"

Possibility hummed in the air. Rhys sat up straight and tall. Neither of them were rushing through to the end of the conversation. They'd been through enough to know that what was said today was constructing the foundation of wherever they went from here. It deserved to be built with care and attention. "It depends. What are you thinking?"

"Angela put the idea into my head before Christmas. I mentioned that I'm getting tired of the here today, gone tomorrow scene. Remember when I was so stressed about the rehearsal dinner and you said it was because the event meant something personal to me? You were right. But you know what? The satisfaction from planning Callum's wedding was greater than I expected, too. She said what I want is to create something meaningful, and suggested I help plan an upcoming fund-raiser for the Butterfly Foundation."

"That's a great idea!" Rhys smiled at her. "The Diamonds have done a really great thing with that charity. I know they'd appreciate the help."

"What if I took it a step further and used my expertise to work for lots of charities and non-profits? I love what I do and I'd still have the challenge of that, but I think I'd feel like I was doing something important, too, you know?"

"How could you do that and still keep the Vancouver business going? You'd be spreading yourself pretty thin."

"By promoting my assistant. She can do it. She's handled this party on her own since I've been here and it's been one of the most challenging projects we've ever done. She's built her own team. I'd still own the company, and I'd still be involved, of course. But in a different way. Kind of like Jack is with his business. He's far more hands-on with his team-building stuff than with the sporting goods."

"Would you set up the new venture from the same office?" he asked. "It would cut down on expenses."

He hadn't put the two together. The two of them and the business change. "This might come as a surprise, but I was thinking about running it from here."

"From Cadence Creek?"

He sounded so surprised she faltered. Had she possibly misread the situation? "Well, yes. It's close to Edmonton, not that far to Calgary, and an easy flight to Vancouver or even Toronto. I have family here. And…" She looked down at her lap. She was so confident when it came to her work and capabilities, but when it was personal she wasn't nearly as sure of herself. John's words—*Incapable of what it takes to maintain a relationship*—still echoed in her head. Even though she didn't really believe them, they'd left their mark just the same. "I guess I thought you might like it if I were around."

"Taylor."

She couldn't read what emotion was in his voice other than surprise. Embarrassment flooded through her as she felt quite ridiculous. The old insecurity came rushing back. What if the problem was really her? What if she wasn't lovable? She'd spent so much time trying to be strong that it had become a shell around her heart.

"Of course, it's okay if you don't. I mean, we did agree

that this was a short-term thing, and I don't want you to feel pressured."

His hand touched hers as it sat in her lap. She stared at it for a long moment, watched as his fingers curled around hers, firm and sure. Her heart seemed to expand in her chest, filled with so much emotion she didn't know what to do with it all. She drew hope from the simple touch. Felt wonder at the newness and fragility of it all. And there was fear, fear that this couldn't all be real and that it would disappear at a moment's notice.

She put her other hand over his, tentatively, until she couldn't bear it any longer and she lifted their joined hands, pressing them to her cheek as her eyes closed, holding on to the moment as long as she could.

Rhys lifted his right hand, placed it gently along the slope of her jaw, his strong fingers whispering against the delicate skin there. "Taylor," he murmured, and she opened her eyes.

He was looking at her the way she'd never imagined any man would ever look at her. Wholly, completely, his lips turned up only the slightest bit, not in jest, but in what she could only think of as happiness. His eyes were warm, and looked on her with such an adoring expression she caught her breath. The pad of his thumb rubbed against her cheek, and he pulled his left hand from her grasp. He placed it along her other cheek, his hands cupping her face like a precious chalice, and he slid closer, so slowly it was sweet torture waiting for his lips to finally touch hers.

She thought the sweetest moment had to be in that breathless second when his mouth was only a fraction of an inch away, and all the possibilities in the world were compacted into that tiny space. But she was wrong. Sweeter still was the light touch of lips on lips, soft, tender and perfect.

"You're staying?" he asked, his voice barely a whisper in the quietness of the diner.

"I'm staying," she confirmed.

He pressed his forehead to hers and she slowly let out her breath as everything clicked into place.

"I tried not to fall in love with you." Rhys lifted his head, smiled, and patted his lap. She slid off the stool and onto his legs, and he put his arms around her, strong and secure.

"Me, too. I kept telling myself it was a fling. But I couldn't get you off my mind. You're bossy and you drive me crazy, but you're loyal and honorable and you…"

She broke off, feeling silly.

"I what?"

He gave her a jostle, prompting her to finish her sentence. "It's corny." She bit down on her lip.

"I don't care. What were you going to say?"

She leaned against his shoulder. "You make me feel treasured."

He tilted his head so it rested against hers. "And you make me feel invincible."

She smiled, the grin climbing her face until she chuckled. "I'm glad."

His smile faded as his face turned serious. "I won't let you down."

"You couldn't possibly."

He kissed her again, more demanding this time, and when he lifted his head her tidy braid was well and truly mussed. "Hey," she said, running her fingers through his hair. "Now that I'm going to be here on a permanent basis, we can take all the time we need to fall in love."

"Honey, I'm already there."

She smiled. "Me, too. But I want to enjoy being this way a little longer. Is that okay?"

"Look at me. I'm in no position to argue."

She kissed him again, thinking that she could happily stay that way forever when he gave her braid a tug.

"Hey," he said. "I know we're taking our time and all that, and I don't mean to rush, but what are you doing New Year's Eve? Do you have plans?"

She nodded slowly. "I do have plans, as a matter of fact."

"Oh." Disappointment clouded his voice.

"I think I'd like to spend it right here, in your arms. If that's okay with you."

"That's more than okay. And the night after that, and the night after that."

She snuggled closer. "I don't know what the future holds. Changes are coming, adjustments and transitions are going to be made. But I know one thing for sure. You're my anchor, Rhys. Somehow you make everything right simply by being. And for the first time, I don't have to have all the details sorted and everything planned to the last item. Things will fall into place. And do you know how I know?"

He shook his head.

"Because I didn't plan for you. And you were the best thing of all."

He kissed her hair. "I love you, Taylor."

"And I love you."

And that was all she really needed to know.

* * * * *

LET'S TALK

Romance

For exclusive extracts, competitions
and special offers, find us online:

Or get in touch on 0844 844 1351*

For all the latest titles coming soon, visit
millsandboon.co.uk/nextmonth